CONVICTIONS

CARO LAND

Print ISBN 978-1-913419-26-4

To Belinda, Yvonne, Janet and Adele:
the fun, feisty and much loved real Natalies

FIRST DAY NERVES

Natalie gazed at her reflection and took a deep breath. The woman in the mirror looked surprised. Perhaps it was the arch of her dark eyebrows, or maybe it was the foundation and blusher which, replicating her tanned skin, wasn't really necessary. But that's what one did when starting a new job. At least she had that polished, lawyerly mask, which hid the real person, the human inside who didn't approve of her actions half the time. Still, she was older now, if not wiser. Ten weeks off her fortieth birthday, Miss Bach was back in Manchester, living with her mother and starting a new job.

She stared long and hard. Perhaps this time she'd be a Ms.

The sound of flushing made her start. A woman waddled from the cubicle. She'd been a girl with swinging hair the last time Nat saw her.

'Hiya, Natalie.'

Nat smiled in reply. She remembered the nasal Salford accent, but couldn't summon a name.

As though she knew what Nat was thinking, the woman gazed at her for a moment, her lips squashed and judgemental. 'It's Wendy, Natalie. Wendy Manning-Dawn now. It's a good job

I'm here, else you wouldn't have got into the building.' She dangled a set of keys. 'I'm the Office Manager. I open up at eight thirty sharp every morning. It happens I was early today.' She rubbed her huge bump. 'Five weeks to go. I keep telling Wesley and Catherine they'll be lost without me.'

Following her out of the toilets, Nat watched Wendy punch numbers into a key pad at the glass office door. She looked back and chuckled. 'Come on then, new girl, I'll show you 'round, shall I?'

Nat smiled stiffly. New bloody girl; charming. Oh well, she'd just have to get used to it.

Inhaling deeply, she stepped over the threshold. Yup, there it was, that aroma of coffee, polish and paper, both familiar and disturbing. She moved to the window and gazed out. Like a television on mute, the high street below was chock-a-block with morning traffic. The sewing shop had closed and the large café opposite had a new name, but the florist was there and presumably the brothel above was still going strong.

A stab of grief caught her. Some things, surely, didn't change?

Aware she should be listening to Wendy's dreary tones, she turned back to the work area and glanced around. This floor had been refurbished to open-plan, and her old corner room was now a smart cubicle of glass.

Wesley Hughes's office, no doubt.

Feeling a little clammy, she looked up at the ceiling. Presumably Catherine still had the floor above for her team. Would Nat be invited up for a chat later? And how would that go? Her sudden return hadn't included any discussion with Catherine. She might've been the managing partner of Goldman Law, but she didn't have the final say; she never had.

Wendy was still talking, drawling her words. 'So your typing will go into the pool with the other assistants, paralegals and trainees.' She crossed her arms. 'I don't know if you've heard of desk-sharing, but that's what you've got. Each fee-earner has a drawer over there, but everything at this bench is shared: computer, stapler, Post-it notes, chair. So no personal effects on the desk, and if you have a drink, you clear it away before you leave.'

Nat looked at the chairs around the central table; there were six. She'd counted seven non-partner fee-earners on the website last night. So she was number eight. Glancing at the empty corner office, she took a breath to ask what would happen if everyone was in work at the same time, but pursed lips got there first.

'Property's at a premium in Didsbury, Natalie. We have to make do. It'll pay to get in early now you've added to the... maths.' She handed Nat a grey ring binder. 'Here's the office manual for you to read while you wait.' She wobbled away before turning back. 'I'll sort you out a swipe card, and we do check on attendance times. I hope you've remembered to bring a mug.'

Wondering who had decided on open-plan, swipe cards and the need for a flipping office manual, Nat sat at the desk and opened the folder. Jack hadn't mentioned the refurbishment during their occasional chats since she'd left, but why would he? These days he was a partner in name only, the name of the legal firm he'd set up thirty or so years previously. Her job as an assistant solicitor at Goldman Law had been her first after a mercifully short stint trying Family and Matrimonial. Newly qualified, she'd been thrilled with the large increase in her salary, but after a few months she had realised the firm was entirely dedicated to Jack's multifarious business interests, and wasn't the niche corporate and commercial practice she'd thought was employing her.

Her eyes returned to the smart corner cube. Hoping Wendy wasn't watching, she stepped forward and peered in. The blinds were open, revealing a huge abstract canvas taking up the far wall. Expensive and flash, but of course. Before she'd left for her 'new life', Jack had asked her to stay an extra week to show her replacement the ropes, but Wesley Hughes hadn't bothered to hide his desire to be rid of her, so she'd left after just one fraught day.

'I tried to help Wesley, but he's so bloody arrogant,' she'd complained to Jack at the time. 'He isn't interested in listening; he just wants to do everything his own way.'

Jack had laughed. 'That sounds promising. It's like someone I know.'

'Oh really?' she'd replied. 'I've no idea who you mean.'

Returning to the central desk, she smiled wryly at the memory. Was it arrogance, or wanting her own way? Most likely the latter. There had been a few silent tussles with Catherine over the years, at least until she played her trump card. Not even Nat had known she was Jack's mistress, and her elevation to wife was seamless, becoming the new Mrs Goldman almost the moment the ink had dried on his decree absolute.

'Natalie!'

A familiar voice brought Nat back from her contemplation.

'I wasn't prepared to believe it until I saw it.' Looking exactly as Nat remembered, down to the dent at the rear of her back-combed bleached hair, Sharon was holding out her arms. 'I never thought I'd see you back here. I heard about your mum. I'm so sorry. How's she doing?'

'Amazing, actually...' Nat replied, not wanting to talk about it, but realising all the same that it was true. Six weeks ago Anna had been in hospital and couldn't speak a word, but now, save for a droop on one side of her face, no one would know she'd been ill.

The bench filled up with bodies as Sharon talked and Nat listened. Noticing she was on the sixth seat, Nat stood and inched away, making sure to take the office manual with her. She'd forgotten how Sharon liked to talk. She was her secretary once, Wesley's now. Though hard working and kind, she was horrendously indiscreet; Nat had learned the hard way not to tell her anything she didn't want the rest of the office to know. Still, it was useful today. She heard five years of gossip within fifteen minutes: Jack had survived an investigation by the Law Society after a malicious complaint; Catherine had had some surgery on her eyes; Wesley's twin boys were just starting at uni.

Sensing movement behind her, Nat turned as Sharon took breath. Sure enough, the sixth seat had been filled by an employee who'd barely reached adolescence. Still, it was a relief that she'd stood; he didn't look infused with #MondayMotivation and she wasn't up to a fist fight. Not on her first day, anyway. In truth, she didn't fancy tackling any work either; never mind open-plan and swipe cards, God knows what had changed in the law. It was tempting, in fact, just to leave, go home to Anna, and say, 'Tell you what, Mum, working in Tesco is just fine. We'll manage somehow.'

'Nat?' Sharon cocked her head. 'Did you hear what I said? Wesley's still in London on his trial.' Placing her hand in the small of Nat's back, she gently guided her into his office. 'I'm sure he won't mind.' She looked at her watch. 'Heck, look at the time. I'll get you a drink and then I'd better get on.'

Nat hovered at the door. Was she comfortable about this, or should she seek out a stool and hide in a corner? Her eyes swept the immaculate room. The empty desk policy clearly stretched to Wesley as well, though he did have a single framed photograph on the side. Without touching it, she bent over and stared at the snap. His twins as babies; chubby, dark-skinned and beautiful. The last time she'd seen it, she'd felt a twinge of nostalgia, but today it was mixed with sadness, even grief. Pushing the thought away, she turned back to the glass. The fee-earners around the bench looked comfortable, companionable – and at least a decade younger than her. Where was the seventh? She hoped it would be an OAP.

'Sod it,' she said, sitting down and casting her handbag to one side. She tapped her fingers on the desk top. Was someone going to give her work at some point? Anything to stop her checking her mobile yet again. Feeling less guilty in the client chair, she swung from side to side. The garish painting felt warm on her back. The artist was probably famous. Yup, she could imagine it. She could see Wesley Hughes wearing a sharp suit in an art gallery, his finger on his lips, studying the piece thoughtfully, then looking at his simpering blonde wife. 'What do you think, Andrea? No, don't look at the price. Should we splash out?'

Nat shook her head and sighed. She was being horrible; she really must stop. Opening the office manual, she flicked through the tabs: health and safety, data protection, appraisals, time-recording, corporate responsibility. Of course, all the large firms had rules and regulations in office manuals years' back, but Goldman Law hadn't been that type of practice. She lifted another section: internal complaints procedure. That was a laugh; in the old days an employee's complaint had resulted in a swift kick out of the door.

The sudden peal of the telephone made her start. Bloody hell. Should she answer?

'It's Jack,' Sharon said at the door, her candyfloss hair appearing a moment before she did. 'For you.'

Nat lifted the receiver. 'Hello?'

As though the past five years had never happened, her old boss dived in immediately. 'Ask that dreadful woman for the key to my filing cabinet, bottom drawer, red file. Especially for you...'

She couldn't help but smile at his description of Wendy. 'For me? Which means...?' she asked.

'For your eyes only.'

Yup, like she'd never been away. 'Let me guess... Julian?'

'You're a cynic, Natalie, you know that, don't you?'

Her heart sank. First day back; really? Julian Goldman, Jack's flaky son. 'What's he done this time?'

'Read the file, Nat. Get some lunch and call me. Don't let–'

'Catherine know?'

'See why I've missed you?'

Glad to have a purpose, even if it was Julian, Nat headed towards Wendy in her own little pod. 'Jack has asked–' she started, but Wendy pointed to her ear and held out the key.

Flipping heck. Who the hell would've guessed? The dim office junior now had her own 'office' with a cactus and a wireless headphone. But the desire to chuckle and share was swiftly followed by a wave of sadness. What had gone wrong? When Nat last worked here she had mates in this room, people with common gripes and common humour, but they'd all dispersed after her, leaving just Wendy and Sharon and a shared desk full of teenagers.

Heavy-hearted, she retreated to Wesley's office, half closed the door, and opened the red file. She felt ridiculously nervous. What if Catherine suddenly appeared? Unlikely, but not impossible. In years gone by this room had solid walls and a creaking door; many a time she had gone quietly about Jack's files 'for her eyes only' without her heart hammering. What she'd never understood back then was why Jack kept them from Catherine. They were his kids, not hers.

Perhaps that was the point.

Time passed as she read through the file. Astonished at the alleged assets belonging to Jack, she went back to the financial statements.

'I see you've made yourself comfortable, Natalie.'

Almost jumping from her skin, Nat snapped to the voice. His presence was a shock, but his tone didn't surprise her.

Standing at the open door, Wesley Hughes was frowning. Perhaps his dark hair was closer cropped, but he looked much the same as five years ago: well-cut suit, expensive tie; straight back, folded arms… and bad attitude.

She automatically closed the red folder. 'Sorry, I was just…'

'So I see. Something for Jack, I assume?'

'Yes, he…' What to say? Wesley was a partner, as much her

employer as Catherine and Jack these days. Though the thought was galling, if she wanted this job, she couldn't afford to offend him.

He shrugged. 'Whatever, it's fine. I'm not remotely interested.' He stared for a moment, his chiselled jaw tight. 'Jack wanted you back, so we'll all have to live with it.'

The resolution to be amiable short-lived, Nat stood. 'I assume one is allowed a lunch break?' She nodded at the office manual. 'I was so riveted by the eighty-three pages of the firm's policies, plans and procedures, I didn't get as far as the Working Time Regulations.'

The slightest of smiles cracked his obvious irritation. 'It'll be interesting to discover what you remember about the law, Nat, but your sarcasm's clearly intact. Yes, an hour for lunch.' He nodded to the fee-earners' bench, his smile stretching to show his white even teeth. 'Good luck with finding a seat when you're back.'

2

YOU'LL FIND A WAY

G lad of the breeze to cool her hot cheeks, Nat stood on the pavement. She was still getting used to the English weather again, but after a rainy August, September was better, balmy and dry, even if it did have that horrible back-to-school feeling. She turned one way and turned again, surprised to see a homeless man and his dog hunched beneath the Co-op window. A high street with too many eating choices, the smart suburban village had become one line of restaurants, most of them new.

At breakfast her mum had offered to rustle up a sandwich. 'Or maybe not on your first day, eh, Skarbie?' she'd added, using Nat's childhood pet name.

'We're not that flipping poor,' she had wanted to retort, but Anna meant well and her offer wasn't just about their precarious finances. Like Nat, she needed a sense of purpose, even if it was looking after her adult daughter in some small way. Nat had asked her to prepare a tasty surprise for dinner; she hoped that would do it for today. And if she was honest, it was nice to be fussed over a little. For now, anyway.

After emptying her coins into the homeless dog's bowl, Nat opted for the café beneath the office building. It had a large front window, so it was easy to spot any of the staff coming in. Settling herself on a leather sofa, she took some time to order, gazing at the tapas menu and working out the likely profit before remembering to stop herself. It made her think of her mobile, the mobile she'd managed not to look at all morning. Finally ordering a Panini, she sat back and closed her eyes, glad of the sun shining in through the open windows.

Though the red file was safely stashed in her bag, she still wedged it between her feet. The wad of legal documents related to Jack's divorce and financial proceedings; the rest of the paperwork comprised letters written to Jack. It had taken several moments at Wesley's desk to work out what was going on. All composed by Julian, the vitriolic missives were written on behalf of his mum. Apart from the frequent complaints that his father had never been there for the family, the gist was the inadequate matrimonial settlement and his mother's need for more cash.

The aroma of roast peppers interrupted her thoughts. Sitting up, she thanked the waitress and tucked into her lunch. So where was this information going? Over the years she'd been nominated to get Julian out of a fix several times, mostly when he was in his teens. Those misdemeanours had ranged from suspension from his private school to a refusal to take a breathalyser test; from minor criminal damage to alleged plagiarism at uni; but he was now in his mid-twenties and his compositions were quite eloquent.

Reaching for the file, she slipped out the final letter. His bile had expanded to Catherine in that one: 'You were generous to Mum and me until Catherine came along. Yes, the slag you were shagging when I was still wearing pyjamas. I can only assume the spite comes from her.'

Hell, that was below the belt. And it did made sense for Jack's need to keep his wife out of it. But how could Nat help? The letters were over a year old. There was only one way to find out: by calling the master of intrigue himself.

She dug to the bottom of her bag, pulled out her mobile and took a sharp breath before checking it. As usual the blank screen felt like a thump to her stomach. No message, no bloody message. But she *had* to get a grip. Closing her eyes for a beat, she steadied herself, then she rang Jack.

'So?' she began. 'I've read the file.'

'How's the office?' he replied.

'Cramped. If I ever manage to rest half a buttock I'll be lucky. So, these letters from Julian…'

'Just to show you the state of play.'

'Oh?'

'We don't talk; we haven't for some time. His mother's a drunk. She got more than her fair share, as you will have seen from the pleadings, the final order. Those letters hurt but…'

As usual Jack was swinging from straight-talking to cryptic, but she knew not to rush him.

'…he's still my son.' Hearing his deep sigh, she pictured him taking off his glasses and rubbing those strikingly blue eyes. 'I've been tipped off by a police pal at Wilmslow station. There's been an assault. A *complaint* of an assault.' He paused for a beat. 'By Julian's girlfriend, his partner, whatever the phrase is these days.'

Nat waited for more, but Jack remained silent. 'Okay,' she said slowly. 'But you're estranged, Jack. Why would Julian want anything to do with me?'

'He refused legal representation at the station. Then he reluctantly agreed to speak to the duty solicitor, apparently. I need to know what's going on. Talk to him, Natalie.'

'But what can I do?'

'I've no idea. But I know you'll find a way.'

Nat had determined to walk the two miles home each working day, not to lose weight, those extra Mallorcan pounds had fallen off without trying, but to keep fit. A bus to Didsbury in the morning, then don the trainers after work and trot home. That was the theory, but she hadn't anticipated being so bloody tired, both mentally and physically. Of course, that was a good thing; she'd spent too many wakeful hours examining the past, but by the time she reached her neat terraced house in Cheadle village, her blouse was dripping with sweat and her feet were blistered.

New running shoes hadn't been a good idea; like being caught in Wesley Hughes's office, she should've broken them in first.

Though far from a 'surprise', a bacon and cabbage casserole was waiting for dinner. It was just the way she liked it – plenty of potato and just a smattering of meat.

'So how was your day?' her mum asked.

Nat pulled a wry face. 'There must be easier ways to make money.'

Cocking her head, Anna studied her for a moment. 'You enjoyed yourself, though, I can tell. Your eyes are bright. Better keeping busy than dwelling...'

Nat scooped up her last cube of potato. 'Yeah, I know, Mum.'

She understood her mum was itching to say more, but she was weary of talking about it. The thinking was constantly there, whether she liked it or not; at least she could control what she said out loud.

Her mobile rang. As though telepathic, it was Jack.

As usual he launched in without a greeting. 'What happened with The Spaniard?'

'He isn't Spanish, Jack, and nothing happened. Mum...' she glanced up at her mother, who'd discreetly moved to the sink. '... Anna was ill and needed me here. So now I'm back. That's all there is to know, so...'

'The girlfriend. Tomorrow, start with her.'

It took a moment to shift focus. Nat was thinking that perhaps Jose was a Spaniard after all. Born and brought up in

Liverpool but with a Mallorcan grandma. Did that make him Spanish?

'On the assumption they're still living there,' Jack continued. 'Julian will be at work. You could have a chat with the girl. Persuade her to see sense…'

Wesley's face flashed into her mind, that look of irritation and disapproval when Jack's name was mentioned. She could see where it came from; the boss could be impossible at times, his demands often on the brink of unlawful; one had to stand firm.

'I'm not going to strong-arm a witness, Jack. I'm here to earn a salary, not to be locked up for perverting the course of justice. Have we got that clear? If you're in any doubt, you can stick your bloody–'

'But you will have a word?'

She sighed; she had never denied Jack anything, and there was no point starting now. 'I will have a word, Jack, but you need to butt out. Understand? Whatever I do, I'll do it my way.'

3

ALL MY FAULT

It was another bright morning. A little concerned about the strange noises it made, Nat drove Anna's car down Kingsway. She'd organised the insurance cover and checked the MOT was in date, but perhaps she should have taken it to be checked out or serviced, or maybe part-exchanged it for something a little more high spec. However that involved money.

Inwardly she snorted. She'd driven a Mercedes Coupe in the old days at Goldman Law – it was part of her package – and while she hadn't been particularly bothered about cars, driving an old Ford Ka was somewhat of a come down. Why hadn't she negotiated a company vehicle with Jack? Well, she knew the answer to that: discussions hadn't come into it, just a teary phone call about her mother's finances and a need to escape from the house.

He'd cut her off after only a minute. 'Goldman Law, first thing Monday morning. I need someone I can trust. I'll deal with Catherine and Wesley–'

The idea of getting a job hadn't occurred to her, let alone her old one. She'd still been hoping to return to Mallorca. Hopeless hope, she'd known, but still, being gainfully employed had felt too permanent.

Jack hadn't given her time to reply. 'And I know there's only you to look after Anna, but she's probably as sick of seeing you as you are of her. She probably wants her house back, to leave the dishes unwashed, the toilet unflushed, to invite the window cleaner in for a cuppa. Ever thought of that?'

The house was actually Nat's, bought when she'd first started at Goldman Law and thankfully paid off, but she hadn't wanted to be pedantic and Jack had had a point. So she'd surprised herself by saying 'Yes', just like she'd surprised herself five years previously when Jose had told her he was buggering off to Mallorca.

Finally arriving in Alderley Edge, she crawled the car through the village. The shops were as sparkling and glassy as she remembered. Pulling up at the pedestrian crossing, her eyes caught a suited mannequin in a window display. Bloody hell; from the smart-casual outfit to its icy expression, it was a spit of Catherine. Her heart fell. Oh God, Catherine. Despite readying herself for the encounter, Nat hadn't seen hide nor hair of her yesterday. How would she react to Nat's tail-between-the-legs return? Presumably Jack had told her? She shook her head at the thought. Jack, flaming Jack; that's why she was in the 'champagne capital of Britain' this morning. Or was it Prosecco these days?

At the other end of the high street, she peered through the windscreen. Julian's house was near here, wasn't it? Pressing her foot hard on the accelerator to manage the hill, she looked to the right. Oh hell, was that his building? She dived on the breaks. That rasping noise again. She'd definitely speak to Jack about a company vehicle, maybe even discuss a salary. God, she hoped she was being paid. Who'd want the grief? But, as she parked up behind a glossy Lexus four-by-four, she thought of what her mum had said about bright eyes. It was good to have a purpose, it felt great to be nervous, it was a fucking relief not having the time to stare at her mobile and repeatedly replay the last year, yet fail to work out what the hell had gone wrong.

Inhaling deeply, she climbed out of the car, straightened her suit skirt, and tried to deduce which house belonged to Jack's son. Separated into three or four sections, the old white-rendered property was huge and it wasn't immediately obvious which was which. Deciding to start from the left, she tiptoed down steps leading to a wooden doorway. What would she say? She still hadn't decided, but as she entered the small courtyard, there was no time to turn back – a black-haired figure was peering through a window.

The face disappeared and moments later the door was flung open. Oh hell. Nat tried not to stare. Not only did the woman have an obvious grey and purple shiner, she had a noticeable pregnancy bump, and she looked so very young, more a girl than a woman. Her dark eyes welled. 'Not again,' she blurted. 'I've told you everything already.'

Quick on her feet, Nat smiled reassuringly. 'Oh, I'm not the police.' She held out her hand and touched the girl's elbow. 'A family friend, actually. Natalie. Are you all right? Is Julian home?'

The girl shook her head and covered her face with trembling hands. 'He's at the police station again. It's all my fault.'

Nat took a breath. She recognised the young woman's need to talk, but she wanted to be honest. 'I'm a friend of Julian's dad, but I'm a solicitor too. I might be able to help. Should I come in?'

Doubt flicked across her face, but after a beat she stood back, allowing Nat to enter. 'Tissues,' she muttered, bolting away up the stairs.

Studying a neat row of footwear, Nat loitered in the hallway. It was a touching 'his and hers' line, hers as small as a child's. Though the sound of flushing and running taps filtered down, the girl didn't appear, so Nat made her way to a thin galley kitchen, found teabags and cups, filled up the kettle, and waited.

The kettle finally popped. Sniffing the milk, Nat added a slug to the two steaming mugs. Was she on a fool's errand? Probably. But she might as well have a cuppa before hoofing it back to Didsbury. Where was the poor girl? Heading back with the drinks, she stopped in the dining room and looked around properly. The house was actually very tasteful; Julian and his girlfriend had retained all the original features of this high-ceilinged room, the ornate light surround and picture rails, the old-fashioned fireplace.

'Thanks.'

Nat turned in surprise. Perched at the table and looking at her hands, the girl had crept back. Sitting opposite, Nat studied her neat face. She had obviously made an effort to cover the bruise, but the concealer was a shade lighter than her brown skin.

'I'm Natalie,' she repeated. 'And you are?'

'Aisha.'

'What a nice name.' Nat dipped her head. 'Why is it your fault, Aisha?' she asked. 'You have a pretty nasty bruise. That doesn't generally happen by accident.'

'Julian was stressed… it's the baby and money. He's never laid a finger on me before. He isn't like that. He's a good person.' She lifted her chin and gazed with red-rimmed eyes. 'You say you're a friend, so you must already know that…'

Nat thought back to the boy Julian and his teenage scrapes. It was difficult to judge. Reckless and spoilt, certainly, but the letters she'd read only yesterday showed something else. Desperation and hurt, a strange appeal for love – which she recognised in herself.

Jose, oh God. Her phone calls and texts: pathetic and angry, spiteful and pleading, demanding and needy, until he had changed his number and cut her off completely. Though she still desperately needed answers, the gratitude was almost there. His brutal ending had stopped the humiliation of those texts and calls. She had become one of the wretched and broken-hearted divorce clients she'd only managed to endure for three seconds, those weak women she'd wanted to shake and shout: 'He's stopped loving you. Show some pride. Get on with your life.'

Dragging herself back to the present, she tried to focus on today. Aisha was still gazing with luminous eyes. Nat sighed inwardly. Of course she now knew life wasn't as simple as she'd thought. It wasn't easy to get on and show pride. And here was a woman who'd been hit by her boyfriend, but still rushed to defend him. An assault by a man was unforgivable; there were no excuses. Yet there was something about this girl she admired. A strange nobility, she supposed. Not in a million years would she have expected Julian to choose such a plain but exquisite beauty.

She took Aisha's hand. 'Tell me what happened,' she said. 'Start at the beginning and I'll see if I can help.'

Instead of heading back through the village, Nat pulled up outside a sandwich shop, bought coffee and a stuffed baguette, then indicated right, the little car struggling as it chugged up Macclesfield Road. On one of their regular cycling routes, she used to come this way with Jose, past the multimillion pound properties hidden behind walls and electric gates, a round trip most Sundays of at least twenty miles.

Despite his proclivity for weed, Jose had been a fitness fanatic since she'd known him, and on hitting thirty she was suddenly smitten too, becoming super fit with him – biking and running, half marathons and triathlons. Yet when they were by the sea, they never went swimming. They didn't take their bikes to Mallorca; they stopped jogging. They were content running 'Havana', their beach-fronted café bar, making friends, chatting to the regulars, drinking, getting fat. They no longer needed those endorphin highs.

At least that's what she'd thought.

Trying to bat those memories away, she continued to drive

along the dappled, tree-lined road. Further into the vibrant coun-tryside, she parked in a lay-by, changed her shoes for trainers and carried her lunch up a stony path towards The Edge. The sun warm on her back, she stood at the cliff face and gazed out. The smell, the glorious shades of green and brown, the shadows and patterns, the horses, cows and sheep were as rousing as she remembered. There was the inevitable sensation of weakness in her legs from the sheer height of the rock and her proximity to the precipice, but she could feel her batteries charging after two months of being drained.

She wanted to help that poor girl; she wanted to help her unborn baby.

Aware of the vibration from her handbag, she eventually turned away. She knew it was Jack; he'd also called her in the car. She hadn't answered. She didn't have hands-free, but it wasn't just that. She was angry with him; he could wait.

The drink could have been warmer, but the sandwich tasted good and the conference pear was crisp. Still perched on a boul-der, she brushed the crumbs from her hands, then finally called Jack.

'You do know you're going to be a grandfather in two-and-a-half months?'

His silence said it all.

She couldn't hide her annoyance. 'He's your son. Whatever he might have said about Catherine, he's still your child. A new baby, Jack. An innocent new life. You can't just cut him off–'

'Why do I feel this has more to do with you than me, Natalie?'

Nat breathed. Yes, a baby, a new life. Despite Aisha's bruise and her distress, she'd almost felt jealous. How she hated Jack's ability to look into her soul.

She found herself shouting. 'Don't make excuses, Jack. Your son will be a father soon. That's something you should have known about.'

He was quiet again and the penny dropped. 'You did know,

didn't you? Why do you always tell me half a bloody tale? You knew; that's why you wanted me to help.'

'Despite what you or anyone else might think, I do have a heart, Natalie. My police mate mentioned it, but it was only station rumour. I didn't know for sure. What did you find out from the girl?'

Turning to the warm breeze, Nat took a moment to process her thoughts. She pictured Aisha's neatly plaited dark hair, her petite face etched with concern as she'd recounted the story.

'Your son's girlfriend is called Aisha, Jack,' she started irritably. Taking a breath, she relented. 'Apparently Julian came home late on Thursday, totally stressed out. She gave him a hard time about where he'd been all evening. His eyes were bleary so she assumed he'd been drinking, and wouldn't accept that he hadn't. She said she'd shouted and screamed, that she shouldn't have goaded him. He hit her once, his face immediately remorseful, then left the house, crossing with her dad who'd just arrived.' Nat paused, tucking her windswept hair behind her ears. 'The dad's visit was a surprise; he'd left something he needed for work the next day. He saw the damage to his daughter's face, was outraged and phoned the police. She tried to stop him, but he wouldn't listen. When Julian finally came home in the car, the police were waiting.'

'Did she press charges?'

'No. She told her dad to leave. She told the police it was as much her fault as his.'

Jack didn't speak for a moment; she could almost hear the whir of his thoughts. 'Then why take him in for questioning?' he asked.

'They suspected drink driving. And, of course, the assault. That's what Julian told her.'

'Why didn't they breathalyse him there?'

'She said she didn't know, and was beside herself with worry by then. She said they might have done it before they brought him into the house. But that's beside the point, Jack. He hasn't been charged with drink driving. Or drugs. Apparently he wasn't over the limit. He went into the station again this morning to hand in his documents: driving licence, insurance.' She paused before thinking out loud. 'But wouldn't all that stuff be computerised these days?'

There was a burst of conversation in the background, then an apology; where exactly was Jack?

'What was the name of the arresting officer?' he asked eventually.

'I have no idea; I didn't ask.'

'Right, you need to see Julian,' he said. 'We need to find out what's going on.'

Dusting the back of her skirt, Nat stood. 'No problem, Jack, I will. But not until you've seen him first.'

4

BETTER NOT KNOWING

Making a mental note of the new parking restrictions, Nat dumped the car on a side street near the office. It was now three o'clock; she'd have to leave by five, and if that was a problem she'd just have to move it. Catching her windswept reflection in the glass panel of the ground floor entrance, she tried to do something about it, then ran up the stairs – another 'new life' resolution. Finally at the top, she almost crashed into Wesley.

He stared with cold eyes. 'It's good of you to grace us with your presence.'

'I've been working out of the office. For–'

'I know; he's been in.'

She ducked to one side to let him pass, but he went the same way and they nearly collided again.

With his sucked-in cheeks and knitted brows, his handsome face was a picture. It wasn't that funny, but Nat suddenly felt febrile and had to stifle the desire to guffaw out loud. 'It seems I'm getting in the way,' she said with a grin.

He shook his head as he passed. 'You're really not funny, Natalie.'

The door below slammed as she swiped into the office. As though waiting, Wendy was at the reception counter. Apparently listening to someone else, security guard-style through her earpiece, she shook her head, then pointed a finger upward.

Scuttling from her workstation at the rear of the office, Sharon almost tripped on an escaped wire. 'Nat! You've been promoted,' she called. 'Sort of.'

Well that was a relief; Nat had thought it was a summons from Catherine. 'Oh right, so...'

Sharon beamed. 'You've got the conference room as your office. Unless it's needed, of course. It's still a desk share in a way, but a better...' She turned her head and lowered her voice. The bench teenagers were ogling, their ears almost flapping. All six were men; Nat hadn't noticed that before. She'd seen a woman, surely? Number seven, probably.

Sharon stepped closer. 'Yes, the conference room. Still sharing, but a better desk share. I'll come up with you. I have some files from Wesley.'

'Right,' Nat said again. Well this was a surprise. Though perhaps not, on reflection, when one considered her half buttock quip to Jack and his rare presence in the office. She couldn't resist a small smirk. No wonder Wesley wasn't happy.

Each carrying a pile of folders, Nat followed Sharon up the stairs to the hallowed second floor.

Sharon swiped in, then pushed at the meeting room door. 'Home sweet home. What do you think?'

'Nice.' Stepping over the threshold, Nat took in the large oval table, the chrome and leather chairs and the small library of legal books on shelves at the end. She grinned; subject to being thrown out for gatherings, she'd ended up in a room twice the size of Wesley's office.

She clocked Sharon's torn face. 'I suppose this was Jack's idea?' she asked, opening the slatted blinds and peering at the second-floor staff, busy at their workstations. Well, that was interesting. No communal desk in the middle for Catherine; her team had individual pods. 'What did Wes say...?' She corrected herself as she flicked on the bright lights. 'What did *Wesley* say about it?'

Sharon bit her lip. 'I wouldn't say he was thrilled; he likes to come here for one-to-one client time,' she replied. 'But he hates doing the audits, so...' She put down her armful of buff-coloured files. 'So here they are. There's some sort of system for which ones pop up for review and when. Wesley will give you a list, I suppose. When he does, I'll find them for you, but these are the first twenty.'

Nat flipped open the top jacket, peered at the date of the first letter, and nodded. Auditing files was a poisoned chalice, but one that had to be done on each case yearly, according to the flipping office manual. The courts had sped up the litigation process, but with the six-year limitation period, some would have been opened for years, including the bulky folder she was trying not to look at. That particular one had been her bête noire when she'd left. Unbelievable it was still here, waiting to bite her.

She sighed. Reading, auditing and preparing a report à la office manual would be time-consuming and extremely dull. When had Wesley last tackled it? It was a clever move by him, but right now she didn't mind having 'one-to-one' time with these cases. Being busy was preferable to twiddling her thumbs while she waited for Jack's intermittent command. Or staring at her mobile.

Sharon's face was still pink; she was clearly bursting to say more. 'Wesley said if you were swanning around like a partner, you might as well have the grief...'

Nat snorted inwardly. Should she rise to the bait and say something mocking in reply? It was sure to reach Wesley's ears, but probably not worth the fall out in the long run. Besides, this time she had promised herself to behave and keep her sardonic humour in check.

'Okey-dokey, no problem, it's something to get my teeth into and keep me out of mischief. I'll make a start now.' Nat sat down at one end of the table, facing the door. 'I don't suppose you could rustle up a cup of tea? I forgot to bring in my own mug.'

As though it was breathing, she pushed the bête noire to one side. It was better to concentrate on the task in hand rather than allow her mind to dwell on the intense excitement she'd felt when she left that flaming file and the office for the very last time. Life had seemed magical then. She'd shocked Jack, her mum and her older brother by doing it. But most of all she'd amazed herself, upping sticks and joining Jose in Puerto Pollensa as soon as she'd worked her notice. He'd been there at Palma airport to meet her, already nut brown and wearing ridiculous shorts. 'Bloody hell, you've come,' he'd said. 'I really didn't think you would.'

Shaking herself back to the files, she read the first few cover to cover. They were surprisingly interesting. Catherine had always had her own clients and Nat had worked for Jack's or his own companies. But as she flicked through the pages it was clear the client base had expanded, not only to conveyancing, personal injury and matrimonial, but also to several decent-looking commercial and litigation files run, she assumed, by Tom, Dick and Harry at their bench downstairs. It was interesting; Wesley had obviously done things his own way and had been very successful.

'Wesley can be a little anal, but he's the future, Nat.'

Nat looked up in surprise. Dressed as gracefully as ever, Catherine was at the door.

'Oh, Catherine, hi.'

Taking in her wide-legged grey trousers and cowl-necked cream top, Nat took a breath. Oh God, what to say? Catherine hadn't said a word to her since the day she'd handed in her notice; she hadn't joined the other fee-earners on her goodbye do; she hadn't signed the card. Nat had never worked out if she was angry at her leaving, or whether she simply didn't care.

Catherine glanced at the gold watch dangling from her wrist. 'Let's get a drink.' She gazed at Nat for a beat. 'A proper drink. In fact several.'

Nat remembered the car. 'I'm in a car. Mum's car. Shit, I don't want a ticket...'

'Put it in the car park. Park it behind mine if there aren't any spaces. I'm not driving anywhere tonight. Downstairs in ten minutes?'

Nat guided the little Ka to the rear of the office. Save for Catherine's Mercedes SUV, the spaces allocated to Goldman Law were all vacant. Though Catherine's number plate showed it was almost brand new, the paintwork was splattered and the tyres rimmed with dried mud: country living. And, of course, her beloved dogs. She and Jack lived on a converted farm in the Cheshire sticks, the property they'd bought when they first married. Nat had never been invited to visit, but she'd heard it was magnificent, still resembling a farm but with every mod con.

Her heels chafing from yesterday's blisters, Nat dashed to the front of the building. Wearing a belted camel coat, Catherine was waiting. Surely wool was too warm for the weather? Or maybe it was just her, feeling hot under the collar and wondering what her old friend wanted to say to her.

Sitting on the same sofa as yesterday, Nat accepted the proffered gin and tonic and sank back. A G and T was probably a good choice; it didn't get her pissed the same way as wine, and she wasn't used to drinking any more.

Lager, she mused, as she took an icy sip. She and Jose had drunk cold beer in Mallorca before moving on to the local vino each night. She'd never liked it before and now she couldn't ever imagine liking it again.

In her usual eloquent tones, Catherine talked about the client she had seen today and his plans to undercut the pound shops. Listening politely, Nat wondered how on earth goods could be made, shipped and sold for fifty pence, whilst trying not to stare at Catherine's eyes. If she'd had surgery, it was good. She looked her age but in a youthful and polished way, her streaked Lady Di hairstyle the same as always.

'So, the conference room,' Catherine said, abruptly changing the subject. 'Will it work out?'

Back on alert, Nat felt the goosebumps. 'Yeah, sure, if that's okay with you.'

'You know me. If Jack's happy, I'm happy,' Catherine replied.

The leather enveloping her, Nat shifted in her seat. Catherine had said it easily enough, but Jack felt like a dangerous topic of conversation.

'He's got you doing something already. For Julian or Verity, I expect.' She looked at Nat coolly for a second before smiling. 'It's fine. They're his children. I'm better not knowing.' She lifted her arm to attract the waitress's attention, then raised her glass. 'Not home measures, are they?' She turned back to Nat. 'We see Verity when she wants something, but we've not heard from Julian for a long time. I think Julian and his father fell out. Jack protecting my honour, probably, which really isn't necessary, I'm a big girl now.'

The waitress replenished their drinks with doubles. The alcohol spread in Nat's chest. It felt pleasant, relaxing and reassuringly English.

Catherine's wry laugh broke the silence. 'Yes, a big girl now. Fifty. Bloody fifty. I would rather disappear in a puff of smoke, but Jack has organised something at a new hotel in town on Saturday. You're invited, of course…' She seemed to drift before raising her eyebrows. 'Revenge for his surprise sixtieth, I suppose. That was at home; there weren't many of us, but friends, proper friends, it was fun. He feigned surprise, but he probably knew. You missed it, you were in Spain–'

'Mallorca.'

'Mallorca, of course. Sun, sea and sangria. I was jealous when you left. I thought you were brave to be so...' She seemed to search for a word. '...romantic.' She tilted her head, her pale face softening. 'It didn't work out with Jose?'

Turning her glass, Nat didn't reply. When she'd first started at Goldman Law she'd fallen a little in love with Catherine. Ten years older than her, tall, sophisticated, clever and so assured. They were friends for some time, shopping trips, meals, nights out, confiding in each other, having fun. Catherine met Anna, Nat's mother, her brother and Jose; they were close. But then Catherine was made a partner and things changed; or perhaps they already had when she became Jack's secret mistress. That had been a shock, a deep betrayal, if Nat were honest.

Catherine spoke again. 'When I heard, it didn't surprise me.'

Nat looked up then. 'Heard what?'

'That you were back, alone. I know Anna had been ill, but it was obvious that something odd was going on when Jose didn't come back at some point. The stroke was serious; they thought she might not make it at first, didn't they?'

Wondering if Jack told Catherine everything, Nat nodded. It had been a stifling hot July night when the call from her old neighbour came. 'Havana' had closed late; she and Jose had been drinking; they'd struggled to shake themselves awake. Her neighbour's voice had trembled as she'd told Nat the bad news; Anna was in intensive care; she'd had a massive stroke.

The neighbour had heard a noisy bang through the thin terraced walls and then silence; she'd called the emergency services when Anna failed to answer the phone or the door; she'd gone in the ambulance, held her hand.

It had had been a terrible shock, but Nat hadn't focused on

possible death – that came later – she'd been too overwhelmed with feelings of guilt. The imperative was to fly home as soon as she could. Jose had promised to follow.

Now glancing at Catherine's inquisitive face, she lifted the glass and swallowed the last of the gin. There was a pleasant numbing effect. 'Are we having another?' she asked. Then, when the fresh drinks arrived, both needing and not wanting to know, she posed the burning question: 'Why didn't it surprise you? About me and Jose?'

Catherine shrugged. 'You were never in love with him.' Despite her careful enunciation, her voice was starting to slur. 'He just ground you down and you eventually gave in.'

'And I suppose you were in love with Jack?' Nat replied sarcastically, her chest hot and constricted.

Catherine's face looked empty. 'I was actually; desperately.' She stood and collected her coat. 'I'm off to the flat now. I need a night without his snoring.' She took a step to leave, then turned back. 'Do you remember the abortion? You held my hand, wiped my tears? A one-night stand with a builder from Cardiff?'

Of course Nat remembered. Confident, self-reliant Catherine; Catherine who never cried, who'd never wanted a baby. She'd been inconsolable, broken. Nat hadn't known about her and Jack then; she hadn't guessed even after, but realisation now hit like a hammer. 'Oh God, it was Jack's?'

Catherine tightened her belt and took a deep breath. 'And in three days I'll be fifty.'

5

DIRTY WORK

On Wednesday, Nat was snoozing on the bus when her mobile jerked her back to the sparkling River Mersey beyond the smeared window. Aware of the usual buttock-clench, she glanced at the screen, but it was only Sharon.

'Morning.'

'Don't get off, Nat. Wesley needs you in court to sit behind counsel.'

Hmm, a task for a paralegal and Wesley in command. That woke her up very quickly. 'Okay, but what about the file?'

'He said you won't need it. The barrister has been briefed. There's a conference at nine. The client's called…' She heard the tap of Sharon's long fingernails. 'A Mr Jagger.'

Nat looked at her watch. She'd caught the bus from Cheadle High Street at eight, but they were still stuck at temporary traffic lights on Stockport Road, so she was unlikely to reach the courts before nine thirty. Damn, and on Wesley's case too. 'I'll do my best.' Then a notion. 'Who's counsel?'

Sharon laughed. 'Your favourite.'

Pleased at the thought of seeing her old mucker, Nat sent him a text, then changed into trainers and tapped her knee as the bus slowly lurched north. She'd intended to jump off at the central library like she used to, but the 42B took an earlier turn, so she found herself clutching her heels and handbag and pelting across town towards the Civil Justice Centre. Finally reaching the vast Jenga-shaped building, she quickly headed for security and tried not to pant as she was beeped through. Conscious of her sweaty, dishevelled state, she discreetly leaned against a wall, swapping sneakers for shoes, but inevitably was spotted.

'The lovely Miss Bach. No, stay bare-footed, fair lady. The thought of your toes will *Shine a Light* on my morning.'

Nat looked up at the tall, gowned figure of Christopher Aaron QC. He hadn't aged a day since she'd met him as a junior barrister, though he was certainly wider. She supposed he was still as heavy featured, but his easy charm was too dominant. It was difficult to see his 'uncomely' face (as Chris had himself put it) any more.

Her jacket was stuck to her spine. She tried to loosen it innocuously. 'The text said to meet me outside the court, Chris. By then I would've been fully attired, my hair brushed, rather than looking…' Did she know *any* Stones' albums? She might be nearly forty, but she wasn't *that* old. '…looking *Black and Blue*.'

'Ah, your lovely message.' He patted his stomach. 'For which I was eternally obliged. It gave me time for a *Sticky Fingers* bacon butty–'

Nat laughed. 'Did you forget you were Jewish?'

'I'm practising for when I go into politics. It's *Dirty Work*, but someone's got to do it. So, what happened to young Max?'

She shifted her mind from old rocker quips. 'Max?'

'Max, your colleague. Another delightful product of Goldman Law.'

'Ah, the bench boys have names. I was hoping you'd fill me in. Sorry, but I know nothing about him or the file.'

'Perfect. Then let us find the client. The claimant, I believe.'

Mr Jagger was nowhere to be found, but he had booked in

with the court usher, so he had to be somewhere in the building. Though Nat had been called in last minute by Wesley – and without a file, let alone any indication of what the case was about – she still wanted to do her best, so she took a description from the usher (definitely not *the* Mr Jagger) and decided to have a recce in the café. A floor down in the lift, she headed for the aroma of coffee, and was almost there when a text from Chris called her back.

Client has rolled back. Time for Live Licks.

Ready to retrace her steps, Nat lifted her head, but a familiar deep voice made her spin round. Gesticulating as he did when emphasising a point, Jack Goldman was at the far end of the corridor. She smiled; he was wearing the usual elevated shoes to give him extra height. Funny to see him after so long – out of context, too; as a partner he had to be on the solicitor's roll, but she hadn't realised he was actually practising.

A thick-set, balding man was standing next to him. She gave an involuntary shiver. Frank Foster, one half of the 'Levenshulme Mafia', as Jack used to call them. Frank and his sister owned several business and residential buildings in Levenshulme, a halfway township between Manchester and Stockport. They let their own and other properties through their estate agency, 'Foster Homes', an incongruous name, if ever there was one.

She gazed at him for a moment. What was Frank up to this time? And, more to the point, why was the boss dealing with him himself? She turned away with a sigh. God, she hoped Jack wouldn't drag her in at some point. Like his sister Danielle, Frank Foster was attractive and winsome on the surface, but underneath he was harder than nuts, nails and nippers. Pressing the button for the lift, she glanced again. One of the quiff-haired bench boys was standing next to him, looking keen. The absent Max, she assumed. Her lips twitched. Poor Wesley, it looked as though Jack had pulled rank.

6

MY LUCKY LADY

N at smiled on the tram back to Didsbury. She'd had a fun morning and a free tasty lunch. Probably the same age as *the* Mr J, the client was an amiable elderly man with shrewd eyes. The pre-hearing conference had been short and to the point. Chris agreed with Wesley: the solicitor defendant had failed to inform Mr Jagger about a hefty pre-existing charge on his property; he didn't have a leg to stand on; they should proceed with the pre-emptive strike for summary judgment as Wesley had planned.

'In short, nipping it in the bud,' Nat had added when the client looked perplexed.

They had duly entered Court 3 at ten thirty and the defendant's flustered barrister immediately requested an adjournment before putting forward a proposal to settle. It had taken some time for his insurer client to reach the right figure, but, as Chris put it, that was an excellent thing; he needed to appear to be earning his outrageous brief fee. Nat had waved off the satisfied Mr Jagger (who 'got what he wanted', after all), said hello to a few old pals milling around court, then graciously allowed Chris to buy her lunch at San Carlo, her favourite haunt when someone else was paying.

'Come on, dear girl, you owe me some gossip,' Chris said over dessert wine.

Nat knew he meant tittle-tattle about her love life, but she parried his questions pretty well, considering she'd collapsed into bed and sobbed before sleep the previous night. She'd lain there befuddled and pissed, missing Jose desperately. Was it love or dependence or something else completely she wondered? It was all too confusing; it was easier to cry.

She shook herself back to the smooth tram ride: another new addition since she'd left for sunny climes. The area she was sitting in was impressively clean, offered a free newspaper, and the route map showed a stop almost opposite her childhood home in Oldham. Not that she had a reason to go back; on the rare occasions she had done so, the stench of the nearby hospital reminded her of her father, an uncomfortable feeling she didn't like to dwell on.

Taking in the pretty pink flowers either side of a bushy pathway, she followed another commuter. She hurried past orange-brick townhouses towards the shops, stopping halfway to allow a crocodile of chattering school kids to pass. Finally arriving at the office, she ran up the two flights of stairs, swiped in and headed for the conference room.

She had planned to dictate notes from the hearing while they were fresh, but the blinds and the door were closed. Despite the soundproofing, raised voices filtered through. What the...? She rushed to Catherine's room, and discovering it was empty, leaned over her secretary's workstation.

'Any idea?' she asked, nodding towards the apparent fracas.

The young woman pulled off her headset and shrugged. 'No, sorry. It's Wesley and a client. They've been at it for half an hour.'

'Okay, cheers.'

What was going on? There was one certain way to find out.

Trotting down to the floor below, Nat said 'Hi' to Christine at reception, then headed for Sharon, who had her back turned towards her. 'What's happening upstairs in the conference room?' she whispered urgently, 'It sounds fraught...'

Sharon gave a little jump and returned her mirror to a drawer. 'Oh God, is it bad?' Biting her bottom lip, she lowered her voice. 'Brian Selby, remember him?'

'A thick-set Yorkshire man with octopus hands?' Nat replied. 'The guy who started a haulage empire with just one lorry in Doncaster?'

Sharon nodded. 'He stormed in about an hour ago and went ballistic with Emilia over something she'd either done or hadn't done. She started crying, then Wesley intervened and took them both upstairs.'

'And Emilia is?' Nat asked, though she suspected the answer: number seven, poor girl.

'Wesley's trainee. It's his file she's been working on.' Sharon gave a theatrical shudder. 'Can you imagine if Brian Selby sacks us? Wesley has a whole filing cabinet of his files alone – commercial, litigation, employment. Then there's all his workers, so that's family, probate, conveyancing...'

'Right; got it.'

Her mind already strategising, Nat headed for the ladies. She'd felt smug this morning at court and thought that the negligent solicitor had got what he deserved, but in truth mistakes were easy to make in the law; she didn't know one lawyer who hadn't had a hot-under-the-collar moment of one sort or another.

Leaning into the mirror, she tucked her hair behind her ears, pinched her cheeks and applied lipstick. Unlucky number seven. She could picture the bench boys sniggering at her tears, making quips about her being on her period, or a having a 'blonde moment' when she cocked up, the sort of supposed banter that she herself had weathered so often. Hoping she wasn't too late, she ran up the stairs, swiped in and listened at the door for a second. Then, taking a deep breath, she straightened her back and burst in.

Three pairs of eyes stared, one bloodshot, two angry.

'Oh, sorry. I didn't realise anyone was...' she started, all innocence.

She turned, then looked back, making eye contact with the ruddy-faced man squashed in his chair. 'It's Brian, isn't it? From Doncaster, but now living in Worsley, if I recall. Hello, how are you?' Hand on her chest, she stepped towards him. 'I'm Natalie Bach. I was with Jack Goldman when we met at the races–'

'Cartmel.' The accent was still full Yorkshire tyke. The man grinned and leaned back. 'As though I'd forget. My lucky lady. You won me a lot of money that day.'

Nat flashed a bright smile. 'Sadly, I only bet a fiver on that last race. I seem to recall yours was somewhat larger.' She caught Wesley's frown from her peripheral vision. 'Sorry again for interrupting.' Accepting Brian's sausage fingers, she shook them firmly. 'Nice to see you again.' Then, as an afterthought, she tapped her watch. 'The curry mile, Brian, while you're here? Unless Wesley has organised something else? I have one particular favourite restaurant: chicken mughlai to die for.'

Holding her breath, she made for the door. Did Brian Selby even like curry? Or was he a strictly beef-and-Yorkshire-pudding type of guy? She couldn't remember anything he'd said at the races, just that he had smoked fat cigars, was a little too tactile, and had a wallet stuffed with notes.

'Let's wrap this up.' She could hear his gruff tones as the door closed behind her. 'Right, I'll go with your plan B, Wesley, but I won't be so forgiving next time...'

∼

Agitated and homeless, Nat hovered in the reception area downstairs. Brian's accent had reminded her of the elderly fella she used to visit on the other side of the village. He'd come over from 'God's own county' to marry his Lancastrian wife. Nat had prepared the probate when the old girl died; she had never witnessed such grief and she'd found herself popping in to check on him at least once a week until Mallorca intervened.

Beguiling Mallorca.

Wesley's voice interrupted her thoughts. 'He's gone to the toilet,' he said irritably. He shook his head, his face tight. 'He wants to try "one of his lucky lady's curries". I hope you know what you're doing.'

Announcing he fancied a pint 'or three' before food, Brian appeared eventually, so they headed for the Old Cock, Nat slipping her arm through Emilia's as they strolled through light rainfall. Looking more composed, Emilia had fixed her tear-stained face, but Nat could feel her tremulousness, the way her breath caught in her throat. Or perhaps it was just Nat remembering. She'd done her training at a large practice in Manchester; her boss had been a sadistic shit.

Nat glanced behind her. How would Emilia describe Wesley Hughes? Not a brutal bastard, she hoped, though looking at his face, she wondered. He most certainly wasn't happy. His jaw was fixed; his broad shoulders hunched; his fists shoved in the pockets of his raincoat.

They stayed for three rounds in the pub, politely listening to Brian talk – and talk – about his exploits in Bulgaria. He'd spent several weeks there to recruit staff for his business and his general attitude was just short of racist, but definitely sexist.

Nat inwardly sighed. Did Brian know she was Polish? Though she wasn't, of course. Her parents had been born in Kraków, but she'd been brought up in the UK, a Manc through and through, despite the Polish Club as a kid and her mum still chattering in the language with friends. A Polish-Manucinian-girl-woman, perhaps. Did it really matter? And anyway, wasn't everyone 'foreign' in one way or another? Not just on the outside, but within?

The familiar jolt of grief hitting, she threw back her drink. 'The Spaniard', as Jack called him. What was he doing right this minute? Why did alcohol always bring him to the surface of her thoughts? And why the hell was she drinking Bacardi?

Flicking on a bright smile, she turned to Wesley's client. 'Are you ready for your curry, Brian? It's a couple of miles up the road. I'll call a taxi.'

Brian heaved himself from his stool and waddled to the door. 'How about a good old-fashioned double-decker?'

Another Wesley scowl. 'An Uber would be–'

'Come on, lad, where's your sense of fun?' Brian stepped onto the pavement and pointed. 'Is this one going our way?'

As though telepathic, a bus had stopped at the lights. Taking his surprising lead, they ran to the shelter and piled on, Brian heading for the stairs like a kid.

Nat brought up the rear, but Brian had saved the seat next to him. He patted it. 'Natalie, here!' Placing his arm along the frame, he leaned close with beery breath. 'Or should I call you Lucky Lady?'

The restaurant felt dense, thick with diners and music and the aroma of spices. Brian headed for the men's as they waited. Her stomach clenching, Nat tried not to glance at Wesley's terse face; Emilia's animated chatter was emphasising his silence. They were finally led through to a table, then Brian returned with an inane grin, downing another pint before the starters arrived. Wesley drank too, but his smile was so fixed Nat was certain his cheeks would be aching come home time.

The meal dragged on, Brian holding court, his voice loud and slurred. Emilia excused herself eventually, saying she needed the loo and Nat followed.

'I'd like to be a fly on the wall,' she could hear Brian say to Wesley. 'The two of them together; a bit of girly action, if you get my drift. I've long wondered why they do that. Women – when one goes for a piss another follows...'

Trying to exorcise her indignation, Nat stomped to the women's toilets and breathed heavily. When she'd collected herself, she washed her hands and caught herself in the mirror. Her reflection glared back. Quite rightly too. It was the twenty-first century for God's sake. She couldn't believe sexist, misogynistic and homophobic dinosaurs like Brian Selby still existed. Why she'd assumed they'd become extinct, she didn't know. She blew out long and hard. She was trying to play him, but still.

Focusing on Emilia at the next sink, she sighed. 'Oh God, have I done the wrong thing? Pandering to that, to that–'

'No!' Emilia's eyes widened. 'Not at all, Natalie. I'm not kidding, I was scared. He was absolutely going to sack Wesley, I could see it coming.' She took a shuddery breath. 'Thanks so much for...' her fair eyebrows furrowed, '...handling Brian.' A nervous laugh bubbled up from her. 'He's pretty revolting, isn't he?' Her smile faded. 'We shouldn't really be having to deal with behaviour like that, the touchy-feely stuff, not after #MeToo.'

Nat nodded. Would the younger woman understand why she'd always endured it – that it was a strategy of playing the bastards and their male privilege, and ultimately getting equal rights her own way? Sure, no woman should have to, but with age had come pragmatism. Which was actually a damned depressing thought.

Age. In a couple of months she'd be forty.

She slipped her arm through Emilia's. 'Come on, one final push with the three Ls, and then we can go home.'

'Three Ls?'

Nat laughed. 'Lardy, leery and loaded.'

Brian lifted his slumped head as they reached the table. 'Tell him, Natalie. Tell Wesley. He wants to, he knows he wants to…'

She looked at Wesley questioningly. His reply was formal and clipped. 'Brian would like us all to accompany him to a nightclub. He wants to dance.' He stared at Nat coldly. 'He wants to dance with his "lucky lady".'

Three pairs of eyes were on her again. The bloodshot ones now belonged to the client. Oh hell. Another gamble, another bet…

Turning to Brian, she wagged a playful finger. 'Taxi time, Brian. Your missus will be wondering where you are. Curry breath's a misdemeanour, but a 3am return is a felony. Right, Wes?' She bent to Brian's ear and pointed at Wesley. 'Have pity, his wife might look pretty, but she breathes real fire…'

Tired and despondent, Nat sheltered under the canopy and watched Emilia mouth a 'Thank you' as she rushed away through the drizzle. Wesley was bundling Brian into a taxi and waving him off. Time to go home, thank the Lord. She walked off smartly for the nearest bus stop.

'What the fuck was that all about, Natalie?'

The sound of Wesley's voice made her jump. She spun round; he'd caught up with her.

'What was what–?'

'Interfering, for a start. Who the hell do you think you are?'

She gazed. The anger was radiating through Wesley's dark skin. 'I was trying to help.'

'Well, don't.' He spat out the words. 'It's none of your business. Everything was fine. I was handling it.'

Not appearing to notice the rain wetting his hair, he paced for a moment. Then he jabbed towards the restaurant, his voice staccato. 'Here, in the pub, on the fucking bus. How can you humiliate yourself like that? Putting on a coy voice, opening an extra button on your blouse, leaning into his face, re-applying lipstick. What happened to your principles, your dignity, Nat? You were acting like a tart.'

Cold, disheartened and bloody, bloody angry, Nat glared. 'You arrogant shit. I'm nobody's tart, I never have been–'

'That's not what I've heard.'

She pulled up her collar and turned away. It's what everyone had always assumed: that she had slept with Jack Goldman. Wesley's insinuation was as offensive as it always had been, but she was too weary to argue, and anyway, why should she bother putting him straight?

Lifting her arm, she flagged down a taxi. 'A simple thank you would have done, Wes,' she muttered instead.

7

SO MUCH FOR PROGRESS

'Wake up, Natalie love. Shouldn't you be getting ready for work?'

Her mum's face was bobbing, bringing on another wave of queasiness. She wasn't sure if it was the curry, the damned Bacardi, or her feelings of self-loathing. Last night she'd fallen asleep the moment her head touched the pillow, but had woken at three with a jerk, immediately berating herself. In hindsight, Wesley Hughes was right. Who the hell was she? And she had interfered. It might have gone terribly wrong; it could still do so; she may well have exacerbated a tricky situation.

'I think I'll stay in bed, Mum. I'll do less damage.'

Her mum straightened up, her pale eyes sympathetic. 'What's up, Skarbie? Did something happen last night?'

Not wanting to brood yet again, Nat groaned. 'I…'

How to put it? Not just meddling, but sucking up to bulbous, bloody Brian. 'I elbowed in at work when it wasn't my place to.' She hitched up the mattress and scooped her mobile from the pillow. Yup; she thought she'd heard something; a missed call from Wesley. Showing her phone to her mum, she grimaced.

'God knows what I've done. Taking over, basically. I'd be furious if he did it to me.'

Pulling back a corner of the duvet, her mum shuffled in next to her. Nat inhaled that comforting, soapy smell and rested her head on her shoulder. Her lovely mum. What would she do without her?

'Who says it's a bad thing, interference?' Anna asked, her accent creeping into longer words. 'Society needs it. Where would we be without social workers, the police, doctors, teachers, even politicians?' She pecked Nat's hair and smiled. 'Some people call it help.'

Nat sighed. 'You're a saint, Mum, you see the good in everything and everybody. Unfortunately I'm not.' A puff of wet wind blew the curtain. 'And it's flipping raining again.'

'You're too hard on yourself; you always have been. Perhaps other people don't see it, but I do.'

'See what?'

'Underneath your… *muszla*. The good person you are.'

Nat mentally translated the Polish word. 'Seashell', 'shell', 'conch'… 'Clamshell' sounded about right. 'See, Mum, "good" again? I rest my case.' Lifting her thumping head, she kissed her mum's cheek. 'I don't think I've been accused of that before. But thank you.'

They fell quiet and listened to the tinny rain drum the car roofs.

'I'm glad you're back,' her mum said, filling the long silence.

Nat took her hand. 'I am too. Even if it hasn't stopped pouring since.'

Anna turned and smiled. 'No, I meant in here,' she said, tapping her temple.

Inwardly Nat snored. It was typical of her mum, saying something without really voicing it. She'd never said that she didn't approve of Jose, but Nat had felt it. Then, when she met up with an old friend last week, she'd been told a story. It had been Fran who'd insisted on driving Nat to the airport when she left for Mallorca. Before they left the house, Anna had held Fran back and had said quietly, 'If Natalie changes her mind and walks back, don't stop her.'

She'd been frustrated when she'd heard that. 'Why didn't she say something to me?' she'd asked crossly, but Fran had just laughed, 'Come on, Nat. Anna's disapproval would've made you all the more determined to go. Not that I'd call you headstrong or anything...'

The sudden peal of her mobile broke her rumination. 'Oh, God, here we go, Mum,' she said, snatching it up and expecting to see Wesley's name. But it was a number she didn't recognise.

'Natalie?'

'Yes?'

'Can you come?' a soft voice whispered. 'Can you come right now? It's Aisha. I don't want Julian to know I'm calling, but it's sort of urgent. I'll explain when you're here...'

Though all fingers and thumbs as she'd dressed, Nat soon headed for the A34, pressing hard on the accelerator until she hit the Alderley Edge lights, managing the door-to-door journey in a record twenty minutes. A soft-top Mercedes was parked behind the four-by-four this time, so she pulled up on the steep, busy road, hoping the handbrake would do its job.

The rain was full pelt, so she climbed out and opened her umbrella. Why she bothered, she had no idea; the unexpected call from Aisha had alarmed her, so she'd cleaned her teeth, donned clothes and darted out of the house without showering. Still, she had thick hair, no one other than her would know it needed a good wash, and she wasn't likely to get up and close to anyone these days. Except leery clients. Oh God; what had she done? But at least her mind was more lucid now. A *tart*. That's what bloody Wesley Hughes had called her.

She held on to that thought as she trotted through the deluge. He'd been bang out of order saying it; she was still offended and insulted; and the high moral ground made her feel mildly better. Was she 'good' inside her clamshell, though? If only... 'Everything will be fine, just you see,' her mum had said, slipping a banana in her handbag at the door as she left.

Her sweet mother, who was glad she was 'back'. She'd think about that later.

Taking care, she tiptoed down the steps to the courtyard. They glistened and looked slithery; there really should be a handrail; suppose a postman tumbled, or a friend with a baby, even a burglar who might slip?

She smiled wryly. Hark Miss Bach. How easily she'd slipped back into lawyer mode. It reminded her of balmy evenings at 'Havana'. 'What did you do before opening up here?' holiday-makers often asked. 'I was a solicitor,' she'd reply. There had always been an incredulous beat before, 'Really? You must be joking.'

She pictured Catherine and her shrug on Tuesday night. '*You were never in love with him. He just ground you down and you eventually gave in.*' Were the two things connected somehow?

Breathing the discomfort away, she focused on the mission at hand. Lifting the latch, she dragged the umbrella in behind her. She glanced around the enclosure, then looked again. What the hell? His arms folded, Jack Goldman was sitting on the small bench beneath the kitchen window. He'd removed his spectacles, but his hair, his coat and his face were sodden.

'Bloody hell, Jack. What's going on?'

He gave a small smile, a stranger without his trademark black frames. 'It seems I'm not welcome.'

The door opened, and Aisha's face appeared, drawn and tired. 'I'm sorry,' she said tightly to Jack. Then to Nat, letting her pass,

'Julian won't allow him in. He's been here since eight thirty. He must be freezing, but...' She covered her face with her hands. 'It's all such a mess. I hope you didn't mind me ringing you.'

What on earth was going on? Nat tried for a reassuring tone. 'Of course not. I asked you to call me at any time.' She stepped forward and put her head around the dining room door. 'Where's Julian? Presumably he's still here?'

'He should've left for work ages ago, but he'd have had to go past his dad to get out, so he hasn't gone. Come on through...'

Aisha walked towards the rear of the house and Nat followed her into a bright, lofty lounge with a wooden floor and French windows. No one was in the room, but Aisha lifted her dark eyebrows and nodded to the open door. 'Out there...'

Apparently looking out to the saturated countryside beyond, Julian was crouched in a chair on the decked patio area. A dripping canopy umbrella in the centre of the table remained unopened. His expression petulant, he was as wet as his father.

A surge of memories hit Nat as she stared at his face. Why was she even remotely surprised? It was ever thus. Jack and his son were as obstinate as each other. Julian looked like his fair-skinned Dutch mother, but his personality was all Jack's.

'For goodness sake, Julian, come inside,' Nat said crossly.

He turned his head, puzzlement passing through before recognition set in. She was surprised how he'd aged. He was still handsome, but his face was no longer boyish and his hair looked thin, though perhaps that was the downpour, which was now assailing her too.

'Come in,' she repeated when he showed no sign of moving. 'For goodness sake! Is this a competition to see who dies of hypothermia first?'

His frown deepened and he opened his mouth to speak, but Nat cut in. 'You have a beautiful pregnant girlfriend who's close to tears. This isn't just about you, Julian. Come back inside.'

With the bearing of a thirteen-year-old whose pocket money

has been cut off, he followed Nat indoors. Aisha put one towel on the sofa and handed him another, then offered hot drinks. Feeling a trickle of water down her own neck, Nat closed the French window and perched in the armchair. There was no view of the courtyard from the lounge. Was Jack still there? Stubborn and controlling, but in all likelihood torn between anger and love?

With a deep sigh, she looked at Julian. He was sitting silently, his features set and stony. Where to begin? She inhaled quickly. 'Your dad's just worried about you–'

He immediately became animated, his face still wet. 'It's funny, isn't it? Last week he didn't care whether or not I existed. Now I've had a scrape with the police and he's suddenly worried. Or concerned about his pathetic reputation, more like. Either that or what Saint Catherine thinks…' He took a shuddery breath before spitting the words out. 'It's been way over a year since we even spoke and before that… well, let's face it, he's barely had any interest in me or Verity since Catherine dug her claws in. He's never met Aisha, the woman I love. What the fuck does that say about him?'

Nat paused, taking stock. If a person didn't talk, if people refused to communicate, it was so difficult to interpret what was going on in their heads. No one was telepathic. And the longer the silence went on, the more one's imagination invented scenarios of what was being thought. No one knew this better than her.

She felt the usual painful jolt in her chest. 'I'm not coming, Nat,' Jose had said when she'd asked him for the umpteenth time when he was flying over to see her and Anna. Still reeling from his tone, she'd almost not heard what he'd said afterwards: 'And I don't think you should come back here; it's over between us.'

The ache, the sheer agony. His unilateral decision to end their relationship was devastating, but it became even worse when he severed her completely. Silence, insidious silence; cutting off her need to voice her anger, confusion and heartbreak. Even more important, she was now unable to find out why.

Dragging herself back to today, Nat focused on Julian. 'I can see you're offended and upset. Jack told me about the letters – perhaps he is too.' She held out her hands. 'But the point is, I don't know and neither do you unless you ask him. And he doesn't know how much you're hurting until you tell him.'

Julian's face coloured. His expression was similar to the last time she saw him: sulky and angry, even though he'd got away with just a small magistrate's fine back then. 'I'm not hurting. He's just a shit. My life is better without him.'

For a second Nat stared at him. He'd grown up being over-indulged by his mother and in all likelihood bullied by his father. It didn't make for a good combination, she knew that. Not that her mum had been overly-indulgent financially; once her father died they'd been as poor as the mice in her mum's church, but she understood that from time to time Anna should have been more assertive, she should've said 'No'.

Nat stood. 'Well, I'm bringing Jack in, whether you like it or not.' She heard Julian draw breath as she made for the door. 'What? Are you going to call the police, Julian?'

There was inevitably further palaver. Like a vampire, Jack refused to step over the threshold unless his son invited him in. Julian refused and Aisha sobbed, only finally relenting when Nat shouted, 'For God's sake! Both of you, just stop it.' Then the four of them moved to the dining room, Jack back on form as he accepted a towel and shook Aisha's hand, saying that it was a pleasure to meet her.

Nat wanted to belly laugh. She was sitting at a table with a pregnant woman who looked very alarmed, and two sodden men who were glowering at each other like characters in an old western film. She wondered who would draw first, then realised she was in charge – the mother who needed to say 'No'.

'Okay. Well done, both of you. Now, you each get five minutes of uninterrupted time to say your piece,' she said, recalling the community mediation training she'd done years ago, an extracurricular activity that had made her feel better about the ungrateful fat-cat clients she'd represented. 'Uninterrupted, which means the other person bites his tongue until the five minutes is up.' She put her gold watch, an unexpected thirtieth birthday present from Jose, in the middle of the table. 'Julian, you go first.'

'It's been over a year, Dad, a fucking year. This is Aisha, my pregnant girlfriend who I live with. You've never met her before. That isn't normal. But why am I surprised? The way you treated Mum...'

Julian continued, his staccato start soon flooded with emotion. His tearful speech was much as she'd expected: lack of contact from Jack, treating his mother badly, his refusal to help financially, having time for only Catherine... and Nat drifted as she stared at her Gucci watch.

Her thirtieth birthday, nearly ten years ago. Jose had still been chasing her then, buying her presents she was embarrassed to receive, sending her love letters, poems or texts she could hardly bear to read. She'd miss him when he worked away on a new contract, but as soon as he returned to Manchester and they reunited, she'd think, What am I doing? He's far too unstable, obsessed. I don't even like him at times.

She jerked back to Aisha's dark, watchful eyes. Seven minutes had passed, but Jack hadn't noticed. 'Thanks Julian,' she said. 'That was really helpful. Your turn, Jack. Same rules apply.'

Jack leaned across the table. 'What the hell is going on with the police, Julian?'

Goosebumps spread down Nat's spine. 'We can come on to that, Jack. The five minutes isn't meant to be a question, it's your opportunity to explain things from your viewpoint, to say how you feel, what went wrong, how you'd like the future to be–'

But Julian had already scraped back his chair. His expression livid, he jabbed at his father. 'That's what it boils down to, doesn't it? You don't care about me or Aisha or the baby. It's all to do with you and your reputation. Not being embarrassed by your disappointing son. And you told her about the letters–'

They both stared at Nat. 'You told him you'd read the letters?' Jack started, his face puce.

'What the fuck, Dad? You let her *read* them?' Julian replied.

A full-blown argument erupted then, but at least it was to the point. Standing, Nat took Aisha's hand, leading her away from the table and back to the lounge. Closing the door, she fell back against the sofa. Her stomach was churning, no longer from nerves but from hunger. 'I don't suppose we can escape the back way?' she said, nodding at the windows.

'You could try climbing the privet at the bottom and braving the long grass. Or trespassing through next door's garden, but they're both scary barristers...' Aisha replied. 'And it's still raining...' She looked pensive for a time. Seeming to shake her thoughts away with a huge effort, she came back to Nat. 'I bet you're starving. I am. I'll slip by into the kitchen and make us a sandwich.' Rubbing her bump, she smiled. 'Despite this, I'm good at being invisible. Trust me, the silly boys won't notice–'

'"Silly boys"? I like it. I wouldn't tell them, though.'

A gust of raised voices wafted through the door before becoming mute as it closed. Nat gazed at the rain. The blame would probably land at her feet, but she was pleased they were talking. She automatically bent down to search for her mobile, but she'd left her handbag with the 'silly boys'. It was probably just as well. Although the imperative had faded a bit, she still couldn't help checking. She supposed that any communication from Jose would appear as an unknown number, yet she hadn't thought of him when Aisha called this morning. Progress? She hoped so.

The sound of slamming wood brought her back from her

mulling. What the...? Rushing to the hallway, she peered through the window. His face steely, Jack was exiting the courtyard gate.

'So much for flipping progress,' she said out loud. She looked at Julian. 'What happened?'

'Nothing,' he replied, his face pale. 'I need to get to work. Did you call them?' he asked, turning to Aisha who'd frozen with a plate in each hand.

'Yes, I said there was an antenatal appointment I'd forgotten; they were fine about it.' Her gaze was glued to his, and Nat noticed the almost imperceptible shake of his head before he kissed her and said he'd better get changed. When he'd gone up the stairs, Aisha's attention came back. 'Still hungry?' she asked. 'Let's be indulgent and eat on the sofa.'

She said it brightly enough, but Nat had already caught the deep worry in her eyes.

8

FIND OUT WHAT HE KNOWS

Avoiding eye contact with Catherine's secretary and the red-haired Tom, Dick or Harry, who was clearly chatting her up, Nat slipped into the conference room on Friday morning. She wasn't in the mood for chitter-chatter; there had been another missed call from Wesley and she was bloody irritated with Jack.

The former made her uncomfortable, and although she wanted to know the outcome of the Brian Selby interlude, she didn't want or need the grief; besides, Wesley hadn't asked her to call back.

The latter made her blood boil. In fairness to Julian, he had complied with her mini-mediation game. It was a shame his dad couldn't have done the same. It was hardly surprising, though. Jack Goldman didn't play by the rules; he never had. God knows why she thought he might do so this time.

Trying to concentrate on her file audit, she kept her head down. She was probably doing a more thorough job than was needed, but it was interesting to see how two of her own cases had progressed over the last five years. Wesley had a different approach to her: more conciliatory, keen to keep talking to his opposite number. Getting his own way through persuasion and charm, she thought, as she read between the lines of his long attendance notes of meetings and phone calls. Of course, she had charm too, but that was saved for her clients. When it came to the other party, her style had been more 'Rottweiler', as Jack had once put it.

Nat smelt the perfumed breeze of someone entering the room. 'Morning, Catherine,' she said before looking up.

'And to you.' Catherine was wearing the usual wide-legged trousers, but with a stylish, nipped-in waistcoat over her silky black blouse. She nodded at the files. 'Having a good time?'

'Surprisingly, yes.'

Catherine pulled a wry face. 'Best not tell Wesley that and spoil his fun.' She looked at her reflection in the glass, adjusted a few windswept strands of fringe, then turned back. 'Oh, by the way, I've come in with–'

Jack appeared in the doorway. 'What's this? A three-minute warning?'

Catherine plucked a hair from his jacket collar. 'Barely thirty-seconds, darling. Clearly not.' She smiled at Nat. 'They're nice flowers. Who's the admirer?'

'Flowers?' Nat glanced at the large display on the side table. At least a dozen chubby yellow roses mixed with red buds she couldn't name. Now she thought about it, the room had been fragrant even before Catherine wafted in. 'They're not mine. Perhaps they're there to make the room look pretty?'

Jack plucked an envelope from the cellophane wrapping attached to the bunch. 'God forbid Catherine and Wesley have become that frivolous without me here to keep an eye on things.' He slipped out a card and read: '"Dancing next time, Lucky Lady".' He stared at Nat, frowning. Then his expression cleared. 'Got it. Brian Selby from Doncaster,' he mimicked in an impressive Yorkshire accent.

'The very same. Aren't I blessed?' Nat replied, her heart

sinking even lower.

Jack pointed with a grin. 'Mention the wife! Always mention the wife.'

'I know; I remembered just in the nick of time.'

Catherine rolled her eyes and sighed. 'Oh Lord. To think I qualify as "the wife". I'll leave you two to it,' she said, leaving the room.

Nat tried to wipe the smile from her face. She liked Catherine and Jack together, they made a good team, but she needed to reinstate her irritation with the latter. 'What the hell happened yesterday?' she asked, noticing Jack's thick hair was peppered with grey. When she'd seen him in the courtyard, she'd assumed he had started to dye it, but of course he'd been saturated from an hour or two in the rain.

His expression was not unlike his son's; his response the same: 'Nothing.'

'How am I supposed to help if you don't tell me what's going on?'

'You can help.' He closed the door, then handed her a scrap of paper. 'This is the duty solicitor who represented Julian at the police station last week. Find out what he knows.'

'How am I supposed to do that?' she asked, though of course she knew the answer.

'You'll find a way,' he replied, pulling out his mobile and leaving the room.

Willing her exasperation to subside, Nat sat frozen for several minutes. She stared at Jack's scrawl, then at the flowers. There was no doubt about it; men were at the root of all her problems. They always had to prevail and have the final say.

Picturing her mum's gentle face, she sighed. 'Jest więcej niż jeden sposób na skórowanie kota,' as she always said. Hmm, more than one way to skin a cat... Not a very nice expression considering they had two moggies they adored, but her mum did have a point.

Nat looked at the bouquet properly: the exotic red petals were spectacular, actually. She'd take them home; Anna would enjoy them. And the name Jack had written was familiar. She turned to the bookcase, plucking out a dog-eared copy of the Solicitors and Barristers directory. 'Savage' was a fairly common name, but she just might get lucky. Dragging her finger down the thin pages, she spent several minutes at her task. Bingo. It was him, Gavin Cameron Savage had qualified the same year as she had. She'd been acquainted with him a little at Chester Law College, but there was someone who'd known him much better.

Tiptoeing down the stairs, she felt stupidly breathless. Brian Selby had sent the flowers; all was well, surely? Sharon wasn't at her pod but she could see Wesley at his desk through the blinds, so she knocked at his door and walked in before she could change her mind.

Wesley turned. If he was surprised to see her, he didn't show it.

'Could I have a word?' she asked, feeling a hot flush of discomfort. 'A favour, actually.'

Wesley tapped his hands on the table. 'I called you a couple of times...' He paused, then grinned suddenly, his face transformed to the one she remembered. 'I owe you an apology. I called to say sorry for getting stressed out the other night.' His eyes flickered. 'Some of the things I said – they were completely out of order. More than that. I'm really sorry.'

Colour flooding her cheeks, Nat perched opposite him. 'You're right, they really were. Outrageous, in fact. However... it's me who should be apologising. I stuck my nose in when it wasn't asked for. If the boot had been on the other foot, I'd have been really pissed off too.'

'Yeah, but you did well. You saved the day–'

'I'm sure you would've coped without me firing off like an Exocet.' Her lips twitched. 'I wasn't very subtle, was I?'

He didn't smile back. Sighing, he rubbed his face. 'You

turned it around, Nat. There's no doubt of that. It's just...' He caught her eye before looking away. 'It shouldn't be that way. Monsters like him shouldn't feel entitled to treat women like that. Balling Emilia out in front of the whole office. Pawing you...'

Not sure if she was pleased or offended, Nat sat back in her seat. 'There's a line, Wes. Brian didn't cross it.' Then after a moment, 'I wouldn't let him.'

They fell silent. Then Wesley arched an eyebrow. 'And today's delivery? I think I recall a debate a long time ago. Chester, nineteen-ninety...'

She thought back to law school. 'Bloody hell, you remember that?'

'You invited me. How could I forget my first and only invitation to that feminist organisation you were involved with? Receiving flowers from a man was demeaning, I recall.'

'Oh God, that and everything else. Me arguing the hind legs off a donkey.' She reminisced and laughed. 'Me and my convictions...'

'Your convictions were good.' He looked at her thoughtfully. 'And still are.'

Her temperature increased another notch. To hide it, she continued to prattle. 'Well, they are beautiful nonetheless. Huge yellow roses and another flower I need to google. I must be getting old; I've decided to take them home for me and Mum to enjoy. No one else is going to buy us any.' The words came out more self-pityingly than she had intended. 'Besides, it isn't the flowers' fault,' she added, trying to cover her embarrassment with a quip.

Aware of Wes's solid gaze, she glanced at the photograph of his twins and gestured. 'I hear Matty and Dylan have started at uni.'

He picked up the frame. 'Yes, last weekend we took them to Sheffield. Different courses, but they're in the same halls of residence. They still look identical. One's now a veggie, the other's a committed carnivore, but that's pretty much the only difference.'

He looked soulful as he stared at the snap. Nat supposed time had flown; she supposed he missed them, but she didn't feel qualified to talk about kids. She'd supposed she and Jose would have children one day, but neither of them had ever spoken about it.

The thought of babies was uncomfortable. 'Sheffield, eh? Same uni as you and Andrea,' she said to fill the silence. 'Keeping it in the family.'

'Yeah, but not a law degree. I wouldn't have minded, but Andrea was quite against it.'

'Andrea. How is she?' Nat asked, wondering why his wife had been so keen to put the oar in. Unless things had changed, she spent her days at the Women's Institute or Circle or Guild organisations in Cheadle Hulme, making apricot jam and macaroons, putting the world to rights over coffee with her chums.

'Yeah, she's good.' He seemed to shake himself away from his sons. 'So, this favour you want?'

'Ah, that.' She snorted. 'Believe it or not, I need to have an off-the-record chat with Gavin Savage.'

'*My* Gavin Savage? He does crime–' Sitting back, he swung in his chair, his face showing interest. 'For Jack?'

'Yup.'

He stared for a second, then laughed. 'I'm sure Gav will be delighted to hear from you.' He scrolled through his mobile and jotted down a number.

'You're still friends, then?' she asked. 'Still playing football together?'

'No time for footie, just running these days, but we bump into each other at legal dinners and the like.' He massaged his forehead, his eyes sliding away. 'We used to get together more – meals at each other's houses with another couple – but Gavin split with his wife and it got … complicated.'

'Ah,' Nat replied, keen to learn more but not wanting to touch on a subject which might move on to questions about her break-up and how bloody complicated that was. She stood and wafted the Post-it note number. 'Thanks for this.'

'No problem; good luck.' Then, as she opened the door, he added, 'You are coming to Catherine's fiftieth tomorrow? Have you got a posh frock?'

'Posh frock?'

'It's a black tie do. It's at the new hotel in town at the top of King Street. No doubt it'll be Jack's fraternity – you know – from the royal family to the criminal underground. It would be nice to see a friendly face.'

Savage Solicitors was hidden between a bookies and charity shop on Finney Lane, not a million miles away from Nat's house. The smeared front window was obscured by equally grimy blinds, reminding her of the dodgy dental practice she'd gone to as a child. After pressing a buzzer to be let in, she was greeted in the small reception area by a spotty, floppy-haired teenager, who needed to work on his charisma.

'Yeah?' he said.

'Natalie Bach for Mr Savage.'

'Yeah, in the back,' he replied, not bothering to move from his counter.

'Right. Thanks.'

Hoping for the best, she knocked on the first door. No reply, so she tried the handle. Opening it, she saw him, telephone to his ear. Gavin Cameron Savage! He was exactly as she remembered: tall, broad and sandy-haired, his accent as Glaswegian as it had always been.

He gestured for her to sit, so she perched opposite, smiling politely and listening to the gravelly melody of his voice. Glancing around, she took in the threadbare carpet, rickety furniture and a peculiar smell. Wet socks? Rotting mushrooms? How had Julian, heir to the Goldman throne, fallen so low?

Gavin's call finally ended. 'You wanted a wee chat,' he stated, folding his arms.

'Yes. Thanks for seeing me so quickly,' she said.

He shrugged. 'There's not a lot else happening on a Friday afternoon. It all kicks off much later, and thank God I'm not on the roster tonight. Besides, I'm intrigued. It's not often a blast from the past appears on your doorstep. So what can I do you for, Miss Bach?'

Unsure of how to begin, Nat felt a flush rise from her toes. 'It's a little delicate. I wouldn't want you to breach client confidentiality, but–'

'But you're asking anyway?'

'More an off-the-record chat.'

He pointed his pen. 'Shoot.'

'Julian Goldman. You sat in a police interview with him last week…'

His hands behind his head, Gavin leaned back. 'Wilmslow police station. Jack Goldman's son. I did wonder why the big guns weren't there. I supposed they weren't prepared to get out of bed that early.' He gazed at her for a moment. 'Wes Hughes took over your job at Goldman Law. You buggered off with a Spanish laddy.'

She almost corrected him, then changed her mind. Gav Savage had been a horrendous gossip back at law school; it was better to keep him on track.

'So the police interview last week. You were called to sit in–'

'Yeah, eventually. He didn't want a solicitor.'

'Why was that?'

'I don't know, but I suspect it was…' He motioned money with his fingers. 'But there's nothing to tell. It was a damp squib. The breathalyser was negative and the girlfriend didn't want to press charges.'

'So why did the police bring him in?'

He shrugged. 'There was something about the breathalyser not working properly; probably a load of bullshit. The chances are he rubbed the officers up the wrong way. Or perhaps they knew he was Jack Goldman's son and wanted to bring him down a peg or two.'

'What did you say to them?'

'Not a lot. He'd already admitted to hitting his girlfriend, so they were entitled to arrest him. Police wasting police time, probably. Sadly not unusual…'

Nat's stomach loudly rumbled. Wishing she'd grabbed a sandwich before leaving the office, she leaned forward. 'It doesn't smell right. What do you think?'

Gavin cocked his head. 'I assume you mean the case and not this fragrant office.' He stood, taking one stride to a dented filing cabinet. Adjusting the drawer to pull it out on its tracks, he yanked out a file and flicked it open. He read for a minute. 'Yup, I remember now. The detective wanted to know where Julian had been between assaulting his girlfriend and coming home. He said he'd just driven around, simmering down after the argument. Did he stop? No. Did he visit anyone, go anywhere? No. So it went on. Then PC Plod brings out a receipt. Seems it *fell* from Julian's car when he climbed out to the waiting police. It showed that he'd been to a car wash–'

Nat sat back and chuckled. 'Is that illegal now? No car washing allowed in a built up area after ten?'

Gavin grinned. 'Not bad, Natalie.' He lifted his eyebrows. 'Why not mention it though? Something so ordinary that had happened only hours earlier? That's what stank of fish.' He dropped the folder on the desk and grabbed his jacket from the back of his chair. 'Come on then.'

'What?'

'The pub. You owe me a beer.'

Seeing that she had no choice, Nat followed Gavin's long

strides out of the office, across the busy road and into a large Georgian pub. She bought him a pint and a ham butty, going for tuna herself. When the food mercifully arrived, she wolfed hers down as he watched with an amused expression.

'What?' she asked again.

'You never were very ladylike. That's why the lads in my house fancied you. You burped just the same as the rest of us, but you had great–'

She thumped him hard on the arm.

'Beauty! A great beauty living only three doors down that thin road. It was a good job no one had a car in those days.' He beamed with a knowing look. 'Remember coming to our house parties? You and Wes–'

'*Wesley* these days.'

'You and Wes were always finding a little corner when your bodyguard wasn't on duty.'

Nat wiped her mouth with a paper napkin. 'Bodyguard?'

'The beanpole weirdo who thought he was Morrissey. He was always high on something and stalking you.'

Handing her glass to Gavin, she gave him a hard stare. 'That was the Spanish laddy, actually. And I didn't find little corners with Wes. He was dating Andrea. It's your round.'

'Hardly dating. She was just his shag hag.'

'Who became his wife…'

Gavin walked to the bar, turned and laughed. 'It was not a shotgun wedding, no siree, not at all.' He returned with the drinks. 'So you've come back to Manchester without the weirdo, which must mean you're single. As it happens, so am I. Not handsome, not rich, but I am very tall. How about a take-out and a shag?' He looked at her and grinned. 'All right, if you insist, I'll stretch to dinner and a little romance.' He slugged down half his pint. 'An offer you can't resist, surely? Come on, Miss Bach, what do you say?'

9

UNTIL THEY KNOW HER

Nat awoke late on Saturday, feeling buoyant. The previous night she'd had a laugh with Gav Savage. He was physically fit, his rock-like stomach, which he insisted she test several times, was proof of that, and he was funny in a non-PC way, but she didn't fancy him. The truth was that she'd always had a weakness for a handsome face, and besides, there was no chemistry. She'd already tried that old 'you'll grow to love me in time' chestnut with Jose, and look where that had got her. So she'd let him down kindly, well as gently as Natalie Bach was capable of, by blaming his 'baggage'. It turned out he had four kids under the age of ten, whom he looked after most weekends. One little baby that was exceptionally well behaved would've been nice, but why anyone would want to pelt out four, she couldn't imagine.

She'd been in two minds about Catherine's party, but on waking had decided why the hell not? What was the worst that could happen? If everyone was in couples, she could leave. Anyway, it would be interesting to have a nosey at Andrea again.

She ambled downstairs, kissed Anna on the forehead and popped two slices of bread in the toaster. 'I can't believe Catherine is fifty today. She doesn't look it; but then again I'm in denial and feel about twenty, so I'm not a good judge.' She pictured the office teenagers. 'The bench boys probably think we're both ancient.'

Glancing at her mum's puzzled frown, she acknowledged she wasn't being very PC herself. 'Tom, Dick and Harry' or the 'bench boys' was grouping men into an anonymous clump, but that was the trouble with being exiled upstairs: no one had introduced her, so she didn't know their names. And she never could resist a sardonic quip.

'The bench boys are other lawyers on the first floor,' she explained. 'Well, sort of. Most of them haven't reached puberty, so they're probably paralegals. You know, doing the work of a solicitor but being paid less than Buzz Lightyear. They have to share a huge pew...'

Her mum still looked perplexed; Nat didn't blame her; in years gone by, each fee-earner had a work table all to themselves, but a desk share was Wesley Hughes's 'future' for you.

'Anyway,' she said, wafting her hand. 'This posh party tonight. Do you fancy helping me find a dress? Maybe in Wilmslow? I'll treat you to lunch with my first week's pay – if they pay me...' She reached for her mother's hand and gave it a squeeze. 'You told me not to throw everything out when I left. All those lovely gowns for the legal dinners. Why did I never listen?'

Anna smiled without replying, but Nat thought she seemed sad. Or perhaps she was looking at the drooping side of her face. 'Only if you want to,' she added quickly. 'Only if you fancy shopping.' The notion had finally landed; maybe her mum was embarrassed to go out. Her features had dramatically improved, but still, who knew what was going on behind her pale eyes?

They headed for Wilmslow, Anna eventually sharing her concerns in the car, spilling them out when Nat returned with a pay-and-display ticket for the car park behind Hoopers. Climbing back in the driver's seat, she listened patiently, trying not to show her mild irritation that her mum was sharing a problem on expensive parking time. Of course the worry was Philip, Nat's older brother. He and his wife were having another baby, which was lovely, but why did they have to live so far away?

'Oh, Mum, I know. But at least there's Skype and FaceTime. Anyway, you have fun chatting to Lila and Ben each weekend; you can see how they're growing–'

'But it's not the same, is it? Not with little ones. Holding them close, touching their soft hair. And a new baby. They have that smell...' Her eyes lost focus before coming back to Nat's. 'So lovely. I really can't describe it.'

Feeling the usual reproof when Perfect Philip was mentioned, Nat fell silent as they climbed the stairs to womenswear. The golden boy had married an attractive, amiable girl and they'd produced grandchildren, which was nice, but it wasn't as though Nat had deliberately gone away to waste five years of her life.

Her mum wandered off, so Nat glanced at the gowns in the evening section. She was wholly uninspired. Everything looked too dressy: sequins, sparkles and feathers for the build up to Christmas, she supposed. She moved on to fancy trousers. How might she look à la Catherine? She pulled a pair out. Would they qualify as Wesley's 'posh frock'? Nah. Besides, she didn't have Catherine's long legs.

Surprised by a tap on her shoulder, she spun around. Anna had selected four or five long dresses, and being so small, she was struggling to stop them dragging on the floor. 'Here's a few which look nice, Skarbie. D'you want to give them a go?'

Nat tried on three and shortlisted two. 'Not bad, even though I say so myself,' she said to the mirror. She turned to her mum and smiled. 'They're perfect; aren't you clever. The big question is, which colour?'

Anna didn't hesitate. 'The red.'

'Not too tarty?' Nat asked, Wes's accusation prodding her before she shrugged it away.

Arranging Nat's dark hair around her shoulders, her mum shook her head. 'Not at all. It's your colour, Skarbie.'

The dress duly bought, Nat linked arms with Anna. She was pleased with her purchase and glad to get back on track after her previous moodiness. 'You've earned your lunch, Mum. Zest restaurant here, or somewhere else? Your choice.'

They headed down the escalator, her mum describing a nearby café her friend Barbara had told her about. The food was lovely there and the prices were reasonable. Were they all right for time? They wouldn't want to get a parking ticket.

Nat checked her watch as they hit the ground floor. When she looked up, a pair of dark chestnut eyes were staring right back. It took a second or two to recognise the young woman out of place. Wearing the scarlet uniform of the cosmetic brand she was selling, her face was rigid, her unforgiving glare glued to Nat.

'Oh, God, I just saw a…' Nat started the moment she was outside the store. She was going to say 'a client', but of course the woman had been sacked by the actual client; she'd ended up being the claimant in a bitter unfair dismissal claim. Feeling hot and unsettled, Nat glanced at the shop window, torn by a sudden urge to race back, to approach the woman and say sorry.

The empty café was basic, selling white cobbler loaf sandwiches and dry-looking cake. Nat doubted it was 'lovely', or that Barbara had recommended it. More likely her mum was worried about money. When her dad died, Anna had commented they had been 'blessed by insurance', but it turned out there was a huge shortfall in the endowment payout to cover the mortgage. After a whole marriage of not working, her mother had struggled financially, eventually agreeing to sell up and move into the Cheadle terrace when Nat left for Mallorca.

The sound of her voice broke through. 'Skarbie? Are you all right?'

Nat brought herself back to today and her lunch. 'Sorry, Mum, I'm miles away. I was thinking about that woman, girl really, in Hoopers. Do you remember me telling you about the Goldman Law client who owns an estate agency in Levenshulme? Foster Homes? She and her brother own half the rental properties there and they're loaded. Her son went to school with Jack's boy.'

Anna leaned back as a china teapot and two cups were placed on the table. She shook her head. 'With Julian? No, I don't think so.'

'Danielle Foster, she's called. She once bought me a silk scarf at Christmas. We'd never heard of the make, and thinking it was knock-off, we looked it up on the internet and found it cost eighty quid or something ridiculous. Remember?'

Her mum's face flooded with recognition. 'Yes, we bumped into her once when we were shopping in town. She was attractive with auburn hair and very pleasant, I thought. She had a nice smile.'

Her jaw tightening, Nat nodded. 'That's what everyone thinks until they know her.'

10

HE DIDN'T LOVE ME

The water was too soapy. Perhaps Nat had overdone the bubbles, but it was nice to relax in the hot bath thinking of something other than Jose Harrow, even if the thoughts were vexatious. The girl's name was Michelle, she now remembered. She'd met her several times at the estate agency, and though still in her early twenties, she had the title of office manager, in charge of another three young graduates who were working for peanuts, letting and selling houses because they couldn't find other work.

Nat absently topped up the hot water. Perhaps that's what caused her discomfort. She'd met the girl; they'd chatted; she'd liked her. She was amiable, smart and keen; she came in early and worked late. She was Danielle Foster's 'number one worker'; the agency would be 'lost without her'. But, like every other employee, Michelle was sacked just before the employment protection period was up. Or so Danielle had thought. She'd miscalculated by just one day, making the dismissal potentially unfair.

A knock at the bathroom door interrupted Nat's reverie. Shading her eyes, her mum handed her a glass of Prosecco. 'As instructed, more bubbles for your bubbles,' she smiled. 'A pre-drink as you call it. You young people!'

'Sadly not so young on the outside. But there's nothing like a snifter in the bath before going out. I hope you're going to have a glass too, Mum.'

Anna hovered for a moment. 'I'm so glad you're happy, Skar-bie. Now what about food? You can't go out on an empty stomach.'

Nat sipped the chilled wine and went back to her memories of Michelle. Even then she hadn't seen it; hadn't spotted the ease with which Danielle had lied, how skilfully she had manipulated everyone. Instead of paying a small drop-in-the-ocean sum of compensation to the poor girl, she had masterfully turned the other staff against her. She'd fibbed, telling them that Michelle had demanded a high salary, but now she'd gone they'd get the benefit; she worked each employee with a few sandwiches at lunch, or unexpected small gifts, almost tutoring what they should say to show the dismissal was justified. Not only alleging work-related incompetence, but horrible things about the girl's personal life, told in confidence. And Nat went along with it, blithely taking the vindictive witness statements and preparing them for use at the tribunal hearing, because that was her job. Of course it never got that far; humiliated and bruised, the devas-tated Michelle withdrew her claim.

Finishing her glass of Prosecco, Nat sighed and stood. She could picture Jack's shrug when she finally saw the light. What did he say? 'It's our job to do the best for our clients, to act on instructions, Natalie. Sometimes you're left feeling grubby. You just have to move on,' he'd advised.

Reaching for the towel, she shook her head. She'd felt margin-ally grubby dealing with Brian Selby the other day, but this had felt so much worse.

Distracted by Ben and Lila on Anna's iPad, Nat was finally ready by nine. Her nephew and niece were gummy and chubby and sweet, sounding remarkably like Anna, speaking English but mixing it with Polish words or phrases here and there. Even though Christmas was weeks away, they were thrilled to be spending it in the UK with *Babcia*, their grandmother. God knows where everyone would sleep in this tiny house, but she could feel their excitement, albeit electronically, and it was pleasantly infectious.

The bottle of fizz finished, she scrolled down her list of contacts. Should she call Wesley to cadge a lift with him and Andrea? Cheadle Hulme was only a mile away from her house and on their way into town. Her finger hovered over his number; it would be nice to arrive with someone else. She hadn't been to a formal party for years, and certainly not on her own.

After a moment's reflection, she shook her head. Andrea was the sort to arrive on time and she didn't know her that well these days. Not that she'd ever really known her at Chester; she was Wes Hughes's on-off girlfriend, the 'Cling-on' as she was popularly known, inevitably turning up to any shout, even though she wasn't at law school, but still at uni in Sheffield.

Yup, the Cling-on. Nat guffawed at the recollection. Pretty and blonde with prominent teeth, Andrea had always made a beeline for her. 'Oh, Natalie, hi, you look great! You have such fab cheekbones,' she'd gush, hugging or linking arms with her, even though they barely knew each other. Then, 'Let's find a corner and you can tell me all the gossip.'

Taking a final glance at the mirror, Nat smiled. She used to think Andrea's behaviour was bizarre, but in retrospect she understood why. What was the expression? 'Keep your friends close; keep your enemies even closer.' Wes Hughes was the only black guy in their class, and though she suspected some people felt uncomfortable or threatened by his difference, he was very popular, admired by the boys and lusted after by the girls. She grinned again: herself included.

∼

The taxi weaved through the bustling Manchester streets. Nat hadn't been to the city centre at dark for a long time, and it was good to watch its Saturday night bombilation.

Climbing out at the top of King Street, she glanced left and then right, but all the entrances were in shadow. She frowned. So much for buzzing. Where was this new hotel? Her shoes weren't made for walking, for goodness sake.

She stared at the still, inky buildings. It was a sign to turn back and go home. But the moment the thought hit, tinted glass soundlessly parted and a doorman appeared. He held out an arm to guide her into a cool, marbled reception. 'Sixth floor, madam. Here's the lift,' he said before she had chance to speak. 'There's a cloakroom for your coat up there. Enjoy your evening.'

Taking in the redolent mix of perfume and alcohol, Nat inhaled deeply at the entrance to the suite. But she needn't have worried about her sudden nerves. Far from being the first to arrive, the party was in full swing; the room was dimmed, the music loud, the guests chatting and dancing. A tray of champagne immediately appeared in front of her, shortly followed by Catherine who looked stunning in a white silk trouser suit and exceptionally high heels.

'Welcome to my fiftieth. I'm glad you could come,' she said brightly. 'That dress is gorgeous. Red is definitely your colour.'

They air kissed and Nat handed over her gift, a silver framed photo of her, Catherine and some other former employees of Goldman Law from ten or so years previously. Before Jose, before Jack.

'Happy birthday and congratulations, Catherine. How's it going?' Nat asked.

'Commiserations, more like. But I have decided to embrace it. And in fairness to Jack, I'm having fun. He prepared an impressive eighties play list. Not bad for an old man...'

Jack appeared at her shoulder, noticeably shorter today. 'Something tells me you're talking about me.' He gave his wife a peck on her cheek. 'Do you mind if I steal Natalie? There are a few people I'd like her to meet.'

'Absolutely.' Catherine looked at Nat and pulled a wry face. 'Lucky you. Have fun.'

Nat gave her a spontaneous hug. Of course there had been a frosty period when she'd first found out about the affair with Jack, mostly because Catherine hadn't confided in her, but she loved her trust. Most people had assumed, and probably still did, that she and Jack had had more than a boss-and-employee relationship, but Catherine had never shown the slightest concern.

When someone had drunkenly suggested just that, Catherine had replied, 'You're right. It's more than boss and employee. She's the daughter Jack always wanted.'

At the time Nat had scoffed, but when she'd sobered up, she'd thought it was the nicest thing anyone had ever said. She hadn't been close to her own father; he was much older, always critical and prone to sudden, angry outbursts. She'd got a place at university and law school through sheer hard work and determination, but he'd never once said he was proud of what she'd achieved.

She now smiled and relaxed. It felt as though the champagne tray was following her as she moved around the room, chatting to Jack's business friends, one after the other.

'Natalie is back at Goldman Law. She has the sharpest brain I know. Ask for her if you need anything,' he said each time by way of introduction.

Was it a dig at Wes? She didn't know; she'd never really seen the two of them together. How did they interact? Were they friendly or did they rub along because they had to? Perhaps Jack was simply touting for new work and Wesley was too busy to take on more clients. She hadn't spotted him or Andrea yet. Perhaps they hadn't come after all. Surely the Cling-on would have appeared at her side by now, polished and preened and commenting how tired Nat looked – 'poor lamb', before lavishly describing her perfect life with her handsome boys and her charity work, as she'd done the last time they'd briefly met.

Smiling wryly to herself, Nat turned. As though reading her mind, Wes was strolling towards her. Wearing a white starched shirt and burgundy bow tie, he looked lithe and striking.

'Shaken but not stirred, I assume,' she quipped, nodding at his drink.

'To be honest, I'd rather have a beer.' He seemed a little tense, flexing his shoulders as though the dinner suit was too tight. 'How did you get on with Gav?'

Nat laughed. She could feel the loosening effect of the alcohol. 'Well, he did me the honour of asking me out…'

Wes cupped his ear. 'It's loud in here, let's go onto the veranda.'

Feeling tall and quite splendid in her red dress and matching heels, Nat followed him. She weaved through the dance floor, stopping to have a twirl and a few words with Catherine, then out through the rear doors to a canopied area warmed by exterior heaters. Wes was standing at a window, looking out. Turning to see her, he motioned to the glass and pointed. 'It's a fabulous view of our beautiful city. How are you with heights?'

She looked across to the splendour of the Town Hall lit up at night, then down to the pavement. She took a step back; the ground felt a long way down. Or perhaps the bubbles were doing their thing.

Wes cupped her elbow and grinned. 'Maybe best we sit down.'

'So, you were saying about you and Gav–' he said once Nat had adjusted the cushions and flopped down on the sofa opposite him.

'There isn't a "me and Gav", I can assure you,' she replied, aware her voice was starting to slur just a little. She folded her arms theatrically. 'The cheeky sod referred to Jose as my "bodyguard".'

Wes sat forward, cocked his head and grinned. 'Well...'

She groaned. 'Oh God, he was, wasn't he? I spent all that year, trying to give him the slip. He wasn't my boyfriend, I hadn't even snogged him, but he had those proprietorial rights. It was a nightmare.' She laughed, feeling light and carefree, then pointed at Wesley. 'But I did snog you. Several times.'

Wes lifted his eyebrows and gave a small smile. 'I remember.'

Though Nat's mind was becoming sluggish, she suddenly remembered Andrea. Covering her mouth with her hand, she looked behind, convinced she'd be there at her shoulder, listening to every word, but it was only a group of smokers minding their own business.

'Andrea didn't come,' Wesley said, as if telepathic. He spread his arms. 'I hardly know anyone here, so I didn't think it'd be fair to...' He left his sentence unfinished and looked at his hands. 'What happened with Jose, Nat?' he asked.

'He didn't love me.'

Wesley lifted his head, his face showing surprise.

'Or if he had done...' She stopped. There. She'd said it; it was surprisingly easy. 'He phoned from Mallorca telling me not to return and when I asked why, he sent a text saying, "I don't love you." Just like that.'

His expression perplexed, Wesley raised his hands. 'He chased you for years. He was infatuated, obsessed. You gave up your job to follow him–'

'I know.'

Nat barely got the words out; her throat had suddenly closed, clogged with an urgent need to sob. She could feel Wesley's gaze on her, his body lean in, but she wanted him to say nothing, to stay in his seat. She put out her palm and shook her head, took a breath and looked up to a figure by her side. It was a waitress with a tray of canopies.

Sitting back, she placed something salty in her mouth. Had she eaten since the sandwich and cake? It had, after all, been quite 'lovely'. That's right; her mum had gone to prepare a light snack after the bath, but the grandchildren had called, the food had been forgotten.

Deciding she should find more to scoff, perhaps move on to soft drinks, she picked up her handbag. Wesley was watching, his expression unreadable. With a steadying breath, she tried to clear the fug and speak clearly: 'I'm just nipping to the loo.'

A cubicle was vacant, thank God. Feeling the start of a godawful spin, she flopped down on the toilet seat and sat forward. Once the whirling was under control, she stepped out to the sink. Avoiding her reflection, she slugged as much water as she could manage directly from the tap.

A beep brought her back, a definite peal from her handbag. Knowing it was Jose, she wiped her hands and took out the mobile, certain it would be him at last, wanting her, needing her, explaining what the fuck had happened.

The text was from Wes. *Are you okay?* it said.

She had to get out; she needed fresh air. Leaving the ladies, she headed straight for the stairs, clutching on to the banister and carefully placing one foot in front of the other. Her heels tip tapping, she puffed through the nausea and tears. When she reached the ground floor, she lifted her chin, trying to look composed as she walked past inquisitive eyes, out of the door and into the cold night.

After a few paces, she put her hand against the wall, lowered her head and breathed deeply. What the hell was wrong with her? She thought she'd moved on, three or four steps ahead during the past week. But now she'd regressed a whole bloody mile in just a few minutes.

It had to stop; she *had* to move on.

And then: suppose it had been Jose, what then? If he'd said sorry, begged her back?

Spying a metal bench outside the post office, she took another gulp and swayed over, sitting down and opening her clutch bag. She took out her mobile and stared for several moments at the screen, scrolled down the contacts and found Jose's name. Then she pressed the call icon, hating her weakness as she listened.

The number wasn't recognised.

'For fuck's sake just stop it,' she said out loud, hurling the phone at the side of a building. She felt marginally better for thirty seconds, then regret set in. Of course the damned number wasn't recognised: Jose changed it weeks ago. And her mobile was undoubtedly smashed; she couldn't even call a cab now; she'd have to stumble to a taxi rank and stand in a queue. The alcohol was supposed to have a numbing effect, but her feet were killing her. As well as her heart and her pride.

'Looks like this has gone for a Burton.'

She looked up to the voice. Wes Hughes was there, holding her splintered phone in one hand, her coat in the other. He draped it around her, sat down, then pulled her towards him.

'I'm sorry,' he said. 'I shouldn't have brought it up.'

She rested her head on his shoulder and listened to silence interspersed by laughter from groups of partygoers, then eventually the midnight chime of the Town Hall clock.

Wes dipped his head to peer at her face. 'Okay now? Shall we get a taxi?' he asked.

'God, don't.' She smiled wearily. 'I must look dreadful.'

He glanced at the sky. 'You look beautiful. I saw you come into the party. Heads turned…'

'Hardly, I'll be a quadragenarian very soon.'

She wanted to cry; she wanted to say: 'In a few weeks I'll be forty and single, childless, unloved and unwanted.' But she managed to hold the self-pity and the need to scream at the injustice of it all in her head.

'Tell me about it,' he replied. 'Mine's a week after yours.' He was still partially turned away but his expression was shadowy and thoughtful. Then he snorted and nodded towards the hotel. 'It'll be low-key for me when it comes. I wonder how much that lot cost Jack. Top-notch accommodation, free drinks, nice food.'

Nat tried for a smile. 'Food? What's that then?' The spinning seemed to be under control, but she still felt pretty rough.

'Ah,' Wes cocked an eyebrow. 'Even at the ripe old age of nearly forty, you forgot that drinking on an empty stomach isn't wise. We could splash out and buy chips.'

Nat took her smashed mobile and examined it. Multicoloured lines and a shattered screen. Gone for a Burton indeed. She shook her head. 'I've wasted enough money for one night. I don't want to pay for puking up potato in a taxi. Shall we go?'

She fell asleep against him in the back of the cab, only jerking awake when the driver swerved into Cheadle High Street. She knocked on the window. 'Here will be fine, thanks.'

'Are you sure? We can take you to the door,' Wes asked.

'No, it's fine. It's not far and I live with my mum, remember? She's probably waiting up.' She smiled faintly. 'She'll be forcing me to drink a cabbage flavour hangover cure if I'm not careful. The fresh air will do me good.'

A surge of nausea hitting, she climbed out and walked a few paces towards home. Realising she hadn't thanked Wes for his kindness, she turned. She'd expected the taxi to continue its journey towards his home, but instead it made a U-turn, driving him back the way they'd just come.

11

NO PORN ALLOWED, THEN?

Hiding in the conference room on Monday morning, Nat was in deep thought, the sort of needling and prodding contemplation that wasn't at all helpful. Deaf to the office hubbub wafting through the open door, she was still replaying her whole disastrous weekend in her head.

How flipping dire had she been on Saturday night? Looking back, she realised she'd been pretty pissed when she arrived at Catherine's party, let alone when she left. She'd waved Wes and the taxi off and teetered towards home, desperate to throw up, and even though she had the door keys in her hand, she hadn't quite made it inside, throwing up against the brickwork under the bay.

She had tried to clear the mess with boiling water, but the kettle lid had dropped off with a clatter. She'd been lucky not to burn her toes. Then her mum had appeared with a rolling pin, seconds away from knocking her out. It was a relief to stumble to the sofa intact, on the outside at least, blacking out until noon on Sunday when the list of her transgressions was annoyingly crystal clear, the flirtatious mention to Wes of historic snogging being top of the agenda.

Dozing on and off under a blanket for the rest of the afternoon, she'd finally twigged there was no need to lie low; the house was empty. It was the fourth Sunday of the month; Anna would be at her old church in Oldham with Barbara. So eventually she'd surfaced, prepared herself tea and toast, and sat at the kitchen table to examine her mobile. No electronic elves had appeared in the night; the screen was still badly cracked; and there weren't even any stripes or colours remaining: the bloody thing was as dead as a dodo or a doornail or even her dad. She'd felt bereft, as though she'd lost a friend. But of course that was stupid; Jose was already long gone, and anyone who mattered had her landline number. The only real problem was work; she'd just have to buy a cheap handset and slum it. It was punishment for getting pissed; penance for being so damned pathetic.

~

'Sharon to Nat. Are you listening?'

Nat now jolted and snapped back her eyelids. Bloody hell. Sharon had managed to enter the room and was inches from her face. Alcohol poisoning or what? She really did need to get a grip.

Her former secretary had pencilled her eyebrows in a darker shade than usual, and with her bleached, bouffant hair, she looked like an eighteenth-century courtier. It was an effort to tune into what she was saying; something about Wesley and his office.

'Sorry, Sharon. Someone has stuffed my head with polystyrene. Say again?'

She handed Nat a diary. 'Wesley is tied up with something at home. He says can you rearrange his two appointments today and, if all fails, see the client and do what you can? He said feel free to use his office.'

'Yeah, sure,' she replied automatically. Then, remembering

how sweet he had been on Saturday night, 'How come he's at home? Is he ill?'

Sharon stood back and sniffed. 'He didn't say. I asked if everything was okay, and he just said "fine", like he does, so…'

Nat would normally have laughed at Sharon's obvious pique, but she was curious herself. There was only Wes and Andrea in Cheadle Hulme these days; perhaps Andrea had shackled him to her new Parker Knoll dining table for going to a party without her. She couldn't see the Cling-on having changed that dramatically over the years.

Pleased to be of help to Wes, Nat made a strong coffee and turned her focus to work. His clients were chilled about having their appointments postponed, so she stayed upstairs, not feeling it justifiable, or indeed comfortable, to sit in his office and stare at the bright canvas. She couldn't remember Wes being into art, but he was two people in her mind: the Wes whom she'd kissed at law school whenever the opportunity had presented itself, which was rare without the Cling-on and the bodyguard, and the Wesley Hughes who'd taken over her job. She really hadn't liked the latter; he'd been working in London for one of the Magic Circle law firms, and she'd heard on the grapevine that he'd become an ambitious and arrogant bastard. Perhaps as a black man he'd had to try harder, she'd mused at the time, swiftly reprimanding herself for that thought. If someone had said she'd had to 'try harder' because she was a woman, she'd have been mightily offended, even though it was possibly true.

'Judge me on my ability as a lawyer, not on my race, my colour, my creed, my sexuality, or my gender,' she would've said.

Which was all very well in theory.

Going back to a new batch of audit files, she plucked off the top one. 'Foster Properties Limited' was written on the front in Sharon's loopy scrawl. She opened the folder and flicked through the pages. The latest correspondence had been only a few months previously, regarding the purchase of a newsagents opposite the estate agency. Hmm… interesting. Goldman Law was still acting for Danielle and Frank Foster; the two bloody villains were still building their empire.

Her stomach rumbled in sync with the peal of the office phone. She scooped it up.

'Natalie speaking.'

'Can't talk, but expect a package from WMD.' It was Wes.

'WMD?' she asked.

He laughed. 'Work it out.'

'I postponed your appointments, by the way. Is everything okay?'

'I think so,' he replied. 'Andrea and I are in Sheffield. Matty was hospitalised last night, but everything's fine.' He paused for a moment. 'It was Fresher's week antics. He passed out and Dylan was worried, so he called an ambulance. Of course, Matty says his drinks were spiked…'

Nat immediately thought of Saturday night and her dreadful behaviour. She didn't know how to respond. Should she be disapproving, or should she laugh and say, 'We've all been there'? She didn't have kids and didn't know the form, but Wes chuckled and continued to speak. 'I know; we've all tried that excuse. That and the one about not having eaten any food before going out…' She could hear the smile in his voice. 'But don't say anything to Sharon about Matty. I've learned the hard way…'

Grinning, Nat finished the call, then wrote, 'WMD?' on her pad. A Saddam Hussein joke? The stuff mechanics used? No, that was WD-40, whatever that stood for. The answer presented itself moments later when Wendy waddled in, armed with a grey plastic bag.

'Office phone,' she drawled in a monotone. 'Usually for partners only.' Her sucked-in cheeks showed her disapproval. 'Read the office manual: page thirty-eight. Personal use is allowed, but not abroad without permission, or for premium rate calls. The internet is only to be used for work purposes.'

Inordinately pleased at Wes's thoughtfulness, Nat beamed. 'Do I get tested?' she asked. 'You know, on page thirty-eight?' And when WMD's lips pressed even further together, she asked, 'No porn allowed then? Damn.'

12

A REPORTABLE ACCIDENT

For the rest of the week, Wes didn't return to the office, so Nat sat in his chair after all, picking up the pieces. In fairness to Sharon, her assistance was invaluable. She had a good knowledge of each file, paying attention when she typed, rather than the dictated words going straight from the headphones to the tips of her fingers and by-passing her brain. ('New paragraph' and 'semicolon' and 'full stop' typed in full were not unheard of in the office.) If one of the bench boys had already helped on a file, it was passed on to them, but Nat wanted to do the work Wes would've done as a partner herself. There was a tricky court hearing in Preston on Tuesday, a conference with a perma-tanned barrister in London on Wednesday, three interviews in glamorous Grimsby on Thursday. Nat was relieved to see a blank page in his diary on Friday.

'What do you think is going on with Wesley?' Sharon whispered, wide-eyed and every three hours.

Nat was able to answer truthfully: other than what he'd said to her about Matty on Monday, she had no idea. She'd downloaded her contacts onto her new phone and had sent him a text thanking him for it. He'd replied saying, 'No problem', but that was all. She'd toyed with asking if his life was okay, and whether there was anything she could do to help, but that seemed intrusive, so she'd left it. Emilia was as bad as Sharon, asking each morning whether Wesley was in and looking downcast when Nat said she didn't know.

~

Nat was at Wes's desk when Jack appeared in the office on Friday afternoon. At least his voice did. His deep tones reverberated through the first floor like Mr Angry's; he was berating poor WMD. It seemed he'd gone to The Ivy with a client for lunch, but his usual window table had been taken (by someone more important than Jack? Impossible, surely?).

Recalling her own outing to The Ivy, she waited for him to appear. The man himself had taken her to the original in London when she'd first joined Goldman Law. Wearing his retro nerd glasses even then, she hadn't yet worked him out.

Though they'd eaten like kings, he'd asked for a dessert menu. 'The puds are all delicious,' he'd said, 'but I recommend the crème brûlée.'

Despite being stuffed and not fancying it anyway, she'd dutifully ordered it and he'd watched her tackle the caramelised crust without having one himself. The lesson to follow her instinct had been learned, like all his teaching over the years, whether intentional or not.

His face still Mr Angry red with annoyance, he strode into Wes's office and slapped a ring binder on the desk.

'For Wesley or for me?' she asked, not able to see the name on the spine.

'You.' He brushed drops of rain from the shoulders of his raincoat, but didn't take it off.

Instinct set in. 'Me? Okay, so–'

'Any more news about Matty?' he interrupted.

She frowned, perplexed. 'Matty? No. What news? Should I know?'

Jack closed the door. 'He's had tests all week. The last I heard, the hospital thought it might be epilepsy. Didn't Catherine say? She knows more than I do.'

Shaking her head, Nat felt a flip of disappointment that Wes hadn't told her himself. Though that was stupid. Why would he? She wasn't a partner, and though she'd been pleased about the phone, he'd have been thinking about work when he arranged it, what was best for the firm.

'So?' she asked, nodding towards the new file.

'Ah.' Jack rotated it to show the name on the spine. 'Battersby v Battersby' it read.

That made Nat sit up straight. 'The Battersbys? They're getting divorced? You're joking,' she gasped.

An image of Danielle Foster's husband popped into her head. With his athletic body, white grin and boyish dimples, there was no doubt Carl Battersby was attractive, but he'd always been ten steps behind his wife intellectually, docilely doing her bidding and looking a touch uncomfortable in his Porsche and Gucci suit. Yet despite their wealth he'd never given up the day job as a 'sparky', he'd held on to his Stockport friends, his roots and his accent. Nat had always admired him for that.

'Bloody hell, Jack, what happened?' she asked. 'Danielle adored him. What did we always say? That Carl was her Achilles heel?'

Jack lifted a dark eyebrow. 'Looks like we were right. He's run off with one of the young graduates. Danielle's last lieutenant. Everyone assumed she batted for the other side, which apparently she did until Carl persuaded her otherwise. A good-looking girl, tall, slim, clever and twenty years younger than him.'

'Excellent. She's got even more than employment protection,' Nat quipped. She couldn't help but laugh. In fact she wanted to punch the air and call her old colleagues to crow. Of course she wasn't being kind, but it was definitely something to be savoured; Danielle Foster had lost the one thing she loved more than money.

Her smile soon faded; Jack was pushing the chunky file towards her. Instinct, Nat, instinct!

As though the folder might lunge, she leaned back. 'No, Jack.' Her heart was tumbling to the floor at the prospect of representing that woman again. 'We aren't a specialised matrimonial practice. I haven't touched a divorce since I was sacked by some wailing woman two decades ago.'

'But you do have experience; you know how these things work; you'll be great; Danielle likes you–'

'Hardly any experience and no, Danielle does not *like* me. She knows that I know what she's really...' She caught Jack's smirk. 'You're winding me up, aren't you?'

He sat down and opened the file. 'Partly. She has some top-notch matrimonial specialists acting for her as you'd expect. Big guns in the City. But...' He tapped the page. 'She doesn't like the advice they've given her. She thinks their suggested settlement figures are way too high. "London figures" she says. So she wants us to read through the paperwork, the financial statements and so on, and see if a second eye will help chip off a bob or two.' He stood. 'Just up your street. No hurry, next week will be fine.'

'Cheers, Jack.' Nat looked at her watch meaningfully. 'After all, it's only four o'clock on a Friday.'

'Enjoy.' He stood, and then turned at the door. 'By the way, Catherine needs a word. It's a set-to with her mother; they're not seeing eye to eye.' His lips twitched. 'I think I've put that delicately. She's waiting in her office. Ciao.'

Pushing the file to one side, Nat sighed deeply. It felt as though she'd been through a whole gamut of emotions during the last ten minutes, albeit in a small way. Despondency about Wes, euphoria, dread, then relief, even if only partial, and now something else she couldn't quite define.

She took the stairs two by two, pausing at Catherine's door to compose herself before knocking.

'Come.'

Nat stepped into the perfumed office. 'Hi,' she said. 'Jack said you wanted a word?'

Catherine put down the telephone and looked at it. 'Just him now,' she muttered. She seemed to shake herself back. 'Oh, yes. Sit down.' She played with a pearl earring and smiled wryly. 'Do you remember my mother?'

Nat nodded. She did. Rosemary Hetherington. A tall, erratic-haired woman who lived at the end of a country lane somewhere in Cheshire. She, Catherine and another friend had visited mid-hike one year. Her small cottage was a 'toilet stop' and they had stayed for tea and Dundee cake, watched by a morose boxer dog.

'She's had a court summons.' Catherine raised her eyes to the ceiling. 'A magistrate's summons, can you believe? For failure to report an accident.'

'Okay...'

'Don't smile, but she knocked down a goat and drove on without stopping.' She laughed without humour. 'It's an offence under the Road Traffic Act, apparently, a reportable accident. The hearing's next Thursday...'

Nat now identified the final emotion: resentment. She had been qualified as a solicitor for fifteen years, but her job here was basically cleaning; she'd been employed to pick up everyone else's mess. 'You'd like me to do a plea of mitigation?' she asked.

Catherine sighed. 'Well, that was the plan. I was going to do it myself, but Mother has sacked me – or I've sacked her, it doesn't really matter which. We don't agree on strategy; she won't plead guilty. She says she didn't report the accident because she didn't run over the damned goat, and she's determined to represent herself.'

She raked fingers through her hair. 'The thing is, Nat, it's pretty embarrassing. There aren't many Hetherington's turning up at the Chester Mags. The farmer says he's going to sue. I don't know how much a goat costs, and God knows what it was doing in the middle of a road, but we need to keep an eye on what Mother says and doesn't say in court for the civil proceedings.' She smiled apologetically. 'It's something and nothing, but would you mind sorting her out?' Catherine slid over a piece of paper. 'She liked you. It's the same address and same number.'

Nat forced a smile. 'Sure thing.' It seemed that being told someone liked her was enough for her to poop scoop joyfully. She made her way to the door, turning when Catherine spoke again. Her expression was sympathetic.

'Oh, by the way. Jack on the phone just then... Sorry for not telling you about Matty, but Wesley wanted to keep it...' She seemed to search for a word. 'Low-key.'

13

THE ROOT OF ALL EVIL

Tuesday morning and Nat was back in the conference room with the Battersby v Battersby file. She had managed to defer it so far this week, but today she had no excuses. She had busied herself yesterday by driving to a clothing factory in an old Stockport mill, chatting to the owner and seeing how Goldman Law could attend to his business needs.

She'd been introduced to the mill man, or 'Mr DeMille', as she'd called him in her head, at Catherine's party. He'd kindly given her a tour of the storage areas and workshop, introducing her to the seamstresses at their machines. Above the steady thrum, it had been interesting to see the huge reams of material, the industrial-sized scissors and irons, not to mention the textured fabrics – from soft, stretchy jersey and fuzzy velvet to the coolest sleek silk – which she had covetously stroked when no one was looking.

She'd stayed for a chat and coffee, but by the end of her visit, 'DeMille' had peered at her with a perplexed expression. She didn't know if it was because she no longer resembled the red-clad, drunk woman he'd previously met, or if it was his poor eyesight. He was wearing the thickest spectacles she'd ever seen, his disconcerting owl eyes as huge as Wall-E's. She hadn't noticed them at the party, but then again she didn't remember much from that night, just that Wes had been sweet, saying she was beautiful and had turned heads, when she'd really been a disaster.

Now taking a reluctant breath, she pulled the ring binder towards her. The Battersby divorce. Who'd have guessed? Opening the cardboard cover, she peered at the depressingly long index. Oh joy. But she replaced the inevitable groan with a smile, procrastinating a little longer with thoughts of her weekend. She'd got together with her old colleagues, Fran and Bo. They'd met at teatime on Saturday and had nattered without taking breath until the wine bar threw them out at midnight.

'Guess what?' she'd said the moment they'd sat down.

There had been a few humorous replies before she'd relented and spilled the beans. 'Danielle Foster is divorcing Carl.'

'You're joking. Not the handsome sparky, with the come-to-bed-with-me-dimples?'

Fran had guffawed into her Prosecco. 'His *dimples*, Bo? What the hell? I always looked at the size of his wallet.'

It had set the tone of the evening. They had gossiped about the promotion of WMD ('What? The dour, dim office junior?'), Catherine ('Yup, still Princess Di, circa 1989') and Jack ('Still Kenneth Clarke glasses?' 'I think you mean Clarke Kent, Fran'). Then they'd moved on to *FroBo*, the small shop Fran and Bo had opened to sell their handmade jewellery and cushions, the money they didn't make, but the laughs that they'd had.

Money, Nat now mused, coming back to the job in hand. A depressing subject, if ever there was one. And, of course, the root of all evil. Fran and Bo had started their business venture around the time she'd left for Mallorca. 'The three escapees', they'd all quipped at the time, but here she was, captured and back in her cell, inhaling deeply and starting on the first round of the Battersby v Battersby fight.

She went back to the contents. The file contained only the

ancillary relief papers, which dealt with finances rather than the divorce itself. It would've been fun to read the allegations hurled between Carl and Danielle, but the chances were that it'd have gone through on his adultery, very dull in comparison. Jack's wife could have used that ground to divorce him, but she'd chosen to petition on his unreasonable behaviour. Her views on the matter had stretched to twenty-three pages. At the time Nat had thought it unnecessary, hurtful and indulgent, but these days she was older and wiser. Having gone through the grief and the unanswered questions about Jose, she understood the need to go on about 'unreasonable behaviour' at length, both aloud and in one's head; writing it down for all to see was undoubtedly an extension of that.

Wishing her mind would just stop, she sighed. It was a process, she knew, the injured party's talking and writing, the therapy, the shouting and the screaming, sometimes even violence, but she still didn't know if that was the answer to heart-break. Her short-lived matrimonial career had been mentored by a wise elderly colleague. 'Time,' he used to say, 'time is the only cure.' She knew he was right. It helped that she had a new phone and a different number, but she still needed to be patient.

She spent a good two hours on the file, wading through pension rights valuations, financial statements and the expert's reports. Eventually she put her forehead on the table. God it was boring, even worse than file audits. Finally flicking through the appendices, she counted the different companies in which Danielle had an interest. God, she'd been busy, though they were Frank Foster's as well, and her son Lewis also had a finger in one or two. They'd clearly grabbed various Foster names and a couple more using their initials: Foster Properties Ltd, D & F Properties Ltd, Foster Associates Ltd, DFL Financial Services Ltd, and so on.

Sitting back, she smiled wryly at Danielle's canniness. Carl could only benefit from any income earned by her from those companies, which according to the accounts, was pretty much nothing. Foster Homes had a great turnover, but the profit on paper was marginal on account of the constant reinvestment in the Levenshulme empire, a good argument for giving Carl very little from that source. Not that Nat was an expert by any means. How much would Carl get? He had his own income, he was a director of some companies himself, and, of course, there was the matrimonial home, which was valued at £4.75 million. She supposed that would be sold; Lewis was in his mid to late twenties, so there wasn't a minor to consider. Split equally, that alone would make Carl a millionaire. Not bad for a sparky.

She glanced at her watch to check the time; she'd had permission from Catherine to park behind the office so she could drive to Knutsford to see her mad mother this afternoon. Nat's own mad mum had taken to making her lunch, slipping it in her bag each breakfast before she could object. Yesterday it had been a pastrami and gherkin sandwich; today she suspected a salad. Pulling out the pink Tupperware box, she opened the lid, then lifted out a fork and a piece of foil so she could identify the smell. Tuna, not bad, but the lettuce looked pretty uninspiring. If this was going to be a regular thing she could do with dressing supplies.

She looked around the conference room. She might not be sharing a desk with the bench boys, but at least they had a handy drawer to stash their stuff. Gone were the days when one had one's own desk with units which were private and confidential. At the weekend, she'd laughed with Fran and Bo about Geoffrey. He was older than them and had worked as a conveyancing legal executive since Jack started up Goldman Law. He'd suffered from narcolepsy, falling asleep without warning. It seemed cruel now, but they would sneak in his drawer, nicking his cigarettes or lunch while he slept, then feign innocence when he searched for them. He twigged eventually, seeing the comical side and getting his revenge with pranks of his own.

Nat sighed at the memory. Life had been fun then; they'd worked hard but had also had a laugh. When she'd gone down to the first floor the day before, the open-plan was near silent; Max had been sat next to Emilia and they'd stared at their screens, the secretaries in the pool were quietly typing from headsets, even Sharon was preoccupied. The only noise had been Wes in his office, pacing the room with his Dictaphone. He'd nodded curtly through the open door when she'd raised her hand, but he hadn't stopped his flow to greet her.

She now dipped in her fingers to sample her lunch, pulling out a lettuce leaf, then another. Mm, very tasty after all. Additional dressing wasn't needed; her mum had used lemon and olive oil and the fish was delicious. Why she didn't use the damned fork, she didn't know, but when she looked up, Wes was at the door, his face stony.

He got straight to the point. 'I believe the turquoise car is yours.'

'Yes, I'm seeing–'

'Can you move it. You're in my space.'

'Sorry, I didn't realise–'

'I had to park on the road and time's up.'

Shocked at his tone, Nat hadn't moved.

'So, are you coming?' he said impatiently, making for the exit.

She found herself grabbing her keys, scuttling after him with tuna fingers as he paced down the stairs to the fire exit at the back. His black Mercedes was already parked behind hers, blocking her in, so she waited for him to reverse and followed, struggling to get the car into gear. They eventually changed places, Wes lifting his fob as Nat pulled on her handbrake.

She opened her door. 'I won't be long,' she called.

He turned and frowned. 'What?'

'I won't block you in for long. I'm going to see a client this afternoon.' Scampering again, she caught him up. Surprised at his obvious annoyance, she tried to work it out. 'Was everything all right on your files last week?' she asked. 'Did I do the right things?'

'Yup. Thanks.'

Entering the building, he bounded up the first flight.

'I wasn't sure about the case management conference on the Williams' file. They argued about the second expert, but it all turned out well,' she called.

He stopped and turned, his eyes cold. 'Matty is *well* too, Natalie, thank you for asking. It puts work into perspective.' He paused and took a breath, as though he'd speak further, but instead he shook his head and walked away.

14

A FEW MORE MINUTES TO SPARE

Nat drove towards Knutsford. 'What the hell?' she said aloud several times. A new bypass had been built since she'd last come this way, and she had no idea if she was lost. Or not. It was a pretty apt summary of her life.

She groaned again. There was nowhere to turn anyway. Now, if she had a posh car with a satnav... But hey, she was only a minion, driving her mother's crappy Ford, doing everyone's dirty work, and no one seemed to be particularly grateful.

And it wasn't turquoise, it was bloody light blue.

A sign for Tatton Park appeared, so she indicated left, finally finding her bearings. Yup, Mere Golf Club was on the right. She'd been there for one of the million weddings she'd attended before Mallorca. She snorted to herself: perhaps that's why she'd escaped; there was too much pressure to become a happy bride. Yet she'd tied herself to a man just as effectively by changing continents, perhaps even more so. How had it happened? Had Jose really 'ground' her down?

Though she tried not to look, her eyes caught sight of the brown stately home sign: Tatton Park. They'd been running there when Jose told her he was handing in his notice and going to Mallorca. Just like that, out of nowhere.

'For a holiday?' she'd asked, wondering if she'd heard properly as they had jogged shoulder to shoulder along the path which cut a swathe through the trees.

'No, for good. The probate's come through, Casa Feliz is now mine.'

Of course she'd known about the house left to him by his granny. They'd gone to Pollensa for a long weekend and had strolled around it, inhaling the fusty smell, touching the frayed cushions and rugs, and eyeing up the dark, heavy furniture.

She'd stopped running. 'You said you were going to sell it.'

'I probably still will. I'm looking to buying a bar or a café, to make a new life.' He halted too and looked at her then, his blond hair newly cropped. 'Let's face it, Nat, there's nothing for me here, is there?'

She hadn't known what to say. They didn't live in the same house and spent long periods apart when he worked away, but they'd been together forever, really. His abrupt announcement was a surprise – no, a blistering shock. Not a week went by without a declaration of his love; she'd been certain of his constancy, his adoration.

Catching a handsome stag over Jose's shoulder in the distance, Nat had steadied her breathing. The deer was so still. Then suddenly it threw its huge antlers at the ground, bellowed and charged towards its rival.

Moments had passed and Jose was still staring, the sunshine lighting his bony face. He'd shaken his head. 'See?' he'd said, turning and running on.

Now pulling up the car, Nat shook the memory away. She peered at the directions she'd printed at the office. She would have asked Catherine the best route to her mother's house, but it seemed the managing partner's job consisted of swanning around and having meetings and lunches out of the office with her assistant in tow – who undoubtedly did the actual work.

'What the hell,' she said again. But what was the point in feeling cross and downtrodden? It wasn't Catherine's or Wes's fault, or even Jack's. She'd missed five years of her career; she'd chosen to leave. After six months in Manchester without Jose, she'd followed him like Mary's lamb. She'd become a different person, but one who'd been happy; she'd loved being a lamb. Hadn't she? Looking back, however, she was no longer sure. Those five years felt as though they happened to someone else.

She continued her journey. Putting her foot down, she increased her speed along a tree-lined A road, only to suddenly spot the wooden stile she and Catherine had climbed on their hike, so she dived on the breaks to take the left turn. A little more cheery at the prospect of cake, she weaved along the thin lane and opened the window to take in the smell of cut grass. Yes, she remembered it now. The cottage was near the bottom, just above the farm.

A van was approaching her, so she pulled to one side to let it pass. Was this the scene of the goat incident? One that was surely bound to happen when there wasn't enough width for two vehicles. But Mrs Hetherington had denied it had happened at all. This chat was going to be interesting.

The Hetherington homestead finally appearing, Nat parked on the small drive. The pungent smell of manure filled her nose the moment she opened the car door. Two large boxer dogs greeted her as she climbed out, sniffing her for a second before slouching away. Neither were on leads. Was this the norm in these country parts? Loose dogs and goats doing their own thing and putting their lives at risk? A field, presumably belonging to the farm, was adjacent to the wall, and a horse was nonchalantly munching one of Mrs H's grassy plants.

She knocked at the door and waited for a couple of minutes before trying again. The appointment had been arranged, but

Mrs H nevertheless looked surprised when she finally answered. Another boxer accompanied her; it looked pretty old. Perhaps it was the same one as ten years previously, but it was difficult to judge, all three dogs looked as morose as Nat felt.

Taking in the sweet aroma of baking, she held out her hand. 'I'm Natalie Bach from Goldman Law, Mrs Hetherington. We met a long time ago. You probably don't recall.'

'Of course I do. Call me Rosemary.' She stood back, letting her pass. Both her wild hair and her equally wild cottage were as Nat remembered. Catherine's mother clearly liked to read. Save for an old table sporting a huge computer screen, newspapers, pamphlets and books covered every surface.

'This way, dear. I hope you're hungry.'

'I am. Thank you.'

Nat followed her into a bright kitchen, then sat as directed at a table covered with a cloth. Result! A platter in the centre was heaped with glossy scones. The day was not lost after all.

Rosemary cocked her head. 'Tea and Dundee cake, I seem to recall. No cake today, but plenty of tea and these are warm, so do help yourself.'

Nat discreetly sniffed her fingers. They still smelled of tuna despite her having washed them several times. The thought brought Wes's moody face to mind, but she pushed it away, replacing the irritation with the prospect of eating.

'They look delicious, thank you. Just what the doctor ordered,' she said, feeling a little like Gretel as she placed a scone stuffed with sultanas on her plate. Picking up a bone-handled knife, she spread on thick yellow butter, the brightest red jam and gloopy clotted cream, then tucked in, too greedy to be put off by Rosemary's steady gaze.

Mrs H eventually sat down, removed a cosy from a teapot, and poured the strong brew. 'So Catherine has sent you,' she said with a raised eyebrow. 'She thinks I'm an old fool. Do all daughters think their mothers are fools? Do you?'

Nat wondered how to reply, but before she had the chance to do so, the old lady spoke again. 'My other daughter doesn't think I'm a fool and neither should you. Here's what we're going to do.'

Helping herself to another pastry, Nat listened to a long story about the farm next door and 'the vendetta', not between Mrs H and the farmer, with whom she'd got along splendidly, but with his son, whom she didn't. He had wanted to buy the field at the back of the cottage but she didn't want to sell it to the 'little shit', who hadn't been there when his father had needed him, but who'd been more than happy to reap the benefit of the lucrative business when the old man had died. The son was still determined to buy the meadow to provide access of some sort to the farm, and he'd resorted to underhand persuasion, which made her all the more determined not to concede to his demands.

'Long story short,' she concluded. 'If an accident has happened, it was by the little shit's own hand, or more specifically the wheel of his car, and the whole thing is a set up. There's no independent or forensic evidence; it's his word against mine, so I intend to turn up at court and plead not guilty.'

She replenished Nat's drink. 'If you would like to meet me at the magistrates' court and have a word with the prosecuting solicitor and refer him or her to the relevant section of the Criminal Law Act 1967, that would be splendid.'

Finally taking a breath, she peered at Nat. She looked strikingly like Catherine. 'I assume you are au fait with the section I refer to? It states that it is "an offence to cause any wasteful employment of the police by knowingly making to any person a false report". If that doesn't work, you're instructed to mention malicious prosecution. Everything clear?'

There wasn't much to say except, 'Okey-dokey,' so Nat took another scone, already stuffed but too weak to resist. Besides, she didn't particularly want to return to the office today, either to the ungrateful prick Wesley or to 'Cool Catherine', as Jack had once called her.

Nat smiled at the memory; she had forgotten that nickname. There was no doubt Catherine was an attractive woman, but she was indeed cool and icy; it was difficult to discern what was going on underneath her exterior until you knew her, and even then, when you thought you'd sussed her out, perhaps you hadn't.

Maybe that's what gave her the edge.

As she gazed at Catherine's mother, Nat drifted back to the conversation they'd had in the café beneath the office: 'Fifty and childless.' It had been a rare moment of honesty, of laying herself bare. Perhaps this woman was the cause. Reading between the lines, the two of them had never been close. Rosemary had never bothered to hide her preference for Victoria who'd been a headstrong rebel, not toeing the line like Catherine until later in life. Nat could see how this might chafe; the prodigal, badly behaved daughter was forgiven and loved, while the good one, who'd always be there for her, come rain or shine, simply wasn't.

All three solemn boxers walked Nat to her car, suddenly becoming animated when a white sports car pulled up next to hers. Their docked tails wagged vigorously as the driver stepped out. Bloody hell; talk of the devil. If Nat wasn't mistaken, it was Victoria, the *other* daughter. She was walking over and removing her sunglasses.

'Hi, Natalie. How are you?' She smiled thinly. 'I hoped you'd be gone by now, but...' she glanced at the narrow lane. 'Well, to be honest, when I saw your car I couldn't be arsed to do a five-point turn.' She put her hand on Nat's arm. 'It's nothing personal; I just don't want Catherine knowing I'm home. You won't mention it, will you?'

'Of course not.' Nat made a huge effort to close her gaping mouth. Victoria didn't look well. She was more Nat's age than Catherine's, and in fact she looked dreadful. Her eyes were bloodshot and her face blotchy; she'd obviously been crying. Oh God, what to do? Pretend she hadn't noticed, or...

'Hey, are you all right, Victoria? Is there anything I can do to–'

She looked at the countryside beyond Nat's shoulder. 'If only there was…' she started. Then turning thoughtfully and trying for a smile, 'I bet you're leaking tea and scones, but do you have a few more minutes to spare?'

'Of course,' Nat repeated. What on earth now? But she was intrigued all the same, so she and the dogs retraced their steps to the kitchen.

Victoria motioned her to sit, and kissed her mother's cheek. 'It's fine, Mum,' she said. 'Everyone will find out very soon.'

There was an interlude then. For ten minutes or so, Nat watched the silent interaction between mother and daughter. Side plates and china cups were washed, more baking was presented, and dark tea was poured. Finally Rosemary sat down and held her daughter's hand.

Knowing she wouldn't be able to even look at another sultana for many a year, Nat waited for Victoria to speak.

'Right; here goes,' she said finally. She took a deep breath. 'A few weeks ago I was arrested.'

Nat lifted her eyebrows. Two Hetheringtons arrested? It looked like carelessness. 'Okay. Go on.'

Victoria cleared her throat. 'For outraging public decency, Nat. I was arrested for having sex in public.'

WALLS HAVE EARS

K nowing that parking near the magistrates' court might be a challenge on a sunny day, Nat drove straight from home to Chester on Friday. As it was, the M56 wasn't as chock-a-block as usual, and once she'd hit the scenic route, turning splendidly from summer to autumn, she hadn't been stymied by the usual stubborn tractor. Still confused by the wrong time on Anna's clock, she arrived at the smart building too soon. The doors were still locked; it was too early even to collar the CPS solicitor before anyone got to him or her first.

She sighed. Best laid plans... Still, there was time for a latte and a croissant in the car. Perhaps she'd add it to her expenses and see if she could get breakfast past WMD's eagle eyes.

Absently brushing the pastry off her lap, she gazed at the tourists and shoppers as the car park filled up. Her mind should have been with Rosemary Hetherington, but it wasn't. It was with her 'other daughter'. She'd been mulling about her since leaving the cottage on Tuesday, promising again not to tell Catherine she'd seen her, even though 'she'd get to find out soon enough'.

The tale Victoria had told was quite shocking, one of those 'bang to rights' stories you'd see in the *Daily Mail*, glancing at the headline in the newsagents and hoping no one was looking as you read more.

She hadn't beaten about the bush. 'For outraging public decency, Nat, I was arrested for having sex in public,' she'd said.

An ice breaker for sure, Nat had hidden her astonishment by nodding. 'It sounds interesting. Go on.'

Victoria had pulled a wry face. 'It was a wealthy client called Howard Phillips, a city financier, no less.' Then she'd sighed. 'So there was me and a couple of other accountants from the London office. We were taking Howard and his associates out for a celebratory lunch. You must know what it's like, Nat. The boozy meal goes on through the afternoon and into the evening.' She'd put her forehead on the table and softly banged it a few times. 'The thing is, I can't remember that much, but the following morning I awoke in a police cell, horribly embarrassed, hungover and missing my knickers. Charming, eh? And I'm not in my twenties or even my thirties. I'm forty-four and counting. How could I have been so bloody stupid?'

Nat now drank her coffee thoughtfully. Victoria had been told by an officer that she and the financier had gone down a back street to have sex. There had been complaints by members of the public who'd flagged down a police van; they'd been arrested and put in separate cells overnight to sober up.

It was a comical story in some ways, the sort of scrape Nat might have got into in her late teens, high on dancing and alcohol, and with a boy she really fancied. But Victoria was a married mother in her forties. This Howard guy was a client she barely knew. The story made Nat feel horribly unsettled. It reminded her of Wes's comments about Brian Selby and the line he hadn't crossed, the one she'd never willingly allow.

Shifting in her car seat, Nat took another sip of her latte. She could still picture Victoria's distraught face as she described what had happened at the police station. Her mother sat with them at the table, her eyes glassy, but pouring tea and passing tissues without comment.

'The officer in charge was nice, Nat,' Victoria had said. 'Well as pleasant as she could be in the circumstances. She was sympathetic. "Off the record," she'd said, "we've all been there," and she offered us both a police caution. Perhaps thrilled is too strong a word, but I was mighty relieved to accept it, to get out of the station with as much bloody dignity as I could muster.' She'd taken a deep, shuddery breath. 'Anyhow, that was that. I later confessed everything to my line manager. He was prepared to let it go this once, but made it clear that any further misconduct... well, you know the score, Nat, bringing the firm into disrepute and all that stuff.' She'd dragged a painted fingernail across her throat. 'Fair dos. I didn't tell Mike for obvious reasons. Long story short, I kept my head down, trying my best to deal with the bad dreams, the feelings of revulsion and guilt.'

Nat now tapped the steering wheel. The humiliating incident itself had been bad enough, but the real bombshell arrived only this week. A letter from the financier's solicitor: Howard Phillips hadn't accepted the caution after all. He would be pleading not guilty to the charge and Victoria would be named in the trial and called as a witness. More to the point, the press would get hold of it, she'd be sacked, and her husband and kids would find out.

Finishing her drink, Nat looked at her watch and checked the time on her pay-and-display ticket. Switching her focus to Hetherington senior, she climbed out of the car, hoping the goat strategy would go to plan. When Catherine had asked about it yesterday and she started to explain, Catherine had abruptly interrupted, 'Stop, Nat. Don't tell me; when it comes to Mother, I'm better not knowing.' As Nat hurried towards the court, she wondered whether that would stretch to Victoria's dire situation. The whole episode troubled her; it seemed so unfair. Perhaps she too was under the prodigal daughter's charm, but she felt sorry for her and wanted to help.

Deep in thought, Nat trotted past the court steps, eventually doubling back with a sigh. No trainers or sticky suit today, she quickly passed through security and checked the noticeboard for the courtroom lists. Inevitably they weren't any, so she collared a gowned usher.

'Hetherington,' she said. 'Ten thirty.'

The tiny man peered over his glasses. 'Court 2. Hetherington? No relation to–?'

'Cheers,' Nat replied, walking away. There was already one secret she wasn't going to blab to Catherine; best not add another.

According to Jack, the old magistrates' courts were now a tourist attraction in the Town Hall (with the teak panelling, benches and ghostly 'hanging' Justices of the Peace, no doubt). Though this building was relatively new, it still emitted the usual aroma of damp clothes, paper, toilets and possibly dogs. She peeped into court number two. Excellent. Save for a bloke sitting at the first bench, it was empty. He was rustling through a large stack of files in a mildly panicky way. Yup, it had to be the CPS solicitor.

She stood over him. 'The Hetherington prosecution,' she said. 'You need to drop it.'

The man lifted his head. Small, attractive and neat, he looked familiar, but Nat couldn't quite place him.

He didn't seem to mind the aggressive opening; he was probably used to it. 'Convince me why,' he said, going back to his paperwork. He did another take. 'Ah, Natalie Bach.'

'Lack of evidence, for starters–'

He picked up a folder and tapped it with a fountain pen. 'Apparently the sheep has been preserved by the owner.'

'It's a goat, not a sheep, and how does that prove the defendant ran it over, let alone committed the crime she's accused of?'

He pulled a mock serious face. 'She might as well be hanged for a sheep as for a lamb...'

Nat stood back. 'Now you're taking the Mickey. I know you, don't I?' She narrowed her eyes; his voice was definitely familiar. 'Law school. You were a friend of Jose; you lived in the–'

'Yup, the house with the turret. You can probably see it from here.' He held out his hand. 'Joshim Khan. I'm pleased to meet you again.'

Nat remembered him now; he was one of four or five lads who had shared a house bang in the middle of the city centre, though she only visited once or twice because she hadn't wanted to encourage Jose's advances. She shrugged that ironic thought away.

'So, this case against Hetherington…?'

Joshim lifted his hands in a gesture of surrender. 'There'll be an adjournment today, and then I'll look into it. It gave us a laugh in the office; it's not every day a goat is preserved in a complainant's freezer.'

Nat tried not to smile back. 'This is serious for my client, Joshim. She says she's the victim. Trust me, despite her age, she knows more about the law than I do, and she's talking about wasting police time, never mind her back up of malicious prosecution. I wouldn't take it as an idle threat, either. She's quite a woman–'

'And so are you.' She spun around to the gravelly voice at her shoulder. 'But you won't turn Khan, Nat. Small but perfectly formed, he's the only gay in the CPS.'

His aftershave as loud as his voice, Gavin Savage was towering above them and grinning.

'Bloody hell, Gavin, you made me jump. And you can't say that, you homophobe. Joshim, do us all a favour and have him arrested.'

Joshim smiled and shrugged. 'That's what happens when they let in the Scottish: bloody foreigners.' The door banged and he lowered his voice. 'And so it begins, another day, another dollar.' He nodded to the approaching court clerk, who bore more than a passing resemblance to Severus Snape. 'He's not looking happy, is he?'

Hoping to catch Mrs Hetherington before she left her cottage, Nat hurried from the courtroom to the lobby. Victoria answered the call.

'How's everything?' Nat asked.

'Pretty shit, to be honest. I can't stay here hiding forever. I'll give it this weekend and then face the music at home.'

Wondering how Victoria's husband would take the news, Nat wished her good luck and said goodbye. She didn't know him at all, but surely the father of her children would find it in his heart to forgive a one-off aberration? Would Jose have forgiven her? Well, she knew the answer to that; he'd sulked whenever he thought she was too friendly with the holidaymakers and regulars. It had been difficult at times; it was in her nature to be friendly, indeed, it had paid to be friendly. But, as with Brian Selby, there were lines she would never cross. Jose should've known that.

Her sense of smell kicked in before sound. Gavin Savage was undoubtedly behind her. In fairness, the spicy aroma was pleasant, if a little too powerful. She turned and looked up to his amiable, ruddy face.

'Have you been eating girders again?' she asked. 'Anyway, how tall are you?'

'Six six.'

'More like six six six. Right, I'm off.'

'Tonight, seven o'clock in The Crown.'

'What? Satan will be there, will he? Does he know the prices of drinks in Didsbury these days?'

Gavin laughed. 'No, but you will be.'

'Nah, I don't think so.'

'I have information...'

She lowered her voice, trying to ignore his smug expression.

'Info about Julian Goldman?' Gavin tapped his nose. 'Oh, come on, Savage, just tell me.'

He reduced his usual boom a notch. 'Maybe you hadn't noticed, but we're in a court of law. Walls have ears. And in all seriousness, client confidentiality. Seven o'clock in The Crown.'

Pulling an exasperated face, Nat nodded. The things she did for Jack bloody Goldman. She walked away a few paces, watching an usher wheel a television screen into Court 1, then turned back to catch up with Gavin. 'Alleged victims of sex crimes have anonymity, don't they?' she asked him.

'Yup, lifetime as the law stands.' Gavin's lips spread into a smile. 'Thinking of me already? I know I'm irresistible, Nat, but really, I might not be interested…'

Nat tutted and turned away. 'Baggage,' she called, just loud enough for him to hear, before leaving the building with a grin.

DO YOU EVER WISH

Still smiling, Nat drove back to Cheadle. It had been a fun morning. She hadn't known Joshim Khan was gay, but now she looked back, it made sense. At college he'd been extremely good-looking in a boy-band type of way, but she'd never seen him with a girl. And Gavin Savage, he did make her laugh, but she could not imagine what he'd be like as a boyfriend. No wonder his poor wife had divorced him.

She parked up outside her house. The weak sunshine lit up its Cheshire brick façade and the pretty flower boxes her mum carefully tendered were still brimming with colour. She considered popping in to say hello, but she was temporarily annoyed. Anna hadn't supported her over Wes's rudeness the other day.

'Well, you didn't ask about his son, Natalie. Parents worry about their babies, however old they get,' she'd said. Nat sensed she had only just held back the words: 'if you'd had one, you'd understand.'

She'd tried to explain she hadn't asked because she wasn't supposed to know about Matty's illness; it was called being discreet. But her mum had sagely shaken her head in the way she always did when she thought Nat was in the wrong.

Nat now sighed. Thirty-nine going on seven. She really did need to get a life.

Striding away briskly, she glanced back at the car. It was definitely light blue without even a hint of green. The 42B appeared on the high street at the same time as her, which felt fortuitous – until a rotund, middle-aged man sat next to her and blithely clipped his fingernails for the rest of the journey.

Finally in Didsbury, she bolted from the bus, ran up to the second floor of the office, and knocked on Catherine's door. She was itching to tell her the outcome of the hearing, and maybe have a chat about the amusing morning she'd had. After a moment she twigged that the light was off. She peered in. Yup, the room was empty. Her spirits fell just a little. A half-day summer Friday, undoubtedly, even though it was autumn.

She stared at Catherine's chair, tempted to rest her noggin on the executive mesh headrest to see what it might be like in her old friend's shoes. Instead she retreated to the dark conference room and sent her a text. There was no point in embellishing the message: *Case is adjourned. Prosecuting solicitor looking into it* seemed to cover it.

Laying her head in her arms, she was almost asleep when she remembered the Battersby divorce papers. Shit. She was supposed to let Jack know her thoughts by the end of today. Sitting back, she tapped her nails on the table. There was actually nothing to say. She couldn't begin to improve on the figures already wildly manipulated by Danielle's solicitors and expert accountant.

Tired and deflated after the morning's high, she called Jack. He sounded far away, as though he was smothering his handset.

'Sorry, I couldn't find anything to pick at,' she stated. He'd know what she was talking about.

'Nothing at all? Not even if you were to put your smug feelings to one side?' He paused for a minute. 'You did hear about the baby?'

Her mind flittered to Wes and his poorly son. 'Jack,' she said flatly, 'I hear nothing unless you tell me.'

'The new girlfriend has just given birth. A daughter…'

Ah, a baby girl, just what Danielle had always wanted, but Nat couldn't be bothered to feel self-satisfied. Good on Carl Battersby. She'd liked him. She'd seen that bewildered look in his eyes when Danielle was working another lie. She was pleased he'd got away, but she didn't feel smug, just slightly grimy that she was on the wrong side.

'There was only one thing–' she said reluctantly.

'I'm listening.'

'Just something I overheard in the agency between Carl and some bloke, a builder, I think. They called it a "joint venture". I was earwigging, so I can't be sure, but it was to do with the conversion of a mill they'd bought in Ashton, and I didn't see it mentioned in his financial statement. It might be something or nothing, but if Carl has concealed it, it could affect a costs order.'

'What did I tell you?' Jack replied, sounding pleased. 'You never let me down.'

Ending the call, she went back to her arms. Jack was content; she supposed that was something. And the costs of a full-blown financial fight between two loaded parties would be substantial, running into tens, if not hundreds, of thousands. But it didn't lift her mood. Perhaps she shouldn't have returned to the law; maybe she should've retrained in a 'caring' profession, doing some good as a social worker, a nurse, or as a counsellor. But she would've been rubbish; she didn't have the patience or the natural empathy required.

Though she had more than empathised with Victoria Hetherington, hadn't she? Quickly scooping up her mobile, she pressed Victoria's number, chatting idly for a few minutes. Then surprising herself, 'Do you fancy meeting up for a coffee before you travel back to London?'

'Yeah, sure; that would be nice. How about Saturday? I'll text you.'

'Fab, see you then.'

Time passed and Nat drifted. Wishing she hadn't given into Gavin's pub ploy, she pictured her sofa and her *Sex and the City* DVD box set. Eventually she peered at her watch. Though only five thirty, the surrounding lights were switched off. Maybe she had napped without realising. Everyone had clearly gone home to their loved ones. Or out with their boyfriends. Or playing with their kids. Noticing a patch of wet on her sleeve, she snorted. Dribble, how lovely. She bent down to fish tissues from her handbag. When she surfaced again, Wes Hughes was staring at her coolly from the door.

'You're still here, then.'

Nat couldn't be bothered with false niceties. 'Apparently so.'

He walked further into the room and pulled out a chair. 'Look, I wanted to thank you for the work you did on my files last week. It was really helpful, and beyond the call of duty.' He smiled briefly. 'I should've said so the other day instead of snapping. Sorry.'

Nat immediately pictured her mother's face, the small shake of her head. 'I should've asked about Matty's tests. The thing is, I didn't know why you weren't in the office, and it seemed wrong to pry.'

He nodded. 'I know that now. It was a mix up, you know, with Sharon being so–'

'Indiscreet.' She frowned and took a breath. 'But I'm not, Wes; I can be trusted.'

He slid his hand on the table towards her. 'I know, absolutely, I know.'

'So, how is Matty?' she asked, conscious of his dark gaze on her sleeve and pulling it down onto her lap.

Sitting back in his seat, he flexed his shoulders. 'He's fine actually, and now back in uni. They haven't got to the bottom of it yet. He used to have these episodes as a kid – fits, I suppose. Not all the time, but here and there, so they considered epilepsy, among a hundred other things.'

He paused for a moment and Nat thought how tired and hollow he looked.

'Can you imagine how that would affect the life of a boy who wants to go into sport as a career?' He rubbed his face. 'But they've discounted that now, thank God.'

'So everything's good?'

'For now. They're just going to monitor him and get him in every few weeks for blood tests.' His hands moved to his temples. 'It's a bloody relief.'

He stood and made for the door.

'Wes,' Nat called before it closed. 'I don't suppose you'd fancy a quick drink?'

He turned back, his face questioning.

'I've been cornered by Gavin. He's got some info for me, but he's only prepared to divulge it in The Crown at seven.' She smiled wryly. 'Something tells me I might need a chaperone.'

Wes stepped back in and sat down. 'I would if I could. The thing is, Andrea… She's struggling. It was hard to let the boys go in the first place, then this happened. It's not that Matty is her favourite, but he's the one who's always needed her most, if you know what I mean. She'd actually driven over that day, taking a supply of food he and Dylan particularly like.' He glanced at Nat and gave a tight smile. 'I know, it's ridiculous, but Matty was in great form when she left, so it was a huge shock to see him the next day, wired up in a hospital bed. She's been pretty distraught ever since.' He stood and spread his arms. 'Well, I'm sure you can imagine.'

Nat stared through the blinds when he'd gone, thinking: the suggestion that Wes join her and Gavin had been on impulse, but it was an excellent idea. She reached for the telephone and rang the extension for the bench table downstairs. Emilia answered immediately. Sweet. 'Fancy coming to the pub?' she asked.

~

Gavin was already in The Crown, taking up a huge amount of space both physically and verbally.

'Miss Bach,' he called. 'Get your arse over here. What are you having?' He looked Emilia up and down. 'Moved on to female bodyguards these days, have you?' he asked.

Nat chuckled. 'I couldn't have put it better myself. This is Emilia, Gav. She's a nice, quiet girl, so you have to behave.'

'The quiet ones are always–'

'Shut up, Savage, and get the drinks.'

It was difficult to reign him in, and although Emilia looked a little shocked at his crass comments to begin with, a few drinks seemed to relax her, even more so when she discovered he'd shared a house with Wesley at law school. A few funny stories about sporting, drinking and culinary disasters got her completely onside.

Gavin pointed at Nat. 'Notice how she remembers the story about the blaze, Emilia? Someone called Fire Services and the appliance got stuck down our street. Nat and her friends weren't remotely interested in our peril until then.' He mimicked a female voice. 'Officer, officer! Come and help me find my pussy...' He shook his head. 'The fire was Wes's fault. Him and his famous Caribbean stir fries. Adding a slug of rum and lighting it wasn't wise...'

'So Wesley likes cooking? Ooh, tell me more. This is great. He gives nothing away. Is it true about his wife?' Emilia asked, guzzling her wine as though it was lemonade.

Nat glanced at Gavin. 'Careful, Emilia, Gav's wife and Wes's are...' She crossed her fingers to show they were close.

'*Ex* wife.' Gavin also crossed his, as though fending off a vampire. He leaned towards Emilia. 'What do you want to know? I'm prepared to dish the dirt for such a bonnie lassie–'

Nat groaned. 'Oh, come on, Gav. We're not in the 1970s. Ignore him, Emilia.'

But she didn't seem to mind. Her blue eyes were wide. 'Well according to Sharon...' she started.

Here we go, Nat thought, hoping none of the gossip had inadvertently come from her, but still intrigued to hear it.

'...his wife got pregnant deliberately to catch him. Is it true?'

Ouch. That was a bit harsh. Nat looked at Gavin, interested to see how he'd respond.

'Well, you know Wes; he'd never actually put it like that. But possibly true, nonetheless,' he replied. He glanced at Nat and raised his eyebrows. 'I think he'd hoped to shake Andrea off when he came to Chester, change the old model for a new one, and I believe a lot of candidates would've been happy to oblige...'

Nat sat back and folded her arms. 'Do you know how sexist that sounds?'

'I think he does it to wind you up, Nat. You know, like ten-year-olds do,' Emilia said, laughing. 'But go on with the story, Gav. Why didn't he just ditch her?'

The words 'shag hag' popped into Nat's head, and she cringed, waiting for them to appear from Gavin's mouth, but he answered more seriously. 'Andrea wouldn't have accepted it. Trust me, that woman likes to get her own way.'

Clearly disappointed with the answer, Emilia scraped back her stool and headed unsteadily to the ladies. Nat leaned towards Gavin and spoke in a low voice. 'So tell me what you know about Julian Goldman before she comes back.'

'Not a lot–'

She thumped his arm. 'Bloody hell, Gavin.'

'–Yet. What I do know is that the police have asked him to attend another interview next week. It sounds as though they were fairly vague, saying it's to do with the "night in question", the usual generic type of phrase they use when they're digging. Plus the usual implication that it would be better for him to attend voluntarily rather than being arrested.'

'I don't get it,' she whispered. 'He accepted a caution for the assault, didn't he? That's an admission. They got what they wanted. Why question him more?'

Gavin shrugged. 'Search me. But I'm going to find out.'

Nat frowned for a moment, her mind drifting to Victoria Hetherington. 'Can a police caution be set aside?'

'Theoretically, I suppose. But he admitted to hitting her. She had a massive shiner. There's no way on earth–'

She came back to Gavin's inquisitive face. 'Oh, not Julian's caution. I was thinking about something else. So how would you do it? How would you overturn one?'

'God knows. Maybe make an application to quash it?' He tapped his finger on the end of her nose. 'What are you up to, Ms Bach?'

'I hope I'm not interrupting.' The voice sounded loud above their whispering. Nat jolted back in surprise. It was Wes.

'Hughsie.' Gavin stood, a huge grin on his face. 'Long time no see, mate. How did you know I was…' he started, then turned to Nat. 'I see. "Baggage", I suppose?'

Wes dropped his folded arms to shake Gavin's hand and Nat watched their interaction as they playfully argued about who should buy the next round. Gavin won, so Wes sat down but his smile seemed thin, growing even thinner when Emilia appeared at their table.

'Oh, Wesley. Hi! Jeans and a cool leather jacket. Don't you look different…' she said. She looked at Nat and then at Gavin, who was approaching with drinks on a tray. 'Doesn't he look different not wearing a suit, guys?' She twirled a flirtatious finger at him. 'Were your ears burning just now?' she trilled. Then after a small silence and with a lame voice she added, 'Not that we were saying anything bad, were we, guys?'

Gavin and Wes chatted and Nat half listened, interested to hear them catch up after an absence of over a year, but feeling obliged to pay attention to Emilia whom she'd invited along, after all. After the girl's third whispered, 'Oh God, I've offended him, haven't I?' Nat was tempted to scream, 'Yes, you idiot!', but as the evening went on, Wes seemed uptight and moody with them both. It was a relief when last orders were called and the four of them left together, standing on the damp pavement and rubbing hands against the cold.

Nat briefly hugged Emilia and Gavin, then nodded at Wes. 'See you next week,' she called, zigzagging through the traffic to the other side of the road. A sleek Audi clearly wasn't happy to stop, so she had to run the last few paces, almost colliding with a large man stepping down from the door next to the flower shop. He quickly turned and paced away, but not before his eyes had met Nat's.

Bloody hell, that was interesting. What was *he* doing coming out of a brothel in Didsbury? Making a note to tell Jack, Nat lifted her coat collar and headed for the bus stop, but the sound of footsteps behind diverted her thoughts.

'You're not waiting for a bus, surely?' Wes asked.

'I've pretty much got public transport to Didsbury and back sussed,' she replied dryly. 'You know, with the difficulty in parking…'

He grinned, the smile transforming his face. 'Point taken. Can I treat you to a taxi by way of apology?'

She opened her mouth, ready to argue that the bus would be quicker, but Wes had already stepped onto the road, flagging down a black cab.

They sat in the back, Nat remembering how much she'd needed to puke the last time she shared a taxi with Wes. Tonight she felt good; more drunk than sober, but considerably less pissed than that night. She glanced at him. His head was turned away, but the tension in his jaw was clear. 'Everything still okay? The boys and Andrea?'

He turned and smiled. 'Yeah, thanks; it is.'

She put her hand loosely on his. 'Then chill out a little, maybe? Life's too short to be miserable.'

He wrapped his fingers around hers, then went back to his silent gaze through the window without letting go. Finally he moved when the taxi pulled up outside her house. He looked at her intently. 'Do you ever wish...?' he started.

Listening to the hum of the cab, she waited for him to say more, but he released her hand and shook his head. 'Night, Nat,' he said. 'Enjoy the weekend.'

THINK ABOUT IT

Nat woke late on Saturday morning and yawned widely. Despite the booze, she'd taken a long time to drop off last night. Her mind had fizzed with thoughts, bouncing from one to another, then landing back to Wes's unfathomable gaze when they'd stopped outside her house.

In her imagination the taxi had gone around the block a few times, allowing Wes to spill the beans. What was the wish? It could've been anything from which boxer shorts he'd chosen that evening, to climbing Mount Kilimanjaro, but she couldn't help feeling it was to do with her. Despite the flutter, she had no real evidence of that; since coming back to Goldman Law he'd been more hostile than friendly. And it had to be said her intuition was pretty crap. She'd thought Joshim Khan had a twinkle in his eye when they'd chatted in court and it turned out he was gay. She was no longer a spring chicken, and even if there was a frisson between them, Wes was married with kids; she really had to get her shit together.

She'd fallen asleep eventually, but her conscious mind-buzzing was replaced by the unconscious, strange visions about her father and Jack who became interchangeable. The dream dissolved when she shook herself awake and she was left with a cramped sensation of guilt. As children she and her brother had been wary of their dad's sudden eruptions of anger; as an adult the roles had seemed to reverse. She hadn't had outbursts, but she'd definitely been snappy. Her elderly father was both stubborn and frail, and without the bond of love, sometimes it had been difficult to be kind.

As she turned over the pillow, she wished she'd tried harder.

Finally dressed and downstairs, she gave her mum a tight hug and quickly ate a bowl of cereal. Victoria Hetherington was collecting her at noon for their coffee date. Nat had offered to meet somewhere convenient for her, but she'd said, 'I'm guessing that turquoise car isn't yours.' Nat had tried not to bristle at the colour description, or the suggestion that Anna might want to use it herself on a Saturday. But it was a valid point: something she hadn't thought through each time she'd borrowed it.

A beep from outside alerted her to Victoria's arrival.

'Are you sure you don't want to come?' she asked her mum. 'For a bit of fresh air?'

Anna lifted her eyebrows and gave a pointed Paddington-like stare. She'd said her piece the other day, politely but firmly. She wasn't an invalid yet. She'd spent the last five years happily by herself; she had her own friends, and didn't want or need to be mollycoddled.

Nat lowered herself into Victoria's thrumming car. 'Morning,' she said. 'Where are we off to?'

The Porsche was not dissimilar to the James Bond Scalextric vehicle her brother had inherited from an older cousin. She looked at the smart wooden dash. Perhaps she should be thinking about one of her own, but this wasn't it. This was undoubtedly sleek and possibly sexy, but she felt too close to the ground; she'd prefer something higher, albeit not as tall as the SUVs which seemed to be a compulsory requirement for the Cheshire set; she wanted something middling that wasn't turquoise.

'Fancy a challenge?' Victoria asked, removing her sunglasses. She'd already mentioned a walk, so Nat was wearing her trainers, but she didn't own a pair of hiking boots and hoped the terrain wouldn't be too rugged or testing.

As though she were reading her thoughts, Victoria smiled. 'Trainers are fine. Just lots of steps. See if you can run it.'

Nat held on to her seat as they swooped in the fast lane towards Chorley, exiting the motorway near the football ground, then heading towards leafy country lanes, mostly in silence. Midway up a hill, Victoria swerved into a small stony car park, surrounded by trees. 'It's popular for dogging, I believe,' she said, smiling wryly. 'So I'm in good company.' She pointed towards a wide rocky track. 'It's a brisk walk up the hill. Rivington Pike's at the top.'

The dry wind hit their faces as they tramped, dodging muddy patches, ridges and puddles, Victoria chatting intermittently about coming here with her grandparents who lived in Horwich. 'The poor half of the family,' she quipped. 'Don't tell Catherine or she'd kill me.'

Inhaling the fresh, piney smell, Nat turned to Victoria from time to time. Her blonde hair was covered by a bobble hat; her eyes hidden by sunglasses. There were things Nat wanted to ask about the night of her arrest, but it didn't feel right, so instead she enquired about Jack, something she had always wondered about.

'How does your mum get along with Jack? Did she mind his…' The word 'baggage' popped into her head. She supposed everyone her age would have some, otherwise they'd be odd. Oh God, maybe she was just that. Weird, dumped, odd. It was another theory which hadn't occurred to her before.

'His age?' Victoria finished Nat's sentence. 'Not at all. In fact it's mandatory. All the Hetherington women have married older men. A father complex, probably, passed down the generations and in the blood, or some such baloney. There's always an excuse for everything these days.'

When they finally stopped, Nat looked up. Weathered, steep steps led up to a stone tower: the Pike.

'It looks easier than it actually is, even if you're walking,' Victoria said, lifting her glasses and squinting ahead. She turned and grinned. 'Ready for the challenge?' Then she darted off before Nat could reply, taking the steps two by two.

Nat followed, going at a slower pace but still jogging upwards until her chest smarted, ready to explode. Breathing hard, she walked the final steps, taking Victoria's proffered hand at the top.

'Come and look at the view,' she said, pulling Nat to the edge of the large grassy mound. She took off her hat and spun around as the wind whipped her hair, theatrically gesturing to the countryside surrounding them like Maria von Trapp. 'Look, Nat. There's the pigeon tower we passed, the radio mast, Macron stadium, the Lake District, sheep...' Then lifting her hands. 'Oh hell, it's raining, let's run to the tower.' She looked at Nat appraisingly when they reached shelter. 'Not bad for a first timer. Do you run?'

'Not any more. I used to with Jose.'

'Yeah, I remember him. What happened?'

Nat laughed. 'God knows. I still don't.' She mused for a moment. 'He fucked off to Mallorca and I suddenly decided I couldn't live without him. Then I became this different person...' She looked at Victoria's face which appeared mildly interested, like a shrink. 'That wasn't what you meant, was it? You meant why did it end.'

Victoria shrugged. She and Catherine looked remarkably alike, but had such different personalities. 'Whatever, it's interesting. Go on.'

'Well...' It was hard to express how she felt. She was still working it out in her head. 'This different person... I let him completely control her, I suppose. But I couldn't see it at the time. I thought I was happy. Then he ditched me. Story over.'

'Maybe he could see it coming. He finished with you before you saw the light and dumped him.'

'I doubt that,' Nat began. A memory suddenly struck her, one she didn't want to share. Jose's occasional impotence was something she'd forgotten about. And she was here to listen to Victoria, not the other way around. 'It looks like the rain has eased,' she said. 'Shall we go?'

'Yup. The tea rooms, I think, don't you?' Victoria rubbed her hands. 'They do a lovely cream scone, but after Tuesday at Mum's...' She laughed. 'How about a cuppa and red velvet gateaux? I think that we've earned it.'

Aided by the wind behind them, the walk back took less time and Victoria drove down the winding lane, pulling up outside a dark stone church hall they had passed earlier.

'Don't worry, we're not here to pray,' she said. 'Tea rooms as promised. Basic but nice. We'll be the youngest there.'

The lofty hall was filled with pensioners sitting around small benches covered with bright gingham table cloths. Nat sat opposite Victoria at one to the side, taking in the strong aroma of cinnamon and listening to the low hum of conversation as they waited for their order.

'So,' Nat began, taking a breath. 'Talking of praying... Stop me if it's none of my business.'

Victoria sighed. 'Go on. I suppose I'm going to have to get used to it.'

Leaning forward, Nat lowered her voice. 'The night of the incident – or rather, the morning after. You said you couldn't remember anything.'

Victoria nodded, her face tight. 'Not after leaving the restaurant. When I tried at the police station, there were snatches of us sitting in a pub. But to be honest, not remembering the nitty-gritty was a relief at the time.' She put her hands to her face. 'Oh God, the thought of me letting him do whatever he did. You should see him, Nat. It wasn't like I was playing away because I couldn't resist. I don't get it; he's married. Why didn't he just accept the caution?'

'I don't know. To prove something to his wife? To avoid having a criminal record?' Nat paused as the waitress put a tray on their table. 'What's he like, though? What impression did you get him before that day, or earlier in the day?'

Victoria shrugged. 'You know what it's like, Nat; I'm sure you've been there in your line of work too. He's an important wealthy client, charming in a slimy, overweight way. I could tell he liked me and I was dutifully friendly, but that's all. Really, I don't know what possessed me, God knows how much I must have drunk. What a stupid, stupid fool I am.' She took a deep breath and straightened her back. 'But hey, I've got to live with it. It was my own bloody fault.'

Nat poured milk in her china cup. 'But was it, though? Was it your fault? What about the nightmares you told me about, not being sure if it was a bad dream or a memory? Is that normal?' She met Victoria's gaze. 'Maybe your drink was spiked.'

Shaking her head, Victoria leaned forward to protest, so Nat quickly cut in. 'And even if it was just alcohol, who was buying the drinks? You were clearly paralytic. He took advantage of that. Can you really be blamed?'

'No.' Victoria was frowning. 'No, Natalie. I'm not one of those women who make excuses. I hate the way society blames everyone else but themselves these days. I'm not going down that road.'

Nat sat back. 'Okay, fair enough. You want to take responsibility for your actions and I admire that. But consider this. Why are you automatically assuming you're in the wrong? The weak, silly female who was a "stupid, stupid" fool? Could it be that society has conditioned us women to feel that way? Is that fair or equal? He doesn't seem to be blaming himself for anything.' She paused for a moment, almost wanting to smile at her old feminist self. 'But that apart, it seems to me that whatever happened between you two, whether you were drugged or drunk, you didn't have the capacity to consent. So that makes his actions a sexual assault.' She held up her hand to stop Victoria interrupting. 'And as I understand it, alleged victims of sex crimes have lifetime anonymity. It would be unlawful for the courts or the press to name that person.'

Nat took a bite of her cake, then licked the butter cream from her fingers. 'All I'm saying is think about it.'

18

A FOOL'S ERRAND

The Sabbath – a day of rest, thank goodness. Wearing pyjamas and flicking channels on the sofa, Nat wondered if she had enough years left to commit to all sixteen series of *NCIS*. Poppy cat was curled on her lap, purring quietly, her brother Lewie on the prowl, trying to work out a strategy to oust her.

Nat yawned, surprised at how knackered she felt. In Mallorca, save for a few hours in the dead of night, work had been full on all week, but she couldn't remember being this tired. Of course, they'd had help from Hugo, their manager, as they fondly called him. She'd always detected a twitch around his mouth when a demand to see 'the manager' occurred. It hadn't often happened, but even their lowly bar attracted the wealthy, impatient Brits who demanded cheap cava and immediate service.

It was the moustachioed Hugo who'd sold 'Havana' to Jose, saying that at fifty-five it was time to retire and spend his hard-earned money, but he'd pretty much stayed, as an interfering customer at first, then later as an employee when Jose gave in to the inevitable and allowed him back behind the bar.

Nat now smiled at the memory. She had always adored Hugo

and it probably took six months to persuade Jose that it would be sensible to ask him back. He had the looks and the charm of a middle-aged crooner, so the ladies loved him. He'd had forty years of experience in the business and he was local, so he knew who to employ, who to trade with, and who'd try to rip them off. The downside was his constant obtrusion, which sent Jose nuts. 'If I'd wanted a bloody father poking his nose in my business, I'd have brought my own,' he'd complain. But Nat hadn't minded Hugo's constant presence. She was that other person then: happy to let everyone else make the decisions and just do as she was told.

Having a sudden urge to study the photographs, she sat up, offending the cat. During the first year, she'd regularly sent mobile pics to Anna, who'd dutifully printed them off at Boots. Nat had wanted to chuck or burn them only weeks ago, but was stymied by the fact they weren't hers. But she felt stronger now, and anyway fuck Jose. She wanted to look at Hugo's smiling face, to examine the many snaps of him and her on the beach and at the bar, his arm around her shoulders protectively. Kneeling down at the sideboard drawers, she smiled to herself. She and Hugo had been like daughter and father, her Mallorcan Jack Goldman. It was funny how she hadn't seen it that way before.

Opening the old shoebox, she took out a few snaps, but her task was interrupted by a rap at the door. She listened to her mum's exclamation and thanks, unable to make out the identity of the caller for a few moments, but then he walked in.

'A cup of coffee would be lovely, Anna. Thank you. Two spoons for me. I like it strong.'

Nat sat back on her haunches and folded her arms. Jack Goldman was wearing what she hoped was his golfing clobber. 'Go away unless you're paying me double – no, triple. It's Sunday, Jack.'

'It's a social call, Natalie. I was passing. I thought it would be nice to say hello to your mum too.' He smiled. 'She was pleased with her flowers.'

Stepping forward, he took a photograph from Nat's hand. 'The Spaniard's aged badly.'

She snatched it back. 'That isn't Jose, as well you know.' She nodded at his trousers. 'What's this, then, a Rupert Bear tribute act?'

'Has he paid you back yet? How much did you put in that bar? Twenty, fifty, a hundred grand?'

'It's none of your business, Jack. What do you want?'

He sat on the sofa and polished his glasses. 'An update. Walls without ears. Except your mum; she's always been good at not listening.' He called into the kitchen. 'Haven't you, Anna?'

'I'm just putting these beautiful lilies in a vase. I'll be a few minutes,' her mum replied.

Nat sat in the armchair and curled up her legs. 'Look at your mobile, Jack. There are missed calls from me. After the third attempt, I decided it was probably for the best you didn't know. Mainly because there's no news yet.'

He leaned forward, his face pale and grim. 'What don't I need to know, Natalie?'

She sighed. 'The police have asked Julian to volunteer for another interview. We don't know why, but his solicitor is onto it, so—'

Jack immediately stood, his skin flushing. 'Right I'm going there now.'

'Where?'

'To Julian's. He can tell me himself.'

'No, Jack, you can't.' Alarm bells jingling and beeping and chiming, she glared at his puce face. 'You're not being fair to me or my friend. If you tell Julian you know anything, it's a breach of client confidentiality, as well you know.'

Jack moved his head from side to side, then paced for a

moment. 'Bloody child!' he yelled, then more quietly. 'I'll say I found out through my policemen pal–'

'Yeah, but you didn't.' She thought for a moment. 'Why's that, then?'

'God knows, Natalie. Perhaps it doesn't pay to have thirty-five successful years in the law.' He was shouting again, his face a deep dirty red. 'Bloody bastards. I'll think of something to tell him,' he said, making for the door.

'Then I'll come with you. Wait just a moment. I need to get dressed.'

Wearing a hoodie and leggings, Nat finally tumbled from the house. Jack was waiting in his Mercedes, thank God. She'd been ham-fisted and shaky getting washed and dressed. Although she'd managed to rake a comb through her hair, she felt naked without even a hint of make-up. Clutching her handbag, she slid into the passenger seat, then looked at Jack's face. It was now almost white and covered in sweat. 'You need to calm down, Jack. There's nothing we can do for now. This is a fool's errand.'

He didn't reply, but kept his eyes on the road, indicating right onto the high street, then left onto the duel carriageway, picking up speed after several roundabouts. Irritated and hungry, Nat stared at the vehicles ahead. She was glad he wasn't in the mood for talking as she certainly wasn't. But an abrupt movement from Jack caught her eye and she turned. He was clutching his chest and suddenly the car was swerving, spinning out of control, nearly colliding with another driver in the right-hand lane, who blared out his horn. Adrenaline taking over, she grabbed the steering wheel and yanked it hard to the left. Moments later the car slammed into the high grassy bank and came to a thudding standstill.

For an instant there was silence. Then there was noise – the screech of the car alarm – and then a smell, the whiff of burning. The panic was immediate. Oh God, she was trapped. And the firework odour; oh God: the car was going to explode. She had to get out.

It took only seconds, painfully slow seconds, for Nat to realise the thump to her torso wasn't plastic or metal, but the airbag which was already deflating. She looked across to Jack. His was emptying too, but his head was to one side, his glasses swinging from one ear.

Her heart battered her ribs. Oh God, Jack. Oh God, she had to call an ambulance. Trying to focus, she tore her eyes from him to the windscreen. A lorry was parked at an angle in front of the car, its hazard lights flashing protectively. Then her door opened and the breeze smacked her cheeks. A man was on his mobile and another was peering at her face, his mouth moving.

She eventually tuned into his words. 'Are you all right, love? Are you hurt?'

Slowly she became aware of her body. Shifting in her seat, she moved her fingers and toes. No pain, thank God, though her ears were ringing, her chest felt tight and her eyes stung badly. 'Best not move, love,' the man said, his expression concerned and kind. 'The ambulance and police are on their way.'

She looked at Jack again. 'I'm not sure,' she said, finding her voice. 'Something happened just before… I think he might have had a stroke or a heart attack.' Her throat felt raw, the panic rising again. 'Oh God. You need to let them know. You need to tell them as soon as they arrive. Time is of the essence.'

God, she was speaking like a bloody lawyer, but time *was* of the essence. When she was in her twenties her father had had a heart attack, but he'd refused for hours to do anything about it. He'd sat stubbornly in his front room, insisting it was heartburn, shouting her mum down when she begged him to let her telephone for help.

Nat had called the emergency services from her home,

arriving shortly before them. 'What the hell are you doing, Dad?' she'd shouted. 'You are so bloody selfish. Don't you know what you're putting Mum through?'

When the second attack had come, it was fatal.

'Time is of the essence with acute myocardial infarctions, I'm afraid. If he'd come in earlier, he might have had a chance,' the consultant later said.

She now dragged her attention back to the figure at the door. He nodded and went to speak to the other man, still on his mobile, then came back and crouched at her side. 'Five minutes,' he said. 'They are on their way.' He smiled at her sympathetically and nodded at Jack. 'Is this your dad?'

As though dropped from the sky, the police, the paramedic and the ambulance arrived all at once. Nat climbed from the Merc and watched dumbly, holding Jack's glasses as they removed him from the car, heaving him onto a stretcher and into the ambulance. Unsure if she'd be allowed to travel with him, she didn't correct anyone's assumption that she was his daughter. Afraid to look at his prone body, she sat frozen in the back, eventually taking out her phone with trembling hands. Oh God, oh God, what to say to Catherine? She stared at the screen for an age. Then she put it back in her bag. Her mind was too fuddled with shock and anxiety. She'd leave it for now. The police had already taken Catherine's details; they'd know what to say.

She jerked at the sudden screech of the siren. Only then did she realise she hadn't thanked the lorry driver and the other man for their help; they had been so kind, but she couldn't have described them, even if she'd tried.

19

CRYING IS ALLOWED

The hospital was stifling, but Nat waited on a metal bench outside the cardiac ward, feeling shivery, cold and despondent. She fingered her mobile again, unsure when she and Jack had arrived in the ambulance, but wondering why Catherine was taking so long. Listlessly she flicked through Instagram on her phone for something to do, then lifted her gaze at the sound of a door opening. At last. Catherine and Wes were striding towards her, a clear look of surprise on both their faces.

Catherine towered over her. 'How did you know…?' she started. Then her eyes fixed on the collar some chump had forced Nat to wear around her neck. '*You* were with Jack? It was you, not Verity?' She took a step back, the frown on her face deepening. 'Jack was away golfing this weekend. Why was he with you? Why were you in his car, Natalie?'

Wes was standing a few yards behind her. Nat caught his questioning look and sighed. 'He turned up a couple of hours ago with some flowers for my mum.' She could see the doubt spreading across Catherine's features. 'Ask Anna, if you like. Ask to inspect the bloody bunch.'

She stared at her old friend. What the hell? The heat rose to her face. She suddenly felt angry, pissed off with the usual assumption, and from Catherine of all people. 'Look, if he was my sugar daddy, Catherine, and if I were stooping so low as to shag someone else's husband, I would hardly dress like this. I don't sleep with married men, and if ever I decide to do so, I assure you I'll make more of an effort.'

Catherine lowered her eyes. 'Okay, fair enough…' Then after a moment. 'Why were you in the car? Where were you and Jack going, then?'

Nat took a breath. How to reply? Her throat felt like sandpaper; she was bloody sick of the Chinese walls Jack always created. The sheer joy of being told by the cardiologist that Jack was very poorly but wouldn't die, had now completely worn off. 'Why don't you ask him?' she said wearily. 'I've been told he's awake.'

Turning her wedding ring, Catherine stood silently for a further moment, then she nodded and walked into the ward, leaving Wes still leaning against the far wall. When the door clicked shut he moved forward, crouching down in front of Nat, his unfathomable gaze on her face.

'How are you? The collar. Are you hurt?'

She shook her head. 'It's just a precautionary measure. Until they check me out.'

'And have they checked you out?'

She shook her head again, trying to breathe, battling to hold back the flood of tears at the surface. 'No, I've been here, waiting.' She looked into his eyes, still pinned to hers. 'I thought he was dead, Wes. I really thought he'd died. Right until I got into the ambulance and saw his heartbeat on a monitor. And even then, until he was here, safe and sound…' She took another gulp of air. 'A second attack often follows the first very soon after. Did you know that?'

Wes didn't reply. Instead he put his arms around her shoulders, pulling her close gently, as though she was fragile. His tenderness felt too much so she shrugged him away, standing up and apart from him, hiding her face and her tears. In the silence she could hear him walk away, the echo of his shoes down the corridor, the swish of the door. So then she cried more, pulling off the collar, wanting to stamp with frustration and self-pity.

A sudden flurry of activity at the ward entrance made her turn. Some of the nursing staff were emerging, their everyday chatter sounding too cheerful and loud, so she didn't notice Wes had returned until she heard the warm sound of his voice.

'Crying is allowed,' he said, holding out a wad of toilet tissue. 'Especially in hospitals. I was crying two weeks ago myself.'

'Were you?' she asked, wiping her face. She blew her nose. 'Is Matty still okay?'

He nodded and smiled. She could see his relief. 'Yeah, he is, actually. Which just goes to show that Jack's in the right place. What have they said?'

'A minor heart attack. It's a warning, as they put it. They're going to do an angiogram, so I suppose they'll know more after that. They gave me a lecture about his lifestyle choices, drinking, smoking, food, stress.' She smiled a small smile. 'When he was admitted they assumed I was his daughter, and by then it was too late to disabuse them.'

Leaning close, Wes touched her cheek. 'Tissue paper,' he said, showing her the evidence. Then more seriously: 'You should get checked out, Nat. Your eyes and your face look sore.' He frowned, looking soulful. 'Still beautiful, but sore.'

She flushed at the compliment. 'It's the chemicals and dust from the airbag, apparently. They're not usually harmful, but it seems I'm a princess.'

'As well as a daughter.'

Searching for disapproval, she glanced at him, but none seemed to be there. 'Here's hoping I'm a better daughter to Jack than I was to my real father.' She looked at the ward door, wanting to stay longer, but knowing it was no longer appropriate. 'It's time for me to go home.'

Wes caught her fingers. 'I'll drive you. Give me ten minutes with Jack and Catherine, then I'll drop you home.' He squeezed her hand and dipped down to look at her face. 'Is that okay? We could stop on the way and have a drink, or something to eat. Are you hungry?'

Nat nodded, the need to sob again clogging her throat. She waited until he disappeared into the ward before heading to the toilets. She watched another woman carefully apply lipstick, and braced herself for the mirror. The image was pretty much as she'd feared. Dreadful was the word which came to mind. The rims of her eyes were red, her skin was blotchy and her dark hair was knotted with dusty white particles. The hood of her top was still tucked inside, making her resemble a mini hunchback, and her head throbbed with a dull ache.

'Beautiful, my arse,' she said to her reflection, not sure if she wanted to smile or cry. She went to the loo, straightened her hoodie and washed her face, took two Paracetamol, and tried to drag a brush through her hair. Then she went back to the ward, reclaiming the bench and pulling out her mobile to check the time.

Minutes passed as she dozed, too tired to browse the web or play scrabble. Footsteps disturbed her from time to time, visitors, she assumed from the grapes and tight faces. Then the worry struck. Oh God; had someone told Jack's kids about the accident? Julian and Jack were estranged, and Catherine had assumed she was Verity. She pulled out her phone and after a few moment's thought of how to phrase it, she sent Catherine a text: *Sorry to bother you, but just remembered Verity and Julian. Anything I can do to help?*

The reply was immediate. *No thanks. Get yourself checked out. See you next week.*

Ridiculously rejected, she stared at the screen. Yup, she could picture Cool Catherine's straight back, her rigid face as she typed it; unemotional, ungrateful and dismissive. And forty-five minutes had passed since she'd come back from the ladies; matters of business undoubtedly, the skivvy soon forgotten.

And what about Wes? Should she message him and say, 'Is the drink still on offer?' or perhaps, 'Don't say that I'm beautiful and then let me down'? But neither was actually appropriate. He'd only offered her a lift and even if there'd been more to it, as she'd said to Catherine, she didn't chase married men.

She almost called a taxi, but knew her mum would worry about the wasteful cost of such a long journey, so phoned her instead. Walking quickly from the ward, she retraced her steps down the echoey corridors to the exit and the chilly evening outside.

Fearful she'd be seen by Catherine or Wes, and wanting to get away from the damned bench, she had told Anna to collect her at the car park entrance. But it was bloody cold, the wind snapping at her face and thin leggings. Crouching against a low wall, she wrapped her arms around her chest and numbly waited. Her mum finally appeared, and she climbed into the comfort of the turquoise car, shivering, tired and hungry. Then she cried in her lovely mum's arms. Tears for Jack and for her long-dead father, but mostly for herself.

20

I'LL NEED YOU ON FRIDAY

It was Monday morning, and Nat lay in the same position she had lain twenty-four hours earlier, but this time she wasn't comfortable or relaxed on the sofa. Too exhausted to do anything other than clean her teeth and smear her face with hydrocortisone cream (probably well past its use-by date), she'd collapsed into bed the moment her feet touched the bedroom carpet last night. She had dropped off immediately, not stirring until a searing pain in her neck hit in the early hours. Her head had throbbed and she could barely move it. Like a little kid, she had wanted to call out for her mum, but instead she'd managed to reach for the medical collar and ram two painkillers in her mouth. Without water she'd struggled to swallow them down, and it still felt as though they were lodged in her windpipe, as Anna tackled the knots in her hair.

Apart from taking more pills, her main priority on waking had been to stand under a long, bracing shower, but the smarting had spread down her neck to her shoulders, so she'd ended up in the bath, lying motionless for twenty minutes before realising she'd need her mum's help to wash her hair. It had actually been quite comical. She had covered her private parts with a strategically placed sponge and a flannel, but still it was funny and embarrassing to be almost nude and helpless, even with the woman who'd given birth to her. It was sobering too; their roles had been reversed from two months ago when Anna had come home from the hospital, when she'd meekly sat naked in the tub to be washed, pushed and pulled like a dolly.

Ill heath allowed for no dignity at all. Of all people, Jack Goldman needed his. She hoped and prayed he'd be fine. That he'd be up and about, building his bloody Chinese walls and being a pain in the bum, just like always – and that a second attack wouldn't follow.

'This is a huge knot, Skarbie. Tell me if it hurts,' her mum now said, gently pulling at a mass of hair with a comb. Each tug was like a spark of fiery torture in the whole of her upper body, but she tried to be stoical, even though the self-pity had returned in shed loads. She had her lovely mum, so she wasn't completely alone, but supposing Anna's stroke had been fatal? Philip had Sonia, Catherine had Jack, Wes had Andrea, the bench boys had girlfriends, possibly wives. Even Gavin Savage had children; perhaps it made sense to have a football team of kids after all.

Finishing her chore, her mum adjusted the cushion behind her head. 'I could call out the doctor,' she said again. She'd been nagging all morning, but Nat knew there wasn't any point struggling to the local surgery, even if she was still registered, and certainly not calling a doctor out. She had whiplash. All they'd do is suggest a collar and painkillers and she had both at home, even if the pills were an assortment of drugs prescribed for Anna. She'd been through the bathroom cabinet, not recognising the name of most of them, but codeine seemed a safe bet.

Too gloomy to endure overly chirpy morning TV presenters, Nat didn't turn the television on. Instead she and Poppy cat stared at her toes. Always on display in her comfortable sandals, she'd had her nails shellacked in Mallorca to keep them colourful and neat, her one token of vanity there. The small pinkies were clear of colour, but the varnish remained at the tips of her big ones, a deep peachy colour, almost orange. She'd chosen 'sunburst' at the local manicurists, ignorant of what her future would be, not knowing that Jose had stopped loving her. When had it happened? Why hadn't she noticed? Unlike her blinking neck, the thought of it no longer hurt, but it still perplexed her. It wasn't just that her boyfriend had stopped caring for her, but that she'd been too blind to see it.

Other than checking her mobile from time to time, Nat didn't move unless she had to pee. She didn't like having nothing to do: it gave her too much time to dwell, her mind flitting from Jose to Jack, from Catherine to Wes – particularly bloody Wes. She had phoned the office to say she wasn't well and wouldn't be in today. The receptionist had put her through to WMD, as per the office bloody manual, but WMD seemed uninterested in why Nat was indisposed, instead checking that she'd be back for her baby shower-cum-leaving do on Friday, speaking surprisingly fast and gushing at how generous it had been of the partners to organise it.

Nat hadn't known about the damned party, but that wasn't surprising. No one told her anything; no one cared. She had foolishly expected a message or a call from Wes last night, certainly this morning, but nothing had come, only periodic texts from Catherine giving her updates about Jack, and making it quite plain that she was in charge. After stating that the 'incident' was to be kept secret from 'absolutely everyone', Catherine had promised to keep her posted about his progress, but Nat was to 'stay away', she wasn't 'good for Jack's stress levels'. She'd sent that particular text with a smiley face, but the message that Nat was to butt out was loud and clear.

Nat peered again at the codeine instructions and popped two in her mouth. She was to expect drowsiness and wasn't to drive. Well, that was fine, she wasn't going anywhere today. And thank God Jack was fine. It was a heart attack, but only a minor one.

According to Catherine's latest text, the consultant had found the dodgy artery on the angiogram, but it wasn't sufficiently narrowed to justify a stent. He'd stay in hospital for monitoring, and if everything stayed fine, he'd be discharged with a host of drugs to take every day and a programme of steady exercise.

More golf, Nat thought as she drifted, Jack will be pleased.

～

She didn't hear the doorbell, or her mum answering it. Just the sound of Wes's voice, which mingled with her dream. When she opened her eyes, he was sitting in the armchair, his brow furrowed and jaw tight.

His suit jacket was buttoned. 'Sorry,' he said, 'I didn't mean to wake you. I came to–'

A scorching ache passed through Nat's shoulders as she bolted upright. Oh God, the second heart attack. Was Jack…? 'What's happened?' she whispered, her heart hammering in her chest. 'Is it Jack?'

As though to stop her alarm, he lifted his palm. 'No, I'm sorry, nothing. Jack's fine.' He leaned towards her. 'Sorry to just turn up like this, but I've driven here because I was–' He paused, turning his head to the sound of footsteps. What the hell? Her mum was carrying a bowl of something and a basket of bread. Placing them on the small table in front of the bay window, she flashed Wes a smile.

'I thought you looked a little peckish, Wesley. There's plenty more, so don't hold back.'

Nat cleared her throat loudly. Food and a smile. The bloody traitor.

Wes beamed back. 'That's very kind of you, Mrs Bach. It smells delicious. I hope you've not gone to any trouble.'

'Oh, not at all. Do sit down and enjoy.' She looked at Nat. 'Are you ready for some lunch now, Skarbie? I'll bring in a tray.'

Nat kept her gaze on the cross-looking cat, but could see Wes's smirk from her peripheral vision. She wasn't in the mood for being friendly. She felt unbelievably groggy, which had not been helped by the shock of him turning up at her home, let alone the heart-stopping moment of worry she'd just experienced. She carefully lowered herself against the arm of the sofa. 'It'll be cabbage, you know,' she said dryly.

'Well, it smells good,' he replied, taking off his jacket and sitting down at the table. 'I'm starving.'

Materialising again, her mum passed her a tray, then sat down opposite Wes with her own bowl. Nat stared. Bloody hell, fifth columnist or what! What had she said about Wes to Anna over the past few weeks? Nothing nice, she was sure.

Inhaling the undeniable aroma of cabbage, Nat shuffled up and made an effort to eat her soup, but after a few mouthfuls she put the dish on the floor. Waves of tiredness were pulling her down. If she just closed her eyes for a minute, she'd be fine... When she awoke the first time, Wes and Anna were still at the small table, playing cards. When she awoke the second, Wes was back in the armchair, watching her.

'Are you still here?' she asked, sounding more belligerent than she intended.

'Your mum's gone to the supermarket,' he answered evenly.

The idea of him seeing her nap was unaccountably embarrassing, and when she spoke her voice was clipped. 'I don't need a nanny. I have whiplash. It's not a life-threatening condition, the last I heard.'

He sighed and hitched forward. 'You left last night without saying anything. I was worried. You hadn't seen a doctor. Then this morning, when you didn't show at work...'

Avoiding his gaze, she thought about last night's warm anticipation of a drink or a meal with nice human company, which was then snatched away. Followed by a long, cold wait outside the hospital. Then tears. 'There's a thing called a mobile phone, Wes.

Maybe you should learn how to use it,' she said, not bothering to hide her hostility this time.

He stared, clearly puzzled. 'What–?'

She focused on her toes, trying hard to ignore the burning sensation at the top of her nose. 'I waited for an hour.'

'God, I didn't realise it was that…' He spread his hands. 'I know, it took much longer than I'd guessed, and I'm sorry, but Jack was insistent we talked through how to keep it under wraps, from the police to the hospital to the office, considering it from every angle to make sure the news wouldn't spread. God knows it's crazy, but I suppose it's his call. He'll be out tomorrow or Wednesday.' He cocked his head. 'But I texted to let you know. Twice, actually. You didn't reply, so–'

Nat glared at him. 'No you didn't.'

'I did. And I called last night and this morning.' He strode to his jacket, pulled out his mobile, and handed it to her. 'Look for yourself.'

Over the last eighteen or so hours, there'd been seven calls to Natalie Bach. She nodded with difficulty and handed it back, trying to ignore the rush of pleasure which had shot to her cheeks. 'I think you've been calling my old phone,' she said stiffly. 'I have a work one now. You might remember organising it for me. Should I remind you of the new number?'

He stood and donned his jacket, the hint of a smile at the corner of his mouth. 'Yes, I think you should.' He strode to the door and opened it. 'I'm glad you're okay. Except for the whiplash, of course.' Before leaving, he grinned. 'Rest and take your time, little Skarbie, but I'll need you on Friday.'

GRAPES WILL BE FINE

The smell of egg woke Nat at ten thirty. Lifting her head cautiously, she looked at her watch. 'Is that really the time? Why didn't you wake me?'

Her mum put down the tray. Two boiled eggs (lids removed) and toast cut into fingers. 'I wouldn't have roused you now, but your mobile has been ringing: Emilia, Gavin and Jack. I said you'd phone back when you were ready,' she replied, perching on the bed. Her look of self-importance made Nat smile, despite the breakfast being fit for a six-year-old. Anna had been in a strange mood since yesterday, a sort of suppressed excitement, and Nat guessed why.

'So, your friend Wes...' she began, confirming her suspicions. 'What a nice man, though I think he let me win at cards. Three bowls of my soup, Skarbie. I didn't expect him to be–'

Nat gave her a stern look, but she continued doggedly. 'You were always chattering about him at law school. With a surname name like Hughes, I thought he'd be Welsh.'

Nat was momentarily thrown. 'I wasn't always "chattering", as you put it.' She came back to the surname. 'Perhaps he is Welsh,

I've never asked him. My name is Polish or German or Czech, or whatever, but I'm not.'

She looked at her mum's raised eyebrows; she was right the first time, the point was the chattering (and his cabbage appreciation, no doubt). 'He's married, Mum, with two boys at university. And I'm a crabby old spinster who should've been at work two hours ago.'

Her mum nodded at the food. 'Eat up while they're warm. Shout if you need more soldiers.' She paused at the door and lifted those damned eyebrows again. 'Wes said to make sure you stay put until you're fully better. I'll bring up your phone and then I'm popping out.'

Gently hitching herself up, Nat tugged off the collar and tested her head. Ouch. It was a struggle to move it from side to side, let alone lower her chin to the tray. Lifting the egg cup with one hand, she dipped the toast in the yolk with the other. Perhaps soldiers and beheading hadn't been such a bad idea after all.

Breakfast dutifully consumed, she stepped from the bed. What the hell? The dull ache had gone lower, into her shoulders and upper back, and when she trudged to the bathroom the wooziness was still there. She had to stop taking the damned pills. They made her feel out of control, her body ruling her mind, or was it the other way around? All night she'd had strange visions, a mix of all the men who were plaguing her life. Dreams far more action-packed, alarming or rousing than real life were not uncommon; she'd usually pull out and shake herself back to reality, but the codeine had dragged her back and she didn't like the parts she could still remember.

Similar to Victoria Hetherington, she mused, as she sat on the loo. That druggy sensation, the disorientation, and strange patchy memories. What had she decided to do? Had she confided in Cool Catherine? And what did Jack want today? Jack bloody Goldman who was currently in hospital. The last text from Catherine had 'suggested' that Nat shouldn't visit him yet, in case she 'over excited' him. There had been another smiley face. Not that Nat blamed her; after all, she was Jack's wife.

Nat stared in the mirror. After yesterday's ennui, she'd decided to go back to work, albeit late, but her reflection put paid to that. The toothpaste foam, which was dribbling from her chin onto her pyjama top, was not a pretty picture. If it was too painful to bend over a sink, sitting on her non-ergonomic chair all afternoon would not be a good move. And apparently she'd been given permission by the current boss to stay away. Though she was to be back on Friday when he'd 'need' her. What the heck did that mean?

Her new daytime attire, a zip-up hoodie and leggings, smelled of lilac washing powder, so there was a positive, but her hair was still a problem; she could brush the front but not the back. That made her smile; she'd end up with candyfloss hair like Sharon if she wasn't very careful.

Clutching on to the banister like an old lady, she trod gingerly down the stairs, made herself comfortable on the settee, then looked at her mobile. Emilia, Gavin and Jack, her mum had said. Which missed call worried her the most? Yup, Gavin Savage. He'd promised to let her know the date of the police interview with Julian, so she called him first.

'Gavin. It's Nat. I missed your call.'

'Why are you skiving?' was his opening. 'Your office said you were ill.'

Wondering what the party line was, she took a breath. Enthused by her baby shower plans, WMD hadn't asked what was wrong yesterday. But then again, as things stood, Nat wasn't going to let go of her collar-crutch any moment soon, so the reason was going to look pretty damn obvious when she returned.

'Whiplash,' she replied. 'So, why were you calling?'

'Miss Whiplash, eh?' Gavin laughed. 'How's the other poor sod? Mind you, your car isn't exactly a lethal weapon. Does it go over thirty?'

Nat would have shaken her head if she'd been able. 'Why do you assume I was driving?'

She could hear a court announcement in the background. 'Well, Natalie, with you being the fairer sex…'

'Is there any "ism" you're not guilty of, Gav? I would count them up, only I don't have enough fingers. I was actually a passenger–'

'Well that's good news; you can sue. You should see a solicitor; I believe they're very helpful.'

'Very droll. So why did you call?'

She heard the tannoy again. 'I've got to go, but the police interview's tomorrow morning, I'll call you after. You'll owe me big time.'

Absently stroking Poppy, Nat spent a few moments musing about the long, and often baffling, arm of the law. Her thoughts were briefly interrupted by the boy cat, who tried to snuggle in. Or so he pretended. Poppy jumped off and he stared at her triumphantly before getting comfortable in her place.

'That isn't nice, Lewie,' she said, thinking it was ever thus; however hard women tried, men never quite allowed them to be equal. But then again she was cuddling the cheeky tom, so perhaps she was colluding.

Flipping her mind back to Julian Goldman, she stared at her phone. Another police interview. Surely that was odd? He'd been given a caution for Aisha's black eye; it should all be done and dusted, shouldn't it? And look what had happened when Jack had insisted on finding out more. It was best to have ready answers before his next apoplexy.

Decision made, she picked up her phone and made the call.

'Hi, Aisha. It's Natalie Bach. I'm sorry to bother you, but I thought I'd just give you a bell and see how things are going…'

'Oh, Natalie, hi.' Relief seemed to flood into the woman's voice. 'Thank goodness. How's Jack? Verity told us he was in hospital, but Julian didn't want to… Well you know what he thinks about Catherine. But Verity said she didn't know much either, just that her father didn't want anyone to find out he was ill. Apparently Catherine said it would be better for her not to visit just now. The hospital said minimum visitors or something…' She paused for a beat. 'I don't mean to be horrible, but does that mean it's serious? You know, could he…? Julian hasn't said anything, but I think he's too afraid to ask.'

'As far as I'm aware he's doing well, Aisha. I think they're calling it a warning; so as long as he's sensible and takes his pills, he should be fine. I really wouldn't worry too much. If there's any news, I promise to keep you posted.'

Nat felt the heat rising. Couldn't Catherine see how selfish she was being? After all, Verity and Julian were Jack's children. From what Wes had said yesterday, he would be discharged fairly soon, but his poor kids were under the impression he might die. And if that were likely to happen, shouldn't they be at the hospital to say goodbye?

Trying to shake away her exasperation, she came back to the reason for the call. 'So, did the police thing go away? Has everything settled down now?'

There was silence before Aisha replied. 'Oh, they've got a few more questions, apparently, but it's nothing to worry about. Everything will be fine.'

The words sounded more confident than her quavering voice. 'Are you okay, Aisha?' Nat asked. 'Is the baby still cooking nicely?'

There was a sound of deep inhaling. 'Yeah, everything's great. In fact I have an antenatal appointment soon, so I'd better get ready. Thanks for your call.'

Rising stiffly, Nat made a coffee before calling Emilia. She sensed there would be a long, gossipy conversation, and she wanted to postpone the call to Jack.

'Nat! You've been off work for two days. What's wrong?' Emilia asked.

'A bad neck,' she replied evasively. 'What about you? I got a missed call at the weekend.'

Emilia's voice dulled. 'Oh that,' she replied. 'I'm trying not to think about it. You know when you get all the signs that somebody's interested, and you think you're getting together, then he ignores you when other people are around. That.'

'It doesn't sound as though he's worth it—'

'But when he's lovely, he's so lovely, Nat. Protective and kind. And sexy and knock out good-looking, obvs.' She lowered her voice. 'Let me find somewhere quiet. I'll phone you back.'

Nat tapped her fingers as she waited. She felt vaguely uncomfortable, not really wanting a conversation about Emilia's love life, or lack of it, but when the call finally came, she was on a different tack. 'Wendy has just reminded me about Friday again. As though any of us can forget. You can't get through the door without her blocking the way. Max says she looks like a space hopper; he's not even convinced she's having a baby; he thinks she pumps up her stomach every morning. And which partner would've suggested a party, let alone "organised" it, as she says? We reckon she's played Wesley and Catherine off against each other, saying that the other gave the go ahead. Or maybe Mr Goldman sorted it. You know him better than anyone else, Nat. Would he have suggested a baby shower? It's all very Kardashian.'

Nat doubted Jack would have heard of the Kardashians, let alone pay for a baby shower, but the penny had finally dropped about Wes's 'need' for her on Friday. With Jack indisposed and Catherine having his illness as an excuse, he'd be the sole partner there, the only other person as old as her. Nearly bloody forty. Deflated at the thought, she listened to Emilia's prattle about one of the bench boys and Catherine's secretary, then a long-winded complaint about Sharon.

She pictured Emilia's blonde hair and her pretty flushed face as she sat in her conference room chair. Bloody hell. It hadn't struck her before, but she looked very much like Andrea had done at the same age. Shaking the disagreeable notion away, she ended the call and pressed Jack's number with a deep sigh, as though that would make a difference to the inevitable request.

She could have written his opening line: 'I've been looking at the same four walls since Sunday. Why haven't you visited?'

'Because I cause you so much aggro, you have a heart attack and crash the car. I think that's the theory,' she replied, not bothering to hold back the irritation which had been brewing for two days.

She had been the innocent passenger; she'd been traumatised and injured through no fault of her own; she'd hung by Jack's side until his wife finally arrived – and it hadn't for a moment occurred to either of them that a 'Sorry', or even a 'Thank you', might have been in order.

There was a long pause from Jack. 'I'm sorry I put you through it, and I'm grateful that you, of all people, were there to hold my hand. Are you hurt?'

The familiar prickle was there behind her eyes. 'Some whiplash…'

'Then you must make a claim against me.'

'Jack–'

'How many times have we said it? "It's not really your husband you'll be suing, Mrs Bloggs, it's the insurers…" So, when are you visiting? Come on, Natalie, I'm as bored as I've ever been. I actually look forward to the horrendous food, just to break the tedium.'

'Seriously, Jack, Catherine has banned me. And to be honest, she's right. You can do without the stress and I can do without the grief. Can you imagine what will happen if the headmistress finds out I've visited without written permission?'

She could almost hear his smile. 'Sexy, isn't she? But as luck would have it, she's gone to the office this afternoon, so you're safe from the birch. No stressful talk, I promise. Grab a newspaper, a bag of liquorice toffee, and a taxi. Of course I will pay.'

'I'm sure you mean grapes.'

Another smile, knowing he'd won. 'Thank you. Grapes will be fine.'

NOT JUST A PRETTY FACE

Anna insisted on driving Nat to Didsbury on Wednesday.

'I don't know why you're going into work. Another day of rest would be far more sensible. And suppose you slip in this drizzle?' Anna complained on the way. 'I'm coming back to collect you at one o'clock sharp. I won't answer the telephone, so don't bother trying to cancel.'

Still not knowing what to say about her two-day absence if anyone should ask, Nat walked rigidly up the stairs to the second floor. She was wearing the medical collar under a polo-neck jumper dress, with a pashmina thrown casually over the whole ensemble. The brightly coloured scarf was Anna's, bought for a wedding. If she didn't die of over-heating, she was sure to qualify for Andrea's Ladies' Circle, or Christian Temperance, or whatever her coven was called.

She'd only just found a comfortable sitting position when Emilia burst in the conference room, pink-cheeked and fresh. 'Nat! So you're back...' She took a second glance. 'It's an interesting scarf.' Then, 'Ah, to cover the collar. Does your neck really hurt? Poor you, you look really tired. I bet you've slept badly. I've never suffered, but I believe whiplash can be really painful. Anyway, this hearing I've got later, you'll never guess…'

Though a reply clearly wasn't required, Nat immediately felt the heat rise. Someone had told Emilia about the accident. Wes, presumably, which made her feel even hotter. Jack's heart attack was the secret, not her injury, but still. Wes had obviously felt the need to tell his pretty twenty-something trainee-wife-clone all about it.

Bloody secrets and Chinese walls, she fumed inwardly, once Emilia had left. Inevitably she'd given in to Jack's request yesterday afternoon, glad Anna wasn't in the house to give her a lecture about needing to rest. Fearful it would be evidence for Catherine to find, she hadn't bothered with the liquorice toffee or the grapes. She'd furtively climbed out of the taxi with a newspaper beneath her arm, walked for what felt like miles to Jack's floor in the hospital, only to bump into Danielle and Frank Foster leaving the ward as she entered. It had been quite a shock. Not just seeing Danielle again after such a long time, but the idea of the Levenshulme mafia being near Jack at all, when there was a three-line-whip not to tell anybody about his heart attack.

Of course Jack Goldman had always worked in mysterious ways, but of all people, those two? Really? The Jack she knew wouldn't want to show his vulnerability to anyone, let alone them. Frank Foster had caught her eye, quickly turning away and striding down the corridor, just as he'd done on Friday night, but Danielle had stopped, all charm and smiles. Nat wasn't sure how old she was these days, maybe in her early fifties, but she'd looked annoyingly good, still petite with pearly teeth and those doll-like brown eyes.

'Oh, Natalie, how lovely to see you. How's your boyfriend? Jose, isn't it?' she'd asked sweetly.

So the bloody woman had heard. 'He's fine, thanks,' Nat had replied. She'd pulled a sympathetic face. 'I'm sorry to hear about Carl and the divorce.'

She had been tempted to mention his new baby, but felt that was a dig too far, even for Danielle. Instead she'd asked after Lewis, her son. He was a financial adviser with flashy offices in Wilmslow, and he'd recently wormed his way out of a charge for sexual assault against some poor girl in a nightclub who'd dared to take a stand.

'How's Lewis? Still gadding about Wilmslow and having fun?'

Danielle's smile had stiffened, but only for a moment. 'He's very well, thank you, Natalie. He has a lovely new wife. The Alexander-Jones family. Lovely people, though I doubt that you'd know them.' She'd put a gentle hand on Nat's shoulder. 'We have to shoot off, but it would be lovely to catch up properly. Perhaps when you're feeling a bit better. I'll send you a text.'

Just like that, as though they were friends. *Lovely* friends, Nat supposed. She'd found Jack in his narrow hospital bed, her face obviously intrigued and questioning. 'Don't ask,' he'd replied. 'Come and give me a hug. Or as much of a hug as you can.'

So she'd been none the wiser; the Chinese Wall had remained.

Now realising her ploy with the scarf had been pointless, Nat carefully removed it, wondering if it was possible to adjust the heating in the room. Situated in the middle of the second floor without any outside windows or natural light, she doubted it would be possible. She looked at a dial near the door: air conditioning, she guessed, but she wouldn't be asking anyone how to operate it. Today she wanted to maintain a low profile, mainly because she both looked and felt like shit, but also because Gavin was due to telephone at some point and she wanted to have a conversation with him without other ears. It was what Jack still wanted her to do, she supposed. In fairness, he hadn't discussed Julian or any work-related matters at the hospital yesterday. He'd been more interested in nagging her about the money she'd invested in the Mallorcan café bar.

'Ten grand, twenty, fifty?' he'd asked again. 'Don't say it was a hundred, Natalie. How much of that have you got back from The Spaniard? Nothing, I can tell. What are you going to do about it, then?'

'Stop asking, Jack!' She had pointed to the collar meaningfully. 'It's stressful. I might have my own episode if you're not careful.'

'Well, you're in the right place,' he'd retorted – the inevitable reply.

Opening her laptop, Nat got stuck in to some graft. Between short bursts of working on the files she was slowly amassing, she glanced at the silent phone, trying to keep her head steady on the two occasions it rang. It was the same eloquent voice from downstairs both times. 'Oh, sorry, Nat; just checking if the conference room was free yet.' From the Red Bull cans and crisp packets in the bin, she suspected the bench boy had taken advantage of the room in her absence. She assumed it was the good-looking one called Max; he seemed to have the most 'chutzpah', as Jack would describe it.

The call finally came through from reception at noon. 'Nat, it's Mr Savage–'

'Thanks, put him through.'

'He's actually here in reception.'

'Oh, right. Send him up.'

Perhaps it was her imagination, but Gavin Savage's spicy aftershave materialised thirty seconds before he did. He strode into the room like Goliath, a frown creasing his forehead. Bloody hell, his expression felt ominous. But his features cleared when he spotted the pashmina, which she had again draped around her shoulders.

'What the...? A Russian doll lookalike competition?'

Despite his quip the alarm was still there. 'How come you're here instead of phoning? What's happened?'

Pulling out a chair, he sat and made the motion of drinking from a cup. 'I'll get you a drink in a minute, Gav. Tell me first.'

His face thoughtful, he tapped the table with a pen. 'Nothing specific, to be honest. I told Julian to answer the questions minimally, and if there was anything he wasn't sure about, he should just say he couldn't remember and would need to check at home. It's a sixth-sense thing. They're definitely digging; something's going on.'

Nat gingerly leaned forward. 'So, take me through it. What were they asking about?'

'Ownership of the Lexus RS; where he'd been all that day – the evening and night. I suspect they already have ANPR–'

'Which is?'

'Automatic number plate recognition. There are cameras everywhere these days, Nat, you wouldn't believe it. It's a bloody police state.' Gavin sat back and folded his arms. 'Then they moved on to his finances. He looked a wee bit uncomfortable then.'

Nat frowned, trying to make sense of it all. The police investigation seemed to have strayed dramatically from a domestic assault. 'As far as I know, Julian is comfortable financially. He has a good job, the house in Alderley, which must be worth well over a million, the flash car, the lifestyle...' she mused.

Gavin grinned and lifted his eyebrows. 'Well...' he began.

'Go on, surprise me.'

'It seems that's not the case. The house is mortgaged to the hilt and the Lexus is a company car. That's as far as I got with him after the interview before he clammed up. My guess is that the police will apply for an order to access his bank statements. I don't think I'll get any further with him, but to be forewarned is to be forearmed.' He paused. The smile had gone, he was looking at her solidly, and for the first time she recognised a bloody good lawyer. 'In all seriousness, anything you can do to help him see sense, Nat... I can't do my best for him with my hands tied. Bank statements, loans, financial worries, debts... I've no idea where the police are going with this, but I need as much background as possible.'

Standing, he stretched his long arms. 'My stomach is calling. Fancy a ploughman's over the road?'

Nat pulled a mock serious face. 'Thanks, but my mum is collecting me. None of the other kids like me so I'm having school lunches at home.' She put her hand to her neck. 'In fairness, it seems to be getting worse rather than better. I'll be glad to lie down.'

'That's normal, it'll start easing tomorrow.' Gavin grinned. 'And while I'm not one to discourage an attractive woman from lying down, don't. It's better to move rather than keep still. Your neck will be painful, but keeping it mobile will improve its function, it'll speed up your recovery.' He pointed to the collar. 'So take that off.'

'Not my collar, Gav. I've grown to love it.'

'In the bin.'

'And the Russian doll outfit?'

'In the bin too.' He opened the door. 'Ibuprofen and Paracetamol, codeine if you need it.'

'How come you know so much about whiplash?' Nat called as he disappeared, leaving only the comforting smell of his cologne.

'I'm not just a pretty face,' she heard as the door clicked shut.

As though it might hiss, she warily pulled off the collar, but rather than putting it in the bin to be found by the likes of the young pretender Max, she stuffed it in her handbag, then walked to the window to look out for Anna's car. For a moment she couldn't see anything except her tired and rain-splattered reflection. Shaking away another surge of self-pity, she focused on the building opposite. The curtains were closed. Was it really a knocking shop or just Didsbury folklore? And, more to the point, what had Frank Foster been doing there when he was happily married to his society wife?

She glanced down at the street. The rain was bouncing off the pavements, but Gavin and Wes didn't seem to mind. Both grinning and holding umbrellas, they were crossing the road, their arms interlinked each side by a fair-haired woman. For a second she assumed it was Andrea, but the mistake lasted only a moment. The laughing blonde wasn't an old crone the same age as her, but somehow, inevitably, it was sweet bloody Emilia.

SO MUCH FOR POSITIVITY

Back in the conference room on Friday morning, Nat gently moved her head from side to side. She wasn't sure if it was Gavin's pearls of wisdom or just wishful thinking, but her neck felt much better today. She was trying to stay positive, despite Wednesday's niggle. It didn't really matter who'd linked arms with Gavin and Wes; in truth she was suffering from FOMO, so she'd decided to bugger the whiplash and self-pity; Natalie Bach was back, armed and ready for action, and, dare she say it, almost looking forward to the WMD party tonight.

Her mobile beeped. The text was from Wes. Trying to ignore the spread of anticipation, she opened the message, but the pleasure was short-lived.

In London on a trial, it said. *Feel free to use my room. Hope you're feeling better.*

She couldn't put her finger on why, but she felt cross, so she continued to sit stubbornly where she was, pulling out a new file for the mill man. Most of his workers had been at the clothing factory far longer than him, but he wanted employment contracts drawn up for the seamstresses. To enhance their working lives, she hoped, rather than to restrict them.

Remembering the women's chatter above the steady trill, she pictured the bustling premises and the general vibe of contentedness. But the two darkly-clad women she'd bumped into in the loos had looked away with flickering eyes. They had returned to their bench, sitting apart from the others and whispering. The sixth sense Gavin had mentioned suddenly chilled her. She hoped she was wrong; a fine of up to £20,000 for each illegal worker would not be a good start to a new solicitor-client relationship. She shook the idea away; she was probably making assumptions; the correct pre-employment checks had been carried out, surely?

'I hope DeMille knows myopia isn't a defence,' she quipped aloud before reprimanding herself. Bloody hell, sixth senses and non-PC comments; she was slowly morphing into Gavin Savage. She'd be wearing shouty aftershave next. Smiling at the thought, she opened the file cover, but before she got past floor plans and equipment guarantees, there was a knock at the door, followed by Max's glossy hair.

'I hear you're using Wesley's office today. Would you mind?' He nodded to the table and smiled an attractive and very young smile, 'I'm preparing trial bundles today; it's much easier if I can spread them out.'

'Yeah, sure,' Nat replied, scraping up her papers and hoping he hadn't caught her 'resting bitch face'. She'd heard one of the associates use the expression last week. It was a new one on her since returning from Mallorca, but she had a damned good idea what it meant. She'd seen it in the rain-splattered window on Wednesday and it was not a pretty sight.

She walked down the stairs carefully. Her whiplash was undoubtedly improving, but there was no need to be rash. She beeped through to the first floor, heading for Wes's office, but two secretaries were chatting to Christine on reception. The baby-shower-cum-leaving-do, of course. What was Nat wearing? they asked. She'd look good in red. It started at seven, a minibus was collecting everyone at six thirty. It would be a laugh without any of the partners. There would be food, but probably best to eat something first.

Eventually escaping, Nat managed to bypass WMD at her pod, but there was no avoiding Sharon. 'Wesley is in London on a trial. He says you can use his room,' she said, stating the bleeding obvious. She slipped her lipstick in her desk drawer and smiled. 'You and me together for a few days. Just like old times.'

Nat opened the office door, a thought suddenly striking her. 'How long is he away for?'

'The trial is listed for ten days. I wouldn't be surprised if he stays over the weekend. He and Christopher Aaron are thick as thieves these days. They usually stay.' She looked wistful. 'The theatre and what not, I suppose.'

The pound coin finally dropped. Bloody Wes wasn't going to WMD's shower. The crafty bastard had found a way out. Never mind just the two of them facing the youth of the office; he'd 'needed' Nat to be the sole adult there tonight.

So much for positivity. Studying the abstract of rich colours opposite, Nat swung in Wes's chair. She'd already lifted the blinds and peered at the world outside the window, but the canvas still distracted her, mainly because she was almost coming to like it. Closing the door from prying eyes, she explored its rough surface with gentle fingers. She couldn't remember the artist's name, but Wes had mentioned there'd been a play about him locally. He was a recluse, and his paintings had only been discovered when he was sectioned; the social workers had found a trove of over two hundred canvases, paintings of different locations, created with oils and acrylics, sawdust and grit, anything he could lay his hands on to add texture, and all done from memory. It was a sad story in many ways, but the hidden depths of the painting felt hopeful. It reminded her of last night. She'd gone home on the bus feeling dismal, self-pity creeping in big time. She was very nearly forty; she had no boyfriend or kids; the guys she'd assumed were her fans had soon deserted her; and she was surrounded by younger people who were attractive and funny and bright.

She'd trudged home in the drizzle, the thought of cabbage 'something' almost welcoming, but her mum must have had an inspired spell of misery telepathy. The house was in darkness. No cabbage, no mum. Not that Nat blamed her; she was tempted to throw back half a dozen codeine just to stop boring herself.

Delving in her bag, she'd finally found keys, opened the door, then–

'Surprise!'

Flowers, fizz, several pizzas and Fran's open arms. 'Why didn't you tell us about the whiplash? Come here. Poor you. Are you up for a hug?'

Then Bo had appeared behind her. 'Maybe just air kissing? Come on, girl, get this down you. We need a blow-by-blow account of what happened.'

'Blow account. Hmm. That could well cause an accident, put off the driver…'

Nat had laughed. 'It was Jack actually–'

'Ew, *not* a nice image–'

'But you're both sworn to secrecy.'

'Ooh, I love a Jack Goldman secret, bring it on.'

Glad to escape their 'toddler jailers', Bo and Fran had chatted solidly for two hours, telling tales of post-birth bodies, grizzly children and hairy-backed husbands. It had been so good to laugh.

'Go to the party and show them the real Natalie Bach,' they'd said. 'You are still young and gorgeous. Look in the mirror stark bollock naked and see for yourself! You've got to promise you will. You are *so* going to the party. You'll knock them out, girl.'

Later she'd lain in the bath, wondering about her new addiction to bubbles, both drinkable and soapy, as she'd tried to get in a comfortable position. Eventually remembering her promise, she'd laughed self-consciously and climbed out, wrapped a towel around her hot body and headed for the mirror. Ridiculous, she'd known, and thank God no one was there to witness her alcohol-induced frivolity, but still she'd lifted her chin and dropped her shield.

She'd turned one way, then the other. 'Okay, life's plusses...' she'd said to her naked self: she hadn't had babies, that was true, but she hadn't got a 'blubber stomach' (Fran) or stretch marks either; she hadn't fed her own child, but her boobs didn't look like 'puppies ears' (Bo); she was 'slim but curvy', as Fran had put it, and if she could manage a whole night's sleep, her face might not be bad either.

Coming back to today and the painting, Nat shook her head at the memory and laughed. She wasn't about to show herself in the buff to anybody soon, but the funny side gave her cheer. As she'd said to Wes a few weeks ago, life was too short. There was no point being miserable.

Her tummy grumbling, she looked at her watch. It was lunchtime already. The conversation at reception suddenly surfaced. What had Christine said? She'd look good in red.

Bobbing her head around the door, she tapped Sharon's shoulder. 'Are people actually getting changed for this... thing later?'

Quickly retreating to the office, Nat sat again. Sharon hadn't bothered to answer; her shocked face said it all. *Of course* the girls were getting changed. Was Nat completely deranged?

She tapped the desk. It *was* her lunch break... Then: Oh come on. Surely she didn't need to rush out to the clothes shop in the village? Not Natalie Bach; come on!

She pictured Bo's face, it was egging her on. Knock them out, girl.

Nat stood and smiled wryly. Maybe she couldn't beat the young, funny and bright people, but she could damn well join them.

~

The noise outside Wes's cube reached a peak at half past four. Opening the door, Nat was hit by the unmistakable smell of hairspray. Sharon was moving away with a small suitcase on wheels. 'Just off to get changed,' she said, patting her hair which now had an extra bouffant layer.

Through the fug, Nat watched her teeter off. How old was Sharon? It was difficult to judge as she'd always looked the same. Nat had bought her birthday presents year after year, but never knew her actual age. As old as her, perhaps even older. It was a comforting thought; she was so conscious of approaching the dreaded 4 – 0, she'd forgotten everyone else aged too.

Closing the window blinds, she quickly swapped her top. There had been a crispy autumnal frostiness at lunch when she'd bought the new one. Cheap as chips, it had been. A good thing with her precarious finances, but still she hoped neither the cheap nor the chips came across too strongly. More ruby than crimson, so not too obvious, though she'd have to find a safety pin, she didn't want her boobs completely hanging out.

Still feeling a little absurd at having changed at all, she opened the door and peered out. Save for two departing bench boys, the whole floor was empty. The women were in the ladies' toilets, no doubt. When she was twenty-something, one didn't swap outfits after work. One went out and got pissed in one's suit like male colleagues; changing clothes was for bimbos and airheads. Disparaging, of course, but in those days it had felt important to stand shoulder to shoulder with the men, to prove herself, she supposed. Perhaps times had moved on. Maybe one could wear something eye-catching, or even pretty, and still be taken seriously. Or maybe she was softening with age.

An eloquent voice interrupted her reverie. 'Are you ready for a drink, Nat?'

It was Max, the smiley, handsome young pretender, raking his hand through his flaxen hair and exuding confidence in a rugger-bugger type of way. Not that she was being judgemental, of course.

'Yeah, sure. Though isn't there a minibus or something?' she asked.

'There's plenty of time,' he replied with a grin. 'The pub first.'

OUTER SPACE

Almost recreating the one in the office, Nat sat at a wooden bench with the boys in the pub.

Thinking that introducing herself might be a subtle way to elicit their names, she opened her mouth to speak, but Tom, Dick or Harry got there first.

'So we're all intrigued...'

'About what?'

'Everything,' the freckled, red-head said. 'Catherine and Wesley, for starters. Then Jack Goldman. We're expecting you to dish the dirt.'

Nat slugged the bottled beer that had been put in front of her. 'Fair enough, but it's a two-way street,' she replied, her expression serious. 'I'll need to know everything about you from the colour of your undies to the size of your... pay packet.'

Her joke raised a cheer and the inevitable quips soon followed:

'It's not the size of the dog in the fight, but the size of the fight in the dog,' Tom quipped.

'Not the length of the wand, but the magic in the stick,' Dick replied.

'It's not the meat, it's the motion,' Harry suggested.

'What do you think, Nat?' Max asked.

Where was Gavin Savage when you needed him? It took a few moments to think. 'I'd prefer a grower to a shower,' she tried.

A loud cheer, more banter and beer ensued. Nat relaxed, feeling good. Despite vowing never to drink it again, it was fun to quaff lager, eat too-salty nuts and chat with four amiable young men who were happy to go with their newly christened names. Fending them off with light gossip about Catherine and Jack, she put the ball back in their court when they asked about Wes, saying they knew more than she did.

'Nah, you don't get much out of Wesley,' Max said. Then with a grin, 'But did you hear about Chris Aaron?'

'My Chris Aaron QC?' Nat queried.

Max laughed. 'He's mine too. Such a darling. So, did you hear about *our* Chris Aaron? He's on Hornet and–'

'What's Hornet?' Nat asked, watching their faces and regretting the moment it was out of her mouth.

'Bloody hell, Nat. Where have you been? You've heard of Tinder? God, don't say–'

'I have! I've just not got around to using it… this week.'

When the laughter died down, Dick explained. 'Hornet's a gay dating app, Nat. Like Grindr?' He studied her expression. 'Where *have* you been?'

Nat wanted to reply, 'Outer space'. That's how it felt. Another world she no longer missed.

Max tapped her bottle with his. 'Don't bother with Tinder. You don't need an app to get a date.'

'So back to Chris Aaron…' she said hurriedly, hoping the little fillip in her belly wasn't showing too obviously.

'Well, this app. It's basically for sex. You can have your actual photo on it if you want, but if you're a Queen's Counsel, it probably isn't wise. So Chris gets a date incognito, excited to see if the young man in question is as delicious as he sounds, but it only turns out that it's the junior clerk in his chambers. So he's out of the closet, poor lad. But the best part of the story is–'

'Shit, look at the time, we've missed the minibus,' Tom interrupted, looking at his watch.

Dick stood. 'We'll go in a taxi. My round while we wait.'

Time passed and Nat's cheeks ached from laugher. It turned out that Harry was an excellent mimic, playing out a scene between Emilia and Sharon: 'But he's so handsome. I think I love him!' he said in Emilia's high Home Counties' voice. 'Oh, so do I. And I was here first,' he replied in Sharon's flat Mancunian. Then he did Wes with a frown. 'I know I'm charismatic and God's gift to women, but control yourselves. I'm deep, and I'm thinking.'

Nat wiped away a tear. 'Very good. So what is he "thinking" about?'

'It beats me,' Max replied. 'I've been his assistant for four years and I've never got below the surface.' He did a zipping motion to his mouth. 'Tight-lipped, which makes you wonder what he's hiding.'

Nat immediately thought of Jack and his Chinese Walls. 'Do you do work for Jack too?'

'Yup. He pulls rank from time to time. It clearly riles Wesley, but he doesn't say anything.'

'I saw you in court with Jack a few weeks ago. What was all that about?'

Max grinned and looked at his watch. 'Maybe I'll tell you later.'

At some point they bundled out of the pub and into a black cab, Nat squashed in the middle on the back seat. She felt mildly guilty for turning up so late, but what the hell, she was enjoying herself; it was nice to be the centre of so much attention, especially with Max, who turned out to be thirty-three and who made a point of telling her he'd just split up with his girlfriend.

The pulse of the music was loud, even before they entered the wine bar back room. To the left a table was littered with wrapped gifts, balloons and enough teddies for a whole nursery. Putting a hand on her shoulder Max spoke in Nat's ear. 'Shit, I haven't brought anything. Did you?'

'No, I put a tenner in the collection, but I didn't think to buy anything else.'

Pulling a strand of hair behind her ear, he leaned forward again. 'Possible breach of the office Bible, I fear.'

Conscious of his touch, she chuckled. 'So it wasn't just me who had to learn it by rote.'

The office manual reminding her of why they were here, Nat scanned the room for WMD. It took several moments to realise the manic hand mover in the centre of the dance floor was her. She was wearing a pink baby grow with a huge dummy to boot. Flipping heck, what dodgy internet site had that outfit come from? One of the divorce cases Nat had long ago abandoned involved the petitioner's eminent husband's penchant for wearing man-nappies; nothing surprised her after that.

Nat laughed at the gyrating vision. Perhaps WMD did have a sense of humour after all. She was surrounded by other women raising their arms to a song, but Emilia didn't appear to be there. She watched Dick and Harry bomb the stage, scattering the girls like skittles before they all rallied, then she turned towards Max, aware of his arm draped over her shoulders.

Wondering how to extract herself, she nodded to the bar, ready to offer a drink. But an unexpected figure leaning against it caught her short. His arms folded, Wesley Hughes was looking back. 'Oh, there's Wesley,' she said. 'I didn't know he was here.'

Max glanced too. 'Nor did I.' He stared for a moment and snorted. 'She's not giving up, is she? She's like bloody velcro. Maybe she made Wes an offer he couldn't refuse. He's bound to give in eventually.' He lifted his eyebrows. 'If he hasn't already.'

Wes had turned his attention back to sweet bloody Emilia. And Max was right; she either had personal space blindness or the recipient didn't mind. So it was going be like that, she thought, the burst of delight from seeing Wes all gone. Bloody hell, the Cling-on reincarnated or what? She was fond of Emilia, but really, what the hell was he playing at? She wasn't much older than his sons. And now she was dragging him by the hand to the dance floor.

'Here we go, ladies and gents; we're off.'

The sound of Dick's voice made her start. He was peering at Emilia and shaking his head. 'She does this every chance she gets. Embarrassing herself. She'll be in the ladies soon, sobbing.'

Nat turned. How to put it? And did she really want to know? 'Does he… does Wesley reciprocate?'

'I've no idea,' Max interrupted. 'Bloody clingy women are a nightmare. He should tell her to push off. I would.'

Nat inspected his face. There was something in the way he said it. 'Is that what you've said to your girlfriend?'

He ran his fingers through his quiff. 'Possibly.'

'And now you're regretting it?'

He smiled. 'Possibly.'

She shoved him affectionately. 'You blockhead.' Then she looked at her watch. 'It's Friday night at eleven o'clock. Now's a good time to say sorry, before either of you does anything stupid.'

He pulled out his mobile. 'You reckon?'

'Go!' Nat pushed him again, watching him weave through the room, already speaking and smiling, presumably to his personal Cling-on.

The notion occurred then. Had she been like velcro too? Was that why Jose had needed her gone? It was an unpleasant idea, but possibly true. Not when they lived in Mallorca, she hoped, but later, when he ditched her and she'd cried and pleaded and begged. When she'd become the sort of woman she'd always despised.

Those thoughts still heavy, she turned to Wes's voice.

'Nat?' His cheeks clenched, he studied her. 'Is everything

okay?' He nodded to the exit. 'With Max? He hasn't upset you, has he?'

'Oh no, that was…'

She could see how it might look from across the dance floor, but it was too hard to explain above the blaring music and she wanted to shake off the gloom before it set in. Listening to the women's chorus, she laughed at the irony.

'So many survivors.' Catching Wes's inquisitive frown, she explained with a smile. 'The song. Men coming "Back from Outer Space".' She nudged him. 'Did you enjoy your dance with Emilia?' His frown deepened. 'Come on, Wesley Hughes, what did I tell you about chilling out?' She took his hand. 'A dance or a dance? Not this one. The next?'

'So long as it isn't "Lady in Red", I'd be honoured.' He lifted his eyebrows as they made for the floor. 'I missed out on having one with you at Catherine's party. I can't think why.'

'Don't remind me about that night. I was so nearly sick in your lap. You don't know what a close shave you had.'

He moved closer. 'I think you were a lady in red that night. How's the neck? It looks very… healthy.'

Nat laughed, pleased to see the famous Wes Hughes dance moves and the sparkle back in his eyes. 'My shoulders still ache, but Gav says I have to keep flexing.'

'Does he now?'

They danced a little while longer, then moved to the bar for a drink. Feeling slightly pissed, Nat looked around for anything resembling food, but gathered from the soggy remains of a quiche and a bitten scotch egg that she'd missed the buffet boat. When she spun back, Catherine's secretary was speaking to Wes, pointing tearfully to the exit. Nat watched them walk away, jumping at the sound of Dick's voice at her side.

'What did I tell you? It's all kicked off in the loos, apparently. Emilia versus Sharon round eight…'

'And that is…?'

'Fisticuffs at every office social. Last time Emilia grabbed Sharon's hair and wouldn't let go.' He laughed and did a swelling motion with his hands. 'Which was particularly below the belt. But never fear, Wesley will charge in, put them in separate taxis, and come Monday it'll be as though it never happened.'

Sipping her drink, Nat watched the heedless dancers as they smiled and swayed, thinking of how other people's lives always went on. Desperately needing a pee, she headed for the toilets. She almost brushed shoulders with Wes coming towards her, but, wearing his overcoat and a frown, he seemed oblivious. Turning, she watched him speak to the barman. Settling up, she supposed. He was clearly off home to his wife, which was fair enough, but it wouldn't have hurt him to acknowledge her or say goodbye.

Trying to dispel the disappointment she wished she didn't feel, Nat stood at the sink to wash her hands. A water fight, this time, perchance? The floor was puddled badly and someone's attempt to dry it with loo roll had been pretty ineffectual. She glanced at a pallid secretary, wondering whether to make a quip about WMD and the health and safety section of the office manual, but the woman spoke first, managing to say, 'I think that was your phone, Nat,' before bolting into a cubicle.

Thrown back to the memory of her mum's stroke, Nat dug for her phone with a catch of concern. It was late; who would be texting at this time of night?

Chips? the message said. *Top of King Street. A bench you might recognise.*

The secretary returned to the mirror and wiped her mouth. 'Are you coming for a boogie?' she asked. 'I feel much better after that chunder.'

Nat replaced her mobile. 'I think I might just get off,' she said, trying for nonchalance, but checking her face for smudges nonetheless.

Wes watched with folded arms as she walked towards him. She tried to hide a stupid grin, but couldn't, taking his proffered arm and strolling along without speaking. Finding a small take-out in Piccadilly Gardens, they sat on high stools and ate fries, hers smothered in gravy, his with a luminous curry sauce. Still a little drunk, she took a breath to mention how chips had come full circle today, but Wes leaned down and removed her right shoe.

'The latest in power dressing, I assume?' he asked, removing a clod of damp toilet paper from the heel, and then slipping the shoe back.

Feeling herself blush, Nat lowered her head. It was ridiculous, she knew; they were in a bus station café, but it felt strangely intimate. A quip wanted to burst out about him being her handsome prince, but that felt too playfully suggestive, even though she wanted to be precisely that.

He waited until she met his eyes. 'Do you fancy a drink?' Then he lifted his empty Coke can and smiled. 'A proper drink?'

'I'm not sure where at this time of the night, unless it's a club.'

'Pockets,' he said, pulling out a slim bottle of whisky from one side of his coat and a bunch of keys from the other. He selected one key and placed it on the bench. 'We could have a wee dram in the office flat, if you fancy? It turns out that it's a partnership asset, so a third of it belongs to me.'

'So we're just to stick to that third?' Nat replied, stalling for time and trying to catch the dissolving vow of what she'd always said about married men.

A hot spread of excitement, danger and downright desire overwhelmed her. She knew she'd say yes, but she still tried for humour. 'You've sussed me out; you know I can't resist a midnight tipple. But no funny stuff, okay? Just a drink.'

Dodging the trams, the partygoers and the occasional cyclist, they crossed Piccadilly Gardens towards the Northern Quarter.

Stopping at a black entrance, Wes punched numbers into a keypad. 'Here we are,' he said. The door closed with a soft thud and he turned in the hallway. 'Remind me. What's the definition of "funny stuff"?'

Nat was glad of the darkness. 'I think you remember.'

Leaning forward, he gently pecked her lips. 'So this is allowed,' he stated. He lifted his eyebrows. 'And if I recollect correctly, this…'

He slipped his arms around her waist, drew her close and kissed her deeply. Pulling away eventually, he unbuttoned her coat and put his lips to her neck and her throat, working down to her breastbone. 'And this?'

She nodded and smiled. 'But not that.'

'Okay, I promise,' he replied, taking her hand firmly and climbing the stairs.

25

THE ONLY LIGHT

Waking abruptly in the early hours, it took Nat several seconds to work out where she was. Wes Hughes was lying next to her in a king-sized bed, his arm under the pillow. Dim street light crept through the voile curtains, catching his face, the high cheekbones, defined jaw, and those beautiful lips.

She chuckled quietly. He'd kept his promise: they'd kissed, they'd cuddled, he'd massaged her back and covered her entire body with his mouth, but that was all. Thou shalt not commit adultery. Exodus didn't define it, though the law did, of course. Contentedly, she sighed. The distinction between committing it or not was pretty artificial, but it had felt right.

The smile spreading, her mind drifted back to law school and a house party the Cling-on had astonishingly missed. Perhaps Andrea's antennae had been faulty; maybe Wes was improving his frequent attempts to bin her. Nat had spent the night with him then, the two of them in a rickety bed with her drunk friend and some random guy who'd already passed out. They had locked lips and canoodled, exploring each other intimately under the duvet, trying to feign sleep just in case, holding in the sighs and the laughter.

'Oh God, that was better than sex,' Wes had whispered in the morning, 'I do *like* you, Natalie Bach.'

Her friend had teased her the next day. 'You finally slept with him, didn't you? Right next to me in the bed!'

'I *slept* with you and AN Other last night,' Nat had responded dryly. 'But we didn't have sex.'

'What? You fancy each other like rotten. Why didn't you just do the dirty deed?' her friend had asked. 'If not the bed, on the floor, in the bathroom, in the bushes?'

But the truth was that the ghost of the Cling-on had been with them even then.

Nat now slipped from the bed, nearly tripping over a large holdall. As her eyes adjusted to the gloom, she padded to the kitchen. She knew the flat was used for client stay-overs and occasionally by Catherine, but she'd never been here before. The kitchen was new, compact but swish, and when she opened the cupboards to look for a glass, there were five of everything one would expect, a whole range of glassware from champagne flutes to decanters, then plates, bowls and mugs, the sixth of each on the drainer.

She filled the tumbler at the tap and made her way to the bathroom. From the vantage of the loo, she inspected the toiletries in the shower tidy and lined on a shelf. Luxury hair, body and facial care. They were Catherine's, of course, which made her wonder about the sheets and pillowcases. When she wanted time out from Jack, did she change them, or didn't she care that some sweaty guy like Brian Selby had slept there, using her shower, soap and shampoo and rubbing his dick dry with her soft, peachy towels?

Yawning, Nat returned to the bedroom. Wes was propped on one arm, looking sleepy. 'Is everything okay?' he muttered. Then with a languid smile. 'Look at you. You're beautiful.'

Suddenly conscious of her nakedness and their strange situation, she slipped into the bed and turned away from him, but he pulled her towards him, his arms hot on her skin as he cupped her and sighed.

It was such a perfect moment, she almost felt weepy, but sleep took over as quickly as she'd woken.

~

The sunshine through the voiles alerted Nat to morning. Mercifully free of a hangover, she stretched and yawned, remembering exactly where she was. Feeling warm, excited and shy, she turned slowly with a smile. She had expected to see Wes's face, defined and dark against the white pillow, but the bed was empty.

'Wes?'

Sitting in a wicker chair next to the window, his elbows were on his knees, his head in his palms. At the sound of her voice he looked up. 'Morning.'

Oh God. What had happened? What was he thinking? He looked sad, his expression unbearably soulful. Pulling the sheet, she wrapped it around her body like a toga, then perched on the side of the bed.

'It's okay,' she said, reaching for his hand. 'We didn't do anything we shouldn't have done. Well… not really.'

He slotted his fingers through hers. 'It was lovely.' Then smiling faintly, 'It was better than sex.'

Not knowing what was wrong, what she'd done or not done, Nat held her breath and watched his face, waiting for him to speak.

He breathed out long and hard. 'There are things you don't know, things I haven't told you. I wanted to tell you last night, but everything was so perfect.'

Releasing his grip, she sat back. Oh God, Emilia. Surely not Emilia? 'What?' she asked, readying herself for the blow. 'What haven't you told me?'

He gazed at the floor, taking moments to speak. 'I've left

Andrea.' He sighed. 'I didn't tell you last night because it felt like a cheap shot to…' He smiled thinly. 'I don't know, persuade you to do the "funny stuff".'

He was trying for a quip, but Nat's thoughts were shattered. Whatever she'd expected, it wasn't that. Andrea would never let go of Wes. Never. 'What?' she said, trying to release the breath stuck in her chest. 'You've left her? Really? When?'

He stood up. 'It's such a long story, I don't know where to start. Let's sit down and have a drink.'

Wearing T-shirts from the holdall, they sat either end of the white kitchen table. Wes was silent for a time, sipping his coffee contemplatively, as though organising his mind.

'I could say I have never been happy in my marriage. That's how it feels now, but can it be true?' he said eventually, focusing on Nat. 'It can't, can it? Having the boys, watching them grow and develop, loving them more than I ever realised was possible. She gave me that gift. Whatever happens or happened, I'll always owe her for that.'

He suddenly scraped back his chair and paced around the small area before finally turning. 'It was my thirty-ninth birthday. It's silly that; you'd think I'd have the crisis at forty. But on my thirty-ninth I looked at her and I thought, I can't stand another day. I couldn't bear the idea of still being stuck with her at forty…'

Sitting again, he continued to talk, his voice low and precise. Nat listened and gazed, almost too gobsmacked to take it in. He'd tried to leave when the boys were younger, several times, but life had seemed to conspire against him; something had always happened – one of the twins got a sporting injury; Matty's illness had flared up; their exams were looming – and he'd felt too guilty to see it through. But on his thirty-ninth birthday, he'd been determined. He'd told Andrea how he felt: he was fond of her, of course, but the love wasn't there. He felt it was better to build new lives now while they were still young.

He'd always be there for her, but he needed space, to live on his own.

Rubbing his face, he smiled wryly. 'I told you it was a long story.' Then, taking a deep breath he said, 'I tried to be... to be kind, but it was horrendous. Her reaction was dreadful, distressing, alarming. It was a shock I suppose. I don't think she'd seen it coming, not for a moment, despite my past attempts...' He paused. 'So I agreed to stay – a weaning period, I guess. I promised to live at home until the boys left for university.' His eyes seemed to glaze. 'She agreed, but she hasn't made it easy. She's... needy.' Giving a shuddery sigh, he gazed into the distance. 'I finally moved out and Matty was ill again. Well, you know this, but it felt like it was my fault. A shit dad, a shit person...'

Absorbing the information, Nat thought of the past weeks and his moodiness. The image of last night's oblivious dancers as they smiled and swayed hit her. Other people's lives always went on. Oh God, poor Wes. The love and sympathy were immediate. But there were feelings of pique too. He hadn't told her; he hadn't trusted her.

'Where are you living now?' she asked after a while.

'Here some of the time. At my brother's house the rest.'

She frowned. Here at the office flat? The holdall, of course; the sixth bowl and plate on the drainer. It took a while to process her conflicting emotions. 'So Catherine and Jack know about you and Andrea?'

He spread his hands. 'Yes, Catherine, presumably Jack–'

The punch of hurt immediate, she stood. 'And Gavin and Emilia? And bloody Tom, Dick and Harry as well, I suppose?'

'No, they don't know.' He stepped over, put his hands on her shoulders and peered at her intently. 'We've only just reconnected, haven't we? I was going to tell you everything. The drink after the hospital that never happened? The mix up with mobile numbers?' He lifted his eyebrows. 'I abandoned Chris Aaron and belted back to Manchester to see you at the party last night. You weren't there. Then you appeared; stunning and laughing with Max…' Slipping his arms around her waist, he rested his head on hers. 'Don't be angry with me. The last few weeks have been a horrendous dark nightmare. The only light has been you.' He dipped his intense gaze to her face. 'I do… like you, Natalie Bach. I really, really like you a lot.'

His erection was hard against her. Her body stirred in reply. 'I really like you too,' she replied.

26

TELL HER RIGHT NOW

Wearing her cheap-as-chips purchase, Nat put her key in the latch and took a deep breath. She was nearly forty, not fourteen, but still. Thank God she'd remembered to text Anna at some point during the night.

As expected, her mum rushed from the kitchen, holding a tea towel. 'Oh, Skarbie, you're back. You look bright. And a new top! Did you have a nice time at the party?'

'Yeah, it was fun.'

Nat tried to avoid her gaze. It was loaded with that bottled delight she'd had the other day. Flipping mind-reading mother. What had her text said? Something about staying at Emilia's, which felt a little ironic today. Wes had no interest in Emilia or anyone else. He liked her and only her. He'd left the Cling-on, for God's sake! Then this morning when they'd retreated to the bedroom...

Her mum's look was pink and knowing; Nat needed to speak before she read more. 'I'd better get a shower, Mum. I'm off out again in a bit.'

That prompted a flurry of the kitchen cloth. 'Oh how nice. Just the right weather for a walk. Wrap up warmly, though, it's quite chilly.' Her eyes shone; she looked fit to burst. 'Oh how lovely, Skarbie. Barbara's collecting me in half an hour, but I can make you something to eat first.'

Still convinced there were remnants of airbag in her locks, Nat scrubbed them with shampoo, then she lathered soap on her skin. Her body was still tingling, more sensitive to her own touch than it had been for a very long time.

Crumpets were waiting on her bedside table, and though her stomach was already stuffed with butterflies, she dutifully nibbled one as she dressed and carefully applied make-up. Then she brushed her hair like she'd done before Sunday school.

Her mum had left by the time she returned to the lounge. Yet still Nat hovered by the window, eager to dive out before Wes could knock. It was stupid really. It's what she'd done with the Sunday school boy. Why she'd regressed to twelve years of age, she didn't know. She wasn't doing anything wrong, and Wes could act as he liked. He was all but single.

Bloody hell, he'd left the Cling-on. The discovery was still incredible.

His Mercedes eventually pulled up, half an hour late. After the thirty minutes of heart-clanging agitation, Nat let out her breath and scooped up her handbag.

Unsure if she was irritated, relieved or simply bashful, she climbed in the car. Wes immediately spoke. 'I'm late. I'm sorry.' He took her hand and shook his head. 'Don't ask. But I managed to buy a few bits and bobs of food. I don't know what Sid will have in.'

Sidney was Wes's brother, apparently. Nat supposed he had a mum and dad too, the people who'd created this stunning stranger beside her. The notion was both scary and exciting, but today's plan was to drive to his brother's house in the country-side and go for a stroll. The thought made her smile. She hadn't mentioned walking to her mum, but she'd seemed to know. Perhaps Nat was simply transparent. If her expression betrayed her happiness so obviously, she'd have to try harder at work, replace the satisfied smirk with a... well, with her 'resting bitch face'.

Wes was still gazing. 'You look lovely. Are you ready to go?'

Wondering about his earlier frown and what she wasn't to ask, she nodded. She knew he'd promised to pop in on Andrea en route, but it was better not to know, at least for today. This morning's lovemaking was still pleasurably fresh in her mind. Quite frankly, she wanted to jump Wes again as soon as practicable, to feel those knowing fingers and soft lips. And the rest.

Wes followed the route she and Jack had taken just a week ago. From a snippet on the local news, Nat knew the bypass had been closed for a few hours, much to the chagrin of shoppers at the nearby retail park. An abandoned yellow cone on a grassy bank was all that remained from that day. It could have been so much worse; she and Jack had been lucky.

As though reading her mind, Wes broke the silence. 'Did Jack crash around here? Thank God you were safe. Of course I didn't know you were in the car at the time, but afterwards, when I thought of what could have happened... It feels a lifetime ago.' Then he grinned. 'Talking of which, how are your shoulders? Was Gav right? Did you have to keep flexing them?'

Moving in her seat, Nat smiled. 'He was. They're fine, thank you. I have a private masseur, actually.'

'Oh yeah? Any good?'

'Oh, yes. Very.'

Aware of her hot blush, Nat gazed through the windscreen. Memories of Jose filtered through. Was it just them, or did all sexual relationships end up like theirs had, him dominating, her submissive, just wanting it over?

Shaking the uncomfortable images away, she opened the window a crack and inhaled the country smells, focusing on the view and her happiness. The lanes were autumnal, the trees on the turn to orangey red, the fields beyond yellowing.

Eventually indicating left, Wes pulled in at an entrance and stopped. 'Here we are.'

Nat peered through the windscreen. How lovely; a 'kissing' gate, as her dad had called them on the few occasions they'd ventured out to the hills.

Leaning over, Wes pecked her lips, then studied her face. 'Don't worry, I checked, Sidney is definitely away. I'll get the gate.'

He climbed out, opened the barrier and shooed several eager chickens back into a pebbly yard. Uncertain, excited and glued to her seat, Nat gazed at the scene. The cottage beyond was picture-postcard-perfect. If she had been asked to describe her dream home as a child, this was it. Rendered white with paned windows, it was surrounded by vibrantly coloured bushes, shrubs and late flowering plants.

Watching Wes stride back, she snorted and clambered out. 'Sorry, I'm in dreamland. Wow. I'm stunned. Not exactly Oldham, is it? I'll close the gate when you're through.'

Once he had parked, Wes held out his hand and they ambled down a patchwork path to the front of the house. Inevitably it had a stable door. Yup, that had been in her fantasy too – for the unicorn, of course. She laughed at the memory and her weight-less contentment.

'Very Cheshire,' she said, taking in a slightly dank smell as Wes dipped his head to enter. He led her down the narrow hallway to a small, tidy kitchen. She had already decided the dream house had an Aga and she wasn't disappointed.

Wes followed her gaze and twitched his lips wryly. 'I'm still getting used to the bloody thing, but determined not to let it beat me.'

Almost tearful, Nat swallowed and nodded.

'This way to the lounge.' Turning her around by the shoulders, he gently pushed her through the door opposite. Dominated by a long sofa and a huge television screen, the room was surprisingly large.

'So this is home, temporarily at least.' Wes's features froze and he looked around as though seeing it through fresh eyes. 'No mess. New computer, turntable and TV. A wine fridge in the corner.' He snorted mildly. 'What makes you think Sid's divorced?'

Feeling a catch of concern at his tone, Nat stepped away to the lattice-style window and gazed out. Surrounded by beds of blue and purple pansies, the lawn looked as though it had been cut with nail scissors. In contrast, a goat and a sheep munched long grass and thistles companionably in a rough field beyond. She craned her neck to the side. Ha! An apple tree; she'd known there would be one.

'A goat and a sheep,' she commented, automatically thinking of Mrs Hetherington and Victoria, Joshim Khan and Gavin – all those people from another world right now. What had become of Victoria? What did she decide? And what of Julian, Aisha and their baby? These people and their problems had all but disappeared.

Slipping his hands around her waist from behind, Wes held her tightly. 'For Sid's kids, when they visit. He's older than me but they're younger than mine.' He propped his head on hers. 'It's crap isn't it? Failing relationships. Even if it's what you want, even if it's what you've longed for, walking away still makes you feel crap. Especially for the children. My boys seem all right, but his kids have taken it hard.'

A surge of emotion flooding, Nat nodded. What he'd longed for. Was that how Jose had felt? Had he *longed for* her to leave, biding his time until Anna had the stroke? She didn't miss him any more, and she felt a hardening resolve whenever he popped into her head, but what had made her so unlovable?

As though reading her mind, Wes turned her in his arms. 'Hey, sorry. I'm not thinking. I'm a selfish bastard, a miserable git. Stop me when I go on, tell me to chill out as only you can.' Holding her face with soft fingers, he kissed her forehead, her cheeks and her nose until she couldn't help the spread of a smile and much more. Then he stepped back and rubbed his hands. 'Okay, beautiful, what's the plan? A walk while it's nice, or a cuppa and a bite to eat first?'

Nat gazed. Would it be unseemly to jump him right now? Putting a finger to her lips, she looked at him wide-eyed. 'Well...'

Adjusting the crotch of his jeans, he grinned. 'Who am I kidding?' he laughed.

The smell and the silence made the difference, Nat mused as she dozed. It seemed that her Cheadle street was occupied by singletons or older people, but still there was noise – muted toilet flushing, or pipes from either side of her terrace, the rumble of cars parking in the pay-and-display car park behind the high street and chatter from people passing outside the bay.

She stared at the intricate knots in the wooden beams. They were like faces, almost. Some smiley, some not, one or two uncannily similar to Lord Voldemort. She felt relaxed and sleepy, her mind flittering from one easy thought to another as she waited for her high tea in bed. It swung gently from Joshim Khan and his sheep joke, to how young Max had fared with his girlfriend; from her mum's solid, telepathic love to how hungry she was. But mostly she mused about the sex she'd just had, conventional missionary position intercourse, face-to-face, lips-to-lips, exquisite and wonderfully satisfying. Making love rather than having sex. It was so different to Jose in the later years, but she wasn't going to think about that.

The door opened and she turned, pulling the duvet with her to cover her modesty. Expecting to see a tray, she did another take. Frowning deeply, Wes was clutching his mobile.

'What's wrong, Wes?'

After a moment, he focused. 'That was Dylan. It's Matty.'

'What's happened?'

He rubbed his head. 'I'm not entirely sure. Dylan says he collapsed playing football just now.' Taking a breath, he closed his eyes. 'A seizure. The coach called it a seizure, whatever that means.' He strode to his jeans and roughly pulled them on. 'He's fine, he came round, begged Dylan not to tell us. But Dylan was pretty freaked, as you can imagine, so...'

As though noticing she was there, he sat and took her hand. 'God, I'm sorry...' Then he drifted again. 'The thing is, Matty doesn't want his mum to know. She's already driven over this week; he doesn't want to worry her.' He shook his head. 'She's fussing as usual. Dylan says it's getting pretty embarrassing. So I'll just–'

'You need to tell Andrea, Wes.' The words were out before Nat could stop them. 'Secrets are horrible. Can you imagine how you'd feel in the same position? Hopefully it's nothing, but suppose it is something?'

Watching the emotions flicker through his face, Nat wished she could lie and pretend Andrea didn't exist. But she wasn't just a phantom: she was the boy's mother. 'She needs to know, Wes. You need to tell her right now.'

27

PRICKING OF MY SKIN

Pear-shaped, Nat thought as she waved at the mannequin in the Alderley boutique; last weekend had definitely gone pear-shaped. Of course, she couldn't influence the gods or fate or the stars, but it felt that way. She'd been on top of the world and had fallen to the bottom in the space of eighteen hours. Though it wasn't that bad, not really. The high was so wonderfully high, that was all.

Watched by the goat and the sheep, she had hurriedly dressed in the cottage bedroom on Saturday. She had done the right thing; she'd tried to stop the construction of more Chinese walls. 'Barriers to avoid conflict of interest', Jack would say, but really he meant keeping secrets. Whitewash was never good, even from the Cling-on. So she'd advised Wes to tell Andrea about Matty's latest episode, which had thrown them together again.

Bloody hell, was she mad?

Wes had gazed for some time without replying. 'Sorry, it's none of my business,' she'd said.

He'd pulled her close then. 'It is your business and thank you,' he'd replied.

That was good, surely? But his eyes had been distracted.

186

Tight-faced, he'd dropped her back in Cheadle and she'd jumped out before he could say, 'I'll text you.' Or not.

A blaring hoot brought her back to the well-to-do high street. Hazard lights flashing, the glossy-haired driver of a Range Rover climbed out, her raised arms demonstrating her annoyance with the one behind. Peering at the equally glamorous parking-space-stealer, Nat deduced this might take some time, so she tapped her nails on the steering wheel and went back to her crappy weekend. Not satisfied with following her around the house with anxious eyes for the rest of Saturday, her mum had interrupted her Sunday lolling by reminding her of her promise to cut the lawn while it was dry.

'It'll be the last chance before Christmas,' she'd said several times.

Nat had doubted that. 'Doesn't your flipping telepathy extend to the weather forecast?' she'd wanted to say, followed by, 'God knows how we're going to fit everyone in the house, let alone the garden for an inspection. And it's still weeks away.'

Of course she hadn't said either. Anna was counting the days to Philip and Sonia's arrival – at least when her worried peepers weren't tracking her daughter.

In fairness, the mowing had turned out well; the small patch looked smart, her mum was pleased, and the rhythmic hum of the lawnmower was therapeutic. She'd put thoughts of Wes and the Cling-on to one side and concentrated on the legal world, in particular Julian Goldman and how to extract the information Gavin required.

The road suddenly clear, Nat came back to today and that very task. Putting the car into first, she pressed down her foot in readiness for the hill. The mound wasn't going to defeat Anna's car today. Natalie Bach and the old faithful were on a mission. Slowing down at Julian's white building, she flicked on the indicator. Oh bugger. The Lexus was parked in its usual spot, which wasn't the plan. Her ploy had been to call on Aisha alone, an 'Oh,

I was just passing' type of visit. She doubted it would wash on a Monday morning, but a personal approach would surely work better than the last call's abrupt ending.

Thrown by Julian's car, Nat didn't turn right, but continued up the hill.

'What a waste of time,' she tutted, slamming on the breaks and searching for the horn when the van in front suddenly stopped to make a U-turn. That's when she glanced in the wing mirror. Bloody hell, there was Aisha. Wearing a cerise jumper, she was walking the other way towards the village. Lifting her hand by way of an apology to the motorist behind, Nat turned too, following the truck as though giving chase.

Crawling back the way she'd come, she looked at each pavement, trying to spot her quarry but stymied by the usual plethora of four-by-four vehicles parked where they shouldn't. Only yesterday, she'd taken Anna to John Lewis for a coffee and a man had admonished them about 'bloody children' who touched the 'damned revolving doors', causing them to halt. They had raised their arms to show they were hands free. Appearing satisfied, the man had marched away, but then he'd turned back, his face not unlike Jack's the day of his heart attack. 'And I'll tell you what makes my blood boil,' he'd raged. 'Women driving SUVs. Overpaid footballer's wives from Alderley Edge, no doubt.'

Nat snorted at the memory, but the man had a point. Most Lexus drivers living in the champagne capital were loaded. Why wasn't Julian Goldman? That was precisely what she was here to find out. Where the hell was Aisha? Had she popped into a store?

Aware of the irony of parking where she shouldn't, Nat pulled in at a bus stop and scanned the likely shops. Inevitably a double-decker appeared in the mirror moments after her transgression, so she rejoined the traffic with another 'Bugger' of frustration.

Finally through the village, she sighed and muttered, 'Mission not accomplished.' Then, catching a glimpse of pink down a side road, 'Oh, perhaps not.'

Ah, the local GP's surgery. Turning left, Nat gave chase, bumping the car on the curb and opening the window before Aisha disappeared.

'Aisha, hi,' she called. 'I thought it was you. How's it going? I'm killing time for an appointment. I don't suppose you'd fancy a coffee?'

Acting had never been her strong point, and the look on Aisha's face was evidence of that. She put a hand on her hip. 'Why are you following me?'

Bloody hell, that was impressive. Though turquoise was perhaps not the best camouflage for undercover ops. 'I'm not following you. It's just...' How to put it? She didn't want to get Gavin into trouble. 'Look, I was in Wilmslow police station the other day. Julian didn't see me, but I saw him. He looked pretty fed up but I didn't want to embarrass him by saying "Hi". Then later I remembered you mentioning another interview. You don't have to tell me what's going on, but is everything okay? Does Julian have a solicitor?'

Squinting with suspicion, Aisha's dark eyebrows knitted.

'Don't worry, I'm not touting for work,' Nat continued. Oh God, she was blathering and needed to get to the point. 'Look, I'm sure he has a solicitor. Maybe the one from before, which is great. Those duty solicitors really know what they're doing. But it's really important to tell them everything, to be honest. Give them any documents they ask for. The police will get hold of anything they want behind your back anyway.' Oh hell, the girl was turning away. 'Julian's solicitor can't do his best unless–'

But Aisha had stalked off before she could finish the sentence, leaving, 'It's none of your business, Natalie,' wafting back on the breeze.

❧

With only her mum's sandwich of the day giving her cheer, Nat trudged up the stairs to the conference room.

'What the...?'

Jack was in her chair, flicking through her diary.

'It's fine,' he said before she could protest. Stretching out his legs, he propped his Hush Puppies on the side table. 'See? I'm resting...' He pulled at his garish golf jumper. '...and I'm wearing civvies too. Besides, I have permission. The headmistress brought me and she's taking me away again. So you have fifteen minutes to bring me up to speed.'

'About what?' Nat asked cautiously. Pulling out a chair, she clocked that Jack looked well. His eyes glinted and the glow had returned to his skin.

Shrugging, he held out his palms. 'Anything and everything.'

'You mean Julian.'

'If you like.'

'The last time we touched on the subject, you had a...' she lowered her voice, '...a flaming heart attack.'

'Caused by a rogue artery, not stress, however much you and Catherine might insist otherwise, but let's change the subject.' He picked up her lunch box and lifted the lid. Expecting a culinary question, she watched him sniff. 'Have you got in touch with The Spaniard about your money?'

'Very clever, but we're not talking about that either. You sue him if you like. I can't be bothered–'

'Who are we suing today?'

With a jolt of apprehension, Nat turned to the voice. Holding out his hand, Wes was striding towards Jack. 'You're looking much better than the last time I saw you.' He glanced at her and nodded. It was the first time she'd seen him since Saturday and she felt ridiculously nervous and shy.

Jack removed his glasses and polished them with his Pringle sweater. 'We're talking about Natalie's ex. Being dumped by text is one thing, being ripped off is another.'

A flash of annoyance passed through Wes's eyes, but he deftly changed the subject to office matters. Then Catherine wafted in.

She nodded at Nat's sandwich. 'No fat or sugar if you're feeding the invalid, and nothing to worry him.' Then to Jack. 'Times up. Come on, no procrastinating.'

Jack did as he was told and stood up. 'She keeps the cane in the car...'

When the door clicked, Wes sat next to Nat. She already knew from a text that Matty was fine. He'd been seen as an outpatient by a younger doctor, coincidentally called Dr Wesley, who'd taken on his illness as a challenge. But she thought Wes looked tired.

'Are you okay?' she asked, feeling edgy and unsettled from Jack's indiscretion and Wes's close presence.

Taking her hand beneath the table, he smiled. 'Nothing that lying down and not having sex with you wouldn't cure,' he said quietly. Absently running his fingers through hers, he fell silent. Then he looked at his watch. 'I'd better go. I'm off to London to take over from Max.' Returning to her, he lifted his eyebrows. 'I'd prefer to stay for a number of reasons, but it's a complex case; it isn't fair for him to manage all on his own. Of course, my office is yours.'

He stood, his expression pensive when he turned at the door. 'I'll text,' he said, and then he'd gone.

A splat of disappointment hit Nat's chest. So much had happened since Friday, she'd forgotten about his trial. Though she'd cocked up with Aisha this morning, she'd travelled back expectantly, lifted by the prospect of seeing him. He hadn't been in his office when she'd popped in to say hello, and now he wouldn't be there for several days. Life was definitely going pear-shaped and it was only bloody Monday.

Her malaise was soon curbed by the sound of her mobile. Gavin Savage was calling. Sounding particularly gravelly today, he didn't bother with niceties. 'What did you do?'

She sighed. Oh hell, here it was, on a hiding to nothing as per usual. But before she took breath, Gavin had continued. 'She's dropped them off just now, the girlfriend–'

'Aisha?'

'Yeah, Aisha. Bank and mortgage statements, some loan documents. I've had a brief look. This is just between you and me, Nat, but Julian is in the shit financially. His overdraft's up to the hilt, the building society only just holding off repossession, some sort of payday credit accruing interest like you wouldn't believe, and a loan company crazy enough to accept a second charge. Only fifty grand, but Julian remortgaged not that long ago, so there's probably little or no equity.'

'Wow.' She couldn't help feeling sorry for Julian. He'd been a spoilt brat, but still… 'And a first baby on the way,' she said, voicing the aspect which bothered her most. 'Where's the money gone?'

Gavin guffawed. 'One of two reasons for the feckless Cheshire set.'

'Which are?'

'Drugs or gambling. I'd put my money on the latter.'

Nat nodded. It made sense of the letters to Jack. Presumably Julian had been borrowing from his mum and the money had run out. What a shame he hadn't asked his dad rather than getting himself into a financial hole. Jack could be difficult at times, but she was sure that if Julian had approached him and respectfully asked, he would have bailed him out.

Respectfully asking was the rub, of course. Stubborn pride was a corrosive thing; she'd seen it first hand when she'd tried her mini-mediation between the two men.

She came back to the call. 'Gambling away your hard-earned money is bloody stupid, but the last I heard it isn't illegal. Why are the police interested in Julian's finances? What's it got to do with anything?'

'I've no idea,' Gavin replied. 'But the prickling of my skin tells me we'll soon find out.'

28

WHICH ADDS UP TO WHAT?

Waiting for an update from Gavin, Nat thrummed her fingers on Wes's desk and stared at the canvas. Was that really a silver wink she hadn't noticed before? Surprising really; she'd been gazing at the flipping painting for the past year. Or so it felt. The astonishing news had come through yesterday afternoon, a text from Gavin which had arrived immediately after a flurry of affectionate ones from Wes, sent during his court lunchtime break:

Yeah, a good night, thanks. Chris was using his incisive cross-examination skills on me, Wes's text had said.

Oh yes? she'd replied.

He accused me of looking at my mobile too often. Dreamy, apparently. Smiling far more than was necessary. I'd no idea what he meant...

So what was the charge?

Pretty serious, I'm afraid. I was accused of being in love. I think he means 'like', so I might have to plead guilty. What do you think?

Almost squirming with pleasure, she'd taken a deep breath to compose a suitably coded reply when her phone beeped again. Grinning stupidly, she'd opened the message, but it wasn't from Wes.

Julian Goldman was arrested this morning, Gavin's text had read. *On my way to Wilmslow police station. Attempted murder.*

What the…? She'd sat motionless for several minutes. It didn't make sense. Julian had hit his girlfriend once; he'd confessed, and had accepted a caution. Aisha hadn't made a complaint; she was having a baby in a few weeks, for goodness sake. Then the worry had set in: What should she do about Jack? Should she tell him, or stay quiet until she knew more? She didn't want him to have another heart attack, but surely the stunning development wasn't something she could hide? More than anyone she hated secrets and Chinese walls.

She'd stared at the artwork, looking for an answer. It had come through another beep.

At the traffic lights, Gavin's second message had read. *Nearly there. Will let you know the score as soon as I do.*

The football analogy hadn't been a reference to Gavin's beloved Celtic that time, but it had helped her decide what to do: nothing. She'd wait until she knew the result. Then she'd call Jack. Little had she known the final score wouldn't materialise all day yesterday, and so far this morning.

The peal of the office phone brought her back to today. 'Hi, Nat. Mr Savage–'

At last, thank God. 'Thanks, Christine.' Then to the receiver, not holding in her irritation. 'About bloody time, Gavin. I've sent you a hundred messages. Why didn't you text or call before now?'

'Nat?' It was still Christine on reception.

'God, sorry. Has Mr Savage gone?'

'No, he's on his way to your–'

'Looking for me?'

Gavin moved from the doorway and slumped into the client chair. Nat stared. Unshaved, erratic hair, a crumpled suit and not even a trace of spicy scent. Bloody hell; things didn't look good.

'That was a damned tough one,' was his opening. He rubbed his face as she waited for more. He hadn't replied to her increasingly irascible texts of last night or this morning, but in fairness he looked shattered.

He leaned forward, so she inched towards him, bracing herself for bad news. 'Coffee, Natalie,' he croaked theatrically. 'I need coffee. I only had a few hours sleep. I can't think without coffee, especially Nero coffee.'

She considered refusing and demanding a full account of the last twenty-four hours immediately, but the poor man's eyes were pink-rimmed with tiredness.

'You win.' Nat stood and grabbed her coat. 'After you.'

Finally in a far corner of the coffee shop, Nat cocked her head. 'So?' she asked, tempted to tell Gavin about the froth stuck in his stubble, but deciding against it.

He gulped down the last of his cappuccino. 'Yeah. So… it was the police station half last night, and Stockport Magistrates this morning to apply for bail. The CPS argued against it, of course. She's a barrister I've come across before, and she's ferocious. She batted on about the compelling evidence, the seriousness of the case and Julian's previous convictions…' He eyeballed her. 'Which I believe you already knew about. You know, having actually *represented* him, Natalie–'

'Oh yeah, those,' she replied, stirring her coffee. She hadn't mentioned them, not intentionally, but things had moved on so suddenly. 'But they were a long time ago, when he was a juvenile. Besides, you were incommunicado, so–'

Gavin grinned. 'Yup, I rallied impressively along those lines. The chairman was shaking his head, lost to the cause, but the other two magistrates were women, so I upped the old Savage charm–'

'Gav–'

'The usual trump card. Julian wasn't a flight risk as his girl-friend was about to give birth.'

'It's another three or four weeks, isn't it? It's hardly imminent.'

He lifted an eyebrow. 'Trust me on this one. I'm a father of four. I think I know about pelting them out. So, job done; bail granted...'

It took a moment to recover from the image Gavin's 'pelting' summoned up. No wonder his poor wife had divorced him. 'Any-way,' Nat said, 'enough of your heroic efforts to get Julian bail. I'm sure you were terrific. What the hell is a charge of attempted murder all about?'

Gavin yawned and shook his head. 'You tell me. They have a man in a coma; they have a witness who saw a Lexus SUV at the scene; they have number plate recognition showing Julian's car in the area; and they have a car wash receipt.'

She sat back, perplexed. 'Which adds up to what?'

'Coma Man's injuries are consistent with being knocked down by a four-by-four vehicle and he's a... how did they put it? A "known debt collector" from Stockport.'

'But you said all Julian's loans were legit.'

'They are. From the way the questioning went at the police station last night, they're assuming there was another loan or loans, but unofficial. Their theory is that Julian defaulted on the payments and Coma Man was sent to enforce it. The laddie didn't have the money to pay, so he mowed him down, then drove to the car wash to remove any evidence.'

Nat took a deep breath. Bloody hell, what a nightmare. 'Pre-sumably there were no dents on the bumper?'

Gavin laughed. 'Nah, those vehicles are designed for women to run over plebs and not even notice.'

Ignoring the usual sexist dig, Nat mulled for a few moments. It was unbelievable; there was so much to take in. 'Where did this happen?' she asked eventually. 'And there was a witness, you said.

So they're saying they have someone who actually saw Julian run this debt collector down?'

Gavin yawned again. Finding herself copying him, she wished he'd stop. 'No, some lorry driver pulled into a lay-by for a nap to keep his tachograph happy. As he drove in, a Lexus drove out. There was something on the ground behind a parked vehicle, but he wanted his nap, his sandwich, to phone the wife, whatever; it was dark and he assumed it was fly-tipping rubbish. It wasn't until he was ready to set off again that he put on his lights and decided to have a look. Found Coma Man and called it in. That's why the police have a fairly accurate time frame. Between ten and eleven on the Thursday night.'

'What about the… the debt collector now?'

'He's one Lee Malloy. Still in a coma.'

Nat suddenly felt cold. 'Bloody hell. What if he dies?'

'Potentially murder.'

Taking a breath, she thought back, vaguely remembering her criminal law lectures from uni days. 'What about a year and a day?' That was right; they couldn't charge someone with an offence of murder if death hadn't occurred within a year and a day.

Gavin laughed and stood up. 'Leave the law to the expert, Natalie,' he said. 'That common law rule was abolished a long time ago. Thanks for the coffee. I'm off home for a kip.'

Still reeling from shock, Nat returned to Wes's office and rested her head on the desk before calling Jack. There was no good way to impart bad news, that was for sure, but she wanted to try.

A beep from her mobile interrupted her disquiet. It was a text from Wes, but she'd save that for later. Feeling a little guilty at the flip of delight, she picked up the office phone to call Jack.

'Hi, it's me,' she started when he answered. She took a deep breath. 'I'm really sorry, but–'

'I've already heard. He was charged yesterday. What took you so long?'

Stumped for words, Nat listened to a sudden squall batter the window. 'I wanted to wait so I didn't have half a story–' she began, but stopped after a moment. Jack was quiet, not raging, not questioning, not demanding; it felt worryingly strange. 'Shall I tell you what I know, Jack?'

He remained silent, but eventually cleared his throat. 'He ran over a villain who was threatening him over a debt. Is that a correct summary?'

'Well, yes, I suppose that summarises the police case, but Julian denies it. He admits having financial difficulties, but–'

'Why didn't he ask me for money, Nat?' Jack's voice sounded flat. 'Why couldn't he have asked his own father? We've had our differences, but...'

She considered mentioning pride and bloody stubbornness, but knew it wouldn't help. 'I've no idea, Jack. Perhaps he was ashamed; maybe he felt he'd let you down.'

Feeling hopelessly inadequate, she sighed. She wanted to help, but didn't know how. She thought Jack might hang up, but he stayed on the line, so she found herself rabbiting on just to fill the silence. She told him about the party on Friday, not even needing to exaggerate what had happened in the toilets. 'Apparently the water fight was quite comical at first, both girls got drenched, but things turned nasty when Sharon's crowning glory got involved. The hair retaliated with savage ear-pulling. Emilia was deaf for half an hour...'

Then she told him about WMD's baby outfit and her crazy dancing. He interrupted her then. 'WMD?' he asked.

'Your office manager. Wendy M something, D something.'

'Very good,' he replied and she could feel a small lift in his mood.

'Oh, and the other thing I forgot to tell you about was Frank Foster–'

'Go on.'

'Guess where I saw him a couple of weeks ago?' Jack didn't reply. He was not in the mood for guessing games, she supposed. 'He was coming out of the brothel in the village. I'm assuming he's still married to his horsy wife.' She paused. 'Is it really a knocking shop? It's a pretty dull story if it isn't.'

She heard the smile in his reply. 'The fragrant Lady Tamara. The "massage parlour" opposite the office? Really? Are you sure?'

'Yeah. I was avoiding a car and nearly thumped him off his feet. He clocked who I was, then turned and made a quick exit the other way.'

Jack sighed. 'You're a good girl, you know. I don't appreciate you enough.'

Pleased at the unexpected compliment, it was on the tip of her tongue to make a quip, and ask for it to be reflected in her pay packet, but now wasn't the time. She could sense his despondency. 'Julian's in good hands, Jack, really good hands. I'm sure everything will work out.'

'And how about you, Natalie?' he asked. 'How's your life working out?'

She turned over her mobile to read the message from Wes. *Tomorrow night x*, it said. Short and to the point; he didn't need to embellish.

Hoping her voice didn't betray her giddy excitement, she concentrated on the downpour outside. 'Yeah, I guess it's okay,' she said.

'Are you fully over The Spaniard?'

She glanced at the glint in the canvas. Yes, she was. She bloody well was.

'Yes, Jack, I am. I thought I'd never say it, but I finally am.'

29

SMOOTHING THE ROUGH PATCH

F eeling hopelessly bouncy on Friday morning, Nat swung on Wes's chair far more than was seemly, trying to look sensible and industrious whenever Sharon popped in with a coffee and her suspicious shrewd eyes.

During the week she and Wes had kept in touch by text during the day and by talking at night, doing the teenage thing of not wanting to end the call first. She was sure she looked terrible; after finally saying 'sweet dreams' each evening she hadn't slept for ages, her mind buzzing with that stupid happiness she tried to rein in but couldn't. Wes Hughes *liked* her, he *really*, *really* liked her. The cottage was free all weekend. He had plans for the Aga, champagne, long walks, and whatever else took her fancy.

It was the 'fancying' bit that especially kept her awake. Wes Hughes' moves were not just confined to the dance floor. Busy with clients, it had almost been a relief he was unable to chat last night; she'd gone to bed with a large brandy and had slept eight solid hours, hopefully enough to look half decent for their get-together tonight.

Aware of a door-opening blast of chatter, she quickly dragged her gaze from the canvas to the computer screen and her study of recent case law. Expecting to see the usual courtesan thatch, she glanced up with a suitably assiduous expression, but her visitor wasn't Sharon. Looking particularly slim and sharp, it was Catherine. Though she was wearing the usual trouser suit, there was no flowing scarf or soft jumper today.

Surprised to see her, Nat sat back and smiled. 'Catherine. Hi, how's Jack? Is he still improving…?' she started before noticing her expression. Catherine's face was pale, her cheeks almost sucked in.

Arms rigid and knuckles white, she gripped the client chair. 'You knew about Julian, didn't you?' she hissed, almost spitting the words. 'Why the fuck didn't you tell me?'

Shock kicking in, Nat stared. Sheer anger was radiating from Catherine's whole being. But before she could formulate words to reply, her old friend had slipped out as silently as she'd arrived.

Sitting frozen for several minutes Nat tried to exhale. Bloody hell. What was all that about? Jack Goldman, of course, with his exasperating Chinese walls. She'd been too winded to respond, but what could she have said? What went on between man and wife was none of her business.

She looked at her hands. Flipping heck, they were trembling. She hadn't clashed swords with Catherine for a very long time. Even back then she hadn't liked it; she'd always wanted her friend on side, she'd craved her approval. And she'd never seen her as hostile as that. Whatever *that* had been about.

Her breath had barely surfaced when the door moved again. Bracing herself for another onslaught, she groped for a reply.

'Natalie, hiya! Long time no see.' Slim arms were reaching out, so Nat stood to accept them. 'Don't you look fabulous!' Then kisses on both cheeks and a sugary perfume aroma. 'I've been meaning to bob in and say hello for yonks. How are you? God, how *are* you?'

Nat gaped at the polished face, too disconcerted to speak. The Cling-on had had her teeth done. That's all she could think of until her mind finally rallied.

'Fine, thanks, Andrea, I'm fine.' Then after a moment, trying to steady her thrashing heart, 'Sorry, Wes isn't here; he's in London. He's on a trial. I'm just using his office while he's…'

Her voice trailed off. Andrea had turned to the painting. Though still drizzling outside, she was wearing a short-sleeved triangular-shaped dress. Or a tent, as Gavin would put it. Though at least two sizes bigger than she'd been at Chester, her arms and legs were still as skinny as they had been then. She spun back to Nat. 'We had this at home, a present from my in-laws, but I never really liked it. What about you? Do you like modern art?'

Thrown by the conversation, Nat ogled again. Andrea still had the slightly turned up nose and pretty blue eyes, but her new teeth made her seem different, though how, she couldn't say. Trying to remember the question, she took a breath to answer, but Andrea spoke first.

'Oh, Wesley – I know, he came back last night. He's probably still asleep.' Flushing, she put her hand to her mouth. 'We had a late night.'

Gazing blindly, the cogs of Nat's brain were painfully slow. No, that couldn't be right; Wes was in London. He'd texted to say he was going out with clients in the evening. He and Chris Aaron were finalising their paperwork for the judge this morning; he hoped to leave at lunchtime to be back for their date tonight, then their Aga weekend.

That's what he'd said.

Trying to focus, she came back to his wife. She'd sat down in the client chair; she'd crossed her thin legs; she was peering at Nat with a sympathetic smile. 'I was really sorry to hear about you and Jose, Nat, but we all got together pretty young, didn't we? It was never going to be plain sailing. The grass is greener and all that.' Her eyes flickering, she frowned. 'Was it someone else? That's usually the way. You stick together until or unless something better comes along. Or so it seems until you realise that it isn't. It isn't better at all.' She gazed through the window with a pensive expression. When she turned back, she leaned forward, her face caught with emotion. 'Don't tell Wesley I've mentioned it, but we've been through a rough patch ourselves, so I do understand. It's nothing we can't mend, but still, it's pretty difficult, isn't it?'

Realisation slapped as Nat gawked. Oh God, she was genuine. Sweet and vulnerable, this woman's words came from the heart.

'It makes you feel crap,' she almost replied. Wesley Hughes's words which had seemed so sincere. 'How are the boys?' she found herself asking instead, her eyes glued to Andrea's troubled frown.

It cleared and she smiled. Her teeth really were perfect. 'Oh, they're great, Nat. Thanks for asking. You've probably heard about Matty's episode, but he's bounced back. I know I'm a fusser and that it drives the boys nuts at times, but what they say about mothers and sons is true. I absolutely love them to death. Of course it was hard having twins, double trouble and all that, which is why we didn't have more but...' she lowered her voice, her cheeks colouring again, 'we're going to try for another. I know it could be twins, but the boys will be at uni and Wesley has always been a really hands-on dad.' Her eyes shone, clearly happy. 'It was something he'd always wanted and when he suggested it again, I could see it was a way of mending things, a way of smoothing the rough patch. Now I've got my head around the idea, I'm really excited too. You never know, it might be a little girl this time.'

Feeling punched and yet numb, Nat nodded and stood. A baby, a new baby to smooth the 'rough patch'. She needed to go home. She had to leave this office now and never return. She picked up a random file, a pad and a pen, then groped for her briefcase.

'Sorry, I've just noticed the time. I have a court hearing, Andrea, so I have to go. Was there something you wanted?'

'God, sorry! You should have stopped me chatting.' She looked around the room. 'A Dictaphone?' she asked. 'A spare Dictaphone, Wesley said. In one of his drawers? He wants to dictate his notes from the trial while they're still fresh.'

Knowing she was a danger to passing cars, Nat crossed the busy road at the pedestrian crossing. Deciding to walk, she ignored the bus even though it was waiting. Exercise was the thing to clear the fog in her mind. Not that she particularly wanted to think. She already knew the truth. The reality was that Andrea Hughes was nice; she'd always been nice. Whereas Natalie Bach wasn't. She'd broken her own rules by sleeping with Wes. She'd been weak and greedy, foolish and eager and pathetic and a whole host of other adjectives, none of which were good.

It drizzled of course, the fine spray invading her collar and her pockets, her mouth and her shoes far more effectively than bog-standard rain. She plodded mechanically towards Fletcher Moss, past the pubs and the cricket club, then by a tortoiseshell moggy staring malevolently as though it knew what a stupid cock-up she'd made, not just this month or this year, but since forever.

In a bike lane without a bike, she continued to tromp, sure her shoes were rubbing but not feeling it yet. A bus pulled up on the final stretch home, so she felt compelled to catch it, greeting the smiling driver with a 'one stop, please'.

'Cheer up, love, it might never happen,' he said, but still charged her a pound.

The house was mercifully empty when she arrived. The cats

demanded food, but Nat threw off her wet shoes and headed for the stairs and her bed. She had thought she might read through her texts with Wes over the last few days, to try and make sense of what had happened, but there was really no point, so she took two codeine and turned off her phone.

30

A HORRIBLE LOW BLOW

Nat's nap was black and deep; she found it difficult to wake.

'Skarbie, you have a visitor,' she eventually heard her mother say.

She peeled back her eyelids. It was dark through the window, a downpour battering against it.

'Who?'

'Wesley.'

'Tell him to go away.'

Her mum's gaze of concern was too much to bear. She pulled up the duvet and turned. 'Really, Mum, I'm not well. Please tell him I can't see him. I just need to rest.'

Like the rain, the stupid rain, her tears wet the pillow. How she wanted to see him, to run down the stairs as though everything was fine. But it wasn't; it really wasn't. She just needed to sleep, to hide, to disappear.

Dozing again, Nat became aware of light pressure on the bed eventually. Anna of course, her eyes pale pools of worry. 'What has happened, Skarbie?' And then. 'Could I ask him in, love? It's been half an hour. He's still out there and it's so wet.'

'What on earth...?' Dizzy from abruptly standing, Nat waited for the nausea to pass, then swayed to the window. Stripes of heavy rain were lit by the street lights. And there was Wes, perched on the low car park wall, his arms folded, head down.

Irritation pierced the drowsiness. 'For God's sake it's pouring. Why doesn't he sit in his car?'

A hand on her arm and her mum's soulful face. 'I don't know, love. Go and talk to him.'

'He's not a bloody child,' Nat replied, her anger giving her the impetus to run down the stairs, burst from the door and march to the wall without bothering with shoes.

'Get in the car, Wes. You're soaked.'

He straightened up, his face terse as he stared. 'You've been crying.'

'Get in the car. You're being ridiculous.'

'I will if you'll talk to me.'

'We're not twelve years old.'

He crossed his arms again.

'Fine,' she said, tiptoeing to his car. Yanking the door open, she thumped down, the leather seats cold and unforgiving.

Wes did the same. He looked at her fixedly for moments before speaking. 'We were meeting tonight. You didn't answer my texts. You turned off your mobile. Why?' he asked.

She took a breath; his gaze was guileless, boyish, troubled. Her annoyance was evaporating, usurped by stupid longing. Stealing herself, she replaced his face with his wife's. She just needed to say it and then it would be over. 'Sorry, I've changed my mind.'

'About?'

'About going out tonight.' She looked at her hands. The rain rapped the bonnet. 'And about us.'

She couldn't look at his expression, but she knew he was glowering. The tension was tight in his voice. 'Why?'

'Nothing in particular. It just doesn't feel right. So please go now. Go home and let's forget what happened.' She turned, blindly searching for the door handle, but he reached out an arm to stop her leaving.

'It's Andrea, isn't it? She's done something, hasn't she? What? Has she called you?' He leaned in to search her face. 'She's been to the office, hasn't she? What's she been saying?'

Nat pushed him away, then found herself shouting. 'You were with her last night. You said you were in London. You spent the night together in your home. It's hardly a fucking marriage that's over.'

'It is over. It's…'

She stared. His eyes were flickering; oh God, he was lying. 'Were you with her last night, Wes?'

Blowing out a long breath, he sat back. 'I was, but not like that… The day in court was wrapped up earlier than I'd thought. Everyone wanted to get home, the client included. I was lugging two boxes of trial bundles. It was easier to drop them in Cheadle Hulme than travel all the way to Sid's.' He lifted his hands. 'It's still my home, Nat–'

'So you stayed with your wife and had a "late night".'

He frowned. 'I spent the night in the spare room, Nat.'

She pictured Andrea's pink, bashful face. 'And a nice lie-in this morning?'

'Yes, for a bit. I dictated the judgment notes, then came into the office with the sodding bundles. You weren't there. Sharon didn't know where you'd gone. She guessed it was the usual mystery mission for Jack.' He stared, his jaw tight. 'It is over, Nat. Are you listening? Andrea and I are over.'

Genuine, so genuine; his gaze was steady and sincere. But so were Andrea's: her words had come from the heart. 'Sorry, I can't…' she began, but Wes put his hand on her cheek, his eyes soft and concerned. 'What has she been saying? Tell me, Nat. What has she said to upset you so much?'

She whispered, the words spilling out before she could stop

them. The one thing Andrea had said, the one thing above all that Nat couldn't bear.

He bent closer. 'I can't hear you. Say again?'

'That you're trying for another baby. She said it's what you've always wanted.'

Falling back, he laughed. 'That's actually funny. We haven't had sex in years. I was chained to her for eighteen long ones because of babies. It would be a double life sentence to have another.' He took her hands in his. 'Look at me, Nat. It isn't true. Okay? It's absolutely not true.' The humour abruptly fell from his face. 'What the hell?' he said, frowning. 'Why would she say that?' Snorting sharply, he nodded. 'She must suspect us. My mobile this morning... She brought me in a coffee at the crack of dawn. I've been stupid, bloody stupid; I should've been more careful.' He turned, his face stony. 'She wanted to hurt you, Nat, and she knew the best way to do it.'

Her heart clenched. 'What do you mean?' she asked slowly. 'What do you mean, "she knew the best way"?'

He lifted his hands. 'Babies of course; the one thing she's had and you haven't.'

A low blow, a horrible low blow. 'Fuck off, Wes. You know nothing about me. You have no idea what hurts me and what doesn't.' Reaching for the handle she quickly climbed from the car.

He opened his door. 'Natalie, don't go.' His anger was palpable, clamped in his cheeks. 'See how clever she is? Did she put on her sweet and vulnerable face for you? She's a master of lies and manipulation. Don't let her do it. Come back and talk to me. Let's go out as planned and sort this out.'

Nat stared. Andrea's shiny blue eyes flashed in her mind. Was she really emotional or just plain calculating? Oh God, she didn't know anything any more, but the fight was all gone. This was hopeless. Her tears mingling with the rain, she shook her head. 'Truth or lies, Wes. It makes no difference. She's here; she'll always be here, the mother of your kids, the wife you can't quite be weaned off. I'm sorry, it isn't going to work. Please go home and don't come back.'

The grit stabbing her bare soles, she pelted to the door. Though her heart was already in spasm, her head knew she was right. No relationship with Wes would work. Just like Chester and her shattered hopes back then, the ghost of Andrea would always be there.

∾

It was only eight thirty, but Nat went straight to her bedroom, avoiding Anna's gaze. She didn't want to be unkind, but it was difficult to explain what had happened and how she felt about it. A dangerous and uncomfortable sensation was rising, hot in her chest. Something she'd missed or just wasn't seeing, not only about Wes and Andrea, but Jack and Catherine, Julian and Aisha. It felt like they were gods peering down from Mount Olympus and toying with her for sport.

Not sure she could get any wetter, the brisk shower felt ironic but helped clear the codeine fug from her head. Then she lay on her bed, wide-eyed and restless, her mind prodding and poking as she listened to the rain.

Was it really only seven days ago? Just one week since she'd been at the party? Despite her attempt not to rewind it, the film was there in technicolour – that heartbeat moment when she'd noticed Wes at the bar, the rush of pleasure she'd felt just because he was there. She'd had no designs on him then; it had just happened, a night of perfect love, even more special without sex, though she wouldn't have stopped him if he'd tried. He'd promised not to. 'No funny stuff, I promise', he'd said.

Oh God. Nothing was going on between him and Andrea. She believed him, she did. But…

'I have done the right thing,' she said to the ceiling. And she definitely had. It was just that…

She turned on her mobile. Maybe Wes had texted since she'd run away. If he had, she'd delete it, she just needed to know. The messages popped up one by one, but they all pre-dated their conversation in the car. He had left, stony-faced, without looking her way. She'd stood at her dark window, watching for minutes, just in case he returned.

That feeling of disorientation hit her again. The world was at a strange angle; nothing added up. Andrea had been so believable, her confession so genuine. Yet she knew from Wes's spontaneous laugh that it was a fabrication, a fantasy, a Straight. Fucking. Lie. Or perhaps *he* was the actor. Who knew? Natalie Bach was losing her touch, the nous that Jack had always admired. It was drifting away, lost.

Like she'd lost it for five years.

Five bloody years. Sitting up, she crossed her legs and picked up the packet from her bedside table. It contained the snaps she'd flicked through on the day of Jack's heart attack. Did that really happen? Not long ago, but it felt like aeons.

Spreading them on the bed, she searched for images of Jose. There weren't many, but she gazed at the few, mostly of her and him together and a couple with Hugo, the two men looking away from the camera and at each other, as though sharing a joke over her head. She studied a close up of Jose. It had always been her favourite. Willowy with tanned skin, his blond hair bleached almost white by the sun. She tried to feel something, but nothing came, not love nor hatred. Not even anger.

She heard Jack's nagging voice in her mind. God, she hoped he'd just drop the subject of The Spaniard and money. She'd willingly given a stack of it towards the purchase of 'Havana', but there was nothing in writing between her and Jose, and she was pretty sure her name wasn't on the deeds. Perhaps she had been 'romantic', as Catherine had put it, but she'd also been a blind optimistic fool; she'd gone against her own sage advice, but she wasn't about to launch a feeble recovery claim under a dodgy Spanish law. It had to be put down to experience. Like Jose himself, it needed to be written off in her head. After all, it was only flaming money.

A soft knock at the door made her turn. Anna's wispy hair was followed by a hesitant smile. Ah Mum. Her lovely mother; thank God for her. 'The light was on. Do you want something to eat?' she asked.

'Thanks, Mum, but I'm not very hungry.' Nat lifted a photograph. 'I'm looking at these. Do you want to join me?'

Anna sat on the bed, picked up a bundle, and went through them with a mix of emotions passing through her eyes. 'Look at handsome Hugo. There are more pictures of him than you!' She smiled. 'A nice man, though. He always made me dance. Quite forceful but smooth, if you know what I mean.'

Nat smiled too. 'I know exactly what you mean. I felt as though I could dance, but really he was manoeuvring me seamlessly across the dance floor.' She pictured the girl she used to be, that stranger dancing arm in arm with Hugo and the other locals. Tactile without being invasive, they weren't like the Brits who gyrated without touching. Though Wes had held her hand in his, warm and solid, when they'd danced last week. Only last week. Oh God.

'Your dad and I used to dance.' Nat came back to her mum's voice. Her expression was misty. 'He was quite forceful, too. It was a good job he was so insistent, otherwise I wouldn't have said yes to our first date at the pictures. He was very handsome, but he seemed quite old to me then. Of course later I couldn't tell the age difference. You just see the person once you know someone, don't you?'

Nat nodded, bizarrely thinking of Chris Aaron's imperious face which belied his cheery personality. Did he ever met Jose?

They fell silent for a time and her mum blew her nose.

'What happened to Dad in Poland?' Nat asked, suddenly wanting to know.

'He was in a camp. He never spoke about it. He had terrible dreams and cried out. That was enough. I didn't need to know more.'

Nat nodded and kissed her soft cheek. 'I will talk to you about what happened, Mum, but at the moment it's all too fresh.'

Her mum squeezed her hand. 'You always do tell me when you're ready. But I'd like you to eat something, please. I don't want my Skarbie wasting away.'

31

SHE'LL ALWAYS BE HERE

Nat's mobile alarm jerked her awake. 'Go away,' she mumbled. 'It's Saturday.'

She tried to open her eyes, but they protested. It felt far, far too early. And the dim light peering through the curtains was evidence of that. But it was her own stupid fault, like everything else. She'd forgotten to disable the damn thing, even though the plan had been to lie in bed all morning, all week, all month, preferably unconscious, so she didn't have to dwell on her final, crushing words to Wes. Not that she hadn't mulled on them all night, swinging from an aching desire just to call him, to other negative emotions she couldn't fully describe, but one of them was hurt.

That blow, that low blow to her stomach.

'Babies, of course,' he had said, as though it was nothing. Well it wasn't fucking nothing. Everyone had been blessed except her. She was nearly forty with no prospect of a steady relationship, and even if there were, she'd probably left it too late to conceive. Putting on the maiden aunt jolly smile was bloody exhausting. She didn't want to do that, or anything else any more; she just wanted to sleep so all the heartache would disappear.

The alarm still nagging, she put out a blind arm and searched the bedside table. It must have fallen on the floor. Oh hell. There was no alternative but to flick on the light and wake up completely. Protecting her eyes from the glare, she reached for the phone.

She stared at the screen. My God; it wasn't the alarm; it was an answer from heaven! Prior to finally nodding off last night, her mind had flipped to her parents and their love against the odds. So she'd prayed that Wes would call her today. If he did, she'd meet him to talk things through rationally and see where it took them. At seven forty on a Saturday morning it was a little too early, but her devotion had been answered.

She took a deep breath. 'Wes–'

'Nat, just listen. I haven't got long. If the police ask, you were with me all last night. Just like we'd planned. All night at the office flat until we left this morning at seven. I dropped you home fifteen or so minutes ago. I'm sorry to ask, but you're the only one I can trust. Here's the ambulance. I have to go.'

Alarm and adrenaline tore through her body. What the hell? What the hell? She bolted from the bed and dashed to the bathroom, splashed cold water on her face, scrubbed her teeth and raked her hair. Scurrying back to the bedroom, she quickly dragged on jeans and a jumper, the blood pacing through her veins. Something was wrong; terribly wrong. An ambulance, he'd said. What had happened? Why did he need an alibi?

She perched on the bed and tapped her foot. What to do? What to do? She couldn't do nothing. But Wes had asked her to fib. Lies had to stack up. She couldn't risk doing something odd in case… In case what? What the hell was going on?

Her mum was hovering at the front door when she finally came down. 'Oh. You're up early. Barbara will be here any…' Then that gaze of pale concern. 'Are you all right? Has something else happened? I can tell Barbara–'

'No, it's fine. I'm just tired. I'll perk up after some food. I think that's Barbara's car.' Then, virtually pushing the poor woman out of the front door, 'Have fun shopping, buy something frivolous on me. Enjoy your stay-over. I'll see you tomorrow.'

No breakfast of course. She just paced from the lounge to the kitchen and stared at her mobile, willing it to ring. What to do? What the hell should she do? Phone Jack for a casual chat to see if he knew anything? Or Gavin, yes Gavin, but what could she say?

The call finally came at noon. Her heartbeat was so rapid, she struggled to speak.

'What's happening, Wes?'

'Remember what I told you before?'

'Yes.'

'Will you do it if necessary?'

'Yes.'

'Thank you. Now call Gavin. Tell him to come to Wythenshawe police station.'

'Why? What's happened?'

'I've been brought in for questioning.'

'Come on, Wes. Tell me.'

'Andrea fell down the stairs. She has a fractured skull. I have to go. Call Gavin now.'

With clumsy, damp fingers she scrolled down her contacts and pressed Gavin's number. Bloody voicemail. She tried again, then again. Bloody, bloody voicemail! So, what now? Wythenshawe police station, Wes had said. She'd go there herself.

She pulled on her boots, then scooped up her jacket and keys. What else? Oh yes, her handbag. She would try Gavin just one last time...

'Hello, Miss Bach. What do you want on a Saturday? Three missed calls, eh? Let me guess. You can't live without me.'

Finally. She almost sobbed with relief. 'Gavin! Where have you been?'

'I'm at a park with the kids. Why, what's up?'

'God knows, but Wes needs you. The police want to question

him at Wythenshawe police station. It's something to do with Andrea falling down the stairs. He wants you to go there now.'

His voice immediately changed to professional, efficient. 'Right.' She could almost hear the cogs of his mind. 'You need to come here.'

'Where's "here"?'

'Wilmslow Park. I'll see you in the car park.'

'Why?'

'Social services might be upset if I leave Ruthie in charge. Not that she wouldn't cope if Cameron decided to go on another biting spree...'

Panic was already setting in. Gavin's three hundred kids. Bloody hell, the frying pan or the fire? 'You want *me* to look after your children?' she croaked.

'Yup. It's my weekend. The ex is away. A dash of the old Savage charm and her mum would be delighted to look after the kids, but if speed is a priority, you'll need to man up.'

'Okay, okay. Wilmslow Park. It's huge, isn't it? Where exactly is the car park?'

'Look for the swings. You'll find it.'

Climbing into the car, Nat tried to focus on where she was headed. Thank God she'd spoken to Gavin. On reflection, turning up at the police station herself would've been pretty stupid when she had to think through an alibi. A *false* bloody alibi. The notion caught her breath. Why the hell did Wes need one? A fall down the stairs, he'd said. Oh God.

She replaced that thought with one a little less stressful, but worrying nonetheless: Gavin's kids. He was joking about the 'biting spree', wasn't he? And she was fine with children, she was a spinster aunt after all. Her nephew and niece were really sweet. On an iPad screen, at least. Shit, Gavin's were real flesh and blood. Savage blood. If they were anything like their dad...

∼

Lined up in height order, Gavin and his offspring were leaning against the ice cream van when she arrived. He lifted his hand, climbed in his old battered Volvo and turned on the engine.

Bolting from her car, Nat knocked on his window. She nodded to the van. 'Your children, I assume. Aren't you going to introduce me?'

'Nah. You'll work it out.' He put the car into gear. 'You can count to four?' Then he was off without even a promise to keep her posted.

With a sinking heart, she turned to the kids. The two older boys had already darted to the play area, ascending a metal climbing frame with astonishing speed. A small, red-haired girl and an even smaller boy, who had most of his mitt rammed in his mouth, regarded her solemnly. Nat looked at the boy cautiously. The biter, she assumed.

After a few moments inspection, and apparent approval, Gavin's daughter took Nat's hand. 'Cameron,' she barked to the boy.

Looking remarkably like a Lilliputian Gavin, he extracted his fist, looked up at Nat with a runny nose and a shrug, and took her other.

They stayed at the playground, an hour speeding by without time for deep thought. All four children darted from slide to climbing frame to swing to see-saw. Only having two eyes, Nat kept them on the younger two, the breath high in her chest as Cameron wobbled across various hurdles that were more suitable in an Olympic-standard gym, only letting out a stream of hot air at the jangle of the ice cream van, which rounded the kids up like greased lightning.

After an intermission for a Mr Whippy hidden entirely by chocolate sauce and sprinkles, the two older boys disappeared behind the privet. For a pee, Nat assumed, until she was enlightened by Ruthie.

'They're going to the river,' she said. Then, slipping her fingers through Nat's, 'Come on, let's go.'

The word 'river' more than alarming, Nat grabbed Cameron's sticky paw and ran after the boys. The weak sunshine lit up the shades of red in their hair, almost matching the autumn carpet. Though they wore wellies, she struggled to keep up with the two older children as they darted through the trees, crunching on fallen leaves and throwing sticks.

At the peak of a mound, Cameron broke away, trotting down the bank and splashing the glinting water before Nat had chance to react.

'Hold Cameron's hand,' Ruthie commanded at the water's edge. Then she turned to face Nat. 'Don't worry, it's shallow here, but it's really deep further down.'

Oh, that was all right then. But Cameron's brothers had each grabbed a shoulder and Nat finally breathed again. It was a relief to have Ruthie in charge. Sitting on a bench with a sigh, Nat finally had a chance to study her freckled features. She had a button nose, pink lips and glorious auburn hair. 'How old are you?' she asked.

'Six, of course. Nearly seven.'

The small child said this as though Nat was slightly stupid, which was possibly very true. An alibi. An alibi! What on earth was going on? But she didn't have time to work that out right now. Ruthie's arm had slotted through hers and she was chit-chatting about their usual Saturday routine, the places they went to and the things Daddy let them do that was forbidden by Mummy, the river included. She sagely explained that Cameron wasn't allowed nuts, that Alistair had a girl who fancied him 'rotten', and that they all hoped no one fancied Daddy because they wanted him to re-marry Mummy.

'Well, I don't fancy your daddy,' Nat assured her, not sure from Ruthie's frown whether this was the right thing to say.

His boots spilling water, Cameron eventually trudged back

from the river. 'I'm hungry,' he said. Then his eyes welled with tears. 'I can't feel my toes. I want to go home!'

While Ruthie rounded up the others, Nat emptied Cameron's wellies. Though she'd done nothing but watch, she was exhausted. She padded his feet ineffectually with a tissue which happened to be in her pocket and sighed. Perhaps she wasn't cut out for motherhood after all. She checked her mobile for messages. There was nothing. So what now? Well that one was easy, a cure for every kid. 'How about a happy meal, Cameron?' Then to the others. 'Are you allowed to eat at McDonald's?'

The older two children eyed each other before vigorously nodding, so Nat scooped up little Cameron without meeting Ruthie's wide knowing gaze.

'Okay, McDonald's it is. But–'

A choral reply. 'Don't tell Mummy!'

Discovering Anna's car wasn't designed for five people, Nat drove home from McDonald's super sensibly, fearful she'd be spotted by the police. Unlikely, of course, when they were preoccupied with interrogating Wesley Hughes, upright and law-abiding solicitor of the senior courts of England and Wales. She shook her head yet again. It was surreal, too surreal.

By the time they arrived in Cheadle, Cameron was asleep, so she carried him into the house, lined the others up on the sofa, handed over a large bag of crisps and the TV remote, then finally sat down to think about the whole bizarre situation.

She sipped her coffee absently. An ambulance had been called because Andrea had fallen down the stairs. That didn't just happen, did it? Oh God, an argument was the obvious thing. Her heart thrashing, she pictured Wes's face yesterday. She'd seen anger, almost fury. And what had *she* said about Andrea? 'She's here. She'll always be here.' Had Wes taken that to mean he should do something stupid? No, she was being stupid; he wasn't like that; he was measured and calm.

But why the hell had he asked her to lie?

Gazing at the flickering shapes on the television screen, she tried to stop her mind jumping from one wretched thought to another. Wes's tight face; Andrea's emotional smile. The police. The bloody police! An alibi. A lie.

Stop, just stop, Natalie. Even hurtling after Gavin's kids was less terrifying than this.

Her stomach churning, she stared at her mobile, willing it to ring, then nearly jumped out of her skin when it did. It was Gavin, thank God.

'What's your number?' he asked.

'You're ringing it,' she replied.

'Your house number, numpty. I'm here.'

The kids barely turned their heads when he noisily strode in.

'Cameron hasn't had nuts, he's just asleep,' Ruthie said, her focus still on the screen.

'Well, that's good to hear, though he'll never sleep later.'

Gavin moved away. 'There'll be no peace for this dad tonight. Still, I've not been in a police interview room all day.' He lifted his eyebrows. 'Or been questioned about assaulting my wife.'

Nat followed him to the kitchen. 'Don't joke, Gav.'

'I'm not. Wes has been released on police bail, but that's where they're headed.' He rubbed his face. 'It doesn't help when the victim points the finger.'

Oh God. Like a hand grasping her throat, Nat's voice emerged strangled. 'What? What do you mean?'

Gavin stifled a yawn and sat down. 'Andrea, the victim. When she regained consciousness she said something to the doctors implicating Wes. But she's confused. She's cracked her skull and there's been a bleed on the brain. It isn't unusual to say crazy things.' He cocked his head. 'Talking of such, Wes says he was with you last night.'

Not knowing what to say, Nat nodded. She'd been too busy to think it through at the park, and too agitated since arriving home. 'So what happened? What did Wes say?' she asked, trying to ignore Gavin's clearly dubious gaze.

'Well, you'd know if you were with him, Natalie.'

Heat flooded her cheeks. 'I meant what happened this morning. After he dropped me off at seven?'

Gavin looked at her pointedly, then he held out his hand and counted on his fingers. 'Okay, let's see if I've got this right. Wes went to work Friday lunchtime. He came home at the usual sort of time, had an argument with Andrea during the evening. He wasn't very specific about that, but he was certain it didn't involve pushing her down the stairs. He left the house, drove into town, met you at the office flat...' He snorted. 'Nice work if you can get it.' He went back to his thumb. 'You stayed together all night. You left in the morning together, he dropped you here, at *seven*, I believe, drove to his house, opened the door and there was Andrea in a pool of blood. He called an ambulance.' He stopped speaking and peered at Nat again. 'I shouldn't be telling you any of this, but he said it was fine to tell you. Funny, that.'

She ignored his sarcastic tone. She needed to get to the point. 'But what exactly did Andrea say to the hospital staff? Why did the police get involved?'

'She told a nurse, then repeated what she'd said to a doctor.' Gavin raised his hands. 'Something about Wes pushing her. The fact is, the medics always have to treat stair falls with suspicion, and if something doesn't add up, they are duty bound to report it to the police.'

Still spinning, Nat stared. 'Why would she say what she said?'

'I don't know, Nat. Was she confused? Did Wes *push* her in a way other than physically? Unless he did shove her down the stairs, of course.'

He stood, stretched and hollered to the children. 'Wake up, Cameron, Ruthie. It's time for home.' Then he turned, his face serious. 'He hasn't given a formal statement to the police yet, but you need to think carefully before he does. He says the two of you are involved, and to be honest that doesn't surprise me. However, you need to think of yourself here, Nat. I'm not saying either of you is lying, but... perjury is bad enough, the courts are far from soft, but you're also a solicitor. They'll come down very hard on you, and you'll be struck off. I've also told him this. He doesn't need to bring you into it. If he was where he says he was last night, the car park CCTV will show his time of arrival and exit.' He pulled Nat into a tight hug before releasing her. 'Think about it, Nat. Really think. And thanks for minding the kids. You looked like a natural.'

32

TALKING IN CLICHÉS

Heads down, low mumbles, just the occasional 'Oh fuck,' the first-floor office was quiet the following week. Were the bench boys and other staff aware of Andrea's accident, or was the despondency just in Nat's head? She gathered from Sharon that Catherine was back in her upstairs office, but she didn't see her, thank goodness. Though in truth Cool Catherine and her unexpected outburst weren't at the forefront of her mind at present. She was back in cahoots with the canvas, searching for answers when she wasn't overseeing Wes's files.

What the hell was going on? It felt as though Nat had been holding her breath since Saturday. Save for one text she hadn't heard from Wes, but she knew through Gavin he was at home with the boys, driving them each day to spend time with their mother at the hospital. Of course he wasn't allowed to see her himself. He was a suspect. A bloody suspect! Her condition had deteriorated, apparently, but this was to be expected, and until she was lucid and could answer police questions, the cloud would remain.

Nat deeply sighed. The cloud. Bloody understatement of the year.

She'd had to interpret Wes's message. It had said in a round-about way that he was sorry he'd asked her to lie, that it was stupid and selfish, and that he wouldn't put her in that position again. At least that's what she hoped. She understood it had to be guarded, that mobile data could be accessed by the police, but still she felt extremely unsettled. Part of her wanted him to tell her straight what had happened, to explain why the hell he'd needed an alibi, but a greater part of her didn't want to know. She had believed Wes's declarations of 'like', but she'd also been convinced by Andrea. They couldn't both be right. Only one thing was certain: Natalie Bach had got *someone* horribly wrong.

The peal of her mobile interrupted her malaise on Wednesday afternoon. As usual, she tensed and took a breath before peering at the caller ID, but once she saw who it was, she relaxed. The 'only gay in the CPS' as Gavin had described him.

'Good news,' Joshim Khan began. Nat couldn't help but smile. Hallelujah! She needed some of that. 'The Hetherington case,' he continued. 'We looked into it and we won't be pursuing her for the sheep death, so–'

'A goat, Joshim. The deceased was a medium-sized Billy Goat Gruff, I fear…'

'Well here's a coincidence. This very night I'm meeting a terrifically terrifying terrible troll. This one's a variety of rabid Scottish. A drink and then a curry? Meet at SS at six?'

'SS?' Nat asked.

'Savage Solicitors.' Joshim laughed. 'Yeah. You couldn't make it up, could you?'

Figuring she could extract a Wes update from Gavin before

Joshim turned up, Nat arrived early in Heald Green. She pressed the SS buzzer. Someone let her into reception, but the musty smelling front room was empty.

'Hello?' she called, hoping for a closer inspection of Gavin's surly man-boy assistant. There was no reply, so she followed the warble. A female voice was belting out 'Crazy in Love', so it was a surprise to find it was coming from Gavin's office. 'Hello?' she said again as she pushed open the door.

Wearing huge headphones, a dark, voluptuous woman was turned towards a filing cabinet. Gavin's secretary, Chantelle, Nat assumed. As though sensing her presence, she abruptly turned, her hand on her huge chest. 'God, you made me jump,' she squawked.

A movie star face, Nat immediately thought. The young woman was stunning, and not a million miles away from a youthful Elizabeth Taylor. She modelled for a website selling clothing for ladies with 'a fuller figure', Nat recalled. Gavin had mentioned that most of the clothes were bought by men for themselves. How he or Chantelle knew that, she didn't like to ask, but she smiled, still wondering who had buzzed her into the office.

'Hi, I'm Natalie; I'm here for Gavin.'

'Take a pew,' Chantelle replied. 'I'm just finishing up. I can't wait to get home and have my feet up with a Baileys and crisps.'

Hopefully that meant Gavin would appear at some point. Nat flopped into his chair and watched his secretary go about her business for a while. Then she focused on the messy desk top, the chipped mugs doubling up as pen and highlighter holders, the pile of Post-it pads in every colour, and an array of art and craft items clearly made by his children.

The sight gave her a jolt, a mixture of regret and anxiety. His kids had been lovely on Saturday. They'd been well behaved and accepting of their parents' separate homes, but optimistic too, convinced that their daddy would come back to live with them one day. She wondered if he knew this. Then there was Wes and his sons. They were older, but still, what on earth was going through their heads? Did they know what their mother had alleged? And what if it were true? How would they cope living with the knowledge that their dad had harmed their mum, even if it was an accident, even if he'd lost his rag in a moment of madness and pushed her?

Oh God. Is that what had happened?

Absently opening a desk drawer, her eye caught Julian Goldman's name on the front of a green folder. Her fingers itching, she slipped it out and placed it on the desk. Sensing Chantelle's gaze, she glanced up, but she lifted her dark eyebrows and shrugged, so Nat opened the file and flicked through Gavin's illegible handwritten notes. Then she moved on to the bank statements and the other financial documents, the ones Aisha had provided, presumably.

Bloody hell, Gavin was right. Julian's financial situation was dire, the mortgage payments crippling. She was glad she'd paid hers off before disappearing to Mallorca. Not that her tiny terrace in Cheadle was in any way comparable to a large house in Alderley Edge, but still, keeping a roof over his and Aisha's head must have been worrying.

Tapping the desk with her fingers, she sighed. She was no expert, but it seemed that while no one could specifically put Julian at the scene of the crime, the circumstantial evidence was fairly damning. She had a feeling in her bones that he'd done it. She'd seen for herself how he loved Aisha, his baby was nearly due, and he was estranged from the one person who could get him out of the mess. She could picture Julian's desperation, meeting the debt collector at the lay-by and asking for more time, the man getting aggressive, perhaps even threatening to come to his house, to tell Aisha or harm her. Julian might have lost his temper, and had a moment of insanity when he climbed back in his car. Like Wes with Andrea, manipulative Andrea, if that's what she was. But also like Wes, Julian would have to admit to the crime if he wanted to rely on mitigating circumstances and get his custodial sentence reduced.

Possible life prison sentences for them both. Oh God.

Breathing back a wave of panic, Nat picked up Julian's mortgage deed and the loan documents, and began reading the small print for a few moments. Rotten pay day loans, taking minutes to apply for – and years to pay off. Bloody crooks with their unconscionable interest rates. Why hadn't they been banned? But then again, if the thieves tried to sue, they couldn't get blood out of a stone. If they tried to enforce the debt, even if they sued and got a judgment, a debtor was only as good as his worth. She'd had plenty of cases over the years when some poor sod was owed money. He'd come to Goldman Law and ask her to sue the defaulting bastard, but the first thing she'd ask is, 'What is the bastard worth?' If he or she didn't have an income, a house with equity or other assets, the poor client would be throwing good money after bad by paying her to pursue it. She was sure Jack hadn't been keen on her turning business away, but she liked to think she'd always been 'of the highest integrity', the phrase describing what solicitors should be, drilled in at law school…

Nat groaned inwardly. Providing a false alibi was the polar opposite, of course, but she didn't want to think about that right now. Speculating why Wes had asked for one had been like a persistent thirty-degree washing cycle, and she wanted it to stop. Besides, she was here to chill out with Joshim and the rabid Scot.

As she gazed at the name of the second loan company, a distant bell rang, but she smelled the Scot in question moments before the file was snatched from under her nose.

'Cheeky sod. You're not working here yet,' he said, closing it.

God knows where he had appeared from, but he was wearing chinos, a bold tartan shirt, and even bolder aftershave. 'Not that you don't know what's in there,' he added, slotting it back in the drawer.

'And you've come from...?' Nat asked.

Gavin looked up at the stained ceiling.

'Heaven? Are you sure about that?' She laughed, feeling chirpier from seeing him already. 'A fallen angel, perhaps?'

'Very droll,' he replied. 'Upstairs. My humble abode.'

She reached for a quip, but caught a passing shadow in Gavin's amber eyes and so quickly changed the subject. 'Are you offering me a job, then?'

'You could do worse: minimum wage, maximum hours,' he replied.

Chantelle slammed a cupboard. 'Don't do it, Natalie. He's not even joking. He's never heard of birthdays, let alone Christmas.'

'I expect we're talking about the tight Scottish bastard,' a voice said at the door. Wearing close-fitting combat trousers and a leather jacket, Joshim Khan was grinning. His hair was gelled into a quiff and he'd grown a neat designer beard since the last time Nat saw him. He nodded at Gavin. 'Make sure he gets his hands in his pocket tonight–'

'Says the man who never takes his out,' Gavin retorted, raising his eyebrows.

Chantelle hadn't yet torn her gaze from Joshim's face. 'God, you are so incredibly gorgeous,' she said slowly. Then, apparently shaking herself from the spell, she flashed a bright smile and held out her hand. 'Hi, I'm Chantelle. And you are–?'

'Gay,' Gavin interrupted.

'Who cares.' Chantelle laughed, linking arms with Joshim. 'Are we off to the pub?'

Little and Large, Nat thought at the bar. She and Joshim at the small end of the spectrum, the Scot and his secretary at the other. She was glad Chantelle had invited herself along; she was noisy and funny, encouraging Nat to match her astonishing consumption of two-for-one cocktails. 'What haven't we had yet?' she said each time they consulted the menu, prodding Joshim with her elbow and almost propelling him from his stool. 'Oh I know: a screaming orgasm!'

A couple of hours of chat and laughter rushed by. 'Reading between the lines, I reckon your Mrs wants you back,' Nat said to Gavin at some point.

The frown was fleeting. 'You must be joking. She can't bear the sight of me. She hides when I collect the kids.'

'Did she throw you out or did you leave?'

'What do you think?' Putting his glass to his lips, Gavin threw back the rest of his pint without apparently swallowing.

Nat watched and guffawed. 'Bloody hell, I don't blame her.' Then, with raised eyebrows, she added, 'Listening to your kids chat, though, Gav... Children don't get ideas from nowhere, do they? I mean, most kids want their parents back together, but...'

'But what?'

'I don't know; it's a sixth-sense thing.' Flipping heck, she was using Gavin's lingo again.

He snorted. 'Sixth sense? Your talents know no end.'

'Yeah, but would you go back?'

He stood with his empty glass. 'Nah,' he said. He looked pensive for a beat. 'Nah. Who needs another drink?'

Looking a little unsteady, Joshim returned from the toilets and took Gavin's place. 'How come you get better looking with age?' Nat asked, a touch wobbly herself.

Joshim stroked his soft beard. 'It must be my holy life. Fighting for justice, prosecuting sheep murderers, sleeping around–'

'Really?'

He laughed. 'Pretty much. Why?'

Nat shrugged. 'The sleeping around bit sounds like a cliché.'

Joshim played with his beer mat. 'We're all clichés to an extent, don't you think? Chantelle is overweight, so she's bubbly,

I'm gay, so I'm promiscuous, Gavin's straight and Scottish, so he's sexist, tight and–'

'And the rest.'

'And as for you…'

'Oh please don't say anything which includes the words "bitter" or "missed the boat". I do have a piercing scream.'

Joshim's dark eyes were watchful. 'What went wrong with Jose? Did you meet too young? Greener grass and all that?'

Flinching at the expression, Nat pictured the Cling-on's soulful face when she said that. She had believed her; she'd thought her so genuine. It was a version of the truth, perhaps. Everyone had those. Which brought on another burning question, one she'd been mulling over since studying the Mallorca snaps. Jose, her Jose. The man she'd lived with for five years. Happily, she'd assumed.

She came back to Joshim to answer his query. 'Maybe, though we didn't actually get together properly until we were in our thirties.' Then cocking her head and feeling surprisingly nonchalant: 'You lived with him for a year, Joshim. Do you think he was gay?'

His face showed surprise. 'You're joking, aren't you? He was obsessed with you. Bordering on mentally ill, but not gay.'

'Okay, but did you ever get the impression he might be attracted to another man, that he could…' She couldn't help laughing, 'That he could turn?'

'And I would know this, how?'

'Gaydar.'

Almost spitting out his beer, Joshim snorted. 'Bloody hell, now who's talking in clichés? Or do you really mean did he look at me a little too long over the Weetabix packet at breakfast, or accidentally walk in when I was wanking in the showers?'

'Well, did he?'

'No, and nor did he make a pass the few times we met after

Chester.' Joshim narrowed his eyes. 'You think that's what happened? That he's fallen for a man?'

'You're the one who suggested the grass might be greener.'

'Come on, Nat, spit it out.'

Though she hardly knew her confidant, she just said it, surprising herself at how easily the words flowed. 'At the bar we had a manager called Hugo, an older Mallorcan guy. When I looked at the old photos, Jose seemed more interested in him than in me.' Now it was out, it sounded plain stupid. 'Does that sound as idiotic to you as it does to me?'

'Pretty much.' He took Nat's hand. 'Maybe Hugo is the love of Jose's life; maybe he's shagging a fifteen-year-old *prostituta*, or maybe he's just a complete arsehole. Does the reason really matter? He ended it; he's a bastard; move on.'

'You sound like me when I had divorce clients–'

'Then take your own advice. Tell him to fuck off. If you can't do it in person, do it in your head.'

Gavin appeared with a large bag of crisps. 'Who are we telling to fuck off?' he asked, sitting down and splitting the packet to share.

Joshim lifted his glass. 'Anyone who deserves it. Cut them out of your life.' His voice was starting to slur. He clinked glasses with Nat. 'Fuck off, Jose.' Then he lifted his drink towards Gavin's. 'Fuck off... Sorry, I can't remember her name.'

'Heather,' Gavin replied. He drained his pint and stood up. 'Enough of this stupidity. It's time for curry; crisps aren't enough for this big man. Drink up, I'm starving.'

It wasn't unreasonably late when Nat arrived at her front door, but the frosty evening air made her footsteps seem loud. Or maybe she was still pissed from the cocktails. She'd had a fun evening, made all the better by taking a break from the constant conjecture about Wes. She'd moved on to water at the restaurant, eating so many poppadoms before the main course that she'd only been able to eat a small portion of her creamy chicken dopiaza. She had intended to bring the rest back in a doggy bag for Anna, but Gavin had predictably demolished it. 'What?' he'd said when he'd piled it into his bowl. 'Do the maths. I'm twice as big as you, I need to eat twice as much.'

She glanced at the strip of dull light between the bay window curtains. Her mum had left on the lamp as a welcome as usual, so she slotted her key in the lock, standing aside as one cat darted in and the other sped out. They were twins, she supposed. Funny, she hadn't thought about that before. Like Wes's sons, the difference between his being their eating habits rather than gender, or indeed, species. Chantelle had turned out to be a vegetarian too; that had surprised Nat at the restaurant. Another cliché or assumption, she supposed.

Pushing open the lounge door to turn off the lamp, she almost jumped out of her skin. Anna was sitting at the small table with a fan of playing cards in her hand. When she stepped in further, Wesley Hughes put down his deck and stood up.

'Hello, Nat.'

Her mum's yawn was far from subtle. 'You take my hand, love. I'm ready to drop, so I'll say goodnight.'

Wes smiled politely. 'Goodnight, Mrs Bach. Thanks for the delicious meal.'

If she wasn't so damned nervous, Nat would have laughed and asked how long he'd been there. But Wes's jaw was clenched, his cheeks sculpted and tight.

The door clicked shut. 'There's something I need to tell you,' he said.

His eyes held hers. Oh God this was serious. The breathless panic was immediate.

He's done it, she thought, he's come to confess. What will I do if he blurts it all out? It's too much responsibility. I don't want to hear.

'I was going to tell you last Saturday morning, after the party.'

Her mind speeding up, her heart started to slow. Saturday, Saturday morning? That was nearly two weeks ago. Before Andrea's visit, before the accident, before everything.

He was still speaking: 'But I chickened out. I was a coward.'

She stared at his face, his tight, steely features. What? What was this now? His gaze was still steady, his expression grim.

'Over the last year or so I've had an... affair, a relationship... God, those aren't the words... an understanding...'

Nat tried to say something, but her throat was constricted. What? Wes? An affair? No, that couldn't be right.

He spread his hands and continued. 'Affair isn't the word. That sounds sordid. A friendship. A mutual need...'

Dumbly, she stared. A fucking *mutual need*? What did that mean anyway? Then, her mind suddenly rallied. Of course. Emilia; bloody Emilia. A woman almost young enough to be his daughter. Oh God. When her voice finally emerged, it was cold and clipped. 'I see. This "mutual need", Wes. With whom?'

He tried to take her hand, but she stepped away. 'With whom, Wes?'

'Catherine.'

The shock robbed her of words. What? *Catherine*? Cool Catherine? Jack's bloody wife?

His eyes pleaded. 'I'm sorry, Nat. I've done this all wrong...' He took a shuddery breath. 'She... Catherine was with me on Friday. At the office flat. That's why I panicked. She was so fearful that Jack would find out... It was stupid, I should've thought things through, but when I found Andrea at the bottom of the stairs–'

The hurt was almost sickening, a hard blow in the centre of Nat's chest. Catherine. Of all the people in the world. Cool, icy Catherine.

Her shell-shocked mind eventually found a sentence. 'You slept with Catherine on Friday? We had a fall out, so you left me and fucked her?'

'No, we didn't sleep together. We didn't have sex–'

She found herself screaming then. 'What? Like *we* didn't have sex? No "funny stuff"? Just everything but?'

He reached for her arm. 'Listen, Nat, it's complicated, let me explain–'

'There's no need for explanations, Wes. I understand you completely.' Nat pushed him away, then shoved him again. 'Fuck off! Get out of my house. Fuck off. I never want to see you again.'

33

A BLOODY NIGHTMARE

'It's complicated, let me explain,' Wes had said. It had repeated in Nat's head like a mantra all through the long, sleepless hours and was still doing it now at breakfast.

Wild horses couldn't have stopped her from demanding he leave immediately last night, but as ever, the lack of information was far worse than the half tale she'd heard. By refusing to listen, she'd created her own bloody Chinese wall. Too agitated to rest, she shuffled around the house, examining what little information she knew from every angle.

Wes had had an affair with Catherine. If the words hadn't come from his lips she would never have believed it. They were so different in every way. She was ten years older than him for starters. And Jack was supposed to be the love of her life. He adored her, poor man. What the hell were they playing at? With fire, that was for sure. Jack wasn't just Catherine's husband, for God's sake; he was her and Wes's business partner. What a mess, what a complete mess.

Then there was the hurt; bitter, smarting pain which brought tears to Nat's eyes. He was supposed to love *her*, Natalie Bach, he'd all but said so many times. The news that he and Catherine had a relationship was shocking, but she'd have got a handle on it once the disappointment had dampened down. But he'd spent Friday night with the bloody woman in the flat. Wes had stood in the Cheadle rain for the best part of an hour just to talk to Nat, yet it had taken only a slight setback for him to turn tail and run back to his lover.

Finally there was Andrea. What was going on there? Wes had found her at the bottom of the stairs, he'd said. Well, she'd pretty much worked that out already. How Andrea had got there was the thing. And why did she tell the hospital she'd been pushed?

Oh God, what to do? Her eyelids were still gluey with exhaustion. She'd roused herself at seven and checked her mobile for messages. Nothing from Wes, but two texts had waited, sent from Joshim in the early hours: *Fuck off, whoever. Cut them out of your life!'* Then the second: *You haven't missed the boat, Nat. No way Jose!*

Now picking at her scrambled eggs, she smiled sadly at Joshim's thoughtfulness. If only the former was that easy. If only the latter was true. Her mum's judgemental eyes across the table didn't help. 'I'm not deaf,' they said. 'So I heard enough last night. Oh, Natalie, sometimes you are your own worst enemy. Knee-jerk's never the best way,' they added. In Polish, probably.

Nat threw back her coffee and sighed. 'Okay, I concede, Mum. You're probably right.'

'Am I?' Anna didn't seem surprised by Nat's first words all morning. 'A good thing, I hope,' she added with a small smile.

'Yes, annoyingly so.'

Her mum patted her mouth with a paper napkin. 'Well that's nice to hear, but I expect you're really talking to yourself. You're a good girl, Skarbie. Sometimes it's taken a day or two, but you've always done what's right.'

Pushing her plate away, Nat grimaced. Of course, 'taking a day or two' was a euphemism for ridiculous knee-jerking, then regretting it soon after. Perhaps telepathy was hereditary. But that didn't matter; she'd already decided. A meeting with Wes was the thing. Somewhere neutral. A café seemed the obvious place, but not a Nero or a Costa with the rest of humanity listening in.

Scooping up her phone, she thought for a moment before composing the message. The only independent café she could think of was a mile away in Gatley, one she had visited for a cream tea with her mum, their first outing after the stroke. They had sat opposite each other on leather sofas that sunny day, chatting, drinking tea and eating triangular sandwiches stuffed with tuna, cheese and ham, almost too full to manage the cherry scones and clotted cream. The other selection of cakes had come home in a hat-like box, and they'd been surprised to find they'd had enough appetite to scoff them straight away. But today she wouldn't be eating buns; she wouldn't be happy or relaxed. She needed the truth; although she didn't want to put herself through the trauma, she knew her mind wouldn't settle until she had it. She was sick of persistent guesswork, so she sent a text: *Meet me at the Roasted Coffee Lounge, 9.30.*

Inhaling sharply, Nat pushed open the café door. She didn't see Wes at first, but he was already there, his back to the large window, hunched up at a side table beside the book-lined wall.

Pulling out a chair, she glanced at him briefly, but the spat of hurt was still there, stuck fast in her chest, so she sat down and looked at her hands. 'Right. Tell me everything,' she said, her voice as hostile as she felt.

He took a deep breath to speak, but the waiter interrupted, so they ordered lattes and remained in silence until they were served. Then Wes dipped his face to meet hers. 'About–?'

The desire was to shout. It was knee-jerk, of course. Instead, she blew out and said the word calmly. 'Everything.'

Nodding, he picked up his teaspoon and absently stirred his drink. 'So, the... the thing with Catherine–' he started, then sighed. 'I should've told you sooner, Nat. I'm sorry I didn't. It was cowardly. I should've been–'

'Wes, just tell me.' Oh God. Did she really want to know? 'Just tell me the truth. All of it.'

He rubbed his face and was silent for a few moments. 'Okay. I needed...'

They both turned to a clattering sound at the door. A young, windswept woman was struggling to pull an old-fashioned Silver Cross pram over the step. 'I'll just...' Wes said, scraping back his chair to help carry it in. When he returned to his seat, he lowered his voice. 'I needed someone to talk to. I was lonely. I think she was too...' His eyes flickered towards Nat before looking away again. 'Something was missing from her life.'

'Like what?' Nat asked, though of course she knew the answer from Catherine's gin-induced confession all those weeks ago.

'She wished she'd had kids.'

'So what? You offered a donation?'

Wes sat back and frowned. 'No, not at all. Nothing like that.' He reached for Nat's hand, but she snatched it away. She didn't want to cry, she really didn't.

'Whatever. Go on.'

He continued to speak slowly, as though working it out. 'So, yeah, Catherine... I like and respect her, but it wasn't ever more than that. Not for her, either; she loves Jack, really loves him.' He paused. 'It wasn't an affair, really. We didn't meet that often. Just from time to time. At low points, I suppose.' As though thinking back, he squinted. 'It was like therapy, almost. Maybe some marriages don't allow room for friends. Mine certainly didn't.' He fell silent for a moment, rubbing the table. 'Then you came back to the office and she could see it before I did–'

'See what?'

He lifted his head and gazed intently. 'You, of course. The one that got away. She could see the pull, the attraction, even when I was fighting it.' He smiled faintly. 'Perhaps she was a bit irked at first – she "forgot" to pass on the message about Matty being ill to you – but she's not a bad person. She was fine when I said I wanted to end it. She understood.'

Absently watching the harassed mum scoop her wailing baby from the pram, Nat scanned the last few weeks in her head. 'When was this?'

Wes rubbed his forehead. 'I'm not sure; I knew I had to do it the moment you walked into her party. You looked stunning. The one woman I always wanted; the one who slipped through my fingers because…' His jaw tightened. 'Because I was a coward back at law school.'

Nat should've felt some pleasure at his comments, but she didn't; she was picturing Catherine and Wes when they arrived in the hospital corridor. 'You were with her when Jack had the heart attack, weren't you? That's why you arrived together at the cardiac unit.' She clenched her teeth. 'It was as plain as day, but being stupid as usual, I didn't register it. I was just pathetically pleased you were there; someone who seemed to care–'

'I did and I do. Very much.'

He frowned. 'Yes, you're right; Jack was away golfing; we met at the office flat on the Saturday night and I told her then. She was completely accepting; she'd seen it coming. We parted as–'

The pain of betrayal was there. 'Don't bother saying it. It seems you were still devoted *friends* on Friday. What was it, Wes? Didn't you get the shag you expected from me, so you arranged a rendezvous with Catherine for old time's sake?'

He stared, a flash of anger in his eyes. 'No, Nat, not at all. You asked for the truth and I'm giving it to you. Do you want me to tell you or not?'

His face was tight, and though she was being reprimanded, a fillip appeared from nowhere. His honesty, his honesty: she could *feel* it. Or perhaps it was just desire. 'Yes, I do. Go on,' she replied, hoping the tiny burst of pleasure wasn't showing in her face.

Wes took a breath. 'So, last Friday. I had checked with Catherine that the flat was free for us, but it was a surprise when she turned up. She said she was looking for you.'

That brought Nat back. 'For *me*?'

'Yes, she was wearing a dark suit, so I assumed she'd been to a business meeting, but she said she'd been in a bar for four hours.' He frowned. 'Catherine can drink, but this was ridiculous: she couldn't stand properly, she was rambling and ranting, asking where you were, saying that you'd tell Jack, that he would never forgive her if he found out. I tried to reassure her, saying that you didn't know about us, and that even if you did, you were discreet, but she wouldn't have it. She said he'd always had a hold on you, that you'd tell him to punish her.' He shook his head. 'It was shocking to be honest. She was virtually incoherent, not making any sense.' He spread his hands. 'That was it. She soon passed out. I slept on the blow up, checked her out from time to time, then left in the morning to collect Andrea.'

Aware of increasing chatter in the background, Nat leaned back in her seat. What the hell? She frowned, trying to process the information about Catherine's strange behaviour, but Wes's words floated back. Andrea.

'Why were you collecting Andrea?'

He massaged his temples. 'For an early start to Sheffield. The boys needed their Lacrosse kits. She'd done their washing, cooked them food, and bought stuff, the usual. I had said no to driving her in the week because I hoped I'd be with you, but–'

'But what?'

He sighed and met her eyes. 'After leaving you in the rain, I was angry, furious about what she'd said and done, especially those lies about us sleeping together and trying for another child. So I drove straight home and confronted her. I was horrible, and shouted like I'd never shouted before. I said some dreadful things, brutal home truths.' He snorted. 'Cruel honesty. But...'

The door opened again, bringing in a cold burst of air and laughter, but Nat didn't turn.

'But?'

Wes shook his head. 'I went too far. I brought in Matty and Dylan; I said she embarrassed them with her suffocating behaviour, said they'd been counting the days until they escaped to university. That they couldn't wait to get away. It was wrong of me; completely out of order and I immediately felt guilty. She's always been a good mum. All the weird stuff she's done to me, the underhand behaviour and manipulation – it's never spread to the boys. So I calmed down and apologised. I said we'd go to Sheffield together in the morning.'

Silent for a moment, Nat finally spoke. 'Then you left?'

'Yes. A neighbour was in his driveway packing up his car, so I nodded. He could probably verify the time, but in all likelihood...'

'He heard the argument, your shouting?'

Weary and tense, Wes nodded. 'It's a bloody nightmare. Shall we get another coffee? Are you hungry?'

There wasn't much more to tell. Wes had turned up to collect Andrea on Saturday morning as planned. He'd let himself in the front door, and there she was on the limestone hallway, wearing the same clothes she'd worn the night before, unconscious and with a pool of blood around her head. Frightened to move her and cause any further damage, he'd immediately called an ambulance. He'd tried to think and breathe as he'd waited for it to arrive, but panic had set in. He couldn't risk mentioning Catherine, so he'd stupidly called Nat.

Nat sipped her cappuccino, the caffeine and her mind working overtime. 'Why, Wes?' She stared at his face, needing that raw honesty back. 'Andrea was unconscious. Why did you assume you'd need an alibi?'

Wes covered his face with his hands. When he eventually removed them, he sighed. 'She'd told me she'd do it. It was just one of the things she'd threatened me with over the years. She said that if ever I left her, she'd throw herself down the stairs and say that I had pushed her.' He shook his head. 'I never, even for a moment, thought she'd actually do it.'

'Why this time?' she asked.

He smiled faintly. 'I told her about you.'

Nat shifted in her chair. 'You said she already knew. That she'd looked at your texts,' she said, looking down at her drink.

Taking her hand, Wes played with her fingers before speaking. 'She knew something was going on, but then I told her it was serious, that I was in love with you.' He corrected himself. 'That I was in love with you again, and that there was nothing she could do to stop it this time.' He exhaled and smiled wryly. 'But I was wrong, wasn't I? She could and she has. The thing is, I've never told anyone about her threats. No person in their right mind is going to believe me, are they?'

34

CONSEQUENCES

Her brain and body undoubtedly making up for lost sleep, Nat woke late on Friday morning. Shit, half past nine! Trying not to allow her feverish mind to crank up, she tumbled out of bed and into the bathroom, scrubbed her face and her teeth, wet a chunk of hair which was spiralling to one side, pulled on laddered tights and scrambled into a blouse tinted pink from mixing colours with her whites.

There was no sign of Anna, so she grabbed her handbag, slammed the door behind her and stepped to the Ka. The key fob didn't work and the driver's door protested when she tried to unlock it manually. Her mum's little car didn't like the cold and she didn't blame it. She had forgotten how the English weather could turn on a sixpence. Mallorca could rain, that was for sure, inundating the green hills without warning even in August, but there had never been this biting chill in the air.

Having finally settled in the driver's seat, she looked at the windscreen. Her side of the window was obscured by rivulets of frozen water. Typical. And today she'd forgotten her coat.

When she'd finally scraped off the ice with a credit card and persuaded the engine to co-operate, she said 'rabbits' out loud. It was the first of November. Rabbits for good luck, and boy did she need it.

~

The office was like a greenhouse compared to outside.

'Morning,' she muttered as she sidled past Sharon.

'Hiya,' she replied, giving her a curious look, but this time not asking where she'd been. Nat suspected she was fed up with evasive answers, and perhaps speculation was more fun. It had forced Sharon into rekindling her friendship with Emilia, so at least that was something.

Quickly opening Wes's diary, Nat was filled with relief. Nothing had been missed; no appointments or court hearings this morning, thank God. She could focus on catching up with his incoming post and do her best to help with the backlog.

Like the painting, it felt as though she'd become a permanent fixture in his office. Throughout the week, the bench boys had popped in and out as though it was the norm, updating her on files they were working on, complaining when one of them was given yet another mortgage repossession claim. The official line was a vague 'Wes is still in London. It's something to do with his trial.' If Max thought that was odd, he didn't say so. Perhaps he was too busy being loved up with his girlfriend. Nat would've been 'loved up' herself if the man in question hadn't had a mutual need with one of his business partners who was married to the other.

Oh yes, and who might have attempted to murder his wife.

Her emotions were still mixed, bubbling away like the three witches' cauldron. Toil and bloody trouble just about summed it up. Still, she was glad to have seen Wes yesterday, and relieved to have cleared the air as far as one could in the circumstances. He'd convinced her that nothing had happened with Catherine last Friday and, crazy though the idea was, she believed that Andrea had carried out her threat. The Cling-on was back in her rightful place in Nat's mind. The dreadful woman had always been manipulative, materialising like a phantom, and causing trouble in her almost imperceptible way.

Nat sighed. God knows why she had fallen for the sweet, vulnerable face. Andrea had used it back in Chester often enough. Causing unease so very gently. It was really a rare talent, but this time one that had consequences, potentially dire consequences, for Wes. Throwing oneself down the stairs was insane enough, but doing it to spite someone else was pure madness. Surely the woman would see sense when she was lucid again? Surely the Cling-on wouldn't put her sons through more turmoil?

She fired up Wes's desktop. He'd said that he loved her; he'd even told his wife. That was good, wasn't it? A glint of colour in the gloom? But Catherine of all people; why her? Nat knew it wasn't the worry at the top of Wes's agenda right now, but it was the one that bothered her the most. She kept telling her obstinate mind that it wasn't a betrayal, but it felt like it. When she'd stood to leave the café, Wes had caught her hand. 'What now for us?' he'd asked, his expression vulnerable and tense, but she shook her head; even if she'd had an answer to give, she couldn't voice it. She had needed to escape from him before she cried.

Sniffing back the emotion, she turned to a pile of folders on the floor. Sharon had helpfully attached outstanding correspondence to the relevant file. The top one was a letter addressed to Jack with a Post-it note affixed saying, 'pass to Natalie'. She looked at it briefly: the Battersby v Battersby divorce.

She shook her head. Danielle Foster. The usual goosebumps spreading, she pictured her sashaying down the hospital corridor the day of Jack's admission. That fake bloody smile. God, please say the divorce file wasn't coming her way again; however hard she tried, she never quite managed to escape the woman. But it didn't appear to be urgent, so she pushed it to one side. Picking up the next one, she stared at the memo, digging into her memory to see if she knew anything about transferring a licence for a pub. No, not really; just that it involved applications and sessions. And time limits, of course, the curse of all lawyers. Oh joy. She would have to swat up and do it pretty fast. Of course, she could just ask Wes. He wasn't dead; weirdly, it just felt that way.

The peal of the telephone interrupted her thoughts.

'Mr Savage for you,' the new girl on reception said.

'Here in person?'

'Er, no. He's on the line…' From her tone, she clearly suspected Nat had lost the plot, but with Gavin one never knew, and a few of his non-PC jokes would have lightened her spirits today.

'Guess what?' he opened the call.

'I've run out of guesses, Gav. It turns out that truth is stranger than fiction after all.'

'Chin up, girl, this one is looking good. It's our friend Julian Goldman. Using my undeniable charm I've got some inside info…'

There was the usual dramatic pause.

'Gavin! To the point. I'll give you a clap later.'

'Apparently a witness has come forward giving young Mr Goldman an alibi for the time in question. The file is still with the CPS, but a guy I know has given me the heads up.'

An alibi? That was a surprise. Bloody hell, it seemed her nous had been wrong about Julian. 'What? Who?'

'The clap, eh? Is that a promise?'

'Gavin…' She could hear excitement in his voice. Gavin Savage was having fun.

'I don't know yet, Natalie, but I'm going to find out.'

'And as soon as you know, you'll call me?'

'For you, the very moment. Speak later.'

~

'Later' was like a ball of wool. Its length and strength were uncertain, the same as everything else in Nat's life. By lunchtime she couldn't bear to be cooped up a moment longer. And she was starving. Not caring how absurd she looked, she swapped heels for trainers, then trotted past Sharon and through reception before anyone could stop her for a chat.

It felt odd to see WMD's empty pod. She had never got to the bottom of who'd promoted her to office manager, but in hindsight she realised how efficient Wendy had been at her job. The answer had to be Jack, surely, a finger in every bloody pastry, patty and pie. She hadn't spoken to him for a while, but her fingers and toes were crossed in the hope that Gavin would have good news 'later'; there was no doubt they all needed some.

A little more cheery at the prospect of food, she ran down the stairs and yanked open the door. The chill hit her immediately, and not just the weather. Catherine was at the entrance, digging for something from her huge Mulberry handbag. She stared at Nat when she finally lifted her head, her green eyes more frosty than the pavement outside.

'Hi,' Nat said. What else was there to say? They were hardly going to do a socialist fraternal kiss. This woman, this ex-friend, this wife of Jack's, had had an affair with the man she loved. And the last time they'd spoken she had made an unexpected verbal assault against her about Julian. What that was about, she still had no idea.

Catherine unhooked her coat collar; it was a beautiful camel cashmere that Nat couldn't help but covet. As though intending to say something, she opened her mouth before changing her mind. Instead she smiled a tight smile, brushed past Nat and walked to the stairs.

Something naughty but nice had been the plan before leaving the office, chocolate preferably, but even that didn't appeal as Nat walked listlessly around the local Co-op. Bumping into Catherine had taken away her appetite. She was just too blinking perfect, clever and detached, always in control. Yet Nat had liked her so much when she'd first joined Goldman Law. Perhaps being a newbie was why; it was the first time she'd met her and there were no preconceptions. Catherine was just another solicitor a few years older than her who seemed to be fun. She had been a laugh too, hadn't she? They'd been close friends, really tight at one time. Stopping in the dairy aisle, Nat strained to remember. The images were all there like a photo album, but the past seemed uncertain, her memory unreliable.

Leaving the shop empty handed, Nat crossed the road and headed for the park. A walk and fresh air was the thing. Assisted by the breeze sweeping through her thin jacket, her hot agitation died down, leaving her contemplative. About Julian, about Wes, about bloody everything. Nothing seemed to add up.

'Seems, Madam? Nay it is. I know not seems,' she said out loud to a bemused passer-by and her ambling black and white cocker spaniel.

A replica of an owl carved into a tree stump stopped Nat at the gates. She traced the grooves with her fingers. It reminded her of Jose. He was artistic in a multitude of ways; he could paint, play the piano, compose music and pen poems. She used to watch him in awe as a pencil drawing came to life. She smiled inwardly; it was a pleasant memory, the most pleasant she'd had of him in nearly five months. Perhaps in a strange way Joshim Khan's 'fuck off' method of dealing with her grief was working.

She continued to stroll, kicking the damp leaves and wishing she could wrap herself in Catherine's soft coat. It took a few moments to twig that the vibration from her handbag was her mobile and not the wind. All fingers and thumbs, she searched for her phone and squinted at the screen: Gavin, at last.

'Bloody hell, Nat. Guess who?' he asked, his voice unusually high-pitched.

'Gavin...'

'She's given Julian a firm alibi for that Thursday night. She says that he and Aisha visited. And listen to this: she has security cameras at the farm. There's partial CCTV footage of Julian petting a Labrador. It's only a slim time frame, but it's spot on for the data on the lorry driver's tachograph. So, go on, have a guess.'

A farm, security cameras and a dog. Nat pictured her livid face and felt a shiver. It seemed the woman was the topic of all conversations these days. 'Catherine? You're joking.'

'Nope, I'm not. A reputable solicitor with incontrovertible evidence. That was the reason why a Lexus was picked up on ANPR in the area. Yours truly pulled out the old charisma and persuaded them to drop the charges forthwith. What do you say to that, eh? Nice piece of work, though I say so myself.'

Too busy mulling, she didn't reply. Then Gavin spoke again, voicing her thoughts. 'The only thing that puzzles me is why she didn't come forward sooner.'

'Exactly,' Nat replied, trying to remember Catherine's precise words when she stormed into her office last week. It was the bloody Chinese walls Jack had insisted on, of course. Even from his wife. 'She probably didn't know anything about it until Julian was charged...' she said slowly. But why hadn't Catherine told Jack about Julian's visit? If she'd told him, he would've known that his son had an alibi, and the whole dreadful mess would have been avoided. Did he know even now?

She went back to yesterday's chat in the café. What did Wes say about Catherine's excessive drinking on the Friday? She'd feared Nat would tell Jack. Tell him what? Was it just about her affair, or something else as well?

No longer feeling the cold, Nat came back to the phone call. Gavin was still talking. '...and other news: she's had the baby. It's a boy.'

'Who?' It took a moment to adjust. Who might have had a baby? God, Aisha of course. How relieved she must be.

'The girlfriend, a day or so ago. A caesarian section, apparently, so she's still in hospital.'

'Wow, Gav, that's fantastic. Good news all round. Thanks for letting me know.' Then, after a beat, 'Well done. A very nice piece of work.'

Almost tripping on a twig, Nat kicked it to one side. She didn't quite know why – perhaps it was the mention of a newborn, but Danielle Foster and her divorce suddenly popped in her head. 'Gavin, before you go, can you put Chantelle on? I want to ask her a favour. Don't worry, it's just girls' stuff; you're not missing out.'

35

A FAMILY FRIEND

Processing the information Gavin had imparted, Nat retraced her steps along the frosty path. Not everything made sense, but one thing was for sure: she needed to tell Jack the glad tidings. Not just the dropped charges against Julian, but the news he was a grandfather. Rather than phone him, she fancied doing it in person. It was sentimental perhaps, but she wanted the pleasure of seeing the relief and the smile on his face. Catherine was safely at the office, so now was the time.

Her stomach had recovered and was aching with hunger, so she dashed to Gregg's to buy a sandwich, then headed straight to the car, parked behind the office. It was another perk of Wes's absence, but she wasn't going to think about him right now. Her 'rabbits' had worked; today was a good one after all.

She munched her cheese butty as she drove down Princess Parkway. It was tastier than it looked. Or perhaps she was just temporarily joyful, delighted for Jack. Her grin make her cheeks ache. Who'd have believed it, Jack Goldman was a grandfather! She felt happy for Julian and Aisha too. They must be thrilled: the investigation dropped and a brand-new baby boy. Feeling the warm spread of a whim, she glanced at the dashboard clock. Gavin had mentioned that Aisha was still in hospital. It wasn't much of a diversion, so she'd drive there first.

~

Macclesfield town centre was crawling with lunchtime shoppers, but Nat found a pay-and-display car park next to Tesco and someone kindly gave her a ticket, thus saving her a pound. Heading for Marks & Spencer, she browsed the kids' clothes, trying to work out whether the modern mother still chose blue for a boy and what size would be suitable for the average newborn. Not that it really mattered; as her mum always said when the spinster pyjamas arrived each birthday from her brother, 'Don't worry, love, M&S is always good for an exchange.'

Her high spirits ebbed as she approached the Birth Centre. She'd been there before, hiding a sense of loss behind her smile each time she'd greeted a friend's new baby. She wasn't entirely sure why she was visiting today, given her last communication with Aisha had been false and embarrassing, but still, she was pleased the young woman's traumas were over, not just the Julian saga, but the inevitable worries surrounding childbirth.

Nat paused at the unit's intercom. How to introduce herself? She wasn't a pal, but in a strange way she wanted to be, sort of spreading the affection she couldn't help having for Jack. The description 'family friend' got her through to a ward with pale orange walls. Taking a breath at the entrance, her gaze swept across four beds. Four women, four babies; how lucky they were. As though sensing she was there, Aisha turned.

Searching for her maiden aunt smile, Nat held the carton of chocolates and a gift box aloft. 'A peace offering as well as congratulations,' she said. She caught sight of what looked like a doll in the cot by the bed. Though not usually a person to gush over newborns, she couldn't help it. 'Oh, Aisha, he's perfect,' she declared. She fleetingly thought about the Cling-on's visit and her 'we're going to try for another', but she brushed it aside. 'Just gorgeous. He's so tiny.'

The flash of pride on Aisha's face was immediate. 'Thanks. He's been shuffling so I think he's due for a feed. You can hold him if you like.'

Nat took a step back. 'Thanks, but no thanks; I make babies cry. I'm not staying long. I just wanted to say that I'm glad all the bad things are over.'

Aisha nodded, but didn't meet her eyes.

Both gazing at the boy, they fell silent for several seconds. Then Nat took a deep breath. Of course she knew why she'd come: she was trying to fix things as usual. It was worth a try, surely?

She watched the new mum deftly lift her little one from the cot. 'I know it's none of my business...' she started. 'But if you have any sway over Julian, it'd be great if he gave his dad some slack. He doesn't always show it, but Jack's heart's in the right place.'

Aisha coolly met her eyes. 'Of course I have sway, which is why that isn't going to happen.' She lifted her chin sharply. 'And as you say, it's none of your business.'

Shocked at the open hostility, Nat nodded. 'Okay, fair enough.'

She stayed for a moment longer. It had been a mistake coming; she should've learned long ago to butt out of people's lives. There were other things she wanted to say, such as, 'Julian obviously has a problem with money; he needs to get help,' and 'Jack's still Julian's father; suppose the next heart attack is fatal?' but she'd already said too much. 'Send my love to Julian,' she said instead. 'He'll be a great dad.'

She'd almost reached the ward door when Aisha called her back. 'Look,' she said, her face still steely. 'I know it's not your fault, but that man refused his own son a loan, let alone actually giving him any money when it mattered. Julian begged because I made him; I forced him to come clean about his problems; I made him humiliate himself. And for what? For nothing.' She turned back to her child. 'Goodbye, Natalie. Thank you for the gifts.'

BLOOD MONEY

S till winded and shaky, Nat drove along the winding country
roads towards Mobberley. The sensation of disorientation
was back. Was it her imagination or did Aisha really say those
things about Jack? It was unbelievable, surely?

Nat hadn't spoken to Jack since Julian's arrest. He'd texted
occasionally, asking what she was up to and when she would
visit; she'd composed answers, but deleted them. Why was that?
Because she hadn't wanted to tell him either the truth or a lie, she
supposed. Just like with her dad. In the end she'd sent a message,
saying, *I'll come and see you when I have something good to say.*

Today was that day, surely? She'd forget about the hospital
encounter for now; she didn't want the brilliant news to be
tarnished by what Aisha had alleged.

Her thoughts splintered, she gazed at the passing countryside. White tips of frost still clung to the hills. Cling-on, bloody
Cling-on. Had she come round yet? Had she put her husband
and boys out of their misery? And how about Catherine? Had
she clung on too, begging Wes not to break up with her? Nat
doubted it; as evidenced this morning, it wasn't her style. Still,
from what he'd said, the façade had cracked big time on Friday

night. With fear, it seemed. Fear of what? Jack's disapproval? His anger? Of course she'd fret about him finding out about the affair, but was her real anxiety something which cut much deeper?

As though reading Nat's mind, her mobile pinged a message. Pulling up, she held her breath, but it wasn't from any of her current mental contenders. It was a message from Gavin's secretary with the attachment she had asked for. Efficient Chantelle. She'd look at that later.

Instructed by 'Maps', Nat eventually turned off the B road, heading down a thin lane which cut through a huge field of brown corn rows. She pulled up the car halfway down. She had reached her destination, apparently. Glancing around, she saw nothing but dry stone walls, meadows and a sprawling farmstead in the distance. Maybe today wasn't the day after all. But, as she drove on, the main barn of the farm became palatial. Surrounded by high brickwork, its entrance was gated.

Nat stopped and stared. So this was where the Goldmans lived. Wondering if she should call Jack to open up, she looked at her mobile, but seconds later the barriers smoothly opened. Oh right. Presumably there was a security camera indoors, a button of approval he had pressed to let her in. Like the footage Catherine had given the police. Only that was of Julian petting a dog. On cue, two Labradors bounded towards her, coming to a halt at Jack's order. Their obedience was impressive, but Nat still preferred cats; she liked the way they suited themselves, feigning love to be petted and fed rather than jumping about clumsily, trying to please, behaving only at their master's command. A dog was too much like her.

Already regretting her foolish haste, she climbed from the car. Jack didn't look angry, but he didn't seem pleased to see her either. Or surprised, now she thought of it.

'Natalie,' he said. 'Come on in.'

Taking in the grand glass-fronted building, she followed Jack.

The dogs scooting ahead, he led her into an equally glassy kitchen with a huge central island.

'Sit,' he said. Without asking what she wanted to drink, he spooned fresh coffee into an old-fashioned cafetière, even though a gleaming Nespresso machine was set next to the oven.

Nat perched on a bar stool, inhaled the heady smell of roasted java beans, and surveyed the open-plan room. A spiral staircase separated the glossy kitchen units at one side and a sofa suite the other. Against the dark wooden floor, the white leather looked particularly spectacular, but not homely at all. She snorted to herself. It was Catherine all over.

Hearing Jack sigh, she turned, studying his drawn features as she waited for him to speak. He looked tired and distracted; he was unusually quiet.

'My one proper coffee of the day,' he commented as he poured from the jug. Then he focused on her, his hair looking greyer than she remembered. 'So, you have something *good* to say?'

She blew her drink and sipped. Jack was wearing his poker face; it was impossible to judge what he knew and what he didn't. About Catherine, Wes, Julian. WMD's baby, the mill man, the Battersbys. About bloody anything. Still, she was pleased to be the deliverer of great news for once. She had wanted to add an invitation to see his new grandson, but Aisha had put the kibosh on that.

'The charges against Julian have been dropped.' She cocked her head and grinned. 'Will that do?'

His reaction was unexpected. Though he gazed steadily at her face, it was as though his body was rebelling. Like an electric shock, his relief was visible, running through to his fingers which trembled around his mug.

He nodded several times. 'Thank God. He came out of his coma.' He took a tremulous breath. 'The... the victim came out of his coma and said it had nothing to do with my son.'

Needing to break his strange stare, Nat looked at her cup and watched the swirls of cream disappear. It was too strong to drink; the sip she'd taken was glued to her throat. What was Jack on about? She wasn't sure what to say; she'd heard nothing about Lee Malloy regaining consciousness. She thought of correcting him, but wasn't sure if he'd been making a statement or asking a question, so she said nothing, eventually changing the subject.

'How's the pill popping going?' she asked, trying for a chirpy tone.

Jack jerked, his gaze clearing. 'Pill popping? Oh, yes. Six a day.' He seemed to rally and smiled thinly. 'When I move, I sound like a box of Smarties. The beta blockers are interesting, though. They give a strange sense of calm.'

She laughed. 'You're always calm, Jack.'

He took off his glasses and polished them. 'Am I?' he asked, before replacing them and looking at her with cloudy eyes. 'Am I really?'

Feeling a jolt of panic at his tone, she touched his arm lightly. 'Are you okay, Jack?'

He put his hand over hers and patted it. 'When I came round in the ambulance, you were there and I will always thank you for that, Natalie. But I was frightened. No, petrified. I thought I was dying. It brought everything into sharp focus. Nothing mattered more than my life here, Catherine and my children. I would have signed the Devil's contract to live; I would have agreed to any terms.' He picked up a jar of tablets and shook them. His expression was soulful, reflective. 'I pretty much did. But it helped me to focus and make decisions. By the time I was wired up in that hospital bed, everything was crystal clear. Things needed to be done. I wasn't going to die. I was still here, still strong, still determined to win. No one was to know about it; I wouldn't let them see any weakness.'

'And now?' she asked.

'Back to crippling fear. Back to valuing the things I love. Or at least trying to.'

She studied his crumpled face. Without the poker, it looked old. He already knew about the baby, she was sure. 'You know Aisha's had the baby?' she asked.

He nodded, a shadow of hurt passing through his face. 'It's a boy. Verity told me.'

Nat willed away the tears pricking her eyes. She'd never seen him look so sad and wistful, almost vulnerable. Wanting to help, she took a deep breath, but she was saved from blathering by the telephone.

Jack took the call so she left the kitchen to search out the toilet, then sat on the state-of-the-art loo, trying to think things through. Jack's mournful mood and his comment about Coma Man. That was the crux, definitely the nub. Picking up her mobile, she searched for the loan document Chantelle had scanned through, then spent a few moments reading it. 'Ha! DFL Financial Services Limited. As I thought,' she said to the apparently tap-less sink.

Hmm. The pieces of the jigsaw were finally slotting into place. She texted Gavin: *Have you heard anything about Lee Malloy coming out of his coma?*

He replied immediately. *No, why? Do you want me to find out?*

No, it's fine, thanks. Speak soon.

She washed her hands absently. She didn't need Gavin to ask about Coma Man's condition. Whether or not he had come out of it was irrelevant. The point was that Jack had assumed it. The reality had been dancing on the periphery of her mind since she'd sat in Gavin's chair and read the second loan document.

Gazing at her pink reflection, she nodded. Yes, the complete picture was there: the terse exchange between Jack and Julian at the mini-mediation when she'd left them alone; the smug faces of Danielle and Frank Foster when she'd bumped into them at the hospital; Jack's apparent lack of interest in the police interviews with Julian since then.

She returned to the kitchen and watched her mentor from a

distance for a while. Sitting on a low sofa, he was staring through the wall of glass to the paddock outside. What was he contriving now? Did she admire him, or was she just bloody frustrated? She flopped on the adjacent chair which turned out to be far warmer and comfortable than she'd supposed.

When he finally turned to her, she spoke. 'You knew all along, didn't you, Jack?' The leather cushions pulled her in like a softly clawed hand. There was no point resisting, so she stretched out her legs. 'Julian confessed to the crime when we met at his house on that rainy day, didn't he? When Aisha and I left the room, he told you what had happened – that he owed money, that he'd met the debt collector and knocked him down with the car. Or something like that.'

Opening the scanned document, she lobbed it into his lap. 'DFL Financial Services Limited, the second loan of fifty grand,' she said. 'The idiots who were prepared to take a second charge when there was no equity. That's what we assumed.' She lifted her eyebrows. 'But they aren't really idiots, are they, Jack? Far from it. They're bloody gangsters. They take the charge to look legitimate, but when the debtor defaults on the extortionate monthly payments, they don't instruct you or me. They enforce by ordering heavyweights like Lee Malloy to collect.' She rocked her head towards him. 'No doubt they carefully choose who to lend to. Reckless sons with rich fathers, for example. How am I doing so far?'

Jack lifted his hands, but he was smiling faintly; his protégé was doing well.

Nat pointed to her mobile. 'I knew the name of the loan company rang a bell, but I couldn't place it. Then finally I twigged this morning. When a twig nearly broke my neck, ironically. DFL Financial Services Limited – Danielle, Frank and Lewis Foster. I saw it in those bloody Battersby divorce documents you made me review.' She took a breath. 'Reading between the lines, the building society threatened to repossess Julian's home, so he went in desperation to his old school mate, Lewis Foster, the debt management guy who appears so very reputable in his swanky offices in Wilmslow.' She looked at Jack pointedly. 'But he's just as much a member of the Levenshulme Mafia as his mother and uncle. Am I right or am I right?'

He nodded, so she continued thoughtfully. 'Let me guess. You paid it off? You paid off the loan and interest, and a hefty sum to keep the mafia quiet? Then more money for the victim, the man in the coma?'

Jack cleared his throat. 'I had to do something for my son. Something.' He looked at his hands. 'Perhaps I'm to blame; perhaps I should've tried harder with his mother, but he was always...' He seemed to search for the word. 'Weak. Needy, I suppose. He couldn't have faced a prison sentence, Natalie. It would've killed him. And he had a baby on the way, my grandson, an opportunity for him to do better as a father than I did.' He sighed. 'It took a bloody heart attack for me to see it clearly, and I needed to do something quickly in case I... So I instigated a business transaction from my hospital bed.' He smiled wryly. 'Blood money. For the henchman when he woke; for his family if he didn't.'

Nat nodded. 'To say it wasn't Julian, I suppose. To stymie the police investigation, and point them in another direction?'

Jack's face abruptly darkened. 'It was an investigation which should never have got off the ground.' He rubbed the arm of the sofa. 'I crossed swords with a cop long ago. His son was the arresting officer.'

That threw her. 'Crossed swords?'

'It was bad blood, a long story. I'll tell you one day.'

She leaned back against the soft leather. 'Bloody hell, Jack, how much have you paid?'

He shrugged. 'It took a while to negotiate the final figures, but it's only money.' Then he grinned. 'Though I have you to thank for being able to negotiate a large discount.'

'*Me*? What did I do?'

'Frank's knocking shop visit. Naturally he didn't want Lady Tamara hearing about it.'

The 'massage parlour' opposite the office. Nat pictured Frank Foster scuttling away. Yes, red-faced, he'd definitely been worried. She laughed. 'So it really is a brothel?'

Jack chuckled too. 'I guess it must be,' he replied.

37

CRUNCHING IDEAS

Lifting her hand as a final goodbye, Nat drove through the gates lost in thought. It seemed she didn't need a winter coat after all; she'd been hot with agitation of one sort or another since leaving Didsbury Park.

Good God, it was a murky world out there: business deals with smiling villains that were just plain wrong. Perverting the course of justice, in fact. But it was difficult to work out who was the victim in this case. The thug who'd been run over, the weak man who'd fallen prey to loan sharks, or the stubborn dad who'd had to face death before realising he'd been a rubbish father.

She had very much been in the latter camp until two minutes ago. She'd been halfway out of the glass barn when Jack called her back. 'You may as well take this since you're here,' he'd said, handing her a large letter. 'It'll save me from paying for a postage stamp.'

She'd looked at the envelope. 'It's addressed to you, Jack.'

He'd shrugged. 'Take it. It's bedtime reading. When you're in the mood.'

It was now burning a hole on the passenger's seat. A letter to

Jack, postmarked Mallorca. What the hell? Mallorca? 'When you're in the mood,' he'd said, the poker once more in his face. Bloody hell. She'd never be 'in the mood' for whatever was in the envelope, and she most certainly didn't have time for it right now.

Lifting the letter by her fingertips as though it was contaminated, she tossed it on the back seat. Bloody Jack Goldman. She'd think about that later.

Instead of driving towards Manchester, Nat sped through the stark countryside, her mind still crunching ideas about Julian, trying to add it all up. Jack had assumed the charges against his son were dropped because Lee Malloy had woken from his coma and duly pointed the finger at someone else, as per the 'business transaction'. He clearly didn't know about Catherine's visit to the police and the alibi she'd given. Why hadn't she told him? There was obviously something she didn't want Jack to know about. What was it? She'd mull on that later too; right now there was something more pressing, a thing she hoped she could actually fix.

She indicated right eventually, her little car protesting as she entered the maternity car park for a second time in one day. She didn't bother with a ticket this time; she'd tell the ward sister she'd left something from the earlier visit. What she had to say wouldn't take long.

Both Aisha and the baby were dozing when she arrived in the ward. Wondering whether to pay for parking after all, Nat sat on the bedside chair, gazed at the seven pounds of perfect child and waited for Aisha's eyes to open. When they did, they showed surprise followed by something else. It was fear, Nat decided, and so it should be.

'Hi, Aisha. I'm back, I'm afraid. And I've been thinking,' she began with a thin smile. 'I've been thinking what a lovely grandfather Jack will be, and how delighted he'll be when you call later and ask him and Catherine to visit. Tomorrow, maybe. And every week when you're back home, of course, so they'll be part of this little boy's life as they should be...'

A flash of defiance passed through Aisha's face. 'Why would I do that?'

Nat lowered her voice. 'Because you owe them both big time. I'm sure you must know that Jack has paid a huge sum of money to... how should I put it? To pay off Julian's debt. But that's because he thinks his son committed a terrible crime. He believes Julian ran over the "loan enforcer", for want of a better expression. The man who's still in a coma, as far as I know. That's what Julian told him when I tried the ridiculous mini-mediation at your house. That he'd driven the Lexus to the lay-by and done the dirty deed.' She cocked her head. 'But he didn't, did he? Jack didn't know his son was lying to protect someone. He didn't know the criminal was you.'

Aisha opened her mouth, but Nat held up a finger, her voice almost a hiss. 'Don't deny it, Aisha. Catherine has security footage showing Julian was at her place when the "accident" happened. The police aren't stupid; they'll have checked it was genuine before dropping the charges. He can't have been in two places at once, can he? And who is the one person in the world he'd want to protect? You, his lovely Aisha. But unfortunately for you, Julian has an alibi from the security camera. Date, time and all that. You don't.'

Nat paused for a moment, letting the information sink through Aisha's shrewd gaze. 'But... but, and this is the thing. You have a friend in Catherine. For whatever reason, she's told the police that you were there too, that you were at her home with Julian that night.' She glanced at the baby stirring in his cot. 'I think friends like that are worth keeping, don't you?'

Aisha didn't reply. Instead she lifted the child and rocked him until he settled. Then she turned to Nat, her eyes burning with hostility. 'Don't look at me in that judgemental way; you have absolutely no idea of what we've been through.'

Nat folded her arms. 'Then tell me.'

~

For the second time that day, a driver gave Nat his paid parking ticket. He left his partner holding her newborn and jogged over.

'How long are you going to be?' he asked as he handed it to her. 'Only thirty minutes left, but it's yours if you want it.'

Quite frankly she didn't know how long or what for. But that was pretty much par for the course these days. And it was worrying how she'd become a car park charity case. Perhaps it was Anna's meek car. Or perhaps she looked knackered. The deranged hair and hole in her tights probably didn't help.

'Cheers,' she called after him, watching as he loaded his new bundle of treasure in the car.

Breathing out a flash of envy, she wearily headed for the day room to meet Aisha. Her limbs felt heavy, her head even more so. Highs and lows. And too much blinking information. She wasn't just a solicitor of the Senior Courts of England and Wales, but a maiden aunt, confidant and bloody counsellor rolled into one.

Catching Aisha's tight expression, she knew there was more to come. A coffee from the vending machine was already waiting on the table. Cold probably. Still, it had to be an improvement on Jack's.

Aisha launched in before she had time to test it. 'You don't understand. You don't know how hard it's been. You have no idea,' she fired.

Nat nodded. The punchbag as usual. But in fairness to this angry young woman, she didn't have any idea, not really. 'Fair enough…'

Though the room was empty, Aisha kept her voice low. 'Julian was already in a financial mess when I met him. Of course I didn't know then.' She smiled thinly. 'He made me love him first. And once I started to love him, I couldn't just stop.'

Nat returned the same smile. She understood that; it made perfect sense.

Aisha stirred her coffee. 'It was gambling. I tried to persuade him to get help, but he didn't want to. It was too embarrassing for him. So I controlled his spending as best I could, but each time we got on top of it, he'd get pulled in again by the two Hooray Henrys he works with; the casino or the races, baiting him in the nicest possible way by calling him a "dominated wimp" when he tried to resist.' She looked at Nat pointedly, the dissent still there. 'Which, of course, he had been all his childhood. He tried to live up to Jack Goldman's standards and was knocked down brutally when he couldn't.'

Looking at the baby in his mobile cot, she sighed. 'Anyway. I'd met Lewis Foster a few times. I thought he was creepy, to be honest, too touchy-feely, but he was a friend of Julian's from school and ran a debt management company. He specialised in finances, so we hoped he'd be the answer to all our problems – well, at least stave off the house repossession. So that was that. I left Julian and Lewis to sort everything out. The next thing I knew was a knock at the door one morning and it was...' She put a hand to her chest and flushed deeply. 'It was a man called Lee who said he'd been instructed to collect interest payments in cash. Thinking he was some loony, I got rid of him that day, but when Julian contacted Lewis, he said the loan was out of his hands; he'd done his best to get the advance in difficult circumstances; it was how these people worked. The guy had to be paid.'

Thinking she should say something, Nat took a breath, but Aisha was leaning forward, her eyes hard and shiny like jet. 'That's when I persuaded Julian to approach his father, to confess everything, to humiliate himself. To save face, he did it through Catherine, grovelling and baring his soul about everything, but the answer was a flat no, the man refused to give him a penny, not even a temporary loan.' Almost spitting the words, she continued, her voice sizzling. 'A man with his heart in the right place? I don't think so. Do you?'

Nat sipped her coffee without replying. It tasted disgusting, but she hadn't consumed anything since devouring the Gregg's butty and that was a lifetime ago. Aisha was standing, so she guessed that was as much as she was willing to share, but she abruptly turned back. 'Remember the black eye and the bruising?' she said, pointing to her face. 'Do you know how that felt?'

She gazed at Aisha's smooth, glowing skin. God, yes, she'd almost forgotten about that. It was the reason the police had got involved in the first place. Did Julian lose it when he'd found out what she'd done? And what *had* she done exactly? From Aisha's tight, angry face, it seemed doubtful she'd spill the beans, but as Nat waited she sensed some uncertainty pass through the woman's petite frame. 'Tell me what happened, Aisha. I promise I'll be the sole of discretion.'

Aisha sat down again. 'The loan enforcer came back, of course, several times. He wanted whatever cash I had in my purse and asked what I could sell; who I could borrow from. He said he'd return. I was pregnant for God's sake! That's what really got me. I loathed him. You can't imagine how much.' She took a breath. 'So that Thursday was a deadline. We hadn't even met the interest payments, so the whole loan had to be repaid. I didn't tell Julian as he couldn't cope. He was already sick with worry, physically puking every morning, so instead I told him I needed the car to meet a friend. I persuaded him to try his dad again by turning up in person and begging if necessary. He agreed, so I dropped him en route.'

Though she lowered her voice, her chin lifted. 'Instead of a friend I met Lee Molloy in a lay-by. I wasn't sure how, but I wanted him gone. When he saw the money wasn't there, he belted me hard across my face, telling me there'd be more where that came from, so that made my decision plain sailing...' She peered at Nat and shook her head. 'The impact threw me to the ground, Natalie. My baby could've been hurt.' Then she shrugged. 'He made it easy. The grinning fool stood and watched me struggle to get up and hobble to the car. Then he lit a cigarette. He got what he deserved.' She glanced at her sleeping child. 'Do you know what I really hope? I hope he dies.'

38

NOTHING UNTOWARD

Like a light switched off, it was inky outside the hospital. Nat drove home on autopilot, more exhausted than she'd felt for weeks. Emotion, she supposed, it had always been more tiring than exercise. Finally parking the little car outside her equally little house, she felt a surge of affection for them both. Inanimate objects, of course, but infinitely more reliable than human beings right now.

She opened the front door, glanced in the kitchen, then called up the stairs. 'Mum? Are you home?'

No sign of Anna, so she put the burning envelope face down on the sideboard, then flopped on the sofa and closed her eyes, hoping to drift without thought for a while. After five minutes she sat up and sighed. Who was she kidding? She'd managed to suspend speculation for the thirteen miles home, but that was only because she'd been afraid of napping at the wheel and running over a sheep or a goat. Or perhaps a debt collector who 'deserved it'. Bloody hell, that was a story. She'd never really seen Aisha's steeliness before today, though she had been drawn to something the first time she'd met her. Vulnerability, she'd assumed, but of course it was courage mixed with fear.

Appearing from nowhere, Poppy cat jumped on her lap. Nat absently stroked her and pictured Aisha's face. She was no longer sure if she liked her, but she certainly admired her. There had been no need for her to say that she loathed Lee Malloy. Like a lioness protecting her young, the naked hatred was etched on her classical features. She'd set out to stop him that night. Bloody hell, an action with intent; she must never ever mention that to the police. Not that she would have to. Between them, Catherine and Jack had wrapped everything up nicely, the huge Chinese wall between them firmly in place. Oh God, she hoped so. If one of them moved even slightly, the wall would wobble and teeter, crash down, in fact. And who'd be beneath the rubble? Natalie Bach, but of course.

Poppy heard her stomach rumble before she did, politely jumping off and looking at her inquisitively with glowing round eyes, so Nat stood and ambled to the kitchen, rewarding her with a sprinkle of dry food. Opening the fridge with a sigh, she tried for inspiration. Home before her mum, she should prepare something for a change, but she was struggling to concentrate. The image of Aisha's lifted chin was still haunting her. *'He got what he deserved. I hope he dies.'*

Not an iota of remorse; bloody hell.

Whether she applauded or disapproved of Aisha's actions, she couldn't quite decide. A midwife had appeared, asking her to return to the ward for a check-up, so the story had more or less stopped there. Remembering Jack's stony expression and his mention of 'bad blood', Nat had quickly asked how the police became involved, but it was as before: Aisha's dad had turned up by a quirk of fate, seen the bruise and called them.

Piecing together what she knew, Nat had stayed sitting in the dayroom for a few minutes. She guessed that Aisha had collected Julian from Catherine's as planned and confessed to the crime. Presumably he'd dropped her back home and immediately taken the Lexus to the garage to wash off any evidence.

Would Jack tell her his long 'bad blood' story one day? Who knew? He was a law unto himself. And what about his son? Being falsely accused of being a wife-beater by Aisha's dad and having to accept a caution must have been challenging, then worse was to come. Perhaps he wasn't so weak after all. There was definitely something commendable about protecting his love and their unborn baby. Nat liked that. Would they have got away with it had Aisha's father not arrived by chance? But even then, the police might not have taken it further than the ticked boxes of a caution and a report to social services had it not been for crossed swords and bad blood. Clearly destiny or misfortune had played its part.

Nat sighed. The whole episode felt like a game of consequences, connected but random, and out of anyone's control.

The fridge's soft hum brought her back to dinner. With an effort she focused. Eggs, gammon and cheese. A quiche was the obvious choice; she could make one without pastry like the Spanish tortilla Jose had often rustled up.

A bloody Mallorca postmark. She grimaced and shook her head. Flaming Jack Goldman. The envelope was waiting, but she was too hungry and tired think about that now. Joshim Khan's 'fuck off' therapy had been working a treat, but as only Jack Goldman could, he'd put a spanner in the works.

She wanted to stamp her feet like a child, but instead she tried to concentrate on food. She snipped the glossy ham, grated more cheese than was healthy and cracked open six eggs. Then she beat everything together. Hmm, that just made an omelette. A potato. Yup, a spud was the thing, sliced thinly so it wasn't too heavy. She started to peel one, but the agitation was too much. Giving a howl of frustration, she picked up her mobile and called Jack.

'Natalie. I'm glad you've called.' He sounded in good spirits. 'I've been thinking...'

Bloody thinking. That was all she needed.

'About what?'

273

'Don't worry. Something nice.'

That threw her. 'What?'

'That car you were driving–'

'Yes.'

'It's Anna's, isn't it?'

'Yes…'

'Right. Have a browse at the weekend. The C-Class would suit you. They do a lovely metallic mink–'

'Jack. That sounds amazing, but please stop.' She took a deep breath. 'The envelope you gave me. What's in it?'

Glad of the distraction, she heard the scrape of her mum's key in the door.

'Hi, Mum. Do you fancy quiche for supper?' she called from the kitchen. 'It's nearly cooked now.'

Anna appeared, her button nose resembling a raspberry. 'It's gone really chilly out there. There was no heating on the bus; you'd think in November they'd turn it on.'

'God I'm sorry. You should be driving your own car. I've added so many miles too.' Through the fug, Nat remembered Jack's offer. 'Actually, Jack has offered me a company Mercedes, which would be perfect.'

'But?' her mum asked, removing her coat.

Surprised, she frowned for a moment. Anna was actually spot on; there was a 'but', but what was it?

'Oh I don't know. I'm not sure if I'll stay at Goldman Law. The last two months have been great for getting my teeth sharpened again, but it might be better to move on.'

Bloody hell, where had that notion come from? It was a sudden light-bulb moment, but probably a good one; she'd mocked Gavin about his 'baggage', but all the impedimenta in her life came from Goldman Law.

Her expression pensive, her mum was sitting down. Nat tried for a smile. 'Have you always read my mind, or is this telepathy a recent thing?'

'Leaving Goldman Law,' she replied. 'I suppose that might be a good thing. Where would you go?'

'Manchester again, maybe?' She kissed her mum's cheek. 'Somewhere around here, so don't worry. I'm not buggering off abroad again. Ever. Well, not for good anyway.'

Busying herself at the oven, Nat removed the flan and tested it with a skewer. 'Cooked to perfection,' she mumbled. Then she added a handful of cherry tomatoes to a bowl of rocket leaves and searched for the olive oil. She could still feel the heat of her mum's questioning gaze.

Eventually she turned. 'Okay, Mum. You win.'

Placing the food on the table, she sighed. She'd gone through the motions of making dinner, but after speaking to Jack, her appetite had clean gone. She looked at her mum. Though waiting patiently with folded hands, her pale eyes were anxious.

'At some point soon I'd better fly out to Mallorca.' Her mum nodded politely, but her cheeks flushed. 'Don't worry, it's only for a flying visit and it won't be at Christmas.' She squeezed her hand. 'Not at Christmas, Mum. I'll be here for Philip and the kids, I promise. But at some point I will need to go.'

She inhaled deeply. With so many other things going on, she hadn't had time to process the information, but she launched off anyway. 'I've just discovered Jack Goldman took it upon himself to instruct an enquiry agent in Mallorca. God knows why. It probably cost him an arm and a leg.' A surge of heat swept through her body. 'Apparently the guy has prepared a report which runs to fifty pages. I've no idea where the documents came from, and they had to be translated.' She glanced at the envelope, still on the sideboard. 'Anyway, I haven't read it; I just couldn't bring myself to…'

Heavy tears suddenly filled her eyes, so she couldn't go on.

Hers welling too, her mum knelt by her chair, wrapping her in steady arms and rocking. When Nat finally pulled away, she gave a dry smile. 'I don't know why I'm crying really. It isn't all bad. It's what I wanted; it gives me a reason. Finally, a reason for, well, everything, I suppose.'

They wiped their faces with kitchen roll and Nat blew her nose before trying again. 'Jack gave me the report this afternoon. It's in that packet with the Mallorca postmark... Anyway, I thought I'd just ignore it, but... Well you know me. So I called him and asked him what was in it. Apart from all the appendices, there isn't a lot to say, apparently.' She took her mum's hand. '"Havana" is still thriving, but it's being run by Hugo. The accounts show everything's as it should be; he's taking his salary and paying for casual labour as usual. There's nothing untoward at all. When asked in conversation what had become of the English owners, Hugo explained that the Señora was away looking after her sick mother in England and that the Señor had been unwell himself. That's as much as he was prepared to divulge, bless him, but one of the documents shows that a Jose Harrow was admitted to the Clínica Capistrano in Palma not long after I left.' She swallowed and nodded. 'Mum, it's a psychiatric clinic.'

39

GOING FOR THE BIG ONE

It was Monday morning and Nat was at the bathroom sink, remembering how painful her neck had been the day after Jack's crash. Cleaning her teeth had been almost impossible, let alone brushing her hair. But Gavin had been right: moving it and using it had helped the healing process.

She smiled at her perky reflection. It turned out that, for all his faults, Gavin Savage was pretty astute. She really liked him too; it was a shame she didn't fancy him. Even though he had a great physique, his girder-like stomach included, she couldn't imagine getting intimate without guffawing. Wes Hughes, however, was another story. Though not as tall or as broad as his pal, he was still around six foot, lightly muscled and toned from playing football and running. Then there was his sculpted face and stunning smile, not to mention his moves…

Berating herself for thinking about him in those terms, Nat looked away from her pink reflection and shook her head. He was in a bad place and here she was contemplating, well, sex. Sexual equality was all very well, but she had to be fair; if she was in trouble, she'd be more than just miffed if he was picturing her naked. She just missed him; that was all. She missed his voice, his laughter, the ease of his company, being held and hugged… Over the weekend she'd tried to block out the longing by imagining him with Cool Catherine, but the resolution of the Julian saga had made her see things differently. Life wasn't straightforward; people were complicated: they needed to be kinder to each other, more tolerant, more forgiving. Or maybe she'd just got used to the idea. Catherine was undoubtedly attractive; Wes clearly had great taste, and whatever had gone on between them occurred before she'd returned to Goldman Law. Or at least Wes had stopped it not long after. That's what he'd said and she believed him. She was also convinced about the Cling-on. That woman was bloody nuts, there was no doubt. But surely not so vindictive that she'd see her allegations through?

Nat splashed her face with icy water, walked to her bedroom and yanked open the wardrobe. New week, new resolutions. Maybe a jacket and skirt that matched; perhaps tights without a ladder, a blouse that was actually white. Maybe she'd even stretch to some make-up.

Alerting her to a missed call, her mobile bleeped. She scooped it up and peered at the screen. Talk of one of the devils. It was Gavin. She called him straight back.

'Of course they do it on purpose,' he immediately started.

'Who do?'

'The police. Early in the morning, just to piss everyone off.'

Her stomach clenched. She'd tempted fate with her lustful thoughts and positivity. Though she knew what he'd say, she mouthed a quick prayer.

'And…?'

'Wes has been charged. They took a formal statement from Andrea over the weekend.' He took a breath. 'Are you sitting down?'

Oh fuck. She sat down. 'Why?'

'She's brought you into it. In a nutshell, she says Wes came to the house that Friday, uncontrollably livid. She says he confessed to having an affair with you. She was devastated and asked him to end it. They argued on the landing. He said he wished she was dead, then he put what he'd said into action by pushing her down the stairs.'

Oh God. It all sounded so plausible. 'And what does Wes say?' she asked.

Gavin paused for a moment. 'That everything is true. Except the pushing, of course.' He sighed. 'It doesn't look good, Nat. The neighbour heard the row coming from an upstairs window. He and Andrea had been chatting earlier, so he remembered the clothes she'd been wearing that day. There are fingerprints in all the right places. The way she fell and her injuries are consistent with falling backwards and landing with some force.'

'Of course there'll be fingerprints; it's his bloody house,' Nat retorted. It was the only lame thing she could think of to say.

'I know. Look, Nat, I'm his friend as well as his brief. No stone will be left unturned. I'm just telling you the worst.'

'And that is?'

'They are going for the big one. The arrest was on the grounds of attempted murder.'

Nat turned the page of the document, glad she was busy to stop the churn of her thoughts. Or reduce them, at least. The files she had acquired over the past few weeks were bubbling at the same time as Wes's, but in fairness Emilia and the bench boys were there; everyone pulling their weight and some more to help out. She hadn't said anything to anyone, but it was clear from Sharon's pallid face that the news about Wes had seeped out. Unusually, she didn't ask questions or gossip. Instead she kept her head down, bashing the keys of her word processor as though it was an old-fashioned typewriter.

Trying to work out the various columns and charging rates

applied, Nat peered again at a claimant's bill of costs. Anything remotely mathematical had always made her eyes glaze from sheer boredom, and in the old days she'd sent such cases to a cost's draftsman, but Wes seemed to do it himself, so she felt duty bound to give it a go.

She tapped her nails on the desk. Frustrated bloody worry! One way to overcome sexual longing, she supposed. Where was Wes now? What was he doing? He'd been given police bail, so that was something. But a charge of attempted murder. It was logical, she supposed, but she'd hoped it would be a lesser one of assault. Then there was herself, the 'Scarlet Woman'. Fearing she'd make things worse, she'd held back from her natural instinct to text or call him. God, she hoped he didn't think her unconcerned. But the charge was incredibly grave. Would the police be monitoring their communications? Would they contact her and ask for a statement? What should she say if they did? She had a whole host of questions for Gavin, but, as he'd put it earlier this morning, 'Perish the thought of me sounding heartless, Nat, but I do have other clients.' They had agreed to meet later. She was saving her queries for then.

40

PRICKLES OF ALARM

Nat felt her buttocks tighten. The usual waft of Chanel had preceded Catherine's entrance. Trying to appear nonchalant, she glanced up. 'Afternoon.'

Her boss looked as pristine as usual, her hair freshly highlighted and her make-up perfect, but her expression was blank so it was difficult to judge her mood. Still, thus far at least she wasn't clutching the client chair with white knuckles and hissing like a demented cat, so that was something.

Catherine gazed for a moment, then placed a tabloid on the desk. 'It seems you get everywhere,' she said, sliding it across until it was under Nat's nose.

Oh God. What had she done now? Her pulse accelerating, Nat cast her eyes at the print. Just when she thought the day couldn't get any worse. What would it be? A 'Scarlet Woman' headline, or a photo of her and Wes in flagrante delicto, perhaps? But when she let out her trapped breath and focused, the newspaper wasn't local as she'd expected. It was the London *Evening Standard* with the usual front page news about commuters' frustration.

Catherine pulled out a chair and sat down. 'Page five,' she said.

Suddenly irritated at her game, Nat pushed the paper back. 'So, what does page five say?'

'Well, it's a follow-on from last week's article.'

Nat sighed. 'Funnily enough, I've been too busy to read any newspapers of late, let alone the whole gamut available in the UK.' She sat back and folded her arms. Where on earth was this conversation going? 'Go on, Catherine, the suspense is killing me. What did last week's article say?'

'A City financier was in court, pleading not guilty to an allegation of outraging public decency,' she started. She paused, then tapped the newspaper with an elegant finger. 'But what outraged him was that the woman he'd been with couldn't be named. She said she'd been sexually assaulted by him and therefore could claim anonymity...'

'Ah.' Nat had almost forgotten about Victoria. Her advice over strong tea and cake felt like years ago. Still unable to work out Catherine's state of mind, she tensed. 'I did wonder what had happened. I didn't like to ask. So what–'

'But the interesting thing about last week's article was the debate,' Catherine interrupted.

'The debate?' Nat asked. Prickles of alarm danced on her skin. A debate? What the hell...?

'The argument about anonymity. Why the victim is granted it automatically, whereas the alleged perpetrator isn't. The City big gun was furious; he said it was a false allegation and that he would personally see to it that the ruling was overturned. The woman had already admitted to the offence and accepted a police caution, so allowing her to effectively hide was unreasonable...'

Nat dropped her head in her hands. Shit. She could see where this was going, but Catherine told her anyway: 'He wanted to name and shame her, making a tiny headline, if at all, into something much bigger. Causing far more stress to the victim and her family than if she'd just taken it on the chin, which, as it happens, had been her gut reaction before *someone* had persuaded her otherwise.'

Listening to the thrash of her own heartbeat, Nat stayed in the cocoon of her arms, only lifting her burning face when Catherine spoke again. 'But what is interesting...' She had stood up and was pacing, reminding Nat that she used to lecture part-time at university. This was exactly the mental picture Nat had of her those days. Glamorous and incisive, the students either drooling or lapping up every word. '...is the moot point. On the face of it, it does seem unfair. It's usually a woman making accusations against a man; why can't a man have anonymity until after the trial, the same as a woman?'

Her cheeks marginally cooling, Nat sat back and listened, unsure if the question was rhetorical or if she was supposed to reply. There was a break and lifted eyebrows, so she gathered it was the latter. 'To encourage more victims to come forward?' she asked hesitantly, regressing twenty years.

'Correct.' Catherine gestured to the newspaper. 'Do peruse.'

Turning the pages sheepishly, Nat reminded herself not to be so challenging until she knew the facts next time. If there was ever to be a next time. Oh God. She had interfered again and this one had really gone south.

Taking a sharp breath, she obediently read the opening line aloud to the class. 'A married City financier who denied sexually assaulting a woman is facing more charges. A further four victims have stepped forward...' She snapped her head up to Catherine, the relief pumping out like steam. 'Bloody hell.'

'All four are professional women in a similar situation to my little sister. She finally confessed everything at Mum's on Saturday.' Catherine nodded, her expression severe. 'You did the right thing, Nat, absolutely. If you hadn't prodded her to think it through and take a stand, that revolting slug would've carried on regardless. Men like him need to be stopped.' She mildly snorted. 'Victoria wants to say thank you in person, but she needed to tackle me first. Charming. I think this warrants a celebratory drink, don't you?'

~

Like a scene on repeat, Nat sunk into the leather sofa at the café below. How life had changed since their last tête-à-tête.

Catherine looked to the bar. 'I would order champagne, but it's gin and tonic time, don't you think?'

'Absolutely,' Nat replied.

Four o'clock on a Monday afternoon was perhaps a touch early, but keeping the boss company gave her an excuse to send Wes's file to the costs draftsman after all. She watched Catherine stride to the counter and chat with the waitress for a while. Then she returned with a tray, two glasses and the mixers. Bloody hell; this establishment was either very generous with their measures, or the spirits were triples.

Flopping down next to Nat, Catherine took a swig of her drink. 'Poor Victoria. She must have been shitting herself for weeks.'

Propelled back to her friend of old, Nat laughed. 'That's true. I guess we've all got ourselves into scrapes over the years, but perhaps not ending up with a sleepover in the police cells.' Like Wes, she thought, the moment it was out. But Catherine was still speaking.

'Yes, she was so relieved and pleased to hear about the other women coming forward. She hadn't lost the plot after all. Mum was high as a kite too. Both of them were like giddy teenagers.' She snorted mildly. 'Mother's favourite daughter, don't you know.' She sighed. 'It seems it was yet another case of "don't tell Catherine".' Smiling tightly, she turned to Nat. 'Am I really so unapproachable?'

Nat sipped her gin. Flipping heck, it was strong. 'Not unapproachable,' she said, sensing Catherine's dejection and wanting to be honest. 'More unreadable. People don't know what's going on inside your head.'

Catherine studied the huge diamond on her slim wedding finger. 'My mask, you mean? If I didn't have one, everyone would see me blubbering and that wouldn't do.'

Nat opened her mouth to protest, but closed it again. Who knew what went on behind anyone's façade. It was a long time ago, but she'd seen Catherine's inconsolable tears herself, never more so than before the abortion. 'I think of you as a cat,' she said instead, trying to lighten the mood. 'And I like cats very much. Whereas I'm a stupid dog, sniffing around and blundering, pissing on everything I shouldn't...'

'But loveable.' Catherine lifted her head and smiled wryly. 'Are we going to talk about the elephant in the room?'

Glad of the warming alcohol which had spread to her head, Nat shifted in her seat. 'Which elephant?' she asked.

'I was going to say Wesley. But you're right, there are others.' Catherine finished her drink and gestured to the waitress. 'Others I'm better not thinking about. They don't make me feel very good about myself.'

The waitress appeared then, taking some time to remove the mixer bottles and wipe the patches of condensation from the table. 'Same again, ladies?' she asked.

Catherine looked at Nat for an answer. Though it was sensible to stick to tonic, Nat was eager to hear the rest of the story, so she nodded.

'So...' Putting her fingers together like a prayer, Catherine tapped her lips. 'Julian came to me twice, begging for cash. He told me he'd got into debt, that he'd squandered all the money Jack had given him over the years, including the hefty down payment on the house. He asked his mother too, but he'd already wiped her out; she had no more to give. So I promised to approach Jack.'

'But you didn't.'

Catherine nodded. 'Julian was quite pathetic. He said he had a gambling addiction he was trying to overcome. I know I should've found some sympathy or understanding, but there was nothing there but disgust. He'd spent all his childhood being spoilt and indulged; he treated me like shit off a shoe. But it wasn't just that. It was his attitude towards Jack. As far as he was concerned, his father was nothing but a pay cheque. He had no appreciation or love for him; there were never any birthday cards, and barely an acknowledgement at Christmas. We didn't know about the girlfriend, let alone the pregnancy.' She looked out of the window. 'A new baby in the family would have been good for us both; if we'd known, it would've been different.' Straightening her spine, she reverted to Nat. 'Julian hurt Jack terribly in all sorts of ways. So, I said no. I told him that Jack had refused.'

Nat turned her glass. 'You couldn't have known what would happen.'

'Perhaps not. But on the second visit he told me he had a girl-friend and that she'd been threatened. I didn't believe him. Or maybe I just didn't have time to hear it through. He just turned up out of the blue on foot. Jack was away and I had… well, I had other plans.' Her face coloured lightly and she took her new drink from the waitress. 'I didn't know about the pregnancy or the arrest until they charged Julian.' She glanced at Nat. 'Well, you know that. It was a horrendous shock. Jack has barely spoken about the whole affair, but when he does, he reprimands himself for being a failure as a person, and particularly as a father. What's the point of life if his only son couldn't approach him when he needed him most? he says. He can take most things on the chin, but this has knocked him badly.'

Leaning towards Catherine, Nat lowered her voice. 'For what it's worth, my lips are sealed. I won't tell anyone about anything I shouldn't. And it seems to me that you've more than made up for it by saying Aisha turned up with Julian that night.' Remembering her conversation with Gavin about the consequences of giving a false alibi, she paused. God, she hoped Aisha understood Catherine's generosity; that the message she'd conveyed to her at the hospital had fully hit home. 'How was your weekend?' she asked casually, sitting back.

Catherine smiled. 'When I got back from Mum's on Saturday, Jack was at the door, thrilled to tell me his news. Julian had brought the baby for half an hour between feeds. Then Aisha telephoned and invited us for Sunday lunch next weekend, though of course I said they should come to us and I'll do the cooking.' She peered at Nat. 'It was very welcome, but completely out of the blue. Funny that, isn't it?'

Gavin's noisy arrival after an hour-and-a-half was a relief. Nat had turned down the last two rounds, but Catherine had shown no sign of moving and instead of cheering her up, the gin seemed to be having the opposite effect.

Nat introduced him. 'This is Gavin Savage.' She wondered whether to say he was Wes's lawyer, but settled on describing him as her friend, which she realised, with a rush of pleasure, was absolutely true.

Catherine stood and held out her hand. 'How do you do. Catherine Hetherington,' she said with a professional smile. Nat had to admire her. Although her voice was a little slurred, the mask was back in place, the moroseness apparently all gone. She offered Gavin the sofa and moved to a chair, chatting pleasantly for ten minutes about their mutual benefits of having an office out of town, before saying she had better get home to her hungry dogs.

'In a taxi, I hope,' Gavin muttered as she left. 'One Goldman Law partner is enough on my plate just for now.' He looked at Nat. 'Are you pissed too? It's only six o'clock.'

'Only a little.' She laughed. 'The need for alcohol is just one of the many downsides of working for Goldman Law.'

'Then maybe you should quit.'

Remembering the reason he was here, Nat laughed unsteadily. 'Maybe I should, but not yet. I'm nursing Wes's files. How is he? Where is he? Is there anything I can do?' She stopped her questions and looked at Gavin's face. 'You need a proper pint, right? Shall we decamp to The Crown?'

Stretching his arms over the back of the sofa, Gavin seemed to think about it for a moment. 'No, this is nice. I am a man amenable to change.'

'Hark you!' Nat smiled. 'You'll be having a gin and tonic next.'

'Steady, woman. Though I am partial to a latte…'

'Latte coming up…' Putting her fist to her mouth, she sniggered just loud enough for him to hear. 'Big girl's blouse…'

Over coffee they settled down to brainstorm about Wes, talking it through from every angle, what had happened so far and what was likely to come next. Gavin finished his drink and looked at her thoughtfully. 'He's at his brother's house in the sticks. It's a nice place. Have you been?'

Remembering that one perfect day, Nat rubbed the grooves in the table. 'Yeah. My dream home…'

They were silent for a while. 'How about the boys?' she eventually asked.

'They're back at university, trying to get on with their lives.'

'God, how awful for them. How have they taken it?'

'Dylan is supporting his father, but Matty is torn. He's always been close to his mum.'

Nat swallowed back a sudden need to cry. 'Yeah. Wes said he was a sickly child, so it's understandable.'

Gavin turned to the cushions supporting his back, looking a little unsure as he adjusted them. 'That's true. I'd forgotten, but Heather mentioned it last night.'

Glad of the change of subject, Nat smirked. 'As in Heather your ex, who hides when you visit?'

Gavin's skin went a dark rusty pink. 'She's just naturally interested, as you would be if–'

'Oh God, sorry, Gav, I'd forgotten,' Nat said, cupping her mouth. 'Of course. They are friends. It had genuinely slipped my mind. Does that make things difficult for you?'

'Funnily enough, they're not any more. They haven't been for a while.' He grinned. 'And for once it isn't my fault.'

'What do you mean?'

He stretched again. 'Quelle surprise; Andrea didn't like me. She was always causing trouble between us. Saying one thing to me, another to Heather, and slowly prizing us apart.'

Nat raised her eyebrows. 'And she succeeded.'

He snorted. 'She's one wilful woman, but I don't think Andrea can take full credit for all my deficiencies.'

Both lost in contemplation, they didn't speak for a while.

'Has Wes told you about what she said in the past?' Nat finally asked. 'Threatening to throw herself down the stairs. That's more than wilful, Gav. It's insane.'

He scratched his head. 'He has, and I agree. But using it as a defence is too weak. No one has heard her say this; Wes didn't tell anyone else. There's no evidence, not even hearsay.' He looked at Nat steadily. 'I think Andrea is nuts; I've always thought so. I have no doubt that she's sitting in that hospital bed, smiling her crazy socks off. But the thing is, how do I prove it?'

41

A TENUOUS NOTION

I nhaling the dank evening air, Nat traipsed towards home. It was Thursday already, and it had been another full-on day at Goldman Law. Weary and despondent, she'd almost nodded off on the bus, but the sight of Anna trying to manoeuvre the car cheered her up. Inching up and down the kerb, she was taking care not to exceed the boundaries of the house. Mrs Bach didn't like to upset the neighbours; she didn't like to offend anyone. Her mum was a passive peacemaker.

Ignoring the rain which suddenly sprang from the sky, Nat rushed to help with the bags. 'I'll get the shopping, you go on in,' she called.

Only just through the door and still in her wet coat, she knew from her mum's expression that the question was coming.

'Thanks, love. This weather is dreadful, but I suppose November always is.' Then, feigning a sudden-thought-face, 'Oh, and have you made any plans about Mallorca yet? Have you decided when you're going?'

It was the same flipping enquiry she made every three hours. Or so it felt. Nat was too distracted by Wes's current trauma and the amount of work she had piled up in the office to think about Jose, so Anna seemed to be doing it for her.

'Soon, Mum. There are things I need to sort out here first. And anyway, Jose has Issa and his parents.'

Her mum shook the drizzle off her hat. 'Issa; that's a name I haven't heard for some time. I remember her, though, a nice girl. Younger than Jose, I think? I liked his father too, but his mother was a strange woman.'

Nat unbuttoned her coat. It was not exactly pure cashmere like Catherine's, but a pre-Mallorca smart one she'd forgotten about. She'd suddenly remembered it was hidden under piles of old anoraks and hoodies in the cupboard beneath the stairs, an expensive purchase she'd made before her ridiculous decision to leave everything behind and bolt to Mallorca. Madness, pure madness. She had no idea who that person was any more.

She came back to her mum's comment. Jose's mother; now that was someone she hadn't thought of for yonks. Picturing her detached, rigid stance, she sighed. 'I agree, Mum, she wasn't the most affectionate of souls. But Jose isn't my responsibility any more. Not really.'

Her mum's face was tense. 'He would be if I hadn't been ill. If you hadn't come back here for me. If you were there now, he might still be well…'

So there it was: guilt. Everything seemed to end up there. Bending down to stroke the cat, Nat tried to summon up sensations of culpability. Bloody hell, that was good. Nothing there; at least not blame. The need to visit her ex felt more like duty, duty that could wait. Like Catherine and Julian, the expected pity wasn't there. Jose was ill: she should feel sympathy, even nostalgic love, but she just felt annoyed. Schizophrenia was extremely serious, she knew that, but she couldn't help concluding he'd partially brought it on himself. How many times had she nagged about his drug use over the years?

'It may only be cannabis, but it can bring on psychosis,' she'd remark when he was stupid enough to smoke it in her presence, or turn up with its distinctive earthy smell on his clothes. 'Don't take my word for it, Jose. Read for yourself. The internet, newspapers, books. It's all there in black and white.'

Of course he wouldn't have it. 'It's only weed,' he'd say, 'it's harmless.' And to prove his point he eventually made a cannabis cake without her knowing, watching her eat every last crumb. Later, when she'd finally come down from her study of the sky, her wondrous description of every shade of blue and shape of fluffy clouds, he'd delighted in telling her what he'd done.

'Oh, come on, Nat, I thought you'd see the funny side,' he'd said.

But she hadn't; she'd been furious at his deception. Like a restraining order, she'd banned him from smoking, swallowing or popping within five hundred metres of her, and he'd seemed to sheepishly comply. God knows what he took behind her back or during the weeks he worked away. But that was before Mallorca. It was the one thing she had insisted on before her mad moment: a drug-free clean sheet.

She finally came back to Anna's comment. Illness or not, she looked fab these days. Save for a nick in her smile, her features had evened up and there was winter pink in her cheeks. 'Who knows what might have happened if I'd stayed, Mum. Jose's situation is no one's fault and most definitely not yours, okay?' Wanting to change the subject, she nodded at the shopping bags. 'How was your afternoon at the shops? Don't tell me. More Christmas tree presents for Lila and Ben?'

The worry cleared. 'Just a few bits and bobs. But I must show you this. You know how Lila likes to dress up...'

Nat absently watched Anna search through her purchases, then lift a shimmery *Little Mermaid* outfit she would've given her right arm for at eight, but her mind soon dragged her back. Bloody Mallorca. What with everything else going on, ruminating about it was something she could do without. But now she was on that track there'd be no peace until she'd poked it to death. God, she wished she didn't have this compulsion to gather loose ends and tie them together until everything was neatly sewn up.

Sighing, she sat down and continued the mental embroidery. So, Jose had been sectioned after she left. If he had been smoking again or using other drugs there, she had been blind to it. Or maybe he'd been routinely adding weed to his Spanish tortillas and that's why she'd been so chilled. She and the hundreds of other customers who'd eaten it; one expensive way to keep the punters happy.

Her mum touched her shoulder. The pensive frown had returned and she was asking a question. What about? Rubbish flaming daughter. 'Sorry, Mum, I was miles away. What were you saying?'

She lifted an advent calendar. 'Is this too old-fashioned?' she asked.

Flipping heck; a blast from her childhood, or what? Joseph, Mary and baby Jesus, duly surrounded by an ass and a lamb. And if Nat wasn't mistaken, gold, frankincense and myrrh too. Not a Santa, let alone a chocolate, in sight. The poor grandkids wouldn't know which planet they were on. 'Not at all,' she replied, trying to stifle her smile. 'It's family tradition and traditions are good…' Anna was lifting her eyebrows; she had to try harder. 'If I had children it would be the first thing I'd insist on. Honestly, Mum, it's lovely. How about a nice cup of tea?'

The bubbling laughter dying down, Nat stood at the sink and filled the kettle. Her own kids, a sobering notion. Why she'd raised the prospect, she didn't know. But it brought her back to Wes and his twins. What sort of Christmas would they have? Dylan, Wes and traditional turkey in one house; Matty, Andrea and nut roast in the other? That was supposing he pleaded not guilty, of course. Gavin had called to say there was a plea and case management hearing in December. A guilty plea would mean Christmas dinner in prison, not just this year but for many.

Eating the other half of yesterday's chicken casserole, they chatted intermittently at the dinner table, her mum's gaze on the pile of cheap trinkets she'd bought from the Polish convenience store, Nat's mind still buzzing like one of Mr DeMille's sewing machines.

Food consumed and cleared away, the whir continued as she dried the dishes with an ineffective new tea towel. Her kitchen was too small for a dishwasher, but she enjoyed the empty time methodically washing and drying the pots, wiping the work surfaces and sweeping the floor while Anna pretended to watch the evening news, but really had a nap.

Opening a tall cupboard, she pulled out a brush, but a sudden hunch struck. No, it couldn't be, could it? Ridiculous, surely? A tenuous idea, it was true, but still... Could she find out if it was at all feasible? She peered at her watch. It was seven in the evening, but not that late. She should probably call Gavin first, but her suggestion might be ludicrous, the guy might not be there. And Gavin had seemed pretty downhearted when they'd spoken this morning. Rather than giving him false hope; she'd make the phone call herself.

Waking after precisely thirty minutes as usual, Anna's eyes focused. 'What's wrong, Natalie?' she immediately asked.

Nat felt the heat rush to her cheeks. 'Nothing,' she replied.

Flipping heck, would she ever be able to hide anything from her mum? And what would Anna think if she knew what her grim speculation was? During the half hour interlude, Nat had done some fevered research on the internet and her wild theory was actually a possibility, but she was no expert, not by a long shot.

Trying to keep her delirium under wraps, she scooped up the remote and flicked channels. 'You nearly missed the start of Corrie, Mum. We can't have that.' She glanced at her mobile, willing it to ring. 'And if I get a call halfway through the programme, don't worry; I'll take it in the kitchen.'

42

A GREAT TEAM

Nat had no idea how she'd managed to drop off last night. The promised callback hadn't come, so she'd turned off her mobile at midnight, needing closure until morning. She had briefly contemplated how resolution hadn't arrived in most aspects of her life, from Chester Law College to Mallorca, from her dad's death to Goldman Law, when the wall of sleep hit. It didn't lift until her mum woke her up with a cup of tea and a croissant at eight.

She arrived at the office on time, kept busy, beavering away methodically at Wes's desk, her head in the files. The buzz of conversation from the bench boys wafted into the room with Sharon from time to time, but she didn't join in their Friday high spirits. Concentrating on work blocked out the anxiety and anger, the excitement and alarm, that were desperate to burst out.

Turning to the final page of a schedule of special damages, Nat sighed and sat back. It was a statement of financial losses for a personal injury claim she'd been studying for an hour. Poor claimant. He was only twenty-four and his total past losses alone came to over three hundred thousand pounds. Travel expenses and loss of earnings; damaged motorbike, helmet, boots and leather jacket; the cost of adapting his home for wheelchair access, the shower, the doors, the paths, the loos – even the plug sockets. She thumped the table with frustration and annoyance. It was just one of many tragic claims in Wes's filing cabinets, and there was bloody Andrea Hughes, taking up a national health bed, wasting all that medical expertise, expense and time. Even worse, she was damaging the well-being of her children, just for her own sweet revenge.

When her mobile finally buzzed, her heart clattered. Dizzy with nerves, she quickly answered, but the call was short and to the point.

'I've glanced at your email,' the guy began. 'I think you might have something here,' he finished. 'I'm only just in, but I'll be in touch with Mr Savage soon.'

A breath later she phoned Gavin. Her mouth was still dry, so she swallowed. 'I have to see you!'

'Whoah. The woman can't keep away. Is it my mind or my body today?'

'Both. Can I come now?'

He laughed. 'Said the actress to the bishop. Okay, if you insist. I'll put on my speedos.'

Nat indicated right and tapped the steering wheel. Of course, every traffic light had been on red. And who had thought it sensible to build a John Lewis near such a tiny roundabout? She glanced at the clock. Twenty minutes to drive three miles! She could have blinking walked. Time wasn't particularly of the essence today, but the knot in her stomach made it feel so.

Finally overtaking the dozy drivers on Finney Lane, she pulled up outside Savage Solicitors and killed the engine.

Ignoring the dodgy-looking crowd outside the bookies, she pressed the buzzer and burst into reception.

She nodded to the charisma-free boy. Though she had no idea why, Gavin called him 'my office ned'. And Chantelle looked different, somehow. But Nat couldn't focus on either right now. She needed to confess to the big man before he got a call first.

'It's fine, he's expecting me,' she said, hurrying past them.

Taking a deep breath at his door, she knocked and pushed it open. 'Hi, I just…' she started.

He lifted his huge palm. Clearly mid-call, he was jotting notes on a heart-shaped Post-it pad, so Nat walked to the window, pulled the dusty blind to one side and absently watched the passers-by. Through the smeared glass they looked distorted. What was going on in their lives right now? If someone had asked her, she wouldn't know where to start. 'Distorted' seemed to cover it, though.

'Result.'

She turned.

Gavin's clenched fist was raised. 'It's a bloody good result, Nat.'

'Oh yeah?'

He couldn't hide his inane grin. 'Hell, I love my job some-times.' Slotting his pencil behind one ear, he sat back and swung in his chair. 'So, Ms Bach, I'm intrigued. Apart from my undoubted animal magnetism, Scottish blood and stunning six pack, why did you need me?'

'Well,' she began. She didn't even reach for the usual joke about cans of beer; the adrenaline had worn off and reality was kicking in. She'd told a white lie. Well, an actual lie. She had to clear that up first. 'The thing is…'

'Spit it out, Bach. Better out than in.'

'Well, firstly I should explain I've… I've been slightly disingen-uous…' She searched for a reaction, but his expression was amused, still smirking from his 'result', whatever that was.

Hoping it looked sufficiently apologetic, she scrunched up her face. 'I'm sorry but I pretended I was your assistant, Miss Brush.'

'Miss Brush. Any relation to Basil?'

'No, it was the first thing that came to mind when I made the call. I didn't want to give my real name, just in case.'

'"Scarlet Woman"?'

'Precisely.' She paused, loving the way Gavin's mind was always in tune and to the point. Telepathic, almost. A quip asking if he was related to her mother fought to burst out, but sudden anxiety set in. Bloody anger too. Now wasn't the time for humour.

She made her way to the client chair and flopped down. 'If I'm right, this is no laughing matter, Gav. In fact it's appalling, dreadful.' She took a shuddery breath. 'You need to prove Andrea Hughes is sufficiently unhinged to hurl herself down a staircase backwards, don't you? Well... I think she is crazy, that she's been insane since the first time Wes tried to leave her. This is going to sound bonkers too, so please bear with me.' She cleared her throat. 'I think Andrea has been intermittently poisoning Matty since he was a little boy.'

Gavin removed the pencil and sat forward with a frown. 'Okay...'

Almost too winded to speak, Nat ploughed on. 'With salt, probably.' Then stopping to let out a long breath of trapped air. 'Wes mentioned a hospital doctor who took a special interest in Matty a few weeks ago. You know, when he had the seizure, playing sport? This doctor took blood and urine samples. Dr Wesley, he's called. I remembered his name for obvious reasons.' She knew she was gabbling, but Gavin's keen gaze seemed to be following so far. 'So I, also known as Miss Brush, contacted him. I said I was your assistant, you being Wes's solicitor and having that authority...'

She paused for a moment. 'Strictly speaking, as Matty is eighteen, the doc should've asked for permission from him, but we can worry about that later.' She came back to the crux. 'Anyway, Dr Wesley was interested in my query, theory, whatever you'd call it. He agrees the symptoms Matty described could be as a result of something he'd ingested…'

Gavin held up a hand. 'And this theory of yours comes from…?'

'Cannabis cake, cats and vegetarians as it happens, but that's not the point. The point is that I suspect Andrea has been making Matty poorly for years. Ill when it has suited her. Basically to manipulate Wes. Are you following me, Gavin?'

He rapped the desk with his pencil and stared. 'She has two kids. Twins. How can she poison just one?'

'I don't know. Slip it in Matty's meals when he was little? Make it more palatable by adding sugar too? I know kids are fussy, but from what I gather, Matty's always been close to his mum, and he's a pleaser. It was the same when he was older, but it was easier then because he ate different food from the rest of the family.' She gazed at Gavin, willing him to follow her hypothesis. 'He became vegetarian, remember? At Andrea's instigation, I bet.'

Calculation cogs seemed to whirl through Gavin's eyes. Then he frowned and shook his head. 'Matty's recent episode. He was at uni in Sheffield, away from home and his mum, Nat, so–'

'I know; two attacks, actually.' She shifted in her seat, the agitation bubbling up through her body. 'Andrea's been taking them homemade delicacies. Popping over every few days, asking Wes to drive her over. Bloody witch. It's meat lasagne for one son, poisoned vegetarian for the other, washed down with love and beer.'

Suddenly jumping up with realisation, Nat covered her mouth. 'Oh God, I've just remembered. Wes said she'd made another batch of food to take the weekend she fell down those bloody stairs. She's been in hospital since; if we're lucky it might still be in the fridge or the freezer.'

Gavin sat back. 'Fuck.'

'I know. I'm sorry. It probably complicates things more than it helps. Maybe I'm doolally even thinking it. But if I'm right, she needs to be stopped.' The anger flared again, hot in her chest. It wasn't just what the woman had done to Wes, but to her boys, her own flesh and blood. It was horrific; unbelievable. 'Not just stopped, Gav; she needs to be locked up forever.'

The silence was punctured by Chantelle bustling in. She placed two mugs and a doughnut on the desk. 'Guess what?' she asked. Then without waiting for a reply, 'You know the lucrative modelling deal that would have put me on the cover of *Vogue*? It turns out it's pretty much pornography.'

'Oh no, that's so disappointing,' Nat said, turning towards her, but Gavin stared into space with folded arms.

Chantelle cleared her throat loudly. 'So I guess I'll have to put up with the minimum wage for now.' She waited for a moment longer before shrugging. 'Intermittent deafness, Nat. Have you noticed? And by the way, the doughnut's for you. Don't let him nab it. See ya later.'

Nat slurped her tea. The slammed door was still reverberating in her ears, so she missed Gavin's mumble. 'What was that, Gav?' she asked.

He seemed to rouse himself. 'Eyebrows,' he said.

He'd lost her there. 'What?'

'Chantelle. Did you notice? She's had them tattooed on.'

'Oh God, yes. That's it.' Nat laughed despite her tingling nerves. 'How do you know this?'

He smiled distractedly. 'I'm not a dinosaur, Natalie. Being down with the kids, I know about these things. Besides it's a wee bit obvious.' He fell silent again, rubbing his chin. Finally he jumped back to their pre-tea conversation. 'No, don't be sorry. It's just the logistics. I can't get my head around it. We need to be sure before calling in the police.'

Nat nodded. She'd tried to do the same as she drove to Heald

Green, but had pretty much gone in circles. Was this a Munchausen Syndrome by proxy type of illness or something far worse? Evil and calculating, for example? 'This Dr Wesley guy said he would email you,' she said, for want of another answer. 'Maybe you could take it from there.'

He cocked his head. 'Seriously, Nat, where the hell did this idea come from?'

She inwardly snorted. Should she confess to eating half a space cake and not even noticing the odd taste or how unusually relaxed she had felt as she'd studied the sky an hour or so later? It was a funny story for another day, really. Instead she said, 'You trust people, don't you? Especially your mum. You eat what you're given.' She pictured all the Polish dishes she'd eaten over the years to please hers, cabbage and more cabbage in every possible guise. 'You eat it even if it tastes a bit dodgy.'

Gavin drank his tea in one gulp. 'And do we trust Wes? Even if we can prove Andrea has been poisoning Matty, there's no causative link; it doesn't mean he didn't push her down the stairs. It would look more probable if he'd found out what she'd done; in fact a bloody good motive.' He shook his head. 'Whatever Dr Wesley ends up saying, she's a manipulative boot. I would've have given her the push a long time ago. God knows how he put up with her for eighteen years.' He pointed his pencil at Nat. 'Then there's you, the "Scarlet Woman", another reason to get rid of her. The lassie he's always loved waltzes back into his life, even if she's topped up with a gallon of gin halfway through each afternoon…'

Nat narrowed her eyes. 'Now you're taking the piss. Come on, Savage, let the cat out of the bag. You've got something up your sleeve, haven't you? Share it with the class…'

The satisfied beam was back. 'Time—'

'Is of the essence?'

'Exactly.' He nodded at his telephone. 'That call when you came in. It was the neurologist, finally back from his jollies. He's as certain as he can be that the bleeding on Andrea's brain was not consistent with a fall which had happened twelve hours before she was found. It was a recent bleed which didn't do half as much damage as an older bleed would have done. He has all the scan results and he's going to discuss it with his team, but he's confident they'll agree with his conclusions–'

'Which means?'

'We can disprove her formal statement that Wes tried to kill her on Friday evening when they rowed.' He stood up and paced. 'She must have planned everything very carefully once he left. She kept on the clothes she was wearing, then waited until the morning, knowing Wes would be back at a specified time to drive them to Sheffield. Presumably she threw herself down shortly before he was due to arrive, even when she heard or saw his car pull into the drive. Maximum impact, minimum damage: *Res ipsa loquitur*, the bleed was fresh.'

'The bitch!'

'The cunning bitch.' Grinning, Gavin held out his hand. 'We make a great team, Natalie Bach. Between us we can show reasonable doubt, but I reckon it won't get that far. My money's on a grovelling letter dropping the charges by the end of next week.'

'How much are you betting?'

'A pound.'

Nat laughed. 'You tight Scottish bastard.'

43

A NEW CHAPTER

Nat looked around the village hall at the interval. Taking the faded artwork with it, the floral wallpaper was peeling from the far elevation, the grimy orange curtains were sagging at the windows and, if she wasn't mistaken, the smell of wacky baccy was wafting from the prompt's corner of the stage.

Though she knew it was pointless, she shifted to get more comfortable in the hard plastic chair. Would the small boy who'd picked his nose with ferocious enthusiasm throughout the first half performance come back? And was it worth braving the ladies to wipe the bogies from the sleeve of her leather jacket? On balance, no. Moving her feet would encourage the arctic breeze blowing up through the gaps in the floorboards.

Smiling wryly, she turned to her six-foot-six companion. 'Please remind me why I've come here.'

'It's been fun hasn't it?' he replied. He handed her a paper cup of almost colourless squash and a digestive biscuit. 'It's not every day you see Joseph fall off the stage.'

The hilarity threatening to surge back, she covered her mouth. 'Oh God, that was so funny. Did I laugh too much?'

'Nah, didn't I mention it was a comedy? And only three broken bones,' Gavin quipped. 'Ruthie was great, wasn't she?'

Nat nodded. 'Never have I seen a little person look more like a lamb. That girl has talent.'

'We were desperate,' he replied.

Sipping her juice, Nat coughed. It was stronger than it looked. 'Eh?'

'That's why you've come. We were desperate for people to cover all three nights. You're lucky you only have to come once. And I bribed you.'

'The promise of a pint in a dodgy pub on a Friday night.' She snorted. 'God, I must be desperate too.'

The lights were abruptly doused, so Nat threw back her drink, tightened her scarf and hunched down for the second half of the action. She inwardly groaned. It was pretty lame that she was spending today of all days watching Gavin's kids in their church nativity play. She had been surprised to discover that he and Heather were Catholic, let alone regular churchgoers, but that was life for you. All sorts went on behind the scenes. Like pregnant women running down debt collectors because they 'deserved it'; like a married, respectable businessman using Rohypnol to sexually assault female colleagues more than a dozen times; like Andrea and whatever venom she'd been using to poison her own son.

The bloody Cling-on. Of course she had flatly denied it. Then, when presented with the evidence, she'd pointed the finger not only at Wes, but at Dylan too, which was particularly dreadful.

As for Wesley Hughes... He hadn't been in touch. Not a visit, a call, or a text. Even though Gavin had won his pound sooner than he'd expected and Wes was back at Goldman Law, their paths hadn't crossed. She had been out of the office on various errands for Jack, keeping her fingers crossed that the mill man's workers could provide the documents she'd asked for, having a cringe-worthy lunch with the lardy, leery and loaded Brian Selby, and a comical one with Chris Aaron. And when she'd been in, she'd hidden in the conference room, sure that Wes blamed her for meddling. Again.

Sighing deeply, she tried to focus on the platform. Not only did Joseph heroically stay on it for the whole thirty minutes of the second half, he recited Mary's lines as well as his own.

'The new Kenneth Branagh, mark my words,' Gavin commented at some point, bringing Nat back from the cusp of sleep. Then before she could reply, 'When everyone stands up, head for the stage door and don't look back. I'll be right behind you.'

'Any particular–?'

'End seat, second row.' He gestured to the aisle. 'I'm a wanted man. She insisted on giving me more than my fair share of biscuits at the break, and virtually jumped me when I came out of the Men's.'

'Maybe she was checking you'd washed your hands.'

He snorted. 'I think I know when I'm wanted, Natalie.'

Nat looked at him and laughed. 'It must be the...' She motioned to his top lip. 'I don't quite know how to describe it. Mouth brow? Doormat?' She thought of the small boy and his need for a hanky. 'Snot mop?' Leaning forward, she peered at the woman in question. Long, shiny hair but possibly too many teeth. 'Ooh, err. She's not that bad, Gav.'

'Sharks have pearlies like that. This body is honed to perfection. I intend to keep it intact.' He nodded to his crotch. 'All of it.'

An old granny in front turned and cleared her throat meaningfully.

When the need to snigger had died down, Nat elbowed Gavin. 'What do they say, Gav,' she whispered. 'About beggars and choosers...'

~

Save for holding Nat's hand, Ruthie stayed in character the whole journey home, manfully ignoring her daddy's quips about having tasty roast lamb for dinner on Sunday.

Pulling up outside a row of triangular houses, Gavin turned to the back seat. 'Okay, little chops?' he asked her. 'It's nearly time for your barn. Best behaviour for Mummy.'

Ruthie looked at Nat and rolled her amber eyes. 'I'm seven now, Daddy,' she said, using a very patient voice.

Gavin flicked her sheep's ear. 'How do you know I wasn't talking to Nat?'

Having promised Ruthie and the older boys a McDonald's very soon, Nat clambered in the front of Gavin's Volvo, watching him usher his kids to the front door of his former home. A woman appeared in the dim light of the porch, stepped out of his huge shadow and lifted her hand. She waved back. Heather, she supposed. Though a distance away, she looked smiley, slim and attractive. Nat said as much when Gavin climbed back in the car.

'Of course. Why wouldn't she be?' he replied. Not in a challenging way, but she thought he seemed quiet.

She glanced at his profile as he drove. He liked to present a one-dimensional front to the world, but she wasn't so sure. Of course she wouldn't actually say it out loud, but she suspected the two of them were similar in some ways; putting on a hearty appearance for an audience and hiding pain and angst with apparent nonchalance and humour. They were particularly rubbish gags in Gavin's case, but she wouldn't want him to be any different. He was reliably predictable; he didn't blow hot and cold like some people.

Like bloody Wes Hughes. One day declaring love, the next total silence.

But she'd interfered, hadn't she? She'd wrecked his whole family. So it was her own damned fault.

'So where are you taking me?' she asked Gavin eventually, trying to sound a whole lot more chirpy than she felt.

'Here,' he replied, pulling up the car immediately outside a pub door.

'Oh right, that was quick.' Then, 'As important as you are, Gav, I don't think you can park here.'

He nodded to the windscreen. 'Rain.'

Nat hadn't noticed. She grinned. 'And Gavin Savage is doing the gentlemanly thing?'

'Yup.' He looked at her hair, then lifted his hands to his own and motioned sideways growth. 'I can't be seen with a bird with Crystal Tipps locks...'

She opened the car door. 'Watch it, Savage. This cassowary might have flown away by the time you've parked up.'

Buying Gavin a pint and herself a large glass of red, Nat glanced around the room.

After the village hall experience, the pub wasn't as grotty as she had feared. In fact she'd been here before, a lifetime ago. It had a different name then, something relating to the nearby railway, which, from the train pictures and paraphernalia, was still clearly its theme.

'I didn't have you down as a railway nerd,' she said when Gavin sat down. 'You like to take in the old choo choo memorabilia with a half of pale ale on a Friday night, do you?'

He sipped his pint, then wiped the froth from his newly grown moustache. 'In the 1960s, steam engine drivers from the adjacent station yard referred to this junction as Platform 5. Hence the name,' he replied.

'Oh God, you *are* a railway nerd.'

He passed her a cardboard coaster and smiled. 'Read for yourself. I've never been here before in my life.' He clinked her glass. 'We make a good team. So when are you coming to work for me?'

She laughed. 'You couldn't afford me.'

'You're still there. I thought you were going to move on.' He sat back and peered at her pointedly. 'But could the lady really leave her beloved Goldman Law?'

'Maybe.'

He studied the beer mat. 'Even Wes?'

'Particularly Wes.' Then before she could stop herself, 'He hasn't been in touch. My meddling fucked up his family even more than they were already fucked up. He's been avoiding me. He blames me.'

Glancing at the ancient couple on the next table, Gavin shrugged. 'Why would he know you had anything to do with it? In the end Dr Wesley reported it to the police, as he was duty bound to do once he was sure. If he mentioned any names it would have been me or Miss Brush, my glamorous assistant with tattooed eyebrows.'

'Chantelle isn't a solicitor and she isn't called Brush. Well, not as far as I know.'

'Wes doesn't know that.' He looked at Nat with a chiding expression fit for a grandma. 'Two words, Ms Bach. View point.'

Not bothering to hide their interest, the old pair leaned forward. Hitching her chair around, Nat blocked them out of view. 'What's that supposed to mean?'

'Maybe Wes thinks you're the one avoiding him. Maybe he thinks you don't like "baggage".' He threw back the rest of his pint. 'Or maybe he's worried you're thinking "no smoke without fire" and that he's a wife killer. Or at least a failed one.'

Feeling soulful, Nat turned her wine glass. How she'd love that to be true, but she doubted it was. Wes knew where she lived; he hadn't held back from turning up unannounced in the past. He had her telephone number; he knew where the bloody conference room was, for God's sake. 'Shall I tell you a secret?' she asked.

Gavin stood with his glass and headed for the bar. 'Can I really take any more of your secrets? Same again?' he called.

Pushing back the need to cry, she finished her drink. 'Why the hell not?'

'So, hit me,' Gavin said once he'd sat down again. 'What's the secret?'

Trying to control her emotion, Nat sniffed and smiled wryly. 'It's my birthday today.'

'Happy birthday,' he said, looking at his watch.

'It's my *fortieth* bloody birthday, Gavin.'

He lifted his half pint. 'Happy *fortieth* birthday, Natalie. I've already been there. You'll get over it.'

After draining his beer he stood and reached for his jacket. Nat looked at her second drink; she hadn't yet touched it. 'Where are you going?' she asked.

He stroked his moustache and grinned. 'Yours truly has a date.'

'Ha. Very funny. You're going to the loo. Why do you need your coat? Have you got some porn in the pocket?'

Instead of replying, he flushed. Bloody hell, she was either right about the porn or he did have a date. She nodded at his groin. 'You said you wanted to keep all your bits intact.'

He seemed to rally. 'Your concern for my boaby is touching, but time's ticking.' He slid his long arms in his parka. 'I've got to go. I can't keep the lucky lassie waiting–'

Nat turned back to the table. Fantastic. It was her fortieth birthday and she couldn't even scrape the barrel of Gavin Savage. 'Oh, right. That's great. Have a nice time.'

He didn't move. 'Aren't you going to ask who?'

That made her look up. 'You mean I know this unfortunate person?'

His cheeks coloured again. 'Not exactly, but I know you'll approve.'

For a moment she floundered, completely lost for ideas. Then she remembered the conversation in the porch light, the bright smile on Heather's face as she beckoned. She put a finger above her top lip. 'So that's why you've grown fluff. It's the ex wife! You dark horse.' But it lifted her spirits. She was pleased for him, and even more for his kids. Standing on tiptoes, she gave him a tight hug. 'A second chance, Gav. Don't go cocking it up.'

He lifted one eyebrow impressively. 'I think you can rely on me.' Then he nodded at her wine. 'I know you're a bit of an alkie, so take time with that drink. If you get into a fight, give me a buzz. I know a good solicitor...'

She waved him away with a smile, then watched through the window as he strode through the drizzle with his mobile to his ear. Returning to the table, she stared at the large glass. Drinking alone on a milestone birthday; that really was tragic. She sniffed. She'd just have to get used to it, just as she'd had to get comfortable as the maiden bloody aunt. She loved her nephew and niece, but it wasn't the life she had wanted. Then there was Jack. He'd invited her to be part of his new happy family by meeting his grandson on Sunday. She knew he meant well, but even the thought of being in one room with him, Julian, Catherine and Aisha, brought her out in hives, so she'd made an excuse. She just hoped all those Chinese walls were made of solid brick, that the new little Goldman would help each member of the clan to hold on to his or her secret super tight.

The excuse had been Mallorca. 'Sorry, Jack, I'd love to see the baby, but I'm heading to Mallorca for the weekend. Just a quick trip to check on the bar. Maybe pop in to see The Spaniard...'

It was funny, really. She'd adopted Jack's term and had come to like it. It felt satisfyingly distant, which is how she had come to feel about the whole surreal situation. Until she'd spoken to Hugo, that is.

She sighed at the memory. It had been Anna's fault, really; she'd needed certainty about when Nat was visiting and for how long. So, like ripping off a plaster, Nat had taken action one evening last week. Without thinking about it deeply, she'd telephoned Hugo at the bar.

Hearing his mellow voice had brought a lump to her throat. His tone had become even warmer when he'd realised it was her.

'Natalie, my *cariño*. How is your beautiful *momia*?' he'd said. 'I've been too worried to ask.'

Then he'd told her about Jose and his increasingly erratic behaviour. It had culminated in him locking himself alone in 'Havana' and smashing up the bar. Hugo had had to call the police, watching with sad desperation as Jose was forcibly removed wearing handcuffs. He was still in the clinic, but progress was slow.

'When will you come?' he'd asked Nat, but she'd had no answer. Despite her mum's need for a date, in spite of her excuse to Jack, she'd known then she wasn't ready to do it: a visit would gouge open old wounds, it would mean a return to the hurt and the anger.

When she'd finished the call, her mum had gazed with those knowing eyes. 'You know I don't want you to go, Skarbie, but you have to face the past to get...' She seemed to search for the word. 'To get an ending. I think you know that.'

She now covered her face with her hands. As ever Anna had been right. Perhaps she needed to be brave and get that closure. Maybe it was time.

Remembering Gavin's quip, she went back to her wine. It was tempting to drink it, then another and another until she felt nothing, but she took a deep, shuddery breath and lifted her chin. She was going to resist, start a new chapter as she meant to go on. God only knew what the story would be, but she had to bloody well try. Standing unsteadily, she reached for her jacket, trying to resist a last stab of self-pity.

A tall figure blocked her way. 'Are you going already? You haven't finished your drink.'

She briefly met his gaze before looking away. 'I haven't even started it,' she replied, dipping her head to hide her flushed cheeks.

Wes Hughes said nothing. Instead he gathered her in his arms and held her tightly. 'You shouldn't be crying on your birthday,' he said eventually. 'You'll make me cry too.'

Aware of the oldies gawping, Nat pulled away and sat down. Then she rustled in her handbag for anything vaguely absorbent to wipe her wet face. 'You're not allowed to hog the limelight; you're not forty for another week.'

He passed her a paper napkin. 'How is it?' he asked with a mock serious expression. 'If I know, I can prepare myself.'

'Pretty shit,' she replied, blowing her nose and struggling to hide her smile. Oh God, he was here and so damned attractive. 'I was going to drown my sorrows; it would be nice to do it with someone else.' She nodded to a huddle of men at the bar. 'Is there anyone there you think might be suitable?'

'Me and only me.' Wes sat down opposite her. 'I'm all yours. Here to whisk you off your feet and to pander to your every wish.'

'I don't suppose Gavin had anything to do with–'

'He's a good mate.' Wes rubbed his head. 'The thing is, the last time we met at the café… Well, I didn't know if you still…'

She hoped her mascara hadn't smudged too badly, but it didn't really matter. The relief and pleasure felt like the fizz of champagne, making her giddy. 'Hmm, every wish…' she said. 'Do I get forty this year?'

'Absolutely.' Wes pecked her lips. 'So, what's the first?'

'Well, you've granted that one already.' She looked at his questioning face. 'You're here.'

He grinned. 'See, I'm good at this wish business. And the next?'

Wes was softly threading his fingers through hers. The heat had gone straight to her cheeks, beacon-like undoubtedly, but what the hell, in for a penny… 'I would like us to cuddle for a very long time.'

He leaned over and kissed her lightly. 'We're on the same page so far. Have you been peeping at my wish list?'

'What else is on yours?'

'Well, I'll be having a mid-life crisis, of course, so a swish new bachelor pad. You know, with all the electronic gadgets? A set of expensive golf clubs.' He scratched his chin. 'And a soft-top sport's car, naturally. I was thinking of a BMW M6 Convertible.'

Nat narrowed her eyes. He was enjoying the tease, the bloody sod. 'You've already had your mid-life crisis.'

His expression clouded. 'Yeah, and what a crisis.' Then it cleared again and he smiled, taking her hands into his. 'But then I thought I'd search out this beautiful woman I've loved for years, see if she'll have me and forgive me for being such a dolt.'

Hoping he couldn't hear the soaring clatter of her heart, Nat tried for nonchalance. 'Oh yeah? Do you think she will?'

He grinned. 'I do actually. And I think we'd want a baby, so we'd need a new house.'

'With a large garden?'

'Yup.'

'In the countryside?'

'Yup.'

'Maybe with an apple tree?'

'Sounds nice.'

A swell of happiness tingling, she gazed at her man, astonished at how certain she felt about their future. But she needed to exorcise the ghost of Andrea and put her phantom where it belonged. Somewhere along the line Gavin Savage had taught her how.

She kissed Wes softly, then pulled away with a rueful face. 'It does sound very nice indeed. There's only one problem.'

Sitting back, he frowned. 'What?'

'Well... just to be on the safe side, it had better be a bungalow.'

The end

COMING THIS SUMMER...

Confessions **by Caro Land**

Dig for the truth and you'll get dirty...

Natalie Bach is facing personal turmoil, legal conundrums and challenges. While trying to make a difference, she walks the fine line between being a help and a hinderance.

Seconded to criminal law firm, Savage Solicitors, Nat finds herself out of her depth when she's handed a complicated and tragic case of assisted suicide. Will she get to the bottom of what really happened?

With a heavy workload to juggle, can Nat untangle her own feelings from another very personal and troubling investigation?

Confessions is the second book in the gripping new legal crime suspense series.

Lightning Source UK Ltd.
Milton Keynes UK
UKHW011354230120
357488UK00002B/146

9 781913 419264